Wonder

I Found My Heart in San Francisco: Book Twenty-Three

Susan X Meagher

Wonder

I Found My Heart in San Francisco: Book Twenty-Three

THIS TRADE PAPERBACK ORIGINAL IS PUBLISHED BY BRISK PRESS, WAPPINGERS FALLS, NY 12590.

COVER DESIGN AND LAYOUT BY: CAROLYN NORMAN

FIRST PRINTING: MARCH 2020

ISBN-13: 978-0-9987907-8-7

By Susan X Meagher

Novels

Arbor Vitae
All That Matters
Cherry Grove
The Lies That Bind
The Legacy
Doublecrossed
Smooth Sailing
How To Wrangle a Woman
Almost Heaven
The Crush
The Reunion
Inside Out
Out of Whack
Homecoming
The Right Time
Summer of Love
Chef's Special
Fame
Vacationland
Wait For Me
The Keeper's Daughter
Friday Night Flights

Short Story Collection

Girl Meets Girl

Serial Novel

I Found My Heart In San Francisco

Awakenings: Book One
Beginnings: Book Two
Coalescence: Book Three
Disclosures: Book Four
Entwined: Book Five
Fidelity: Book Six
Getaway: Book Seven
Honesty: Book Eight
Intentions: Book Nine
Journeys: Book Ten
Karma: Book Eleven
Lifeline: Book Twelve
Monogamy: Book Thirteen
Nurture: Book Fourteen
Osmosis: Book Fifteen
Paradigm: Book Sixteen
Quandary: Book Seventeen
Renewal: Book Eighteen
Synchronicity: Book Nineteen
Trust: Book Twenty
United: Book Twenty-One
Vengeance: Book Twenty-Two
Wonder: Book Twenty-Three

Anthologies

Undercover Tales
Outsiders

Acknowledgments

Many thanks to Aoife for giving the book a good long look for any glaring "Americanisms" lurking about in the Irish characters' dialogue. Any errors that remain were undoubtedly introduced afterward. Tinkering after proofreading is a bad habit of mine!

Dedication

As always, I dedicate this book to my first reader, and most gentle critic, Carrie.

Chapter One

Jamie Evans stifled a yawn, turning her head so the others didn't see. She hated to be the first one to call it a night, but that often happened when she was in a bar surrounded by O'Flahertys.

It was only the first day of the family trip to Ireland, and she was already bone-tired. Oddly, the flight hadn't been the thing that wore her out. It was managing such a large group that had drained her energy. Well, that and taking a long turn at entertaining Caitlin on the very long flight. The next time Jamie searched for a girlfriend, she was going to find someone whose entire family lived in the 415 area code.

Ryan's hand had been on her leg, and one second after Jamie's attempt to disguise her draining energy, it moved up and down slowly. Then warm, humid breath tickled her ear.

"Tired?"

"Parts of me are," Jamie said quietly, "but I'm also kind of wired." She tapped her head. "Everything's a little jumbled up here."

"Just let me know when you want to go to bed, Jamers. If we leave, it'll give the boyos permission to crash."

Nodding, Jamie scooted around in her chair, trying to relieve the discomfort she'd been experiencing for the last couple of hours. Normally, her butt didn't hurt from ten hours in the air. But she didn't often have to sit in coach on a long flight. One day she'd learn, and would maintain sole discretion over their travel plans.

She gave Ryan a pat on the leg, smiling at her when she turned her head a little. It would take a very cold-hearted soul to look into those earnest eyes and complain about a flight. Ryan had wrangled sixteen relatives to Ireland with no significant squabbles or mishaps. That feat deserved only praise.

"Hey, Ryan," Niall called out. "Is this the only bar within walking distance?" He lowered his voice only slightly to add, "I've been to livelier wakes."

Aisling jumped in before Ryan could respond. "There are five decent pubs in Ballina, another five not-so-decent, and another five you'd regret poking your head into."

Niall started to speak again, but Aisling barreled right over him. "All of them are within walking distance of the hotel if you're not paralytic, and if you are…" She shrugged dramatically. "Right here is fine if you're dying of the thirst."

Ryan's muscles had gotten a little tense, and Jamie could see she wanted to jump in. But once Aisling made it clear she wasn't afraid to voice her opinion, Ryan settled back into her chair and took a sip of her pint. Jamie prayed Aisling would boss the boyos around for the entire two weeks they were going to be in town, since that would lessen Ryan's workload. Of course, their granny would be the big boss. It was silly to assume otherwise.

Jamie had finished her own pint long ago, so she took a sip from Ryan's fresh one, with its amber head still sitting atop it like a crown. The sooner it was gone, the sooner they could go to bed.

Idly, she surveyed the bar, noting there were only six strangers in the whole place. But that wasn't odd, given the hotel likely appealed to families. When they'd checked in, Jamie had been surprised that Ryan had chosen such a big place. They only needed seven rooms, since Martin and Maeve were staying at Moira's, and Tommy, Annie and Caitlin were at Ryan's grandparents' home. Seven rooms seemed like a good number to fill up a B&B, the choice she would have made. But now that they were there, she was glad they were in a large property. More choices let Ryan assign rooms in a very specific fashion. She'd placed Aisling at the far end, with them right next door. Then she'd handed out the rest of the keys at random. Jamie wasn't sure Aisling and Colm would be able to have any alone time, but at least the room assignments gave them a buffer from the boyos' curious eyes.

The hotel was nice enough, although a little overdecorated for Jamie's tastes. It looked a bit like a nice doctor's office from her youth, when mauve and teal seemed to blanket everything. While it was good that it wasn't a chain, the highly personal tastes of the owners added to its dated appearance. Large sprays of glaringly fake flowers never worked to warm a place up, although she had to hand it to the owners for making an attempt.

Besides the bar, the hotel had a full restaurant, which closed at nine, a shockingly early time in her book. The owners called the place they were sitting a pub, but that was a misnomer. It was more like an American bar, in that they served mixed drinks as well as wine and beer. But if they'd only served soft drinks she wouldn't have been surprised. The place was lit like a diner, with the light not only far too bright, but unflattering. There wasn't any music playing either, although a sign claimed they'd have a band at the weekend. She was quite sure the O'Flahertys would have found someplace livelier by then. Back home, Conor and Colm usually paired up to find new spots, since both of them got bored easily. But Aisling would kick Colm's butt if he went trolling for a spot with the largest number of single women. How he was going to explain away his lack of interest in local women was going to be interesting.

Jamie let her gaze trail across the three tables they'd jammed together. Colm and Aisling had chosen seats well away from each other, both determined to keep their romantic feelings hidden during the visit. That was a damn shame, but Jamie understood the urge. Once the boyos knew about their relationship, the spotlight would be on Colm in ways she knew he would despise.

At home, most of the boyos hung with the group, and almost all of them were open books when it came to their social lives. But Colm was a little different, a little more mysterious. He disappeared frequently on weekend nights, usually blithely saying he had a date, but refusing to give details. She'd never seen him with a woman around the neighborhood, so he must have ventured outside of Noe for his hookups—which alone made him stand out from his brothers and cousins, who were too lazy to put any effort into chasing women at all.

Aisling's brother Cormac was sitting by Jamie, and he leaned over to say quietly, "I was looking forward to being home for the summer, but I've begun to change my mind. With two of my own cousins and four of the O'Flahertys looking for girls, I haven't a chance."

Cormac expressing himself so boldly wasn't his norm. Then Jamie spotted the two empty pint glasses in front of him. Apparently, his tongue loosened as his blood alcohol level rose. She put a reassuring hand on his arm. "Ooo, don't be silly, Cormac. Not every woman is in the market for—" She stopped on a dime. Finishing that sentence with the truth wouldn't help the guy's attitude. She rephrased. "If I were looking for a guy, I'd turn tail and run if an O'Flaherty tried to chat me up."

Cormac rolled his eyes toward Ryan, his only female first cousin. "If you ran, you didn't get far."

Jamie let out a laugh. "No, I didn't. But it was Ryan's sensitivity and kindness and sense of humor I was attracted to. Not her rugged good looks and rippling muscles." She spent just a second gazing at her, thinking that her looks certainly hadn't hurt. But she was trying to boost Cormac's mood, and acknowledging that Ryan could undoubtedly beat him at arm wrestling wasn't a good idea. "When I was in the market for a guy, I was always attracted to someone who looked like he wanted to get to know me." She let her eyes slide down the impressive specimens around the table. "The boyos just want to show how the sleeves of their T-shirts strain from those big muscles."

Cormac lifted his arm, a perfectly serviceable appendage. He didn't even try to form a muscle, which was wise, since Jamie was fairly sure even her biceps were bigger than his. Instead, he poked at it, with his roomy sleeve showing he had plenty of space for another arm or two to fit inside. "Compared to them, I look like I haven't started shaving yet."

Jamie took a look at him under the unflattering light. With his fair skin and auburn hair, he probably could have gone a while without shaving, but it wasn't going to do him any good to compare himself to the cousins physically. They were hunks. That was a fact. Cormac was going to have to make a play for women the O'Flahertys frightened, or weren't interested in. Jamie just hated to say that in so many words.

Ryan had obviously been listening, because she clapped Cormac on the back and said, "The boyos look for the flashiest women in the place. All you have to do is find the ones who aren't taken by their height or their muscles—"

"Or their looks," Cormac added, pouting a little.

"You have to find a woman who wants to be special," Ryan insisted. "Not just another notch on a bedpost."

He sighed, looking disconsolate. "I wouldn't mind notching a bedpost or two. Everyone tells me to find a nice girl who's as shy as I am, but I want the same girls your cousins want."

Ryan laughed, shaking her head. "Then you're going to have to step up your game, lad. They're significantly older, have significantly more experience, and they don't think twice about going up to any woman in a bar and asking if they can buy her a drink. Some of them will even dance if that's what it takes."

"I'm dead," he said, sliding down in his chair, looking absolutely miserable.

"We'll keep an eye out for you," Ryan promised. "Maybe we'll split up. If the boys stay in Ballina, we'll go to Killala, or Enniscrone." She clapped him on the back again, possibly bruising him. "Just remember, they'll only be here for two weeks. Then all of the women of Killala will be yours once again."

"None of them are mine yet, but I still like my chances better without the Irish Rugby team breathing down my neck." Niall and Donal were in his line of sight, and he narrowed his eyes at them, which almost made Jamie laugh out loud.

"My cousins would never make the Irish Rugby team," she scoffed, "although they did win the San Francisco GAA Championship. They're pretty good."

Cormac let his head drop to the table, with Ryan smirking at the poor kid's dismay. She, like the O'Flaherty cousins, had no idea what it was like to be shy or undersized or lacking in courage. No one could argue that the genetic lottery was fair, but the O'Flaherty boys had been too generously gifted, at least where looks and bodies were concerned. While Cormac ran rings around the whole bunch when it came to brains, a woman walking into a bar likely wouldn't be able to see past the flash of the boyos to be swayed by Cormac's outsized IQ.

Jamie led the way up the stairs to their room, with Ryan walking behind her, playfully pinching her at random spots.

"You know, an eight hour time change really screws with my perception of ti—"

Jamie turned and clapped her hand over Ryan's mouth, stopping her from finishing the sentence. "It's midnight," she said sternly. "My watch says so, the clock in the bar said so, and everyone in Ballina agrees. If you want to drive yourself mad with figuring out what time it is in San Francisco, go right ahead. But do it silently."

Ryan licked her palm, then pulled the hand from her face. "I'm not driving myself mad. Just stating a fact."

"I'm not interested in your facts. It's midnight, and it's been nineteen hours since I got up." She climbed the remaining stairs, then slid the old-fashioned brass key into their lock and jiggled it until the latch gave way. "It's time to brush our teeth, pop off a couple of orgasms, and get to sleep."

Ryan kicked off her shoes, turning her head to gaze at Jamie over her shoulder. "Pop off a couple of orgasms? Is that what making love has become?"

Jamie couldn't tell if her puzzled expression reflected concern or if Ryan was just playing with her. She reached out and grasped the waistband of Ryan's slacks to hold her still. While slipping her arms around her, she nuzzled against the back of her neck. "Normally, I want to make love to you. Tonight, I need a therapeutic orgasm. I don't want to let jet lag slay me like it did last time, so I want to get to sleep fast."

Ryan turned in the embrace, gazing at Jamie for a few seconds. "I've got some work to do, but I can give you a hand."

"Work?"

"Email. I've got a lot of balls in the air. I don't want to let anything slide by."

Jamie put her hands on Ryan's hips and pushed off. "Now it sounds like I'm just another agenda item." She made herself smile, even though her heart wasn't in it. "I guess I'm not as good at separating orgasms from love as I thought I was." She patted Ryan's cheek as she started for the bath. "Go ahead and do your work, babe. If I'm not asleep when you're finished, we'll reconsider."

"Are you sure? I probably only need fifteen minutes."

Jamie laughed to herself. No one was better at falling down the rabbit hole of losing hours to the internet than Ryan was. "Sure. Go ahead and start while I get ready for bed."

Travel always made her feel unreasonably dirty, so Jamie took a quick shower, then brushed and flossed her teeth while trying to think of calming images. She'd convinced herself that their bed was going to be a fluffy cloud, and that the sheets would feel like angel's wings, with gigantic marshmallows for pillows. Ryan was sitting in the only chair, a small upholstered number made for a much smaller person, and her attention was fully fixed on her laptop. Not even a glance to show she'd registered that Jamie was in the room.

After she pulled the bedspread off and folded it, Jamie got in, pleased to find that the bed wasn't bad at all. It wasn't quite the celestial image she'd conjured up, but it was ten times better than their bed at home—not a surprise. She put on the eye shade she'd brought, then stuffed some silicone ear plugs in to mask the rapid tapping of Ryan's fingers gliding over her laptop keys.

She'd been sporadically practicing some mindful meditation techniques, and started with a body scan, going over her body from the top of her head to the tips of her toes, just registering each part and acknowledging it. But her mind wasn't shutting down the way it did at home when she tried this.

The problem was one of unmet expectations. While they'd been in the bar, she'd decided they'd have a quickie, and had spent a little time gearing up for one. The atmosphere hadn't been very sexy, but she loved sitting close to Ryan when they were in a group. No matter where they were, her warm hand managed to touch some part of Jamie, even if it was just to hold onto a few of her fingers. But tonight Ryan had been a little more expansive. Her hand had been on Jamie's thigh for most of the night, and every once in a while it had slipped up to brush against her inseam. None of the touches had been sexual, of course. She didn't do that kind of thing in front of her family. They'd only happened because Ryan was reaching for something or shifting around in her chair. But when Jamie was in the mood, which she definitely was, she could focus on the simple brush of those talented fingers to imagine just where they might travel in the near future.

In her fantasy, they would enter the room, brush their teeth, and have a quick wank, as Ryan might poetically call it. But when Jamie lifted her eye mask, Ryan was still wanking only her keyboard, lost in planning all of the tasks she wanted to accomplish during the boyos' relatively short visit.

Jamie understood her own instincts well enough to know she was on the verge of fixating on her unmet needs, a habit she was working to break. So she stopped thinking of Ryan and started thinking of herself. It had been ages since she'd touched herself, and she'd never done it in Ryan's presence when she wasn't participating in some way. But that was just silly. She had her own needs, and tonight one of her needs was to have a quick climax to help her get to sleep. That wasn't Ryan's responsibility. Still, she was a little reticent to do something so private with her partner just ten feet away. But if Ryan was giving her email her usual laser focus, Jamie could do calisthenics and not distract her.

She'd been in a pretty good groove when they were downstairs, and she tried to get back into that headspace. She'd been thinking of how quickly Ryan could turn her on when she focused on it, and in her imagination they'd no sooner crossed the threshold than Ryan had her up against the wall, probing her mouth with her silky tongue. That image started to work in a heartbeat, making her clit tingle.

She was about to get her period, which always made her breasts more sensitive than normal. Reaching under the covers, she ran the flats of her hands over them, touching them gently to make her nipples harden. That worked too, so she kept going, barely touching herself with her fingers, relishing the sensation she felt in her clit from that direct line to her nipples.

Lifting one knee, she let her hand trail down her body, heading for her favorite spot, when a heavy weight compressed the mattress. An ear plug was pulled out, and Ryan's soft voice murmured, "Can I get in on this? It's totally fine if you'd rather be alone. I just heard a little whimper and I…"

Jamie reached up blindly and grasped her shoulder, tugging hard to pull Ryan across her body.

"I guess that means you want help," Ryan said, with her soft laugh making chills chase down Jamie's spine.

"Put those fingers to work," Jamie said, already imagining how good the sensation would feel. "Perfect," she sighed when Ryan's cool fingers touched her heat. "Next time I complain about your timing, remind me about tonight."

"Aww, you never complain."

Jamie lifted the edge of her sleep mask while raising an eyebrow. "Now I know I'm lost in a fantasy."

Ryan slowly woke from a pleasant dream, with her bladder thinking it was time to get up. She was tempted to ignore it and snuggle up to Jamie, but she cracked an eye open to see that the sun was about to rise. Getting her usual amount of sleep was going to be a struggle on this vacation, with dawn a few minutes after five and sunset at ten pm. She truly couldn't go to sleep while it was still light out, but running right at dawn was a strong preference she didn't really want to ignore.

She tossed the light blanket off and tucked it around Jamie's body. Maybe it was time to reconsider her preferences. If she didn't get her eight hours, she wouldn't be mentally sharp. And keeping an eye on all of her cousins would take every bit of her brainpower and patience.

After using the bath, she got dressed for her run. She had no idea how warm it was, but she'd rarely been overdressed for a run in Ireland, even in June.

Stealthily, she tiptoed out of the room, not bothering to take the key, having every confidence Jamie would still be asleep when she returned.

As she closed the door, she heard a rustling sound to her right, then laughed to herself as Aisling's door open to spit out Colm, clad in basketball shorts, a T-shirt, and running shoes.

"Oh, that looks authentic," she whispered.

His head snapped up and he turned to her with a look of absolute panic before he registered her as a friend, rather than a spy. "Aisling's idea. If Donal wakes up when I go back to our room, I'm supposed to convince him I've started jogging."

"Oh, that'll work. He'll totally buy that you're going to close down the pubs at night, work all day on my granny's renovations, and add an early morning sport to the mix."

"Got any better ideas?" he asked as they walked down the hall together.

"Not really. But I'll put my thinking cap on." They reached his room, and he paused in front of the door. "What time are we starting?"

"I thought nine. Is that good?"

He gave her a big smile. "Perfect. I could really use three more hours of sleep."

She gave him a pat on the shoulder as he turned to slide his key in the door. "By the way, thanks for not telling me you were up all night doing unspeakable things to my poor innocent cousin."

Colm turned his head to stare at her. "Innocent?"

"See you at Granny's at nine," she said, scampering away before she had to give another moment's thought to her cousins doing God-knew-what to one another.

Dawn broke over a clear, cloudless sky, burning a wide orange stripe at the horizon that filled Ryan with a sense of peace. She'd had to drive her rental car over to Killala to reach the long-familiar road, but she quickly got into a groove when she started to move.

She'd spent much of her life convincing friends and herself that she was the fully American daughter of Irish parents. But when she was in Ireland, she didn't feel very American at all. In fact, while sitting at the bar the night before, she could feel the difference between her O'Flaherty cousins and herself.

With Irish-born fathers and American-born mothers, the boyos didn't seem to feel the same pull toward Ireland that she did. Their Irish grandparents had died before they'd been born, and they had no Irish first cousins. But she had both, and was truly torn between two identities, with her Irish citizenship taking over when she was with her Irish family. On previous trips, that hadn't been a problem. But now, accompanied by her very American cousins, she was going to have to find a middle path, one she wasn't sure she could reach.

Flushing those confounding thoughts from her head, she concentrated on her stride, lengthening it to pick up speed. The sun had already lost its orange hue, burning gold in the sky as it rose. The birds were chirping madly in the trees as she cruised down the lightly traveled lane, and a few sheep were already out cropping grass for their morning meal.

As she rounded the corner, she got her first glimpse of her land, with her heart skipping a beat as she took it in. It actually wasn't hers yet, but it would be as soon as her solicitor had the papers ready to sign.

As land to develop, it was worth every dime they'd agreed to pay. But as a site for a single-family home, they'd been robbed. She honestly didn't care about that, clearly the first time she'd ignored overpaying for anything. But it was worth many thousands of dollars to her to keep these acres of land mostly undeveloped. The last thing Killala needed was a bunch of cheaply constructed homes spoiling pastureland that had supported flocks of sheep and a few cows for generation after generation. It made no sense from a financial perspective, but it meant everything to her to live on a patch of land that she was going to keep much like it had been when her granny's family had worked it. While she understood it wasn't easy or even wise to try to stop progress, some things were worth fighting for, or in her case, paying for.

She was really flying when she approached the family church, and she had to put the brakes on to round the corner as she climbed the slight hill to the graveyard.

Panting from the effort, she let out a cry when she saw her father standing in front of her mother's grave, head bent, one hand covering his eyes.

He'd obviously heard her, because his head snapped up as he turned to her. She'd stopped on a dime, and had leaned over slightly, ready to turn-tail and run the other way. But their eyes met and he opened his arms, giving her a wan smile. She raced over to him and fell into his embrace, immediately soothed.

"I had no idea you'd come," she whispered. "At least not at the crack of dawn."

"I wanted to be up and out before your aunt woke," he said, his voice soft and gentle. "I'm sure she'll come later, probably before Mass, but…"

She could feel his broad shoulders shrug. "We each have our own thoughts."

"Want me to leave you alone? I can do another few miles and come back later."

"Stay," he said firmly. He wrapped his arm around her shoulders and turned back to face the headstone. "I haven't been here with you since the day of the funeral."

Sniffling, she nodded, not able to speak. She'd been so sure she could just pay her respects and get on with her day, but now she felt like she might melt into a puddle of tears.

He spoke softly, with a serenity she knew she couldn't match. "I know you'd be shocked at the gray in my hair and the lines on my face, Fi, but will you look at this gorgeous creature we've made?"

Ryan was sobbing, with tears running down her face so quickly she couldn't begin to catch them. But having her father's arm around her while talking to her mother like she was right there in front of them was strangely soothing.

"I don't know how two average people raised such an extraordinary girl. She must have gotten the very best parts of both of us, Fi, but I'm so happy she got your gentle nature and your unlimited patience. She might look like the prettiest O'Flaherty ever born, but she's a Ryan through and through. And for that, I couldn't be more grateful."

He pulled his handkerchief from his back pocket and dabbed at his eyes, then folded it and wiped Ryan's just like he had when she was a little girl, continuing to speak. "I've made mistakes. Hundreds of them. But none of them were bad enough to harm the foundation you created with our little brood. Each and every one of them do you proud, sweetheart, and I promise you…" His voice started to break, but he carried on, his strength amazing Ryan. "I promise you there isn't a day that goes by that we don't long for you." He sucked in a deep, shaky breath. "I'm as happy as a man has any right to be with your sister, but I'd give anything on this earth to have you here by my side, as would she," he added firmly.

He tucked his arm around Ryan tightly and pressed a kiss to her temple. "You won't believe this, but we're here to fix your mam's house, sweetheart. I'm keeping an eye on her, solely because you'd want me to," he added, with a soft laugh making Ryan laugh as well. His head lifted, and he murmured, "Good lord, it's like Grand Central Station around here."

Ryan wiped her eyes to see Brendan loping up the street, dropping his head after they made eye contact.

"Come along lad," her father said. "Let your mother see what a fine man you've become."

Sheepishly, he stood next to Ryan and put his arm around her from the other side. "We can't stay long," he said. "Granny's probably on her way and she hates it when we come."

"You could both take her in a brawl," Martin said, giving them a playful grin. "I'm proud of you both for keeping your mother in your hearts, and if your grandmother doesn't like it, she can speak to me." He turned back to the headstone. "You might not see Conor or Rory, but that's only because they aren't as soft-hearted as these two. They don't love you or miss you a bit less, Fi. I promise you that."

"This is so hard," Brendan said softly. "But I couldn't imagine being here and not coming." He sniffled a little, then wiped his eyes with the backs of his hands. "We have time for early Mass, right?"

"Sure," Ryan said, caught a little flat-footed when they both looked to her for permission. "I've got to get going, but you two go right ahead."

"I'll work on her, Fi," her father said, turning back to the grave. "We might only be able to get her into an Episcopal church, but we'll try to bring her back into the fold."

"I love you both," Ryan said, sidestepping the issue. "And I'm very glad we had these few minutes alone together. I have a feeling the day is going to be a mad one."

As she started to run back down the hill, she realized she'd been speaking with her full-bore Irish accent. Living a bifurcated life wasn't for amateurs, but she knew neither her father nor her brother would mention her gaff. She wasn't at all sure which one had the kinder heart. It actually might have been a dead heat.

Ryan was at her grandparents' home by 8:30, pleased to find her Granny already gone to St. Patrick's to perform her many duties. She was usually there Monday through Friday, but she worked extra hard on Sunday. Other than going to Mass, her grandfather's presence at the parish was much less frequent. This morning he was in the garden, sitting on a wooden chair while he drank his tea and read the paper. "Well, hello," he said, smiling up at her. "Let me get you some tea."

"No need," she said, resting her hand on his shoulder while bending to kiss his cheek. "I've had all of the caffeine I can stand." She flinched, realizing she'd been using her American accent. That brought her up short, having to remind herself it wasn't an accent, it was the natural way she talked. But here in Ireland, where she'd always spoken like her relatives, her California-inflected speech sounded very American to her ear. Right then, she decided to go all-Irish for the remainder of the trip. The O'Flaherty cousins would razz her, but she thought the benefit of fitting in with both her Mayo-born family and the town would make up for that.

Kieran, Donal and Rory rolled up to the house a few minutes before nine. Right behind them, Conor, Aisling, and Kevin arrived. A minute after them, Niall and Colm brought up the rear. While Ryan was walking to the curb to greet them, her father pulled up. "I feel like I'm back in San Francisco," she said, helping Jamie extricate herself from a tiny backseat. "O'Flahertys as far as he eye can see."

Her grandfather was beside her before she'd realized he'd followed along. "John Ryan," he said, extending his hand to Kieran. "I don't know which of you is which, but I can see the O'Flaherty in you."

"Kieran," her cousin said. "And my brothers, Niall, Donal and Colm. I think you're related to everyone else."

"I am that," he said, smiling when he put an arm around both Kevin and Tommy. "I've got the best grandsons a man could want, and this is the first time I've had them all here in many a year."

Brendan and Maggie tooted their horn, and Ryan watched her grandfather cross the street to greet them. "We're going to spend half of the day chit-chatting," she grumbled.

"You're in Ireland, honey." Jamie reminded her. "Chit-chatting is part of the deal."

They were finally acquainted, and the whole group trooped into the house. Maggie came up and pulled Ryan aside. "I hate to do this, but I've got to finish a few things for a case I'm working on. I promised to have everything ready to go today so a colleague can look it over before morning. Where can I find a good Wi-Fi signal?"

"Not here, but my aunt has a good one, since Cormac needs one to even breathe. Why don't you go over there for the morning?"

"Great idea. Sure I won't be bothering anyone?"

"Ha! There will be so many people walking in and out of so many houses, I'd be surprised if anyone noticed you were there."

"Thanks," she said, kissing her cheek. "I'm not sure I can figure out how to drive a manual transmission, but I can't get into too much trouble, can I?"

"Give it a try. If you need help, Jamie can drive you."

"I don't mind a challenge," she said, waving as she took off.

Brendan smirked at Ryan as Maggie left. "She lasted longer than I thought she would. Where did you send her?"

"Aunt Moira's. She's got an internet signal as good as the library in Ballina."

She noticed her grandfather pointing at spots on the ceiling, with Kieran listening to him closely. Ryan walked over, hearing her grandfather say, "You'll take down as little as possible, right?"

"Aren't we going to knock down the whole ceiling?" Ryan asked.

Kieran's eyes grew wide. "No! I won't be able to tell until I get up there and see for myself, but I'm only planning on cutting out the parts where the keys won't hold."

"I thought with the mildew…"

"You can wash that off," he said, unperturbed. "I don't think it looks all that bad."

Conor ambled over. "Who's going to go onto the roof to see what's leaking?"

"I was going to nominate you," Kieran said. "Maybe you and Donal."

"Me?" Donal asked, getting into the circle. "Why me?"

"You're a plumber," Kieran said. "You understand how water moves through a house."

"In pipes!" he said, clearly not in the mood to climb onto a slick, slate roof.

"I'll do it," Conor said, sighing. "Ryan?"

"Great. Just great." She headed for the door. "I brought running shoes. Let me go change into them. They're tackier."

"Where are you going?" Jamie asked, grabbing her by the sleeve.

"Conor and I are going onto the roof to see where the leak is."

"The roof? Why are you going? You don't know anything about roofs."

"I'm going because Declan and Dermot are the roofers in the family, and we didn't bring them. I hope that wasn't a fatal mistake."

Kieran and Niall stayed inside to test the ceiling, with everyone else outside the house, looking up at the roof. Jamie felt a little sick to her stomach having to watch the most important person in her world standing on a roof that from the ground looked almost vertical.

Both Conor and Ryan were blessed with agility and confidence, which helped a lot. They both leaned into the roof as they scampered across it, with Martin, Brendan and Rory following them, ready to catch either of them if they missed a step and slid off.

The roof wasn't terribly high, and Jamie was certain any of the O'Flaherty men could break Conor or Ryan's fall, but it still made her tremble.

Conor held onto the center line of the roof and got down on his knees, pointing to a spot. Ryan managed to squat down and check it out, then she shifted her body to the right, following along a course of tiles. By the time she'd moved over about three feet, the siblings seemed to agree. They started back down the ladder, with Conor letting Ryan go first. By the time she was on the ground, Jamie had her arms around her.

"Um, honey?"

"What?"

"Can Conor come down too? We're kind of in the way..."

Jamie looked up and caught Conor's eye. "Sorry. I'm pretty fond of her."

"I'm not in a hurry. I'd rather stand on a ladder than take down a ceiling."

Jamie grasped Ryan's hand and pulled her aside. "I know you're going to want to fix that roof, but—"

"I really don't," she said, making Jamie clap her mouth shut so quickly she almost bit her tongue.

"You don't?"

"Well, I do," she said, laughing a little. "But you need scaffolding to do it right. Having both of us up there could make the damage worse. I'm going to ask my grandfather if he knows a roofing guy."

"Amazing," Jamie said. "Just when I think I know you, you do something so...normal."

"Ha! I love to keep you guessing," she said, pulling away to go back inside to keep the project moving.

The weather was glorious. Clear, blue skies, moderate winds, and a delightfully warm sun shining down on Aisling and Jamie as they loitered in the back garden of John and Brigid Ryan's home.

They should have been inside, trying to help. But the small home was stuffed with men, along with one woman who was trying to keep everyone in line. Jamie wasn't at all sure Ryan could manage the project, but no one could say she wasn't trying. It was just too painful to watch—especially since neither she nor Aisling had the skills to be any help at all.

"You know what we should do," Jamie said.

"If it involves leaving the premises, I'm in. I can't help, and it's too frustrating to watch."

Jamie stood and held out a hand, pulling Aisling up from the concrete landing she'd been sitting on. "We should follow up with the commercial real estate guy I spoke with last week."

Aisling put her hands on her hips while cocking her head. "Did you do that, then? For me?"

"For you," Jamie said. "I think the price Mr. McNulty is asking for the pub is pretty reasonable, but there's no sense in overpaying. I asked a guy in Ballina to print off listings for every pub for sale in Mayo, and he said he'd drop them off at the hotel on his way to Mass."

"Siobhán says you have an instinct for finding a bargain, so let's get to it. Do you think we can just…leave?"

"I do. We'll go by your mom's house and make sure they don't need help with Caitlin, then we'll take off."

Aisling took her phone from her back pocket, and hit a couple of buttons, smiling at Jamie as she waited for the call to be answered. "Mam? Jamie and I are going to do a little research on what a pub should cost. You don't need me today, do you?" She smiled as she nodded. "Just as I suspected. We'll come 'round after we've finished to help make lunch for the lads. Right?" After another satisfied nod, she said, "Don't let that child wear you out. She has an immense amount of energy." She snapped the phone closed, and put her hand on Jamie's arm to lead her toward the street. "I just saved us an hour. You can thank me later."

Dealing with her grandfather was so much easier than trying to make progress with her granny that Ryan wondered why she didn't always go directly to him. He not only knew a roofer, he'd made some casual inquiries, and the guy had promised he'd be able to swing by and take a look.

Now that the roof was off her agenda, it was time to get down to business and cut out the parts of the ceiling that weren't fixable. Thankfully, there were only four of them, with the largest part about three feet square, the smallest a foot wide by two feet. That wasn't insignificant, but it was going to be a hell of a lot easier than knocking down the whole thing and starting over.

This was when having a lot of help was a blessing. Kieran used a special knife to score the plaster and peel it off where it was still sticking. But much of the damaged part fell in a cloud of white dust, seemingly only held up by many layers of white paint.

They'd moved all of the furniture into the kitchen, and had put plastic tarps over the staircase. Thick rosin paper covered the floor, and Ryan had personally taped plastic over the kitchen door to make sure no dust traveled into the room. But that meant the kitchen wasn't usable, a fact her granny was not going to be happy about.

By the time they'd gotten all of the ruined spots cut away, they were all covered in white dust, with some of it infiltrating the safety glasses she'd made everyone wear. It hadn't occurred to her to bring some kind of eye wash, but she prayed the local shop carried it. If not, she was going to have to travel to another town just to be able to clear her eyes well enough to see to drive, which hardly made any sense at all.

Jamie sat in the passenger seat of Aisling's little car, heading back to Ballina. It was a short drive, but the landscape was so pretty, with the sun shining on the verdant grass, that she almost wished it was longer.

"I'm so glad to be back in Ireland," Jamie said. "How about you."

Aisling gave her a quick look. "You're taking the mickey? If I were happier, I'd surely be committing a few sins."

Jamie grasped her knee, using a rougher touch than usual. Aisling probably had a soft side, but she didn't show it much in Jamie's presence. So she'd decided to treat her more like the boys, with a certain amount of playful roughhousing. "I'm glad to hear that."

"If I could get Colm away from the pack, I'd be blissful."

"Mmm. When Colm offered to come with us, you made a point of saying you didn't want him working all the time. Were you surprised to see him in the lineup this morning?"

"No," she sighed. "I don't know what I thought would happen, Jamie. It would look odd if he and I took off to see the sights. I'm afraid we're going to have to sneak around to have any time together at all."

"But they really don't need him on the project. Only Kieran and Niall and Conor have the kind of experience they need to do the ceiling, and Kieran's really the key."

"Do you know that for a fact?"

"I'm pretty sure. Fixing the ceiling will take some carpentry work, and only Niall and Conor are expert at that. All the rest of them are going to do is trip over one another."

"How can I use that to my advantage? I need some time with my man."

"I'll check with Kieran once they've gotten the ceiling down. Maybe he'd prefer to have fewer helpers. If so, we can do some touristy things. If I work at it, which I will, I can manage to have Colm in my car if a group of us go together."

"Let's join together to split the group up so thoroughly no one will notice if Colm and I both disappear."

"Oh! Ryan needs to rent a van for hauling things. Let's have her put Colm on the rental agreement so he can run to Ballina when they need supplies. That will give him an excuse to be gone."

Aisling gave her a wry smile. "Just how I envisioned getting to know Colm better. Stealthily riding along to the builder's yard."

Ryan's tummy was grumbling by eleven, but she had a feeling Jamie wouldn't bring lunch any time soon. She just didn't seem to understand how hungry you got doing physical labor.

There were too many people in the house, and definitely too many supervisors. Tommy and Brendan were willing to follow anyone's instructions, as would Colm, but Kieran actually knew how to plaster, and Donal was a skilled plumber. Neither of them liked to be second guessed, which Ryan was sure would happen—and happen soon.

She wasn't sure how to do it, but she was going to have to manage her father, Conor, and Niall, men used to being in charge of their own crews, to remove a few of the competing supervisorial voices. She got on her phone and called Jamie, just to make sure she didn't step on her toes.

"Hi, honey. What's up?" Jamie said when she answered.

"Is lunch in process?"

"Lunch?" Ryan could nearly see her take a puzzled look at her watch. "It's only eleven, babe."

"I know. Are you at Aunt Maeve's?"

"Aisling and I are at the hotel, looking at the real estate listings and checking out some towns on the internet. But we'll come back to make sure you guys get fed."

"Why don't you go look at a couple of places? The pubs might have a good Sunday afternoon crowd."

"Mmm. That would help."

"Come to think of it," Ryan said, making sure she was speaking loudly enough to be heard by some of the crew, "would it help to have someone come along who knows something about construction? We don't have a lot for Donal or Colm to do now that we've got the bad parts of the ceiling down."

"If you can figure out how to get Colm over here, you'd make Aisling's day."

"Consider it done."

"We'll keep him until dinner," Jamie said. "You're a peach!"

"No problem." She lowered her voice. "Now if I can get rid of three or four more of these guys, we're in business."

"Leave it to you to have too many competent workers, babe."

"That's me," Ryan admitted. "I can't get enough of a good thing."

Only Colm volunteered when Ryan asked, so she sent him on his way, certain at least he and Aisling would have a nice afternoon. She pulled out the keys to her car and jiggled them. "Who's willing to go with me to fetch lunch?"

"Lunch?" Conor was standing next to her in a second. "I'm in. Where are we going?"

"Aunt Moira's. Da? Want to go with us?"

He'd been standing by the front door, hands clasped behind his back, gazing up at the broken laths that Niall would replace.

"Pardon?"

"We're going to go get lunch. Would you like to go with us?"

"Do you need the help?"

"I think we might," Ryan said, lying through her teeth.

"Then I'm right behind you."

"Oops. Help me collect the curtains, will you? I'm taking them in to be dry cleaned."

He gave her a beaming smile, then picked up a pile of folded fabric. "I love that you know how to do a job properly. It only makes sense to get the soot and the dust off the curtains when you're going to paint the place."

It was a very short drive to her aunt's, and they'd just pulled in when Caitlin ran out the back door, hands in the air, her little mouth flapping as usual.

"You don't ever have to wonder if she's glad to see you," Conor said, while sticking his hand out the window to wave.

"She-bon! Cono! Gampa!"

Turning to give Ryan a sharp look, her father said, "Are you certain there was nothing in that plaster that can hurt the baby?"

"Positive. Kieran was sure they didn't use asbestos in plaster here, but we checked with the guys at the builder's yard to make sure. All we're covered with is dust."

"And there's enough of that to be a danger. I've already spoken to Tommy. He agrees they need to move over to the hotel."

"I should have thought of that," Ryan said. "But he wanted Granny and Granddad to have some time with the baby."

"Your grandparents should be at the hotel too," Martin said. "But I'll not be the one to convince them of that." He tossed his door open, and squatted down to grab Caitlin when she ran into his arms. He was smiling so broadly that it brought a tear to Ryan's eye, watching him toss her a few inches into the air to catch her as she shrieked.

"She-bon! I fly!"

"You sure do," Ryan said, ruffling her hair. "Your grampa used to throw me in the air like that, too."

"Ha! Ha!"

Ryan had to admit it seemed impossible now, but the kid was being a little rude to make a point of it.

They went into the house, with Conor grabbing the sandwich Moira was just about to wrap up.

"Don't mind if I do," he said, his hands nearly white with plaster dust.

"We have water, if you've a mind to wash your hands."

"I'm good. Ryan just assured me there's nothing in this dust that can hurt me."

Maeve was working at the counter next to her sister, and she said, "We've made enough for ten men, but I'm still never sure if it will feed you all."

"It will," Conor said. "We're not working all that hard."

"You're not?" Maeve asked, turning to get a good look at them. "You look like you were in an explosion in a talcum powder factory."

"I only had to climb onto the roof once, so it was an easy morning for me. No complaints."

Her father put Caitlin down, and she ran and grabbed Ryan's hand and pulled her into the living room. "Look!" she demanded. "I make."

Ryan looked down at the obviously new set of Legos that her aunt Moira had probably bought. "That's so cool, Cait." She folded her legs so she could sit on the floor. "What is it?"

"House," she said, giving Ryan a slight scowl. "This me." The set was a cutaway of a two-story house, with a bedroom, a bath, a dining room and a kitchen. A little girl was standing on the bed, and two adults were outside by a sporty-looking car. The child picked up the man and shook him in the air. "Cono!"

"Who's this?" Ryan asked, tapping the woman's head.

"Myra," she decided. Ryan gave her props for getting close to Moira. The poor kid would be in grade school before she could pronounce all of the Irish names properly.

Ryan looked up as her aunt Maeve walked over. "Moira gave you a nice present didn't she, honey."

"Myra," she repeated, picking up the little figure and waving it in the air.

"She's the new favorite," Maeve said. "Caitlin's head is easily turned by a gift."

It took Ryan a second to unkink herself, but she got to her feet and said, "Why don't you all go down to the s-e-a? It's too nice a day to be inside."

"We were trying to decide what to do. But we only have so much time. We'll have to make dinner for everyone."

"Everyone?" Ryan asked, raising an eyebrow. "We could fill the church hall, Aunt Maeve. I think we'll wind up at the pub." She put an arm around her. "I don't want you and Aunt Moira to spend all of your time cooking for this crowd. On a day like today, you should get outside and enjoy the fine weather." She leaned over and spoke a little softer. "Ask my father to go with you."

Maeve looked up at her. "Is it not going well?"

"It's fine. But there are too many people at the house. Once Niall replaces the broken lath, Kieran can really get busy. All he'll need is a single helper who won't complain or offer suggestions, and that's me. I'd like everyone else to clear out to give us room to move the ladders."

"Leave it to me, sweetheart. Annie's ready to do some sightseeing, and I'm sure we could convince Tommy and Kevin to come with us."

"Take them over to the Céide Fields. There's plenty of room for Caitlin to run around."

"Brilliant idea. I'll see how many cars we need and get right on it." She laughed a little. "It didn't dawn on me that we'd need a bus, but one would have come in handy."

"Don't remind me. I've got too many laborers, and too few vehicles. We're going to go rent a van on the way back, but that will only help a little."

"Me go!" Caitlin announced, jumping to her feet to grab Ryan's hand.

"You don't know where I'm going. How do you know you want to make the trip?"

"Me go!"

"How about going to the beach with your grandma and grandpa? You love the beach."

The baby dropped Ryan's hand, then grasped her grandmother's. "Me go beach!"

"It might have been nice to spring that on her once we were ready to leave, but I can't fault you for your exuberance," Maeve said, pulling Ryan over to kiss her dusty cheek.

It took a little time to figure out who wanted to go where, but eventually Kevin and Donal took off to have a look around Galway. A short time after they left, Conor, Brendan and Maggie jammed themselves into a little car and headed for the Cliffs of Moher. With her father gone, she was now down to just two supervisors, Kieran and Niall. Luckily, the brothers were used to barking at each other, and neither took offense at being told what to do. They didn't often obey, but not taking offense was good enough for Ryan.

She and Kieran made the first batch of plaster while Niall got onto a ladder and replaced every broken piece of lath, of which there were quite a few.

Ryan carried their plastering materials outside so they could use the hose. Kieran was right behind her, carrying a bag of lime. "Lime?" Ryan asked. "I thought you used gypsum."

"I usually do, but I thought it would be fun to go old school. Lime, sand, horsehair, and water."

"Really? We're using horsehair?"

"Why not? I've only used it once, but if we're going to do this, we might as well have fun, huh?"

Ryan didn't really think this was the proper definition of fun, but when you asked a guy to spend his vacation plastering your grandmother's ceiling, you had to let him carve out his pleasure where he could find it. "What's the consistency supposed to be?" she said after adding a little water to create a damp mess.

"It should look like stiff peanut butter."

"I have a feeling I'm going to have to burn my clothes."

"Nah. This stuff will come right out. The horsehair will make you itch, though." He laughed. "But it's not dangerous."

Chapter Two

After studying the listings for all of the pubs for sale within two hours of Ballina, Jamie and Aisling had narrowed down their list to just four places. None of them were very close, but two of them were only about a half hour straight south, and the other two were roughly the same distance to the west. After Colm arrived, they took off.

Jamie had struggled a little with bringing Colm along. While she knew that both he and Aisling were very helpful when they had their minds on business, she was worried they'd be more interested in each other than in the condition of the pubs. While she had no qualms about giving Aisling the funds to buy a business, she was simply unable to overpay if she didn't have to.

They arrived at the first place, a tiny town on the west coast named Gweesalia. Aisling was driving, and she muttered, "This makes Killala look like a metropolis."

"Two stores and a bar," Colm said, his head moving back and forth as he scanned the street.

"Two shops and a pub," Aisling said, giving him a sweet grin. "Don't go out of your way to sound so American."

"I am American!"

"I realize that. You just don't have to make a point of it."

Jamie could easily see that Aisling was teasing, mostly because she was usually teasing, but Colm clearly hadn't learned to read her very well. He cleared his throat, while still looking out the window. "Is that a problem, Ais? Are you embarrassed to date someone from the US?"

"Embarrassed?" She looked at him as if he'd lost his mind. "Why would I be embarrassed?" Slapping at his thigh, she added, "Don't be such a plank."

He looked into the rear view mirror to catch Jamie's eye. "A plank's bad, right?"

"I think so," Jamie said, laughing a little. "But I've learned to take most of what Aisling says with a hearty grain of salt."

"Exactly. Follow Jamie's lead, Colm. She'll steer you right."

The town was actually quite neat and tidy. But there couldn't have been more than a few hundred people who lived in the area. They were a proper town, though, since they had a pub—even though it was for sale.

The outside of the pub looked promising, but when they went in the interior was dark, and the lighting dim. Colm looked at Jamie when it became clear there wasn't a soul inside. "Did the owners forget to lock the door when they left?"

Aisling marched right over to a swinging door at the end of the bar, pushed it and called out, "Hello?"

There was a rustling sound, then a young woman walked out. She looked like she'd been asleep, with a pink imprint of her fist on her right cheek. "Hello," she said, straightening her shirt. "Would you like a pint?"

"We'd actually like some information," Aisling said, very businesslike. "The place is for sale, yeah?"

"Oh, yeah. My granddad's trying to sell it." She nodded, putting on a weak smile. "Are you in the market?"

"I might be, but I don't think I'm willing to be this far west. I'm just trying to get a feel for what different properties cost."

"I think he's looking for about seventy-five thousand." She shrugged. "But he'd take less. He needs to move to Ballycroy to be closer to my mom and dad. I'm only here helping out."

"Would you mind if we looked around?" Aisling asked. "I'm honestly not interested in buying, but I'd like to see how you've got the place set up."

"All right," the woman said. "You can stay all day if you'll keep me from falling asleep. I've never been so bored in my life."

"Just a peek, then," Aisling said, giving the woman a dazzling smile. She twitched her finger, and Colm followed her into what was likely the kitchen. Jamie went along too, and watched Colm get down to business.

He ran his fingers along the walls, tapping them against the aged tile and the vaguely yellow walls that had probably once been white. "Mmm," he said repeatedly. "Not good."

Jamie went out into the main room and counted seats. At best, the place could hold about fifty, although even having that big a crowd would probably require everyone within five miles to show up at the same moment.

Aisling and Colm emerged from the kitchen, then Colm took a look at the only bathroom. When he walked over, he said, "It's not bad. I could tile both the kitchen and the bath for about five thousand if I could buy tile for the same price I pay at home."

"So you think it's fixable?"

"No problem. But where would the customers come from?"

Aisling turned back to the bartender. "How many do you draw on a Saturday night?"

"Usually ten, maybe a few more. We can fill up when someone gets married, or when someone dies. But that's not common."

"I hate to leave without buying something," Aisling said, "but I don't want to be caught out for drink driving."

The woman waved her hand. "Don't give it another thought. That was the most excitement I've had all day."

"Thanks so much for your time," Aisling said. "I hope you sell fast."

"Oh, we won't. It's been lingering for months now. I'm afraid we might have to walk away."

"Keep a good thought," Aisling said as the three of them exited and stood for a moment in the bright sun.

"That's exactly where I'll be in fifty years," Aisling said, raising her eyes to the heavens. "Desperate to sell and get off my aching feet, but with no takers for my little business."

"No way," Jamie said, taking her by the arm. "Killala's going to have a renaissance. You'll have a prosperous little pub that will be the talk of Mayo." Jamie opened the door and climbed into the back of the car. "This was a long drive, but it was helpful. This place is slightly bigger than yours, and the kitchen is in better shape. I think we could buy McNulty's for less than they're asking." She winced, reminding herself that the McNultys were just local people trying to make some return on their investment. She was about to pull back from her statement when Aisling got into the car.

"Nothing would make my granny happier than punishing the McNultys for doing such a poor job for these last few years. If we got them down to ten thousand, Granny would do a jig."

Jamie laughed at the mental image. "I hate to be that bloodthirsty, but seeing your granny dance might make it worthwhile."

Once Niall had replaced all of the broken or mildewed lath, Kieran was ready to put the first coat of plaster up. Niall took the car and went back to the hotel to take a nap, leaving Ryan to scamper up and down the ladder, dumping small buckets of plaster to the board Kieran was using as a palette to slide globs of it onto a tool he used to squeeze it into the lath. Having him able to stay up on his ladder until he had to move it saved him time and trouble, shifting the burden to Ryan.

By the time she'd been up and down the ladder about fifty times, she was ready to cry. But Kieran had that grimly determined expression on his face that she often saw when her cousins had a task to finish. You couldn't be a top-notch professional if you didn't have the ability to ignore your aching muscles and focus, and Kieran was one of the best at that.

They finished the first coat on all of the worst spots, then went with more modern materials for the rest of the job. This time, she was able to help a little more. Her uncle Eamon had borrowed two drills from friends, and she and Kieran drilled into the plaster wherever it wasn't snug up against the lath. After they'd gone over the whole ceiling, with her shoulders and back muscles feeling like someone had been hitting her with a bat, they filled in the holes with a caulk material, then applied plaster screws into the lath to hold everything tight. Once the caulk dried thoroughly, they'd remove the screws and cover all of the holes with joint compound. But that was for another day. Now, if she could get her legs to stop shaking, she was going to fill the tub in her room and stay in the hot water until it was time for bed.

Ryan's grandfather had taken off when the house was full of workers, and she was surprised to see him return with her grandmother in tow.

Ryan had gone outside to try to get some of the dust out of her hair before realizing she was wasting her time. She stood up and put her baseball cap back on, then looked down at herself. She'd worn an old T-shirt and her painter's pants, liking the hooks and loops she could slip a hammer onto when necessary. The dust was close to their normal color, but she'd made the mistake of wearing a Cal T-shirt, and the dust had rendered the navy blue shoulders almost uniformly white. She was sticky, and sweaty, and so tired she truly wasn't up for a confrontation. But she was damned certain her granny was going to give her one.

"You look like a raccoon!" her grandmother said, shaking her head. "At least you had the sense to wear glasses." She got close, clucking her tongue. "But your eyes are dreadfully red. Is that from dust?"

"I suppose so. Or sweat. You haven't met my cousin Kieran, Granny, our plaster expert."

"Thank you for coming so far to help," she said, extending her hand to shake. Her smile grew a little when she said, "Do people think you two are brother and sister?"

"When a few of us go out together, people always stare," he said, smiling back at her. "Then they see Jamie and they probably assume we kidnapped her."

"You both look like you're about to drop. Do you need a cup of tea?"

"Um…" Ryan took a breath and got it out. "You're not going to be able to use your kitchen, Granny. At all."

"At all?" she said, with her pale eyes growing wide.

"Not at all. We had to take parts of the ceiling down, and it caused a very big mess. I've got the upstairs taped off, with all of your living room furniture stacked in the kitchen. You can move the plastic to get upstairs, but…"

"Should we go stay with Moira?"

Ryan blinked at her. Who was this reasonable person? "Um, you could, but she doesn't have room since Da and Aunt Maeve are in Aisling's room. I know you don't want to but—"

"Is there room at the hotel?" She was gazing at Ryan with what looked like mild curiosity.

"Yes, there is. I checked earlier when I realized it would be impossible to keep Caitlin upstairs."

"All right then. Can we pack a bag?"

"Sure. Sure," she said, knowing her voice was coming out robot-like.

"We'll be right back." She turned and said, "Won't this be fun, John? We haven't been on holiday for years."

As they walked into the house, Kieran said, "Your granny's sweet."

"I…I agree," she said, wondering who the sweet old lady was who was impersonating her normally not-very-sweet-at-all grandmother.

Jamie sat on the edge of the tub, pouring warm water over Ryan's head, gently urging her to join the group for dinner. "Come on, sweetie. You need to eat. Your grandparents are there, your da and Maeve, Eamon and Moira, and your Ryan cousins."

"Too tired. Too sore. Too..." She submerged herself again, blowing a few bubbles until her dark head popped back up. "I'm afraid of that woman who took over Granny's soul."

Jamie laughed. "No one took over your grandmother's soul, sweetheart. You didn't leave her many options. She and your grandfather would have had to sit in their bedroom for three or four days. No TV, no chairs, no tea. She was giving into the inevitable."

Ryan turned slowly and stared for a few moments. "She never gives in. The more inevitable something is, the more she fights it."

"Well, maybe she's taking on some new traits. Come on now. They're waiting for us."

"Why do we have to go to the hotel bar again? It's weird."

"I know." Jamie reached down to the foot of the tub and removed the stopper that hung on a chain, drawing a scowl from her grumpy partner. "But that's where we're going. If you want to, we can leave early and go join your brothers and the boyos."

"Do you know where they are?"

"Uh-huh. We have a mole in the group. Colm has been texting Aisling with updates."

"All right," she said, rising from the water like Venus. "I'll go, but we're sneaking off the first minute we can."

At 8:30, Jamie took a look at her watch, then discretely nudged Ryan, waking her from a light doze. She jerked, then sat up and shivered.

"Working for a living takes some of the spark out of a girl, doesn't it," her grandmother said, chuckling softly. "You haven't said a word all night, Siobhán, and you've not eaten so little since you were three."

She smiled, but it looked like even that had taken a lot out of her. "I think I have some jet lag, too. Everything caught up with me at once."

"Let's go on up to bed," her grandmother said, standing and taking Ryan's hand.

She looked up at her like a child, then rose compliantly. "I hate to go to bed so early," she said. "It's not even dark out."

"I know. But if you go to sleep now, you'll feel like a new woman in the morning."

Martin grasped the sleeve of Jamie's shirt and tugged on it, quietly saying, "Herself isn't under-the-weather, is she?"

"No, Martin. She's fine. As usual, she bit off a lot more than she can chew. I think she's crashing as much from the stress of all of her planning as anything else." Jamie looked up to see Ryan following her grandmother to the stairs like a puppy being trained to walk on a lead. "I don't think she knows where she is right now, but she'll be fine tomorrow."

"We'll be there at nine in the morning," he said. "As promised."

"I don't think I'll see you. Aisling and I are going to check out two more pubs tomorrow. I'm going to see if Colm wants to tag along again, since he was so much help today."

"Bring one of the others for a little variety," Aisling said, straight-faced. "Maybe Niall. He seems like fun."

"I'll check and see who wants to come," Jamie said, impressed with Aisling's acting skills. "We might be stuck with Colm again." She smiled at Maeve, who always teased her about her crush on him. "Not that I mind."

"You'd better go see about Siobhán," Maeve said. "She'll be sound asleep if you don't rush."

"In her clothes," Jamie agreed, pressing kisses to every cheek before racing for the stairs and her exhausted lover.

Jamie's hunch was correct. When she opened the door to their room, Ryan was lying facedown, atop the bedspread, running shoes still on her feet. Jamie didn't want to wake her, but she thought she might be able to at least delicately remove her shoes, which might let her sleep more soundly. She'd just loosened one of the laces when her phone started to buzz. Pulling it from her pocket, she smiled when she heard Mia's voice.

"If you don't miss me yet, you will."

"I miss you every minute I'm not with you," she said, speaking quietly. "Let me call you back in a minute. I've got to move somewhere I can talk."

"Excellent. Then I don't have to pay for the call."

"Two minutes," Jamie said, then hung up. She looked down at Ryan again, and decided to remove her shoes later. She clearly wasn't going anywhere.

Heading back down to the lobby, Jamie saw that the rest of the family was still in the horribly-lit bar—except for Aisling, who was probably already tucked away with Colm.

Skirting the bar, Jamie went outside, where she found a bench located under the branches of a large tree. It was about twenty feet from the hotel entrance, and on a slight rise. Dialing Mia, she stretched her legs out and took in the night sky, which was clear and bright with stars.

"Where were you that you couldn't talk?" Mia asked, never one for formal greetings.

"In our room. My beloved partner worked so hard today that she fell asleep at dinner. I followed her up to our room not three minutes after she left the table, and she was already asleep."

"I'm not saying you should have looked for a lazy woman, but maybe you should have looked for a lazy woman," Mia said, laughing a little. "She could wear you out!"

"I think I'll keep her, but you're right. If she was just a little lazier, she'd be a lot easier to live with. So? What's going on in your part of the world? Isn't it like lunch time?"

"Uh-huh. I'm sitting at a cafe on Telegraph, having a shake."

"Milkshake?"

"Nope." She made an awful noise with her straw. "Some kind of healthy crap. Jordy makes such big dinners that I've had to cut back at lunch. If I gain weight, I can't wear your clothes."

"Perish the thought! Is Jordan with you?"

"Not yet. She's over at Cal, helping some of the returning volleyball players run drills. She'll be along soon, though. She's only willing to work around twenty hours a week, since they're not paying her."

"She's a good woman. And just the right amount of lazy."

"She is," Mia said, with Jamie smiling at the warmth in her voice. "She's also patient, which comes in handy around me."

"What's up with you?"

"Oh, the usual. I bitched about my parents until we both fell asleep last night, but she never told me to hurry up or shut up, either of which she would have been entirely justified in doing."

"What's the beef?"

Mia laughed. "That doesn't sound like you, but I kind of like it. And the beef is that I went to have dinner with them last night to tell them that I wasn't going to law school in the fall."

"Oh, my," Jamie said, trying to sound dramatic. "Who was more upset?"

"My dad, I think. My mom just used it as a launching pad for how irresponsible I am. I don't think she cares if I go to law school or not."

"Mmm. Was your dad hurt?"

"I guess." She sighed heavily. "Yeah. That's probably it. He's got this crazy notion that we'd work at the same firm. But if I did become a lawyer, I'd never represent big corporations, which is all he does."

"No, I can't see you doing that. Although you're working for big corporations now, and that doesn't seem to bother you."

"We're not trying to get them off the hook for poisoning people, or failing to pay women fairly, or invading people's privacy, James. We're just…" She was quiet for a second, then said, "We just try to make sure they don't look bad once they're caught doing that stuff. It's fine with us if they go to prison. Actually, it's better for us if they do. They'll need more spin-doctoring."

"Ahh. That's a very large difference," she said, trying not to laugh.

"What are you going to do? Corporations have all the money. The ACLU doesn't need good PR very often since they're not poisoning people."

"Um, are you currently working with a client who's poisoning people?"

After a significant pause, Mia said, "I can't talk about our clients' secrets. But if you're buying clothes with a halogenated flame retardant..."

"I'll check the labels. So? Where did you leave things?"

"Worse than I found them. My specialty." Her voice had lost some of its fire, and Jamie was about to follow up when she said, "I made the mistake of telling them that we're thinking about getting pregnant in the next year—"

"Oh, Jesus," Jamie sighed. "That's like poking an angry bull! Your mom must have lost it."

"Kinda. Yeah." She was quiet for a few seconds. "Jordy wasn't happy about my telling them, either."

"For good reason, Mia. She told you pretty clearly that she's not ready to have kids."

"She will be," she said, moving on like they were disagreeing on what time to eat dinner. "But I'm really going to have to work on my parents. My dad was as negative about my having kids as my mom was, which really caught me by surprise."

"Well..." Jamie waited a second, making sure she was going to state her point as neutrally as possible. "You had a few rough years, and they weren't that long ago. They're probably still thinking of you as the young woman who gobbled up all of the Ecstasy she could find—"

"Blah, blah, blah. I got all of that BS out of my system when I was in high school. I've been on the straight and narrow since college."

Jamie pulled the phone away and stared at it for a second. Mia hadn't had a single straight and narrow moment in those four years. But she couldn't keep picking away at her. "Give them a little time. Once your dad gets over being hurt, he'll support you. He always does."

"Yeah, he always has, but he wasn't happy with me last night. And now Jordy's a little unhappy with me. You're all I've got left, buddy. So you're going to have to tell me I'm perfect just to even things out."

"You're the best friend I've ever had, and if you were any more perfect, you'd be insufferable."

"Aww. You're my perfect friend. I'm going to call you like every day."

"Any time. Actually calling me around your lunchtime is perfect. Ryan will be asleep, and since I don't like to go out without her, I'll have nothing but time."

Jamie woke to a leaden sky, unsure if it was before dawn or just raining. As she sat up, she did a double-take when she saw that Ryan was right next to her, still in her clothes, still atop the bedspread, still sound asleep. They'd been sleeping together for two years, and the only time she'd woken before Ryan had been when she was ill. Gently, she put her hand to Ryan's forehead, finding it cool and dry. She took a look at the clock radio, and let out a gasp when she saw that it was already eight o'clock.

That tiny sound was enough to wake Ryan, who batted her eyes a few times, then, when her gaze met Jamie's, a smile curled her lips. "Morning, princess."

Jamie tried to cuddle up to her, but the bedspread didn't allow for much movement. "Are you feeling all right?"

"Uh-huh. I've got to pee, though. Be right back."

Jamie watched her slide her feet to the floor. Amazingly, she turned her head to peer at the clock, then simply shrugged her shoulders and padded off to the bath.

"Um, not to be rude, but why are you still here?" Jamie asked. "Did you get up at five and go for a run?"

"Nope." She closed the door, and when she returned a minute later, she climbed into bed on Jamie's side, enfolding her in a full-body hug. "I need eight hours to keep up with the boyos. If I have to give up running, that's just the way it's got to be."

"Um, honey, you got almost twelve hours of sleep. You were out like a light by 8:45."

"I obviously needed it. I'm not as young as I used to be." She placed a kiss to the back of Jamie's neck, then rolled out of bed. "Want breakfast?"

"I'm not in a rush. I'd rather take a shower and blow my hair dry before I eat. Do you mind?"

"I do not. What time are we meeting with our attorney?"

"I made the appointment for late. Four thirty."

Grinning, Ryan rubbed her hands together. "This afternoon, I'll be the first O'Flaherty to own property in Ireland for generations—maybe ever. Couldn't be happier!"

"Your uncle Leo…"

"Rents. As do all of my da's cousins. As did his father, and his father before him. I truly might be the first person in my line to have enough money to own a piece of land." She leaned over and kissed Jamie gently. "And I've only gotten my hands on the cash by sleeping with you." She laughed a little. "Thankfully, I'd do that for free."

Having a big crew was more of a benefit on the second day. Conor was a self-starter, and he'd spent time in the morning prowling around the house, looking for anything out-of-whack. He'd decided the front door wasn't closing properly, and before Ryan could stop him he had the door off the hinges. That would have been more ideal if it hadn't been pissing rain, but they had enough drop cloths to cover the floor near the entry, keeping it dry.

Kevin was testing all of the outlets and repairing the ones that had stopped working long ago. Then he was going to put a more powerful fixture in the kitchen, which had always been too dark.

That left everyone else to help Kieran and Ryan put on the brown coat. Again, Kieran stayed up on his ladder as much as possible, with Ryan climbing up and down hers to hand him material. But this time, her father would load up a small bucket and hand it to her, letting her keep her journeys to three or four rungs of the ladder.

Colm and Donal went along with Jamie and Aisling to check out the last two pubs, and Brendan and Maggie drove Rory to a gig in Sligo, where he was going to hook up with his bandmates to start their summer tour.

When Moira and Maeve came in at eleven with lunch, Ryan peered at them from her perch. "I've never seen you two without a child attached. Where is everyone?"

"Tommy and Annie took Caitlin to a play center in Castlebar. We couldn't get a thing done with her underfoot," Moira said. "It's only been a few years since I've had a toddler, but I'd clearly forgotten how much trouble they are!"

"That's why I haven't knitted a scarf since the child was born," Maeve said.

"She runs herself ragged," Martin added. "I didn't work nearly so hard when I was an active firefighter."

"Oh, she's the joy of my life, and you know that, Marty. But I'll admit I don't mind a little time to myself." She walked over and handed him a sandwich. "Of course, I like to spend my free time taking care of you."

"The only difference between Caitlin and me is that I appreciate you," he said, smiling at her. "She still thinks the world revolves around her."

"I'm sure the world doesn't revolve around me," Ryan said. "If it did, I wouldn't be up on this feckin' ladder!"

Chapter Three

The solicitor's office was right in Killala, so Jamie arranged to meet Ryan at her aunt's house. Jamie entered the house to find her sitting on the big sofa in the living room, with Cáit on one side of her and Brenna on the other, both still in their school uniforms.

Everyone looked up, with Jamie saying, "Isn't your summer vacation ever going to start?"

"No," Brenna said, clearly sulking. "We don't get out until the twenty-ninth of June."

"Isn't there some human rights organization we can call..."

Moira walked into the room from the kitchen. "Seven weeks of vacation is plenty for this one," she said, pointing at her youngest. "She'll be looking for entertainment every minute." She continued over to the sofa and ran her hand over Cáit's auburn hair. "And this one has three long weeks of exams in front of her. She's doing her Leaving Cert, you know."

Ryan's face paled in a second. "That's now?"

Cáit nodded. "English was today. Irish is on Thursday."

"Shit!" She gave Brenna a quick look. "Sorry. I know I shouldn't use language like that, but I had no idea Cáit was doing her Leaving Cert right now." She turned back to Cáit. "How can I help?"

"I'm fine," she said, looking to her mother for help.

"We've all asked how we can help, but she insists she's as ready as she can be."

"I am, Mam. I've got two days to review, then I can work on my Maths on the weekend."

"I'm so sorry I didn't realize you had an exam today," Ryan said, looking like she wanted Cáit to at least chide her. But the kid seemed tired, but calm, the look of someone who'd studied all year and was as confident as anyone could be when faced with a large number of tests.

Brenna had clearly spent enough time thinking about her sister. She looked at Jamie, with her eyes bright and an entreating smile affixed to her face. "Siobhán says we can go to the solicitor with you if you say it's okay."

"I don't really want to…" Cáit said, trailing off when Brenna reached behind Ryan to pop her on the shoulder.

"We really want to go," Brenna said.

"To meet with a lawyer?" Jamie scowled at Ryan. "What else did you promise?"

"Nothing. Brenna wanted to go, and I couldn't think of a reason to say no."

"I can," Jamie said. "It'll be boring, and I need to concentrate. But after we're finished, we'll come pick you up and take you to get an ice cream. How's that?"

She brightened visibly. "The best ice cream's in Sligo. Can we go there?"

Jamie rolled her eyes. "Yes. We can go to Sligo. But we'll have to take the baby if she's back by then."

Now Brenna made the same expression, but her eyes rolled even more dramatically. "Can't Tommy put her to bed early? You can't talk at all when she's around."

Moira started to laugh, mumbling something to herself as she went back into the kitchen.

"Yeah. That's a real bummer," Ryan said, keeping a straight face. "She's such an attention hog."

"You can't forget about us," Brenna said. "The place I like is open until nine, so make sure you're back in time."

"Nine?" Jamie asked, her brows rising. "It's just after four, and I can't imagine this taking very long. I assumed we'd all meet at the pub for dinner."

Brenna covered her mouth, stifling a laugh. "Oh, that's a good idea. We'll all have dinner at the pub."

Jamie shot a glance at Ryan, who was acting like she hadn't even heard the kid. Something was clearly up, but she didn't have time to grill her. Of course, if they stayed at the house for another two minutes, Brenna would spill whatever beans there were to spill, even if she'd been sworn to secrecy. She was as transparent as tissue paper. Her sister, on the other hand, would barely mention it if she was bleeding from a gaping wound. Sometimes it was hard to comprehend what a crapshoot it was to have kids. There was no way to predict what you'd get.

They drove to the solicitor, which seemed like a big waste of fuel to Jamie. She was going to ask Ryan why she wanted to drive, but thought she might have been climbing up and down that ladder all day again. If she suggested driving rather than walking, she always had a reason.

They arrived at the solicitor a few minutes early, with Jamie looking around the tiny waiting room. The office was on the first floor of a two story building, with what looked like an apartment on the second floor. She'd been to a lot of attorneys' offices in her life, but this was the most modest of them all.

The room was decorated with inexpensive paneling and an industrial-strength carpet on the floor. When the inner door opened, a man in his fifties or sixties poked his head out and waved, using just the tips of his fingers—like you'd do to a baby. "Hello, girls," he said. "Jamie and Siobhán?"

"That's us," Ryan said, standing up and walking over to him. "I'm Siobhán, by the way."

"Fergal Pierce," he said, nodding as they entered. "I've everything ready, so this won't take a minute."

"I'm ready to go," Ryan said, clearly excited. "We've got everything you told us to bring."

"Then this will go even faster. I do love it when clients are prepared."

"You're going to be a happy man, Mr. Pierce," Ryan said, clearly proud of herself for checking her to-do list a million times in the last month. If there was anything missing from their documentation, it was because of someone else's mistake. Ryan had definitely not made one.

They were out of the office by 4:45, and they'd only delayed that long because Mr. Pierce knew her grandmother slightly, and they had to go down their list of other people they might mutually know. It was a time-consuming ritual, but Ryan kind of loved it. Having common friends or acquaintances immediately gave you a toe-hold to a conversation, even if it was a brief one.

She held up her hands once they were on the sidewalk. "Isn't it funny to buy something and not get a set of keys?"

"Keys to what? There aren't any buildings."

"Not yet," Ryan said, waggling her eyebrows. "But one day…"

"I'm just glad I've found a country that compels you to open up your checkbook once in a while. We've spent more money in Ireland than we have in the whole time I've known you in San Francisco."

"I guess that's true. But I've got something to show for this money. Land."

"You're thrilled, aren't you, sweetie."

"Beyond," she said, snapping her wrist to indicate a great distance. "Way beyond thrilled. Can we go look around?"

"At…what?"

Ryan laughed as she took Jamie's hand to urge her into the car. "Sometimes I wonder which one of us is the practical one and which is the artist."

"I'm not an artist," Jamie said, wrinkling up her nose.

"I'm not either, but when I look at my land…" She put her hand over her heart and tapped it a few times. "I feel an awful lot."

"Then let's go look at your land. I love it when you feel."

It only took five minutes to reach the property, with Jamie scanning the stone wall that encircled a portion of the property as they drove along. Ryan pulled over to park on a strip of grass, with Jamie asking, "Is there a break in the wall? If so, I've never seen it."

"Um…" She got out and stood next to the car, with her hands on her hips. "If we don't want to scale this, I guess we'd better look further."

She hopped back in and drove along the lightly-traveled lane, looking for a break—which Jamie knew didn't exist on this side. The wall wasn't very tall, maybe three and a half feet, but the mason had set sharp, thin stones into the capstone all along the length of it. The jagged stones stuck up like a bunch of widely spaced, gruesome looking teeth. If you didn't scale it with enough clearance, you'd catch your jeans—at best.

Ryan turned right when she had a chance, and drove slowly. She'd gotten about halfway down the property when she said, "Right there."

The remains of an old metal gate covered about ten feet of space. Ryan pulled over in front of it and hopped out before Jamie could get her door open. "I'm sure I can bend this if I put any pressure on it."

Jamie stood next to her and took a look. "It's just this sturdy vine that's stopping it from falling to the ground."

"Hmm. I guess we can just climb over it." She smiled. "Better here than on the main road. We can shimmy over this and not wind up in the Emergency Department. But we've got some things to carry."

"We do?"

"Uh-huh," she said, smiling like a fox. She used her key to open the trunk and pull out a blanket and a picnic basket. "While I worked, and you did your pub crawl, my aunts made us a picnic. I'm a little surprised Brenna didn't hide herself under this blanket, but it appears that we're all alone for our first meal in our new home."

Jamie threw her arms around her and hugged her tightly. "Such a romantic."

"I have my moments. If I help you over, can I hand you this stuff?"

"Sure."

Ryan put everything back into the trunk for a moment, then put her hands on Jamie's waist and mostly lifted her over the plant-choked metal.

"Very impressive, Studly. Working construction all year has given you a different set of muscles."

"And I've still got some pop in my legs," she said. After handing the basket and blanket to Jamie, she backed up a few feet and ran toward the gate, slapping her hand onto it to propel herself over it like she was doing the high jump. "Score!"

"You're a studly jock, which is the best kind."

"I'd argue, but…" She took the picnic basket and started to walk across the field. No one had mowed it for a long time, and it was thick with vibrant green grass at least ten inches long. It was actually so long it couldn't stand up, creating a kind of thick carpet.

"Why are there so few weeds? At home, our lawns would be all nasty stuff if we didn't keep after them."

"Well, at home we can't grow this kind of grass. Plus we only get rain for a few months a year—at best. I think this grass is so thick and healthy there's no room for weeds to get a toe-hold. Our sheep are going to love this, aren't they?"

"Our sheep, huh? Are they arriving like…tomorrow?"

"Nope. But I was seriously thinking of buying your horse this summer."

Jamie stopped and stared at her. "This summer? I know you don't know a lot about horses, but they need some tending."

"Aunt Moira said she'd love to watch your horse when we're not here."

"Honey," Jamie soothed, looking up at the earnest expression Ryan wore, "I think we should wait until we have a house and can put up a proper barn. There's…nothing here."

"Sure there is. The lambing shed my granny used to play in is still here."

"Play," Jamie said, rolling her eyes. "I don't think your granny ever had a minute to play. She's had her head down, working, since she could walk."

"No, no, she said they played a little out here. She has very fond memories of this place. I think she and her siblings thought of the sheep as pets…until they sold them or ate them," she said, finishing quietly.

They picked their way across the grass, with Jamie holding onto Ryan's free hand. So far, her footing had been firm, but she didn't want to trip over a gopher hole—or whatever kind of animal burrowed around Ireland.

They came to a small rise, and were able to see the shed, a very rough-looking structure. "You're not planning on raising sheep for food, are you?" Jamie asked. "I mean, I admit that I eat lamb, but…"

"I wasn't planning on it. I thought we'd just keep a few sheep at first, then bring a ram in every year to have a couple more. We could keep the females and give the males away. Nothing very intense."

"Yeah. That sounds like you," Jamie said, chuckling. "Nothing very intense."

"Go ahead and make fun, but you'll see I'm a different person here in Ireland. I'm super laid-back," she insisted, probably believing her own fantasy.

"Uh-huh. And that's why you went to sleep at eight thirty last night. In your clothes."

"Well," she said, showing a small smile. "It's going to take me a few days to get into Ireland mode. Then I'll be super laid-back." She slapped herself in the forehead with the flat of her hand. "I'm not laid-back about not knowing Cáit was doing her Leaving Cert. I didn't even wish her good luck on today's exam. Actually, I'm miffed my aunt didn't mention it, given that Cáit never would."

"There's not much you can do, Ryan. I'd offer to help, since I have more free time, but I have no idea what a Leaving Cert is."

"Mmm. The system is complicated, but I can distill it. To get into university, Cáit has to get minimum scores on a series of exams. They're national exams, with everyone sitting for them over a few week's time."

"Well, that sounds horrid. But when she gets her results she'll know where she's going to college, right?"

"Kind of," Ryan said, waggling her hand. "That part's even more complicated. She won't get her results until August, so she's got a long time to worry."

"August? She's got to sit around all summer, hoping she makes the grade?"

"Everyone does. I think Aisling had just three to four weeks notice before she started at NUI-Galway. Her first choice was University College Cork, but she didn't make it."

"You're serious," Jamie said, stunned. "Mia and I had time to look for houses, buy one, have it painted, then furnish the whole place between the time we were admitted to Cal and when we started classes. Cáit won't have time to buy an advance-fare train ticket!"

"It's kind of harsh," Ryan said, "especially if you're the kind of person who likes to have everything settled."

"When do parents start bribing their kid's way into the best schools? Cassie's mom was ready to sleep with the head of admissions at Cal, and now that I think of it, she might have. Cassie's SATs weren't fabulous."

"I'm sure someone has gamed the system, but from what I can tell, that's harder to do in Ireland."

"Well, let's be available if Cáit wants any help."

"I can drill her on math." She pursed her lips together, looking very serious. "I'm not sure when I'll do that, but I'll figure it out."

Jamie squeezed Ryan's hand and took in a deep breath. "We'll worry about Cáit later. Let's focus on this moment." She sniffed the air again and said, "Why does it smell so darned good around here?"

"Probably because the closest industry is miles and miles from here. No factories are belching fumes into the air. The plants don't hurt, either. They clean the air."

"I bet it won't smell as good once we get some sheep. Unless you're going to come out here and clean up after them."

"It's all part of the cycle," she said, acting like she knew what she was talking about. "Sheep poop helps to fertilize the land."

"It certainly did a good job. I've never been in grass this springy."

"Ahh…" She stood in front of the lambing shed, looking at the ramshackle thing like it was a work of art. "I wonder who put up these stone walls?"

"Or the tin roof—which has more holes than Swiss cheese."

"The roof came a long time after the walls." Ryan slapped her hand onto the substantial stones, each one around a foot wide. "This could have been put up in the seventeen hundreds."

"I suppose… But the roof is a lot newer than that."

"Oh, yeah. They probably had a thatched roof or something like that for a long time. I bet they had the tin roof when my granny was a girl."

The structure was just a back wall of about twenty feet, with shorter side walls. There had been some kind of wooden structure inside, probably to protect the baby lambs, but it had also mostly fallen to the ground. The sun hit the tin roof, shooting down through the holes to land on some of the very old hay. It looked a little like a creche, Irish-style, and Jamie could easily picture a sheep giving birth in there, with Granny and her siblings watching in awe.

"One day, I want our kids to be down here, watching our sheep have lambs." She looked up into Ryan's eyes, seeing they were already damp.

"I'd love that," she said, with her voice breaking a little.

"I truly love it here," Jamie sighed. "I can just picture our house."

"You can? I don't have much of an image."

"I think so. I want it to blend in as much as possible, but I want it to be big enough to have guests. If we have two or three kids, along with Aisling living here, plus your father and your aunt… We need a barracks."

"Maybe we'll build Aisling her own place. She definitely wants kids, so she'll need some room. And we could build a little home for Da and Aunt Maeve. Then we could have guests stay with us."

"We still need a barracks," Jamie teased. "Knowing you, you'll have all of your aunts and uncles and cousins coming and going year-round."

"Yeah," she said, smirking. "That will happen, so we might as well prepare for it." She let out a laugh. "The architect is going to think we've lost our minds. No one builds a six-bedroom house in Killala."

"With two smaller houses on the property."

"We'll hold off on those for the time being. We'll muddle along with six bedrooms until we and Ais have kids."

"If Ais and Colm hook up, you'll have O'Flaherty-O'Donohue second-cousins. Wouldn't that be sweet?"

"Still chewing that one over," Ryan admitted. "But if it turns out that way, I'll get over my…whatever it is that makes me itch when I think about their being together." She took the blanket and snapped her wrists to let it unfold. "I always feel better when I eat. Hungry?"

"Very. We ate at one of the pubs we visited and the food was ghastly. I pushed it around on my plate so I didn't offend anyone."

"I don't know what we've got in this basket, but I trust my aunts to do a better job than a pub in…where?"

"Bally-something or other. I get my Ballys confused."

"Have a seat," Ryan said. "You can occupy yourself by opening this wine while I unwrap the food."

"Wine, huh?" She held up the bottle and read the label. "Who bought this? It's…" She stopped herself from saying it was awfully nice for Killala. "A good bottle."

"Aisling likes wine. She found an off-license in Ballina and bought some yesterday." She tapped her temple. "I've been planning."

"You could take over the world if you set your mind to it."

Ryan folded herself into a seated position, then leaned over and gave Jamie a tender kiss. "I only want to capture your heart."

"It's yours, sweetheart. And always will be."

Grinning, Ryan leaned back, resting with her arms slightly behind her. "I'm still loving this monogamy thing. You?"

"Pretty much," Jamie said, smiling at her. "I still check out every woman who walks by, but I haven't found one I want to trade you in for yet."

"Just let me know. I can step up my game if the competition gets fierce."

After making short work of the cork, Jamie pulled two wine glasses from the basket. They'd been wrapped in tea towels, and she held one glass up to the light as she poured. "Look at that color," she sighed. "I never buy clothing that's anywhere close to the color of wine, but I'm entranced by it in liquid form." She handed Ryan the glass, then poured another for herself. "To us, landed gentry of County Mayo."

They clinked their glasses together and each took a sip. "Nice," Ryan said, looking like she meant it. "I never could have guessed I'd wind up buying property here, much less while I was still young." She tipped her glass in Jamie's direction. "You've made dreams come true that I hadn't even considered."

"Same for me," she said, feeling a smile settle onto her lips. "Three years ago, I was moping around the house, anxious to get back to Cal. I wasn't happy at home, I wasn't happy with my engagement, and I felt like the walls were closing in on me." She tapped her glass onto Ryan's again. "My world opened up when I met you just two months later."

Ryan patted the ground near her hip. "Why don't you scoot over here? We can look out at our gorgeous field together."

Jamie handed her glass over, then did as requested. When she returned the glass, Ryan draped an arm around her shoulders. "Pretty nice, huh?"

"I was sure today was going to stay rainy and gray. But once the sun came out, it turned into a spectacular day." She extended a finger, pointing toward a pair of birds that flew low over the land, then swooped up to perch in a tall tree near the property line. "Do you know what kind of birds those are? I don't recognize them."

"I don't know a thing about birds. But I see those all over Ireland. I'll have to ask my uncle. He knows nature pretty well."

"Don't rush off to do that right now. I want to stay here until it's too dark to see." She turned slightly to meet Ryan's gaze. "This is a peak experience."

"Worthy of a journal entry?"

"A few pages. For sure."

"I'm not sure if there haven't been any cars come down the lane, or if we're far enough away that we can't hear them. I hope it's the latter. We're going to have to test that out before we decide where to place our house. I want it to be in the quietest spot."

Jamie nestled up against Ryan's body, relishing her scent. When she was fresh from a shower, there was no better smell on earth. Just clean skin, clean clothes, and a little natural spice from her body.

"You know what this reminds me of?"

"I can't guess."

"Being in my tree house when I was a kid. It was always really tranquil up there, and being up in the leaves of the tree made me feel like I was in the middle of nature."

"Nice image. I know you loved your tree house, so if this brings back that memory, I'm happy."

"I'm happy too. With this, but most of all, with you."

Ryan turned and gazed into her eyes for a few moments. Jamie already knew she was going to kiss her. But she wasn't quite sure what level of intensity she was going to put into it. Sometimes the heat of her gaze was a good barometer. But sometimes you had to just wait and see.

Keeping her gaze locked on Jamie, Ryan tilted her glass to her lips, swallowing the rest of her wine like it was water. *Ooo.* This was going to be a serious knee-wobbler.

Jamie followed her lead, draining her glass, then putting the cork back into the bottle and setting it aside. The second she'd finished that task, strong arms encircled her, tugging her close to Ryan's warm body.

"We've toasted to our new home, but we haven't properly memorialized the occasion. That requires a little more effort." Her lopsided grin was so cute it was almost silly. Jamie tilted her head and leaned forward, brushing her lips across Ryan's, then returning to linger for a few moments.

"I wouldn't really call this hard work, sport."

"Not hard, no," she murmured. "But vital."

"Oh, yeah. It's definitely vital."

With just a shift of Ryan's hips, they were lying on their sides, then a strong hand started to glide along Jamie's body while Ryan captured her lips again. "Our first time making love at our new home."

"Making love?" Jamie's eyebrows rose. "We're going to make love?"

"Sure are," Ryan said, the essence of certitude. "Right now."

"Out here in the open? Just a few hundred yards from your aunt's house? Within easy distance of Brenna's watchful eye?"

"Uh-huh. Right here. Right now."

When Jamie looked into those cool, blue eyes, filled with a mixture of desire and drive, there was no turning back. If she hadn't already been ravenously attracted to her, that look of complete confidence would have sent her over the edge. "If anyone catches us, I'm going to say you caught me in a weak moment."

Ryan's smirk made her look particularly rakish. "Those are my favorite moments with you." She laughed a little. "You're never weak, but you can pretty convincingly act like you are."

Jamie wrapped her arms around Ryan's body and hugged her tightly. "You know how I know how much you love me?"

"Tell me."

"You want to make love before you eat."

Ryan laughed. "Too true. My love for you is many times greater than my appetite." She dipped her head and pressed a heated kiss to Jamie's lips, so intense and purposeful that her eyes nearly rolled back in her head. Ryan could go from a walk in the park to a full-out sprint in the blink of an eye, always keeping you guessing.

That kiss flipped a switch, and before she knew she was moving, Jamie was astride Ryan's hips, pressing her shoulders into the ground. Looking down at her placid expression, about as carefree as a woman could look, Jamie felt like her blood was about to boil. "When you lie there, looking so blasé, you make me want to climb you."

"Let's go," Ryan said, grasping her ass and squeezing it hard.

"Oh, we're going." In mere seconds, Ryan's T-shirt lay next to them, joined by her bra a moment later. If Jamie'd had to testify under oath, she couldn't have said how she'd accomplished that, but she frankly didn't care. Having all of that supple skin just waiting to be touched filled her head to the brim.

The sun was hitting them full-on now, its warmth heating up Ryan's skin until it released some of its more erotic elements. Jamie tried to fill her lungs, but she was so fixated on Ryan's rock-hard nipples that she wasn't sure she was breathing at all, much less deeply.

Ryan's hands were on her head, neither guiding nor encouraging. She seemed to just enjoy being connected in one more way.

Unable to get enough of the taste of her body or the soft sighs that left her lips, Jamie tried to pace herself. But that was impossible to do when what you wanted was right in front of your eyes, willingly offering itself up for your pleasure. Her head began to ache from the desire that coursed through her veins, but it would take more than a headache to stop her now. The whole family could show up and she thought she might just wave them aside and keep going.

"I've never tasted anything as delicious as your skin," she murmured, licking and nibbling Ryan's breasts, the tender skin of her belly, the muscles in her arms.

Ryan placed her hands on Jamie's hips and shifted so they were on their sides again. Then her hand slipped into the front of Jamie's slim-cut khakis and covered her sex with the flat of her hand. "I'm going to get these clothes off you and bury my face between your legs. I'm going to do that right now," she murmured, with her eyes looking a little wild.

Jamie grasped a hand and slapped it onto her breast, purring when Ryan instinctively squeezed it. She had the best instincts. "More of that," Jamie whispered, eyes closed tightly.

Ryan pressed into her, until she was half on her back, with her breasts being manipulated gently but unceasingly. Their lips met again, and Ryan started to probe her mouth with her tongue, making the kisses even sweeter.

The relentless pressure continued to grow until Jamie's breasts were tingling with sensation. They crossed the threshold from pleasure to pain again and again, until she was moaning low in her chest, while rubbing her sex against Ryan's thigh.

Everything changed in an instant as Ryan stripped her efficiently, slacks and undies tossed away in a flash. In another half of a second, her legs were draped over Ryan's shoulders, and she felt herself opening up to her fiercely determined tongue. She knew she wouldn't last long, but when fingers slid inside her and pressed down, she thrust herself so hard against Ryan's hand it sounded like a sharp slap.

Her climax caught her completely off-guard, and Jamie rode it out as long as she could, with them rolling around wildly as she chased Ryan's fingers for just a little more stimulation.

Finally spent, Jamie tried to relax, but her muscles were nearly in spasm. Ryan was trapped between her legs, and she gently stroked them, quietly saying, "Relax, sweetheart. Let go now. I've got you."

It took some effort, but Jamie finally convinced her thighs to relax. Ryan climbed up her body and covered her with kisses, painting her cheeks, her forehead, and finally, her lips. "That's exactly what I wanted our first time making love on our land to be," she sighed. "We've set a pretty high bar, but we've got to try to top that every time."

Jamie got out a laugh, but she wasn't sure where she'd gotten the energy. "You might kill me, but I'll go with a smile on my face."

The sun was still in her eyes when Ryan lay on her back, completely spent. "I'd stay right here if we didn't have to take Brenna to Sligo," she sighed.

"Oh, shit!" Jamie looked at her watch. "It's eight. Will we make it?"

"Unfortunately," Ryan said, nodding. "If we'd forgotten until it was too late, I'd just stay and accept my punishment for breaking a promise. But since I'd be breaking it intentionally…" She sat up, feeling a little light-headed. "Where are my clothes?"

"I threw your jeans somewhere, but they can't be far."

"Damn," Ryan said, rolling over to get to her hands and knees. "We were on fire!"

"Time, opportunity, a novel spot…"

"The possibility of being caught." She gave Jamie a hearty slap on the ass. "I know your exhibitionist streak heats you up."

"Your streak is easily as wide as mine."

"Just because that's true doesn't mean you have to make a point of it."

"Come on, Buffy. Let's go before Brenna organizes a search party."

"I kept trying to force myself to keep my eyes open," Ryan said. "If she came looking for us, she'd see our car. That would make her come through the gate, and I had a clear view of it." She laughed. "When I was able to keep my little peepers open, that is. She could have snuck in when the top of my head was blowing off."

Jamie got to her feet and started to shimmy into her slacks. "We've properly christened our little patch of Ireland. Well done," she added, helping Ryan to her feet.

"Got 'em," Ryan said when she spotted her jeans. "You should think about taking up shot-put or the discus."

"Shake a leg, O'Flaherty. And come up with a good excuse for why we look like we've been wrestling on the ground for the last couple of hours. Your aunt and uncle won't believe us, but Brenna's still naive enough to buy a good story—I hope."

Chapter Four

On their third day of the project, Ryan only had to go up and down her ladder twenty times, a significant improvement. After Kieran skillfully applied the finish coat of plaster to the areas they'd had to do from scratch, they both stood beneath them and looked up.

"A damn fine job, if I do say so myself," Kieran said. He lowered his chin, then let his gaze travel around the room. "Have you noticed we're the only ones working?"

"You know, I have," she said, chuckling. "Everyone else is sightseeing."

"Sightseeing," he said slowly. "I wonder what that's like? All I've seen is the road between Ballina and Killala, the interior of two pubs, and my room at the hotel."

Ryan nodded slowly. "If Cáit doesn't need help getting ready for her big test on Thursday, we can do something fun. Hold on and I'll call her to check in." She went outside to call, reaching her aunt. "Hi there. How's the scholar?"

"Good, I think. She's at her friend's house today, studying. She said she'd take time for a meal, but that's it."

"Got it. Make it clear to her that I'm willing to jump in and help, okay?"

"She knows that, honey. But I don't think you're going to get a call. Cáit has her own schedule, and she tends to stick to it."

"That makes sense. Just let her know I'll make time for her if she wants me to."

"I will give her the message. Now go put up or take down a ceiling."

"I'm on it," Ryan said, stepping back into the house. "Kieran, this is a good day for us to do something fun. We could see the sights, or go to some Victorian-era seaweed baths in Enniscrone—"

"Like a spa?"

"Um, not like a spa back home. More like a room with an ancient tub that they fill with hot water and seaweed. I love it but—"

"Who's driving?"

"I guess I am," Ryan said. "And there's a good spot for fish and chips nearby."

He was out the front door before Ryan could say another word. She caught him standing in front of the car, clearly ready to go. "So, we've just got to take off the plaster screws tomorrow, fill the holes with joint compound, and paint, right?" she asked.

He nodded. "That's exactly what someone else needs to do. I'm on vacation unless anyone else needs plaster repair."

Ryan got in and started to fasten her seatbelt. "I like the way you think. Jamie and I could finish the rest of this job. It's kind of a snap."

He reached over and gave her a cuff to the arm. "You're like your father. You think you've got to be involved in everything."

"I…" She sighed. "I wish I wasn't like that, but I clearly am."

"You can take your foot off the gas now. Brendan and Tommy and Colm and Donal haven't done squat. Let them finish up. Your da can supervise."

"I don't think they'd even need supervision."

He gave her a smile that showed a little of the fondness she knew he felt for her. "They certainly don't. But that doesn't mean your father doesn't need to give it. Let him have a little fun."

After she and Kieran spent a long time relaxing in their separate baths, Ryan spent the last part of the afternoon going for a long run along the Moy River. She kept to the sidewalk for a while, but that was too boring, so she clambered down a path to reach a strip of grass that hugged the bank. She was muddy and wet within twenty yards, and was afraid she'd break an ankle, so she climbed back up to the sidewalk for a while. It wasn't until she hit the Belleek Woods on the outskirts of town that she finally started to smile. She wasn't sure how long the trails were, but she knew the woods were big—for Ireland.

After a few hundred yards she got into a groove, and let herself relax her stride and take in the scented air, full of all sorts of good-smelling things. The air was heavy with moisture, one of her favorite things. She loved the way her lungs felt cleaner after breathing in damp air—kind of like steam-cleaning them.

She was still getting plenty dirty, since the paths were muddy in spots, and she kicked wet earth up with every stride. But she could worry about cleaning up later. She was having too much fun to worry about the repercussions.

At four o'clock, Ryan sat in the only launderette in Ballina, cleaning all of the clothing she'd managed to turn into a filthy mess in only two and a half days. She didn't bother with Jamie's stuff, since all she had were a couple of pair of undies, and she was particular about how they were washed.

The whole cycle was an hour and a half, which just seemed mad to her, so she set out searching for a place for dinner, having vowed not to have another meal in the hotel.

She was at the end of the main commercial street when she saw a couple of guys standing outside of a restaurant, smoking. They had the look of cooks or dishwashers, with their checked pants and white jackets, and she went up to them and said, "Do you guys work here?"

"Uh-huh," the taller of the two said, giving her a quick once-over that she typically only got in Ireland.

"What kind of food do you serve?"

"All kinds," the shorter, younger guy said. "Are you hungry?"

"Always. But I've got a big group. How many do you seat?"

"About fifty."

"Anyone inside I can speak to about a reservation?"

"You can talk to me," the taller guy said, smiling like he was reeling in a big fish. "I cook the food, so I should get to decide who eats it, eh?"

She nodded, then tried the door. "I'll just make sure there's room."

"Stop by the kitchen later," he said, making her laugh. "I can sneak a naggin or two of whiskey out." He tilted his head to indicate a dirty alley. "Come by after nine when the rush is over."

"If I come to meet you in the alley, it will definitely be after nine," she said, admiring his confidence. It was unwarranted, but she still admired it.

The restaurant had room for fifteen at six, and Ryan successfully wrangled her grandparents, her father and aunt, her aunt and uncle, all four of their kids, along with Maggie, Brendan, and Conor. Even though she hadn't seen much of Caitlin, Ryan was glad Tommy and Annie hadn't wanted to join them. It was hard enough having a conversation with Brenna in the mix. Adding Caitlin was a recipe for chaos.

Jamie was on her left, with Conor on her right. He'd wanted to join the cousins at the pub, but Ryan had convinced him when she'd offered to pay. The boy couldn't resist a free meal.

He leaned over while they were eating their soup, saying, "Have you talked to Colm since we've been here?"

"Not much. Why?"

"Something's going on with him," he said, with his eyes slightly narrowed. "He hasn't been around much, and when he is, he's not himself."

"We've only been here three days, Conor. He's probably got jet lag."

"No, no, I mean back home, too. I haven't been able to get him to go with me to find a new bar since Christmas." He took a sip of his soup, looking thoughtful. "We used to go out every week or two, but he keeps saying he's got something else going on." He gazed at her, with his eyes lowered. "Think he's pissed at me about something?"

"Of course not," she said, giving him an elbow. "Maybe he's seeing someone."

He shrugged. "That's a definite possibility at home, but not here. We've been out twice now, and he acts like the women are radioactive. Won't even sit by me to check them out."

"Mmm. Well," she said, thinking hard. "If he was seeing someone at home, maybe he doesn't want to screw that up."

He gave her a puzzled look. "But the girl's not here. How would she know he was looking at other women?"

She almost went into it, then decided it was a waste of time trying to explain that some people thought monogamy meant not only not touching, but not looking. He'd never buy it. Instead, she shrugged. "Jet lag. Definitely jet lag."

After dinner, everyone staying at the hotel walked back, with Granny leading the pack. She wasn't faster than Ryan, but she'd leave you in the dust if you were only strolling. Ryan pulled Aisling to the rear, and mentioned what Conor had said.

"I think you've got to tell Colm to act like he normally does when he's with the boyos."

Aisling gave her a perturbed glance. "Should he actually charm the knickers off some girl, or can he stop short of shagging her?"

Ryan put her arm around her, smiling at Jamie, who was on Aisling's other side. "I'm not saying he should boink his way through Ballina, but he's acting like he's taken a vow of celibacy. Just suggest he at least look at other women."

"Why do the others care? What business is it of theirs?"

"It's definitely not their business, but they gossip constantly. It's infuriating, since they're so oblivious about so many things, but they keep a close eye on each other—especially when it comes to women."

"Lovely," she grumbled. "I not only have to work to get him alone, I have to encourage him to drool over other women."

"He doesn't need to drool," Ryan insisted. "Just have him act like he's still got a sex drive."

"Oh, he has that," she said, giving Ryan a satisfied smile. "I've no complaints in that department."

"If you don't want me to go into detail about how Jamie and I celebrated our property purchase last night, you'll keep your thoughts about that to yourself." She flinched when Jamie reach around Aisling to pinch the skin right above the waistband of her jeans, a particularly tender spot. "Ouch!"

"Don't you dare talk about what we did last night! Or any night for that matter."

"I bet you tell Mia everything," Ryan groused.

"That's different. I don't know why, but it's definitely different."

"Got it. You can talk about our sex life, but I can't."

"Makes sense to me," Aisling said, smiling at Ryan. "I'd box Colm's ears if he talked about what we do, but I can happily taunt you with details."

"So I can't talk, and I can't bear to listen."

"That sums it up nicely," Aisling said. "I'm glad you're finally catching on."

Around ten o'clock, Jamie was sitting on the bed, reading, while Ryan watched an Irish-language rugby match on TG4. A door closed loudly, and she heard voices, but she didn't pay much attention until a woman's voice rose and it dawned on her that it was coming from next door.

She nudged Ryan with her foot. "Aisling's yelling at someone. I'm guessing it's Colm, unless she's talking to herself."

Ryan took the pillow she'd been using and wrapped it around her head. "All better," she said, with her voice muffled.

Nudging her again, Jamie spoke up. "Come on, babe. Go tell her to lower her voice. The pub closes in an hour, and the boyos will be coming home."

"She can't keep that up for an hour. She'll lose her voice."

"Ryan…" She pulled at the pillow, managing to move it enough to see Ryan's ear. "Your grandmother's just down the hall, you know. She can hear a gnat fly by."

Turning onto her back, Ryan looked up at her. "I don't want to get involved. If they're fighting, the last thing they want is an audience."

"I agree, honey, but they're going to get an audience, and it's going to be people they definitely don't want listening."

"You go."

"Me?" Jamie stared at her. "They're your cousins!"

"I realize that. That's why I don't want to get involved. You're more impartial."

"You're more than infuriating," Jamie grumbled, getting up to put her jeans back on. She walked out quietly, making sure the door didn't make any noise. Then she went next door to tap on Aisling's door as quietly as possible. That didn't work, and she heard her clearly say, "If you'd rather be with Róisín, by all means go on over there right now. You've got the feckin' address!"

Both annoyed and determined, Jamie knocked harder. The voices stopped, then she heard footsteps. When the door opened a crack, Aisling peered out. "Why didn't you stop me when you learned I was lusting after an O'Flaherty?"

Jamie wasn't in the mood to argue about the family from the hallway, so she pushed on the door and slid inside. "We can hear you in our room," she said, feeling awful when she saw the hangdog look on Colm's face. "If you're going to fight, you'd better go outside."

"There's no fight," Aisling said, looking at him coldly. "He'd rather be with a woman called Róisín, and I'm simply telling him to go to her and leave me the feck alone."

"I was doing exactly what you told me to do!" he whispered loudly.

"I didn't tell you to go home with some ride!"

"I didn't go home with anyone!" He looked to Jamie, continuing to whisper. "Aisling told me to act like I normally do in a pub, so I talked to a girl. But I told her the whole story!"

"What story is that?" Aisling demanded, still talking *way* too loud.

"That I have a girlfriend, but I don't want my brothers or my cousins to know, since they supervise me like I'm in prison!"

"And for that, you had to spend an hour talking to the prettiest girl in the pub, then disappear for another hour? Explain that away, ya gobshite!"

He strode over to her and put his hands on her hips, holding her tightly when she tried to squirm out of his grasp. "Róisín was the second prettiest girl in the pub," he said, his voice now sounding not only soothing, but sexy. "You were the prettiest—by far."

"Then why were you talking to her the whole night?"

"Because you told me to act like I normally do, Ais. Róisín said she wanted to peel off from her friends and go home, so I used that as a way to get out of there early." Jamie could see his big, strong arms compress around Aisling's body. "I assumed you'd leave then too, so we could be together sooner."

Now that Colm wasn't acting like a kid in trouble, Aisling softened up almost immediately. She put her arms around him and nestled her face into his chest, and as soon as Jamie saw that, she turned and made for the door. As she opened it, she heard Aisling's soft voice say, "Sorry," and she hustled back to her room.

Ryan was standing right by the door, probably having spent the last five minutes pacing. "Any bloodshed?"

"None," she said, taking her hand to lead her back to the bed. "But you owe me, since I had to hear Colm's sexy voice."

"Oh, God!" She stopped abruptly and Jamie could almost see her shiver with revulsion.

"I know. Now when I fantasize about leaving you for Colm, I'll hear that voice in my head."

Ryan started to laugh. "If you dumped me for Colm, you'd have to leave the country. Everyone from my da to Caitlin would have you on their shit list. Say what you will about the O'Flahertys, but we take care of our own."

Jamie stopped and gazed up into her eyes. "You know I'm one hundred percent kidding when I talk about Colm, don't you?"

"Well, given that you're gayer than I am, yeah. Colm's objectively a great looking man, but you dig chicks."

"One little chick in particular," Jamie said, giving her a push when they were near the bed. "I think we'd better make love so we don't hear them."

Ryan cocked her head. "I don't hear her yelling any more."

"That's over. Those two are like squirrels. They're either fucking or fighting, and the fighting portion of the evening has finished." She tried to waggle her eyebrows like Ryan did. "We need to make our own racket so we don't hear the second act."

The McNultys were selling their pub via what rumor stated was their typical style—haphazardly. Donald was the owner, having run the place for thirty years. But he had a second home in the Algarve, and only returned to Ireland for a part of the summer. Donnie, his son, ran the pub as his schedule allowed. He was a handyman, who apparently had a flair for plumbing, and seemed to prioritize his work over the pub. That might have been because he didn't earn much pouring ale, or he simply didn't care for the work, but even Jamie knew you couldn't run a business when people couldn't rely on you to be open during your stated hours.

She, Aisling and Maggie had decided to go talk to Donnie about the business, and they pulled up at the time he'd agreed to meet. "His van's not here," Aisling said. "I should have expected he'd be late."

"He's not open for lunch?" Maggie asked.

"No longer. A local fella was the daytime barman for a few years, but he moved to Galway. Donnie either didn't try to replace him, or wasn't able to. Since Séan left, Donnie opens at five, if he's in the mood."

Maggie got out of the car and gathered her hair in her hand to toss it behind her back. She'd been letting it grow out, and now it nearly reached her shoulder blades. She had the features to be able to pull off a substantial amount of hair, yet not let it overpower her. Actually, she would have had to try not to be attractive, being a naturally beautiful woman, but she always put the effort in to look her best.

Jamie had always been impressed with the way Maggie dressed. She generally looked her age, but she could also seem a little older, or maybe a little more polished. She was just thirty-two, but she could have easily passed for anywhere from twenty-five to forty, based on her clothing and makeup.

Here in Ireland she wore no makeup at all, and very little jewelry. Just the big gold watch she'd bought herself when she'd made partner at her firm. That watch probably cost half of Brendan's annual salary, but their earnings differential never seemed to bother him. He was generally a little shy and not very forceful, but he had a quiet confidence that Jamie had always admired.

The weak sun caught the watch, and Aisling said, "Will you look at that lovely thing," while clucking her tongue. "Was that a gift?"

"To myself," Maggie said. "My mother has always told me to buy my own jewelry. It takes the pressure off whoever you're dating, and insures you're not wearing something ugly just so you don't hurt the guy's feelings."

"I could have bought myself nice things," Aisling said, sighing. "But I couldn't stand to do the job that gave me the good money." She shrugged. "I'd rather have my sanity."

"Good choice. I'm lucky that I like the work I do, and it just so happens to pay very well."

"You need a high-paying job in your crazy city," Aisling said, laughing a little. "It's as expensive as London!"

"It's getting worse all the time. There won't be any working-class people at all in a few years."

"Oh, yes there will be," Jamie insisted. "Maybe just O'Flahertys, but we're going to keep the OFC going until all of the boyos have a home."

"How are you going to disentangle them from their mammies' apron strings?" Aisling said, batting her eyes.

"Valid point. I'll restate my position. We'll fix up houses for the boys who can stand to leave home. I concede there will be some hangers on."

A horn honked briefly, and a white panel van pulled up. Donnie's last name was inelegantly stenciled on the driver's door, along with his mobile number. But there was no indication of what trade he plied, a strange omission from Jamie's perspective.

Donnie got out and brushed the dirt from his coveralls. When Jamie looked a little closer, she saw that it was mud, and had caked all around his ankles. He took a look and scowled, but didn't try to get any more of it off. "When you spend the morning digging a ditch, you're wise to expect some mud," he said, walking over to extend his hand toward Maggie. "Donnie McNulty."

Jamie thought she'd also peg Maggie as the leader of their little group, so she didn't mind the slight.

"Maggie Reardon. I assume you know Aisling, and this is Jamie Evans, Aisling's cousin-in-law."

"Cousin-in-law," he said, testing the term out slowly. "Must be American."

"Mind if we go inside?" Aisling asked.

"Sure. Sure. I have the keys somewhere." After patting all of his pockets, he went back to his truck and rummaged around, returning after a fruitful search. "Here they are." He got the door open and they entered, with the smell of stale beer assaulting Jamie's senses.

"Do you have anyone come in to clean a bit at the end of the night?" Aisling asked. Given there were still some bottles on tables, along with spent napkins and remnants of chips littering the space, she was clearly being sarcastic.

"I do. Usually on Saturday."

"Mmm. Maybe you can convince people to clean up after themselves Monday through Friday."

He gave her a quick look, but Jamie could see he wasn't able to determine if she was kidding or not, so he let it go. "So," he said, pulling out a barstool and perching on it. "Are you serious about buying the place, Aisling?"

"I'm serious about everything," she said, sitting next to him. "How serious are you about selling?"

"Well," he said leaning back against the bar and letting out a breath. "I hate to let it go, of course. We've had the place since I was your little sister's age."

"Uh-huh," Aisling said, obviously letting her gaze travel around the place. It wasn't in horrid shape, but it also wasn't treated with tender, loving care. Maybe Donald had kept it in better order when he'd been in charge, but even that was doubtful.

"I still earn a tidy sum from the place, of course, and I'd hate to lose that."

"Right. But you'd have more time to ply your trade. I know the pub has to come second when you have a job you're trying to finish."

"Oh, no, never second," he said. He held his index fingers together. "The pub and my plumbing business are both number one."

Jamie recalled Granny saying something derogatory about Donnie's plumbing skills, so he might have been telling the truth about that. Maybe the businesses were equally poorly run.

"So? Are you willing to sell? I'm interested in buying a pub, since I want to own a business in Mayo. I've looked at four other places, all about the same size as this, but ideally I'd have a place close to my family."

"Oh, you'll not find a place with a better reputation than McNulty's," he said, dismissing her comment with a wave of his hand.

"I agree that reputation is critical when it comes to a business. Cleanliness, reliability, consistency..." She let her gaze travel around again, lingering on the trash. "People are particular when it comes to their food and drink."

"And what brought on the thought of running a pub, Aisling? Your people aren't in the hospitality business."

"No, they're not. But I don't want to fish like my grandfather, or teach school like my father. I suppose I could volunteer at the church, like my granny, but I want to be able to support myself." Her eyes took on a certain spark when she added, "A good pub can help a town, Donnie. And I love Killala with my whole heart."

"And this is for yourself, yes? Your da's not leaving the school?"

"My father has no interest in running a pub. I'm buying a business for myself."

"Hmm. What would you be offering?"

Maggie'd been watching silently, and when Donnie asked the question she jumped in. "I suppose I haven't properly identified myself. I'm Aisling's solicitor."

His eyes opened wide. "Not a one of you looks old enough to have a pint, much less buy the place."

"Looks are deceiving," Maggie said, showing what Jamie recognized as the smile of a cold-blooded corporate attorney. "Why don't you tell us what your asking price is, and we'll go from there."

Ryan tried not to supervise while her father and brother worked to fill the holes she and Kieran had previously created, and she thought she'd done a pretty fine job of it. When they'd finished that task, they spent a little time prepping the walls of the room for painting, then called it a day.

They rode together to her aunt Moira's to meet up with their respective partners. When Ryan opened the car door, she stood beside the vehicle for a moment, finally saying, "No one's running out to meet us, so Caitlin must be on an adventure."

"Maybe Tommy and Annie went to Tralee with Niall and Donal. They were going to visit Uncle Leo and Aunt Mary today."

Ryan gave him a puzzled look. "Different side of the family, Da. Tommy's not related to Uncle Leo."

He stared back for a second. "I've lost all sense of who's related to whom! Being married to two Ryan women has thoroughly confused me."

"I'm only half of a Ryan woman, and I confuse the hell out of Jamie," she teased, putting her arm around his waist as they walked down the drive.

Brendan opened the door to a buzz of women's voices. By the time they'd all gotten inside, Ryan heard a can open, then another. She walked into the kitchen to find both aunts, one cousin, one lover, and one near sister-in-law opening tins of beer. "Is this what you get up to when we're laboring like convicts?"

Aisling took one of the tins and popped it open, handing it over. "Congratulate me! I'm a publican!"

Her father and brother started peppering Aisling with questions, so Ryan just tapped her tin against the others and grabbed a chair, happy to let Aisling tell her story.

She held up her hands, asking for quiet, and said, "I'd just gotten through the start of my tale, so I'll continue on from there." She pulled Maggie over and draped an arm around her neck. "Let me start by saying you should never negotiate for anything without this woman at your side."

"I've never won an argument with her," Brendan teased. "I wouldn't even try."

"She was a gift," Aisling continued. "I almost felt sorry for Donnie, but he's such a lazy plank I couldn't find it in me."

Jamie was sitting next to Ryan, who leaned over to ask, "How many drinks has she had?"

"That's the first. She's just in high spirits."

"Got it. I don't want to have to sleep with her like the last time she was lashed."

"That might happen," Jamie said quietly, "but it hasn't happened yet."

"Side conversations may be held in the garden," Aisling said, raising her voice. Ryan sat up straight and held a finger to her lips.

"As I was saying, I was almost sorry for Donnie when he was trying to make his very feeble points. I think we could have gotten away with no money changing hands whatsoever, but I knew word would get out about that, and I'd look like a thief."

"Wait," Ryan said. "You're making it sound like you've actually bought the place."

"I have," she said, sticking out her chest. "He didn't want to use an estate agent, so it was mano a mano, as they say. And Maggie's manos made short work of him. Jamie wrote a check, and he handed me the keys. We've got to get the business license transferred over, but I'm told that's not difficult."

Maggie was smirking as she watched Aisling talk, and she added a bit. "He never should have given Ais the keys when his name's still on the license, not to mention the insurance risk, but he didn't seem to mind."

"Alleged mind," Aisling added. "I think his head's full of fluff and twigs. Like a bird's nest."

"So we can help you get started on repairs," Ryan said.

"Starting tomorrow if the fellas are up for it. The walls seem sound, so I think it's mostly plumbing, electrical, and tile."

"Here's to O'Donohue's!" Ryan's father raised his beer, but Aisling wagged a finger.

"Aisling's," she said. "I don't want anyone to think I'm minding my father's pub."

"They won't think that for long," Ryan said, sure her cousin would make it clear to everyone that she was firmly in charge.

Donnie hadn't bothered to tell his cook he'd sold the place, and when he called Aisling to ask her if she wanted to fire the woman, she decided to pay her for her time and clean out the cupboards while they were at it.

The entire group met at six, with Aisling having already put up a hand-lettered sign saying the place was closed for repairs. No one who walked by would have believed that, though, since the place was shaking by seven.

The cook, a pleasant young woman called Katie, happily fired up everything she had in the kitchen. Aisling told her she'd be looking for a cook when she officially opened in a couple of weeks, and she seemed to be trying to impress her.

Katie kept putting the food on the bar as she finished it, with Aisling pouring the drinks. It had taken her a few tries to keep the heads at the right level on the pints she pulled, but she got the hang of it. Ryan wasn't sure who was going to drive everyone home, but it wasn't going to be her. The one taxi driver in town might have a banner night.

Ryan had called Rory when she'd heard the news, and he and his bandmates stopped by on their way to Dingle, where they were playing all weekend. They didn't unload all of their gear, keeping the entertainment to a spritely acoustic set.

The place was fairly full, and with everyone from her grandparents to Caitlin gathered around, it made it seem like a family wedding, or a very festive wake.

Ryan sat at the bar next to Donal, who had done a brief survey of the plumbing system. "I think I'll have to jackhammer the floor of the bathroom out. I'm sure what I find will be awful, but we might as well get it over with. Do you know where to rent equipment?"

"Ballina. We can get a jackhammer as soon as you need one."

"You know," he said, "some of the tools I need aren't cheap. I should have brought some things from home."

Ryan waved him off. “Aisling will need tools to do minor repairs. We’ll leave her with a good basic kit.”

“I’ll do my best to make sure she starts off on a good foot.” He’d been letting his gaze travel to Aisling as she got up on her toes to find a whiskey from the top shelf, or squat down to fetch something out of a cooler, and he finally said, “You’d shoot me if I made a play for Ais, wouldn’t you.”

She stared at him, dumbstruck.

“I know, I know,” he muttered. “It would be really weird to have one of your cousins chasing another one.”

“No, that would be okay,” she said, carefully choosing her words. “But Ais has a big crush on a guy.”

“A crush?” he asked, laughing. “Are we talking about Aisling or Brenna?”

“The one who sleeps with men,” Ryan said, giving him a poke. “But she just broke up with her long-term boyfriend last winter, and she’s a little skittish…”

“Forget I asked. She’s just so damn cute!”

“She is that,” Ryan agreed. “And she owns a pub. Just think of the money you’d save.”

Chapter Five

At six am, Ryan was flying along a paved road just outside Ballina, working on her speed. She liked to run at full-tilt for around twenty seconds, rest at a slow jog for another twenty, then crank it up again. She could do that for about three minutes, but that was her current max. She ran much faster in Ireland, since the hills around Ballina and Killala were so mild, but she was still trying to be able to do her sprints for a full five minutes, her summer goal. One morning she'd have to convince Jamie to go along to time her, but that was going to be quite the task. Jamie and dawn were not the best of friends.

Her cell started to buzz, and she reached into her nylon jacket to pull it out. "Hello?"

"Ryan? Jim Evans. How's it going?"

"Um…fine. How's it going with you?"

"Good. Good." He was in what she thought of as his sales mode, where he exhibited all of the charm as well as the sincerity of a guy selling fake watches on the street. "Hey, I was thinking we could get together for a chat. Are you available?"

"I'm in Ireland."

"I know. I'm in London, and I thought I could swing by."

She spent a moment wondering how he knew they were in Ireland. Since the night Jamie had found out about his betrayal of Catherine, they hadn't spoken even once. He'd sent a few letters, but Ryan had watched her partner rip them to pieces before tossing them into the trash. So she was sure Jamie hadn't told him they were traveling. The fact that he could undoubtedly call someone in the State Department to check on their whereabouts distracted her, but she focused and said, "Swing by? Are you headed home?"

"I am. But I could catch a helicopter and be there in…oh, two hours or so."

"A military helicopter?"

"You have an airport not far away, don't you?"

"Sure. Galway could work. But…" She took a moment to think. What was his angle? He always had one. "You know Jamie won't see you, right?"

"Of course," he said, clearly exasperated. "That's why I want to talk to you. I thought you could offer some advice."

"I can do that on the phone, Jim. It won't take long."

"Uh-huh. Well, I'd rather talk face-to-face. When's good for you?"

"I could meet you tomorrow."

"Fine. Where and what time?"

"Either Dublin or around Shannon, your choice. But I'd like you to take a commercial flight."

"What? Why?"

"Because a military flight costs a ridiculous amount of money. As a taxpayer, I don't want to see my contributions to the federal coffers spent that way."

"It hasn't taken long for Jamie to rub off on you, has it?" he asked, clearly pissed. "Now I have both of you pulling the moral superiority card."

"I wouldn't mind being influenced by her, but I was frugal long before I met Jamie. And, not to make too big a point of it, but my cynicism about politics is far greater than hers." She paused for just a second. "Sure you want to make the trip? There's every chance I'll say something that makes you feel morally inferior—even though that's not my intention."

"I'm sure," he said, all traces of the happy salesman gone. "I'm sorry for that crack. I don't have a lot of tolerance for being lectured to."

"Neither do I. If you want to come, fly into Dublin. You'll have more options, and we haven't been there yet so…"

"You just said Jamie wouldn't come."

"No, I said she wouldn't talk to you. She can find something to do while you and I talk."

"Fine," he sighed. "I'll let you know when my flight is scheduled to land. Where should we meet?"

"I'll pick a place that matches the time. If it's early, I'll find a good place for brunch. Late? I'll find a handy bar."

"All right. I'll let you know."

"Got it," she said. "I've got to get going before my legs start to cramp."

"See you tomorrow, Ryan. Pick someplace nice. I'll buy."

"Given that I have to drive to Dublin to have a chat, I thought that was understood," she said, thinking that if Jamie inherited even one percent of his genes, it was too damn much.

Tommy and Brendan got to work on painting the living room bright and early that morning. Or rather, dark and early. The sun was completely hidden from view, and it didn't give any hints it was going to come out as Ryan carefully roughed up the paint on the window muntins. She wasn't overly fond of prepping for paint, but she knew she'd do a careful job. Her granny was a stickler for workmanship, and she didn't want to hear any complaints if the paint didn't last for ages.

She was just so glad she wouldn't have to climb up and down the ladder anymore that she would have volunteered for any other job. The climbing was bad enough, but staying up there for a while really trashed your legs, since you were always adjusting your weight slightly, adding to the stress. And having to do that with even a slight hangover was no fun at all. Luckily, Tommy had only had a few at Aisling's celebration, and Brendan almost never drank to excess. Many of the others couldn't say the same, and she was certain a few of her cousins were counting their lucky stars that they weren't on painting duty today. Come to think of it, Jamie was probably still in bed. She hadn't had a great deal to drink, but she'd started early, always something she regretted. But she'd have to be awake to regret that choice, and Ryan was sure that wouldn't happen for quite a while.

Brendan and Tommy finished up just after they'd wolfed down the lunch Ryan had run out to buy them. The boys were taking the drop cloths out to the van when Ryan's aunt Moira appeared, accompanied by two diminutive, elderly women, bearing bright smiles and carrying plastic buckets.

"Morning! Since I didn't have to do any work," Moira said, "I decided to contribute by having Molly and Clodagh in to clean."

Ryan stared at her, too puzzled to speak. The women looked like they were over eighty! "Um, welcome," she said. "I'm Siobhán. I take it you know my grandmother?"

"Your grandmother?" the smaller of the tiny women said. "Who's that, then?"

"Brigid Ryan," Ryan said. "Brigid Kelly Ryan. She was born in Killala. St. Patrick's..."

"The name doesn't ring a bell. Do you know a Brigid Ryan, Clodagh?"

"I don't think so," she said, her voice as soft as a whisper. "We're from Castlebar." She was wearing a type of apron that Ryan only saw in Ireland. Kind of a smock, usually with pockets in the front. She reached into one of them and produced a card. "My grandson made these for us," she said. "Pass it around, will you?"

Ryan spent a second reading it, seeing they were the Castlebar Cleaners. "Come in," she said, giving her aunt a questioning look as the women walked past.

Moira clearly found the situation funny, but she was good at hiding her amusement. "I found Clodagh and Molly on the internet," she said.

"My grandson put us on it," Clodagh said. "We get calls nearly every day."

"They have very good reviews," Moira added.

"I don't know where those come from," Molly said. "They just appear."

"Keith puts them up there," Clodagh said. "I don't know where he gets them, but every time he adds one, he shows it to me."

"Well, I'll be sure to add one," Ryan said. "What can I get you? Mops?"

They both shook their heads like she'd asked if they wanted rakes. "Oh, no. A mop just pushes the dirt around. If you're going to clean, you do it right or not at all. We have our own supplies," Molly added. "Oil soap and rags are all we need. We'll clean the stairs and the floor in here." She scanned the room, seeing the kitchen was taped up. "Can we go in there?"

"No need. I'm sure the dust didn't travel."

"Your floor will sparkle," Molly said. "As will the windows, of course."

"Then we'll let you get to it," Ryan said. "Can I help with anything?"

"Come back in three hours," Clodagh said. She turned to Moira and spoke with a flat, no-nonsense tone. "Cash only."

"You'll have it," she said, with Ryan seeing she was about to burst out laughing.

"See you in three hours," Ryan said, escorting her aunt from the building. When they were near the van, she said, "Did you search the internet for 'oldest cleaners in Ireland?'"

"No! I had no idea they were as old as my mother. But she cleans her floor every Saturday, so age isn't a bar."

"I hope they're not doing this because they don't have enough money to pay the bills."

"I'll tip well," Moira soothed. "And I'll add a review, too. Maybe I'll have them do my house. I haven't had a minute to clean since you all arrived."

"Let's see if they're free tomorrow. Wouldn't it be nice to return to a clean house after a day of sightseeing?"

"I believe that is what they call a rhetorical question," Moira said, affectionately ruffling Ryan's hair.

Jamie had been talking to her mother for over an hour, and when the door to their room opened she looked up to see Ryan, looking remarkably clean. "I think I need to hang up, Mom. My beloved one is here and that must mean I'm needed."

"That's fine, sweetheart. Call me late in the week. I'd rather see you in person, but our phone calls are a very acceptable substitute. Give my love to Ryan."

"Will do. Give Jen a big hug from both of us."

She clicked off the phone and stood up. "What kind of clothes do I have to put on for whatever you're going to make me do?"

Ryan gave her a sweet smile and moved across the room to caress Jamie's cheek. "You're perfect. I've got a couple of hours to kill while a pair of senior citizens cleans my granny's house, so I thought I'd swing by and see what you were up to."

"Nada," she said. "I read the paper while I had breakfast down in the restaurant, then I got caught up with my journal, and read a few chapters of a new book. I had a very long chat with my mother, and I was planning on going over to Moira's to take Caitlin out for the afternoon if her schedule allowed."

"Great. Want me to tag along?"

"Always. Let me get my purse." She found her things and made sure she had the room key, then started to follow Ryan out the door. They'd just started to walk through the lobby when Jamie said, "What else is on your mind? I can tell something is."

"Really?" Ryan gave her a puzzled look. "How can you tell that?"

"Mmm. The fact that you didn't deny it means I'm right. What's up?"

They reached the car, and Ryan opened Jamie's door for her, waiting until she was fully seated before shutting it. When Ryan got in she fussed with her seatbelt for a second, then said, "Your dad called me this morning."

"Lucky you," Jamie said, turning away from her to gaze out the window.

"He asked to have a talk with me and I didn't have a good reason for saying no, so I'm meeting him for breakfast tomorrow."

Jamie turned to give her a long look. "You have many reasons for saying no, but if you want to chat, go right ahead."

"Um…I was thinking you and I would go to Dublin together. I know you don't want to talk to him, so you could sit in a nice cafe and read while I'm busy. We'd have most of the day to hang out."

"And then we'd rush right back?"

"Um…yeah. I've got to help Aisling figure out what she needs to have done while the boyos are still here."

Jamie met her gaze, then slowly shook her head. "How many hours is the drive?"

"About three."

"So that's a six hour drive to have an afternoon in Dublin?" She blew out a breath. "I'd much rather go when we can stay a few days. Maybe when the boyos are gone?"

Ryan's eyes went wide, and she reached over to turn on the car. She didn't respond for a couple of minutes, and Jamie decided to wait her out. Finally, she said, "Is it really asking a lot to have you drive with me?"

"Nope. And I would have happily gone if you'd asked me first and we agreed on our plans. But you didn't, honey. You blithely made plans and now you want me to go with you since you don't want to drive alone. Not great," she added, trying to make it clear why she was miffed.

"I can't cancel now," she said, sounding glum. "He's in London and he wanted to take a helicopter and come over today. I refused to see him if he did that, so he's staying over another night and flying into Dublin in the morning."

"Uh-huh. Again, those are plans that the two of you made. If you want me to go to Dublin, you should have asked me what would make the trip worthwhile for me—not just present it as a fait accompli."

Ryan gave her a quick look as she guided the car around a rotary. "You seriously won't go with me?"

"I'll go if we can stay for two days. Final offer."

"Great," Ryan grumbled. "I guess that's what I get for trying to see if I can help you two have a relationship again."

"Not your job," Jamie said, truly trying to not sound as agitated as she was. "I appreciate that you want that for me, but I'm the one who will make that decision. What time will you leave?"

"Well, since I agreed to meet at ten, I guess about six or six thirty."

"While you're leaving the room quietly, know that I love you," Jamie said, with that sentiment being the most loving she could manage at the moment.

The whole group went to the pub they'd learned to call home in Ballina, with not only Maggie and Brendan joining them, but Tommy and Annie. The pub hadn't been crowded when they'd first walked in, but they took up twelve seats after jamming three small tables together. Now the place seemed much more lively with an infusion of O'Flaherty energy.

Ryan made it a point to sit next to Brendan, since she'd spent less time with him than she'd wanted to. He and Maggie clearly considered this their vacation, and they'd done more sightseeing than all of the other boys combined. But she was glad for that, and glad that Maggie wasn't afraid to ask for what she wanted. If it was up to Bren, he'd happily sit around and chat with his aunts and grandparents for two straight weeks.

"I'm going to run over to Dublin tomorrow to meet with Jim Evans," Ryan said. "Do you two want to tag along?"

Brendan leaned back in his chair and gave her a long look. "Jim Evans? Dublin? How did that come about?"

She shrugged. "He's got the idea that I'll talk Jamie into seeing him. Which I wouldn't—even if I could."

"I got the impression they were on the outs, but I didn't want to pry..."

"Oh, yeah, they're definitely on the outs. She won't even go with me, which makes me regret agreeing to go at all."

"That bad?"

"Pretty bad. Once again, he got caught lying about something important, and she's tired of it." She looked across the room to watch Jamie try to balance five pints on a tray, finding it cute how she stared at them, as if that would help.

"Um," he lowered his voice and leaned close. "How about just you and I go? I want to shop for something, and I think I'll have to go to Dublin to find what I want."

She raised an eyebrow. "Shop? You?" She nodded when he looked embarrassed. "Maybe an engagement ring?"

"Shh..." He whispered. "Maggie hates engagement rings. But I was thinking of buying her something...like a necklace? Something important."

"Well, Jamie would be better at that, but I've learned a little about jewelry. You're on. You'll just have to come up with an excuse for why Maggie can't come."

He laughed. "She'd be happy as hell if she can stay in our room and catch up on her email. I'll tell her I'm going with you in case Jim needs his nose bloodied."

"We're set," she said, laughing at the thought of him popping Jim in the face. "Can you be ready to go by six?"

"I'm up by five thirty."

"Great. I hate to blow through that much gas, but taking the train would take all day."

"Looking forward to it. Well, I'm not looking forward to spending money, but taking a long drive with you is always fun."

"We think alike," she said, clapping him on the back.

At ten o'clock on Friday morning, Ryan looked up from reading the *Irish Times* when she felt someone approach. Lowering the paper, she got to her feet and extended her hand. "Good to see you, Jim." They'd been offering each other tentative hugs and kisses to the cheek for a while now, but at this point she thought they'd both be more comfortable with a formal vibe.

"And you," he said, his salesman affect back in place. "You're looking very well. Have you been here long?"

"We got here late last Saturday."

"Ahh. Going home soon?"

"Not very. We're planning on staying until I start school."

"Really?" He cocked his head. "Won't you be bored to death?"

"Nope." She wasn't going to try to convince him she could stay for three years and not be bored, so she didn't try. "Ready for brunch?"

"I'm famished. I was only in London for a couple of days, and haven't gotten adjusted to local time. I've been waking at four, too tired to get any work done, but too early to go out."

"You sound like Jamie. She adjusted well this time, but normally she has a heck of a time."

"I don't normally have trouble. But I was in California for a week right before this trip. That's too many time zones for me."

"The restaurant's right around this corner," she said. She'd picked the most expensive hotel in Dublin, figuring he'd feel at home with all of the dark wood and sumptuous upholstery.

They were escorted to their table, and both accepted the offered coffee. "How far is your family's place from Dublin?" he asked.

"Around three hours." She snapped her linen napkin out and placed it over her lap.

"Three hours? You're willing to spend six hours to come talk to me? Damn, Ryan, I could have had a helicopter put me down in any open field in your town."

"This is better. And I think I've shown I'll do a lot more than take a long drive for Jamie."

Their server brought their coffee, and Ryan looked up at him and said, "We'll have the full Irish."

"I'll be right back," he said, nodding.

"Full Irish, huh? Is that like the English breakfast I had yesterday?"

"Close. The English usually have beans and mushrooms. We often have two kinds of pudding." She waggled her hand. "Depends on the spot, I suppose. And our bread is usually brown. I'm interested to see how a fancy place does breakfast."

Their server returned with a basket of scones and preserves. Ryan took one and started to add butter and raspberry. "These are good," she said after taking a bite. "Worth the drive."

Jim played with his coffee, stirring it idly. "So," he finally said. "What do I do to make things right with Jamie?"

This was the question she was expecting, and she'd given it a lot of thought. But she still didn't have a great answer. "I'm not sure, to be honest. Her opinion of you is in the basement this time, Jim. It was hard for her to forgive you for cheating on her mother, but this is...this is worse."

He gave her an annoyed glance. "She'd prefer to have a younger brother or sister in rehab? Because that's what she'd have if her mother and I had decided to have another baby."

Ryan popped another bite of her scone into her mouth. "You destroyed the dream of someone she loves very much. Arguing that you know how things would have turned out if Catherine had more children..." She shrugged. "That won't win you many points."

"What will? I need her in my life, Ryan." He took a sip of his coffee, then put the cup down quickly. "I thought I could just let her go—but I can't." He looked like he was going to cry when he added, "You don't know what it was like when she was young. We were like this," he insisted, lifting two fingers.

"I think I understand how close you were. But that's not going to win her back, either. You've got to convince her that you understand that what you did was wrong, and that you'd change the past if you could." She looked him right in the eye before adding, "If that's true. If it's not…"

"It's not true," he snapped. "Catherine was a mess back then, and having another child would have been a crime. Jamie can try to revise history all she wants, but neither of us were ready to be parents. And Catherine wouldn't listen to reason when I told her one child was more than we could handle."

"Um, again, that's not going to convince Jamie you're someone she wants in her life. Have you ever considered going to therapy?"

"Therapy," he said, rolling his eyes. "I'm not about to open up my brain to some quack."

"Okay. Then let's think of what you can offer Jamie to pull her back in. Money? Nope. Prestige? Nope. Power? Not interested." She leaned forward to stare at him across the table. "All she wants from you is an honest relationship. And that's something you've shown no ability to offer."

"No one's honest," he said, sounding more bitter than she'd ever heard him. "Everyone uses other people." He met her eyes. "Including you."

She held up her hands. "Care to explain how I use Jamie? I know you've got a list." She was tempted to laugh, which surprised her. It had only been two years since he'd scared the crap out of her with his threats and tricks. She still recalled how low she'd felt when he'd made fun of her home and how little money she had, predicting Jamie would soon tire of her. But she'd grown up in the last couple of years, and this jerk simply didn't have any hold over her.

He gazed at her for a few seconds, appearing to give the question some serious thought. "I'm still not sure about you. You're clearly using her money, since you haven't worked in a year, but you haven't bought anything big… She's always complaining about how much you hate to go out to eat, or travel, so you're not interested in living an opulent life." He took a sip of his coffee, then made eye contact with their server, indicating he wanted a refill. After he received it, he stirred a little milk into it and said, "I assume you use her like I use women. For sex, but also to have someone pretty on your arm."

"She is pretty," Ryan agreed, surprised he wasn't getting to her, even though he was trying to. "And I'd be lying if I said her looks hadn't attracted me."

He chuckled at that. "I can't see you with a dog."

That made her flinch. Even her cousins didn't refer to women like that—in front of her, at least.

Jim kept going, clearly warming to his subject. "You're going to reach a point—and I hope it's far in the future—where Jamie's a little older, and you're a little bored. You've done everything in bed she's willing to do, and it's all gotten pretty routine." His eyes took on a nearly gleeful shine when he said, "That's when you'll find out how you're using her. You might stay because of her money, or the kids you'll have together, or whatever else means something to you. But it *will* be something." He leaned back in his chair when a different server brought their meals.

Ryan didn't speak for a while, wanting to taste her food before it got cold. It was all pretty good, but the white pudding wasn't like the Clonakilty white pud that her granny made when she had the time. No matter how good a restaurant breakfast was, eating at home was better.

After having several bites of everything, she slowed down to think about her response to Jim's comment. "You know," she finally said, "I've never been with anyone for long, so I can't know how I'll handle it when things get routine, which I assume they inevitably do."

"Inevitably," he agreed, nodding solemnly.

"I guess that's when you have to look at all of the benefits of being with someone you love, and you dedicate yourself to finding ways to make your sex life interesting again."

"What if your partner doesn't want to do that?" he asked, giving her a pointed look. "I've only been with two women for longer than a year, so fifty percent of my long-term lovers have refused to do anything even slightly out of the ordinary."

"That would suck," she agreed. "It would also suck if one of us lost her libido because of illness or injury. That's when you have to drill down deeper, to focus more on the things that matter to you as a couple." She shrugged. "No one gets everything."

He picked at his food, interested only in the fried eggs. With the majority of the meal still on the plate, he pushed it away and signaled for a refill of his coffee. "After all of the women you've been with, you're telling me that you'd basically give up on having a sex life if Jamie tapped out."

"Yes," she said, nodding briskly. "That's exactly what I'm telling you. I'm a huge pain in the ass when it comes to making her talk about things she doesn't want to get into, and if she just had some hangup that was getting in the way I'm sure we could make progress on it. But if her libido got broken in some way… I'd take care of myself. I've got plenty of experience there, too," she added, giving him a wry smile.

He stared at her while taking another sip of coffee, then put his cup down and cleared his throat. "You know, that statement is nothing more than a juvenile belief in your moral certainty. Trust me, Ryan, things aren't as clear cut when you're in your forties. Especially when hot twenty-year-olds are flirting their asses off."

"I'm sure that's true. I used to hook up with anyone who gave me a second look, and there's a part of me that loved that anonymous kind of connection. But I have more with Jamie. She's not just a pretty face and perky breasts." She waited until he met her eyes to ask, "Did you never have that?"

"I guess not," he said quietly.

Ryan's mouth almost dropped open. She'd rarely seen him admit to anything that even hinted at vulnerability.

"I loved Catherine," he said, picking up his fork to idly push his brown bread around on his plate. Meeting her eyes, he added, "You know her well enough to realize how easy she is to love."

"Oh, yeah. I could fall for her in a minute."

"Right. But when we met she was very naive, very closed-off, and I suppose she was depressed. The last thing she was interested in was having a great sex life."

"That's…kind of awful."

"It really was. And once I started to cheat…" He moved his index finger around in a circle. "After the first time, each time was easier. In a couple of years, I stopped even thinking it was wrong."

"It's a little late in the game for this observation, but maybe the key is to not cheat the first time."

"Thanks for the tip. In my next life…"

"I don't mean to sound like I think I'm morally superior, Jim. I'm just saying that I know Jamie and I will have problems. But I'm determined to remain faithful while we work through them. And I'm confident Jamie feels the same."

"I hope so," he said quietly. "I don't ever want her to feel like Catherine did when she found out."

"I don't think I could live with myself if I hurt her like that." Just talking about hurting Jamie turned her stomach, so she got off the topic quickly. "Jamie tells me you and Kayla split up. How…how's that going?" she asked, realizing she'd asked a really stupid question.

"Shitty. She's the one I should have been with. I've never met a woman who loved sex as much as she did, or whose interests matched mine as well. And smart? Damn, she was smart."

"So? Why end things?"

His expression turned cold. "Because Catherine burst into my office and caused a scene. I had to eventually tell Kayla why Cat had been so unhinged, and that made it clear I'd lied about the purpose of her visit."

Rolling his eyes, he added, "Kayla was another one with a huge hot-button about lying. She started packing one fucking minute after I admitted I'd lied. I haven't spoken to her since that night."

"Wow," Ryan whispered. "That's cold."

"Oh, yeah. I'm not sure who screwed her up, but she never let herself be vulnerable. She laughed in my face the first time I told her I loved her."

"But she's the woman you wish you'd made a commitment to?"

His smile reminded her of a lecherous boss, the kind of guy who chased women around a desk. "She was awesome in the sack, and as calculating as any man on my staff. You don't find that combination very often."

"Maybe not, but…" She shrugged. "I'll say it again. A little therapy wouldn't be a bad investment. Loving a woman is honestly more fun than just having sex. And from what you've said, you've never truly loved a woman who matched you sexually."

"And a shrink is going to find that woman for me?"

"No, I don't think they're into that. But a shrink might be able to help you figure out why you're willing to settle for so much less than what you could have."

"Woe is me," he said, smirking at her. "All I have is a decent chunk of change, one of the best jobs in the world, and pretty, young women who are still willing to hop into bed with me and do whatever I want."

"I'm not saying you don't have a good life, Jim. But you don't have many deep emotional connections. And while you probably don't believe this, those fill you up in ways that casual sex can't."

"You're right," he said, sighing heavily. His eyes began to sparkle again when he added, "I don't believe you."

Ryan knew as much about Dublin as she did Chicago, which was next to nothing. Brendan didn't know a bit more, and he hadn't done any research on jewelry stores. So Ryan did what she always did when she needed help with things outside of her usual expertise. She called Catherine.

It was only eight in New York, but she was confident she'd be up. Now that she wasn't drinking to excess, she'd turned into a morning person.

They were at a coffee bar on O'Connell Street, having a good cup of tea when she made the call. "Catherine? I'm not waking you, am I?"

"Oh, no," she said, easily convincing Ryan she was telling the truth. "I use my mornings to get things done while Jennie's sleeping. I'd forgotten that teenagers are either sleeping or hiding in their rooms," she added, laughing a little. "Is everything all right?"

"Sure is. My brother wants to shop for some quality jewelry, and we don't know where to go. I know you've never been to Dublin, but I thought you might know someone who knows someone…"

"I'm sure I do. Let me make a few calls. I'll get back to you."

"It doesn't have to be a rush—" She stared at Brendan. "She already hung up."

He laughed. "You can't say she lets the grass grow under her feet."

While they waited, Ryan went to fetch more hot water for their tea. When she got back, she sat on her stool in front of the counter facing the street. "I could sit here for hours, people watching. I've seen more interesting faces in the last ten minutes than I have in the last five days."

"But you love Mayo," he said, with a hearty dose of affection in his voice. "I think it's your happy place."

"Ireland fits me. The West, especially. If we didn't all live close to each other in Noe, I wouldn't be able to stand San Francisco. Our little enclave has let me turn it into a small town."

"I could live in Mayo, but Maggie couldn't. I think San Francisco is the right size for her."

"Jamie, too," Ryan admitted. "Luckily, she loves the city. I'd hate living down in the South Bay. Way too much traffic, and it's impossible to walk anywhere."

"Are you two going to find your own place?"

"Rumor has it, but we haven't looked. Too many things keep coming up."

"I hear you." He drank a little tea, looking contemplative. "Do you want to talk about your meeting with Jim?"

"Not much to say. He wants my help in getting Jamie back, but he's unwilling to do anything to show he's not a baldfaced liar—which he is."

"Sounds like fun!"

"Oh, yeah, it's always fun to beat your head against a wall. But I didn't mind the trip. Every time he and I talk, it reminds me of how committed I am to Jamie."

"How…?"

Ryan shook her head. "I listen to him talk about his inability to be faithful, and how it's something you can't avoid. But it just doesn't seem like a tough task to me. It's like Noe Valley," she said, smiling when his head cocked in question. "There are prettier parts of the city. Places with better views. More nightlife. Better restaurants. Places right next to MUNI. But I've never considered moving. Noe has everything I need, and having that stability makes me happy. Same with Jamie. The stability of monogamy doesn't feel constricting to me. It actually feels freeing."

"Ahh. One more way we're alike. I know other women exist, and I take a look when I pass them on the street. But it's actually funny to think of giving up on Maggie to get one of them. No way," he said soberly.

"And she feels the same about you?"

"I assume so," he said, looking a little hesitant. "We're very different in a lot of ways. For one, she likes money more than I do, and she's a little flashier. But she loves me, and when she comes home at night she seems really happy to be there. That's all I need."

Ryan put her arm around him for a hug. "I'm so glad you have her."

"Me too. I don't think she wants to get married, but I'm going to ask anyway. I thought this was the best place to do it."

He didn't elaborate, but she knew what he was implying. Being in their mother's birthplace meant a lot to both of them. It would have seemed silly to a more practical person, but Ryan got it one hundred percent. Brendan wanted to be close to their mother's roots and her people when he asked Maggie such an important question.

"You say she's not into engagement rings? She was very complimentary about ours."

"Oh, she likes them—for other people. I think it might be a feminist thing, to be honest. She'd probably want one if men and women both wore them."

"Oh! Got it. Yeah," Ryan said, nodding. "When you're both women, you don't have that same dynamic."

"Right. She's commented a few times that she'd wear a wedding ring, but she thinks a woman's engagement ring is a claim of possession, and no one's going to possess Maggie Reardon."

"But you still want to give her something when you ask her?"

"I do. She likes jewelry, but she's bought everything she owns for herself. I was thinking a necklace or earrings would give her something to remember from this trip, if nothing else."

"She mostly wears gold," Ryan says. "She usually has on a nice gold necklace when she gets dressed up."

"Thirtieth birthday present. To herself," he said, smiling.

"So if you buy a necklace, it should have a gold chain."

"You've already helped me narrow things down," he said. "We're making progress."

Catherine called just before they were going to be forced to leave, after having monopolized their seats for such a long time. "I have bad and good news," she said.

"Give me the bad first."

"I couldn't find anyone who knew a good jeweler in Dublin. I have the names of several in London, though."

"Mmm. That's pretty bad news. Maybe we'll just go to someplace around here that looks nice."

"My good news might interest you."

"I'm ready."

"Is the shopping experience important to Brendan?"

"How do you mean?"

"Will he recall how he felt when he picked out a memorable piece for Maggie?"

"Hold on a sec." Ryan put the phone to her chest and said, "Are you into the shopping part?"

"Not in the least," he said, making a face. "If I could have Maggie pick something out for herself and let me pay for it, I'd be jacked."

"Um, the shopping is not an important element, Catherine. How does that help?"

"I don't have a thing planned for today, and I know an excellent jeweler who always has a very generous inventory. Why not let me pick something out?"

Ryan didn't even check with Bren before she said, "No way. You'll wind up paying for it. I know your tricks."

"No, I wouldn't," she said, laughing. "But you're right to think I might try. If Brendan can give me an idea of what his budget is, I can send you some photos. What do you say?"

"One moment," she said, placing the phone to her chest. "Catherine can go to a guy she knows, take some photos, and let you pick."

He stood up and started for the door. "Done."

The photos came when they were back in Ballina. Bren, Jamie, and Aisling surrounded Ryan's laptop, carefully looking at photos of solitaire necklaces, earrings, and a few bracelets, all tasteful, and all within Brendan's budget.

Jamie had Catherine on speaker-phone, and she said, "You saw everything in person, Mom. What was most striking?"

"I was very impressed by the emerald solitaire with the traditional emerald cut," she said. "The three diamonds that sat atop it gave it some extra sparkle, and it was youthful."

"And this was in my price range?" Brendan asked, leaning close to look at the necklace again.

"Right at the top," Catherine said. "I can overnight it to you if you like it, Brendan. And if Maggie doesn't love it, the jeweler will let her exchange it for something she'd like better."

"I like it," he said. "Emerald green for the emerald isle, right?"

"That would be my choice too," Jamie agreed. "I think she'd love it."

"It's got my vote," Ryan said. "But I'm partial to emeralds." She tapped Jamie's engagement ring with her finger.

"I wouldn't sell my soul for it, but I'd definitely mortgage it," Aisling said. "It's fantastic."

"Let's do it," Brendan said. "I assume I can find someplace to wire you the money."

"We can settle up when we're all back home," Catherine said, "and yes, before you ask, I will present you with the receipt."

"Thanks a million, Catherine," Brendan said. "You've come through for the family—once again."

Chapter Six

Ryan returned from her morning run on Sunday, finding her cousin sitting on the bed, chatting with a tolerant-seeming Jamie.

"What's going on?" Ryan asked.

"I came to see if you wanted to go for a walk," Aisling said. "You weren't home, but your girl here has allowed me to annoy her with my plans for the pub."

Jamie pulled her hand from the covers and patted Aisling's leg. "You aren't annoying me. Now, going on a so-called walk would annoy me severely, but talking? I can do that all day."

"Oh, come on now," Aisling said. "Don't you want to take in some fresh air? The walk we decided on won't take more than two hours—at a good clip."

"Have fun," Jamie said, pulling her hand back in and burrowing under the covers. "It's drizzly, and chilly. I'm going to see if I can talk anyone into going to the seaweed baths after Mass."

"Fine," Ais said, sliding off the bed to stand. "Don't come complaining to Siobhán and me when your sluggish blood stops pumping."

"If that happens," Jamie said, smiling sweetly, "I won't be able to complain. Everyone wins."

"You don't mind?" Ryan asked, on the verge of leaning over to kiss her, then recalling she was a wet mess. "I would have preferred to know about this adventure before I ran eleven miles, but…" She shrugged. "I know now." She stopped in her tracks. "What about Cáit? Does she need help with anything? I know she's got two more tests this week."

"She's fine, Siobhan. I asked her last night. I think she's got a bad case of nerves, but she doesn't need help."

"If you're sure…"

"Colm is pulling Donal out of his bed at this minute, and Maggie and Brendan are meeting us in the lobby."

"Cool! How'd you talk them into it?"

"O'Donohue charm," she said, waving as she went to the door. "Be ready to go in fifteen minutes, Siobhán. No time for even a quick ride."

"The nerve," Jamie said, smirking as the door closed. "Are you going to bother with a shower?"

"I think I'll just put on a dry shirt. I'll be a wet and grimy mess in no time, so why waste the time starting off clean?"

Jamie slipped out of bed, clad only in a T-shirt. "I had to pee the whole time Aisling was here, but I didn't want to parade around with my bare bum."

"Didn't she see your sweet bum when you answered the door?"

"Nope. You left the door unlocked. Not that she paused long before trying it. Yet another branch of your family with no respect for privacy."

"Yeah, but we're stunningly attractive," Ryan said, making the most hideous face she could summon.

The peak was one Ryan and Aisling had scaled during the winter. Then it had been cold and wet, with very little growing on the rocky surface. Now it was cold and wet, but a little less cold than it had been in December. It was actually a little less wet, now that she thought about it. And much more lush, even though it wasn't very lush. Little plants sprouted up alongside the path, and grasses covered the base of the hill. Even though the plants sputtered out when the elevation rose, it was still pretty.

Donal led the way, getting a good lead on Colm after only a few minutes. Ryan had a feeling Colm was walking slower on purpose to stay close to Ais. While she was probably as fit as he was, his legs were many inches longer than hers.

Ryan was dawdling a little, not having any need to hurry to the peak. She'd been stressing her legs climbing ladders and doing speed work, and she decided today would just be a long, tall stroll.

She was still going faster than Brendan and Maggie, though. Neither of them worked out because they both put in so many hours at their jobs that they'd never see each other if they added a session at the gym. Brendan had always been athletic, but he'd never been obsessed with sports like Conor had been. He was more like Rory in that way. He could make a respectable showing at golf or hiking or biking, but he wasn't driven to go fast or hard.

Maggie seemed to stay thin by skipping meals, which wasn't the recommended technique. But Ryan made it a point to not question anyone on their eating habits. It wasn't possible to do that and not create bad feelings.

After they'd climbed about a hundred yards, Ryan looked back to see she had a big lead on her brother already. She would have been ashamed to have the two office drones beat her at anything athletic, but she wouldn't admit that to anyone. Of course, she probably didn't have to. Everyone knew she was one of the most competitive members of the family.

She let Colm and Aisling get a good lead on her, hoping a little alone time would let them chat—something they hadn't gotten to do often during their first week together.

Ryan concentrated on clearing her mind, a practice that she found vexing. Time and again she tried, with random thoughts about Aisling's pub, her relationship with Colm, whether Caitlin was wearing everyone out, how Cáit would do on her comprehensive exams… Around and around her thoughts flowed, rarely ceasing.

She'd been walking for about an hour when Donal came lumbering down the peak. "You finished?" she said, stunned.

"Yup. Ais says there's another trail about a quarter mile to the north. I'm going to try that one now."

"Want me to go with you?"

He raised a dark eyebrow. "You're only halfway finished."

"I can go faster," she said, embarrassed. "I was loafing on purpose."

He clapped her on the back. "This one has a good view. Keep on going. I'll be fine."

She knew he was a much better, stronger climber than she was, but it still shamed her that he'd essentially lapped her. "I'll send Colm after you if you're not back when we get to the car."

"*If* you ever get there," he said, holding a hand over his eyes to act like Maggie and Bren were so far down he couldn't see them. "Those two might not make it by Tuesday."

"They're enjoying the journey," she said. She could hear his laugh as he strode down the hill like it was dead level. *Showoff.*

Ryan reached the peak about five minutes after Ais and Colm had. It was a beautiful spot, with a view that spread out for miles, all of the fifty shades of green represented in the sprawling farmland, pasture, and lakes that surrounded them. The sun wasn't fully out, but it peeked out every few minutes, briefly spreading heat and warmth and golden light across the land.

After Ais and Colm had some water and a couple of energy bars, they decided to descend via the path that Donal was going to tackle.

"I'm going to sit right down and wait for Maggie and Bren," Ryan said. "I think I see them waaaay down there."

"You can come with us," Aisling said. "A different view might be nice."

"No thanks. I might have to carry one or both of them back down."

"If you're not down half an hour after we get to the car, I'm coming back up," Aisling said, giving Ryan a very no-nonsense look.

"I think she loves me," Ryan said to Colm, wrapping Aisling in a tight hug and leaning back until her feet left the ground.

"No smaller person likes a bigger person picking them up," she said, kicking her feet. She turned to Colm and added, "Except for you, of course. And only then when you sweep me off my feet and throw me on the bed."

Colm stared at her, open-mouthed as Ryan dropped her as if she were scalding. "Jesus," she whined.

"Ha!" Ais crowed. "I knew I could make you drop me. You're so easy to trick," she added, slapping Ryan hard on the butt.

"I'll get you back," Ryan called after her. But she knew she wouldn't. Aisling had always been more clever.

She plopped down on the rocky ground, finding a flat rock that didn't hurt her butt. She wrapped her arms around her knees and stretched her back out, then stuck her hands behind her to rest on her locked arms.

Now she really tried to clear her mind, using some of the tricks she'd learned through the meditation training she'd had when she was much younger. The tricks worked—a little. If she tried hard, she could still her mind for fifteen or twenty seconds. Nothing like the peace she used to achieve when she sat in front of her tiny altar and prayed. Back then, she could get into a zone that tranquilized her until her legs got numb.

The sun broke through the grey clouds and warmed her face. Slowly, she opened her eyes and took in the gorgeous landscape. It always amazed her how many variations of green existed in nature, and how all of them seemed to cover vast swaths of Ireland.

California was mostly brown, despite what the tourism ads claimed. That was what Ryan was used to, and the varieties of brown and tan were pretty nice. But the dull sage color she got at home was nothing compared to this green. She closed her eyes again and took in a deep breath of the plant-scented, moist air as a sense of deep peace surrounded her like a hug. A *real* hug. She was alone, on a mountain, but something made her feel like she was being tenderly embraced. Not even tempted to open her eyes, she relaxed into the feeling. Then she heard a whisper, right in her ear. A soft, warm, love-filled voice said, "Mo leanbh."

Normally, hearing a person who wasn't there call her "my child" would have made Ryan leap to her feet, fists raised. But this feeling was so peaceful, so serene, that she just filled her lungs with the sweet air.

She was transported nearly twenty years into the past, to the bed they'd set up in the living room of their home in Noe Valley. Her mother was lying there, and Ryan was nestled up against her. She'd been fading for weeks, and everyone tip-toed around the bed when they visited, not wanting to wake her from her drug-induced haze.

On the day she died, Ryan felt those rail-thin arms embrace her, as she whispered "Mo leanbh," a term she didn't use often, reserved for the occasions when she was expressing her deep love.

The voice—the same voice she'd just heard—spoke that day. Since Ryan had been so young, she might not have the details down pat. But she'd always been sure her mother's last words were to express her abiding love. And now...now she was certain. She would have put everything dear to her on the certainty that not only had her mother spoken those words to her that day—she was speaking them now.

A scratching sound made her open her eyes, certain her mother would be there when she did. But it was Brendan, winded and gasping for air as he bent over and put his hands on his knees.

"Mama was just here," she whispered, so quietly she wasn't sure he'd heard her.

In a second, he was sitting by her side. "Did you just say what I think you said?"

She nodded, unable to speak as she tried to get her bearings.

He blew out a breath, gazing out at the beauty spread out before them. "She's talked to me a few times."

"She has?"

"Uh-huh. It's always been when I'm asleep. I wake up to her voice, but I never know if I heard it in a dream, or if she...was there," he said, shrugging his shoulders. "It doesn't matter, I guess. It feels so good to hear it that I don't really care."

"But if we hear her…" Ryan swallowed, her nerves making her mouth dry. "Does that mean she's…somewhere?"

He answered immediately. "I believe with my whole heart that she's somewhere, Ryan. And I'm just as sure that I'll see her again."

"You really believe that," she said quietly.

"I do. I'm not sure what form we'll be in, but I'm going to connect with Mama again." He faced her, with such a sweet smile on his face her eyes grew clouded with tears in half of a second. "And so will you."

"God, Bren, you don't know how much I want that." She leaned against him, snuggling closer when his arm circled her back.

"I promised her I'd take care of you, and I will always keep that promise. If I can help you regain just a little bit of the faith you used to have…"

"But…" She took in a heavy breath. "I feel like the scales have fallen from my eyes. Once you've convinced yourself there's no one up there…" She sat up tall and looked at him. "Isn't it like trying to believe in Santa again?"

"Maybe," he said after a while. "But what's so bad about believing in someone who brings joy to kids?"

She laughed at the tone in his voice. "I guess you've got a point. Maybe…" She looked around, puzzled. "Where's Maggie?"

He let out a laugh. "I won't tell her it took you five minutes to notice she wasn't here."

Ryan gave him a playful shove. "Where is she?"

"She gave up. I left her sitting on a flat spot. There goes my chance to ask her to marry me in this beautiful setting." He put his arm around Ryan and hugged her. "I was afraid you were waiting for us, so I said I'd go on alone."

"Aww." She leaned into him again. "You've always kept your promise to Mama."

"Until the day I die. You can count on that."

She sat up and retied her shoes. "Hey, Bren? When Mama has spoken to you, what does she say?"

He looked at her for a second, then said, "It's always in Irish."

Staring at him, she whispered, "Me too. She called me her child."

"Is that mo leanbh?"

She nodded.

"My Irish isn't as good as yours, but I thought that's what it was. I've also gotten 'mo pheata.'"

"That's 'my darling,' or 'a mother's darling.'" Ryan gave him an elbow to the side. "I want that one."

"Then you've got to keep your soul open to hearing her again. Have you stopped praying?"

"Yeah," she said, lowering her eyes.

"Do you sit quietly and clear your mind like you used to?"

"No."

He gave her a soft thump to the head. "Then when is she supposed to have time to talk to you? You never sit still!"

"Maybe I'll start doing that again." She let out a sigh. "I felt a whole hell of a lot better when I used to believe."

"You don't have to start off believing. You just have to open your heart to the possibility of God."

"But there's such scant evidence—"

"There's no evidence to prove that love exists, either, but we both know it does."

They looked up at the same moment, with Maggie standing in front of them, also winded and flush-faced. "Made it," she gasped. "I am not a wimp."

Ryan got up and took her hands, twirling her around until she stood over the spot Ryan had been sitting on. "Take some time to catch your breath and take in the sights," she said, holding her hands until she was down. "We're not in any hurry."

"Thanks," Brendan said, meeting her eyes with a smile.

"Thank *you*. As usual, you're here when I need you." She ruffled his hair as she started to walk back down. "You're a stór," she said, hoping he knew how much she treasured him—in any language.

Maggie sat between Brendan's legs, leaning against his chest as they both looked out at the splendor that was rural Ireland in early summer. Maggie had been to Ireland several times, but she'd never been to Galway or Mayo, and she seemed pretty charmed by it.

"Just four generations ago, our great-great-grandparents lived on this island," she said, letting out a sigh. "I'm sure their paths never crossed, but I bet they had an awful lot in common."

"Besides poverty, too many kids and blind obedience to the Church?"

She gave his thigh a slap. "Harsh words for a man whose butt's in a pew every Sunday."

"Not true," he said, gently tickling under her chin. "Just yesterday I went to Mass on Saturday evening."

"My point stands, Bren. You're the only holdout in your immediate family. They've got a whole pew with the Episcopalians now, and you're all alone at St. Philip's."

"True. Just shows how hard-headed I am."

"That's not you." She moved her shoulders around, nestling into him. "You're a man of principle, but you're not hard-headed." Tilting her head back, she met his eyes. "For an O'Flaherty, that is."

"I'd argue, but everyone knows we're a determined people." He was afraid his voice would start to shake, but this was his moment. Tucking his arms snugly around her, he placed his lips by her ear. "I'm determined to marry you, Margaret Elizabeth Reardon. Why not give in and skip the argument?"

She wriggled out of his embrace, staring at him for a moment. "Are you serious?"

"Very." He reached into his pocket and took out the black velvet box Catherine had overnighted to the hotel. Before he got it open, she was already shaking her head.

"Don't even open it," she warned. "I can't wear an engagement ring, Bren. I just can't."

"It's not an engagement ring," he said, laughing at her overreaction. "I *do* listen to you, Mags."

"Then what is it?"

He twisted the box in his fingers, taunting her with it. "You're going to have to open it to find out."

"If it's not an engagement ring, I don't have to open it right now. Let's settle one thing at a time." She scooted around until they were facing each other, and put her hands on his knees. "You know I love you dearly, Brendan, but if we marry, we'll have to answer the 'when are you having kids' question for the next ten or fifteen years." She rolled her eyes dramatically. "I'll never be in the mood for that."

"Tell people it's none of their business—which it isn't. Or have fun with it. Make up a different answer depending on your mood. Like… kids? I'd love to, but I can't. Court order."

She laughed, but he could tell she wasn't finished with the point. "The questions would be annoying, but that's not the big issue. You want children," she said, shaking his legs a little. "I know you do."

"And I know you do, too. But you've decided not to get pregnant, and I'm okay with that." He leaned forward and gave her a quick kiss. "No one gets everything on their wish list, right? We'll have so many nieces and nephews we won't know what to do with them all. Not having kids of our own will let us be the world's best babysitters. Then we'll give them back at the end of the night. Kind of a win/win, right?"

"It's not the same, and you know it. I'm the one who made the decision not to have a baby. If you were with a woman who wanted six, I think you'd be very happy."

"Six is a little much, but yes, I'd like a few. But I'd rather be with you and not have kids, than with anyone else and have the best kids in the world." He put his hand on her cheek, feeling the cool softness of her skin. "You're the prize, Maggie. Kids would be nice, but they're not a requirement. You are." His voice grew stronger when he said, "I'd give up an awful lot to keep you in my life. I'd even move to Chicago if it would be easier for you to be closer to your family."

"No," she said quietly. "I'm too much of a coward to watch my father fade away. Short visits are all I can bear."

"I understand," he said, pulling her close for a hug. "When my mother was dying, I raced out the house the moment I could get away. To this day I have so many more memories of her last months than I do of the previous twelve years. It's awful," he added, feeling a little sick to his stomach just to recall that time.

She gazed at him for a long time, with the wind whipping strands of her long, black hair around, but she was so intent she didn't even bother to grab hold of them. "I don't want you to be in that position with *me*. We don't know that I don't have the Huntington's gene, Bren. If I do have it, I don't want you to have to watch me wither away."

He returned her emotion-filled stare. "What do you think marriage is? A huge part of it is promising to be there until you die. That's the point, right?"

"If you'd known my dad before he started having symptoms, you'd understand what this disease does to a person. To you, my dad's always been a severely disabled guy who can't feed himself or speak. But that's not who he is to me."

Brendan started to speak, but she cut him off.

"I acknowledge that marriage is a pledge to be together until one of you dies, but the implication is that you'll be old and feeble. The gamble is that you'll have a few decades-worth of connection. Of fun. And I don't know that I'm going to have that. We both know the odds are good that I won't."

"We *don't* know that. The odds are equally good that you will. If you didn't inherit the gene…"

"I know the odds, Bren. I've known them since my dad got sick. But if we get married and I *do* get sick, you're stuck with me. Even if I gave you a hundred good reasons to divorce me, leaving a woman with a terminal disease is a bad look for a guy." She smiled at him, but just hearing her attempt to joke gave him a chill.

"I love you, Maggie. All of you. I love you in health and I will love you if you get sick one day. I mean, when you get sick, or injured, or feeble, or whatever. Neither of us is immortal, baby."

"I know that—"

"The fact is that I'd rather have a few good years with you than many with anyone else. So…come on and marry me. I know the risks of marrying someone who might have inherited an awful disease, but I also know the rewards of being with you. The plusses are so much greater than the minuses."

She looked like she was struggling hard not to cry when she said, "Oh, Bren, you don't know that's true. You can't know what the disease will do to me. For most people, it changes their entire personality."

"I know that. But committing to anything involves risks. It's part of the deal."

"Sometimes I wish we hadn't gotten back together," she said, losing the fight as a few tears spilled over her lids to slip down her cheeks. "I was planning on staying single until I had the damn test. I'm still kicking myself for being such a chicken, but now that I'm with you I'm even more afraid."

"I'm glad you didn't have it," he said, taking her hands and squeezing them. "If you'd found out you had the gene, you wouldn't be with me." He scrambled to his feet and pulled her up to stand next to him. After wrapping her in his arms, he said, "Come on, Mags. Admit that none of us knows if we'll get even one more day on earth. Roll the dice with me."

She hugged him for a long time, with her body shaking as she cried. Finally, she looked up at him, with her red-rimmed brown eyes full of emotion. "I wish I could promise you we'll be together for fifty years, but I can't." She took in a long breath. "But I'll love you as well as I can for the rest of my life."

He smiled at her, feeling a little dizzy from the tension. "We're going to be a great team," he promised. "Mr. and Mrs. Brendan—"

Laughing, she put her hand over his mouth. "I know you're teasing, but the thought of changing my name is so ridiculous I can't even stand to hear what it would sound like."

"I love your strength," he said, starting to tear up. "I love that you always stand up for yourself."

"And I love that you'd call yourself 'Mr. Maggie Reardon' if I asked you to."

"Wouldn't bother me a bit. We have plenty of O'Flahertys. Losing one to add to the Reardon clan wouldn't hurt a soul."

"Well now," she sighed, leaning her head all the way back to expose her face to a burst of sunlight. "I think it's time to give me a present. Not that it's an engagement present," she warned. "I'd actually rather not tell anyone outside of the family until we send out wedding invitations. But since you went to the trouble to buy me something…"

"I did," he said, bending to pick up the box he'd placed on the ground. He put his hands on it, hesitant to open it. "I'm going to give you the usual—"

"If I don't like it, you won't mind if I return it," she cut in. "I know, honey."

"Right. So…I bought this because it reminds me of Ireland. Being here with you has been fantastic, Maggie, and I want you to have this to remember the day we decided to marry." He cracked the box open and watched her mouth drop when she saw the necklace, the best reaction a guy could hope for when he bought a piece of jewelry. "It's your birthstone, too."

"Holy fuck!" She stared at him like he'd just dropped to earth from another planet. "That's fake, right?"

"Nope. It's as real as my love. Conflict-free," he added. "I know you won't want to wear this every day, but when you do get dressed up I want you to have something that reminds you of today."

"Like I could ever forget today," she sighed, wrapping him in a tight hug. "I love you, Brendan…only partially for your excellent taste in jewelry." She looked up and grinned at him. "I'm not going to ask what caused you to lose your mind and spend so much money on a gift, because that's just rude. But if you need me to cover your half of the rent…I'm up for it."

"My savings took a hit, but it was worth it to see your eyes bug out."

"It's a gorgeous piece," Maggie said, taking another look at the necklace. "I will treasure it."

"Don't you want to put it on now?"

"Now? Not with sunblock on my neck, and a good deal of grit. I'll get dressed up tomorrow night and we'll tell everyone."

"That works for me. My grandmother will be thrilled. I can tell how much she likes you."

"I can see myself being a lot like her, should I make it to eighty." She grasped Brendan's hand and squeezed it tightly. "I desperately hope we make it that far."

"Whatever we get, we'll make the most out of it. That's all the control we have, sweetheart, and I promise it will be enough."

The whole clan had taken over Aisling's pub once again, with Moira and Maeve deciding it was more fun for everyone if they could eat together while letting Caitlin, and to a lesser extent, Brenna run around during the meal. Jamie had pitched in to help, and assigned herself the task of preparing some vegetable side dishes to go with the Atlantic salmon and potatoes. She'd been vegetable-deprived since they'd arrived, and she went a little crazy, roasting beets, and asparagus, and Brussels sprouts, as well as making a huge salad with radishes and snap peas and red pepper strips.

Granny had come into the kitchen repeatedly, checking on their progress, but she didn't offer to help, which was just as well. She was perfectly able to cook a meal for a crowd, but she didn't do well with delegating or being delegated to.

Everything was ready not long after the hikers returned, dirty and tired from both the trek and the drive. Jamie was setting the salad on the bar when she heard Granny say, "You would have made it up the mountain quicker if your souls had been relieved of your sins. Confession's at four on Saturday."

"Thanks for reminding us," Aisling said, giving her grandmother a kiss on the cheek. Aisling knew just how to handle the woman. Agree, agree, agree. Ryan hadn't learned that lesson, and Jamie was waiting for her to make a point of not having confession on her weekly schedule. But she just nodded, went over to the bar to pull a pint, then sat down by her father.

That was a new tactic. Maybe she was learning a thing or two from Aisling.

Jamie hadn't had any alcohol, so she was able to drive Ryan, Conor and Colm back to the hotel. Ryan had been very quiet throughout dinner, and she continued that on their drive back to Ballina. She didn't seem out-of-sorts, nor particularly tired. Just quiet.

Once they got to their room, Jamie went into the bathroom to turn the shower on to let it warm up. But Ryan called out, "Babe? Can you draw me a bath?"

"Sure." She poked her head out. "Did you hurt yourself on your hike?"

She was busy stripping her clothes off, but she stopped with her tights at her knees. "Hurt myself? Why would I have hurt myself?"

"Mmm. Sometimes you're quiet when you're hurt."

"Nope. Not hurt. Bath?" she asked, cocking her head. "I need to soak the grime off."

"I'm on it," Jamie said. She'd brought some bath salts, and she added them to the water, making it hot, but not as hot as Ryan liked it. She could add scalding water when she got in.

Jamie laughed when Ryan entered the bathroom. She'd obviously put sunblock on, and the grit and dust from the path had stuck to the skin across the back of her neck and by her ears. "You need a stiff-bristled brush to get clean tonight, Pig Pen."

"Maybe my devoted partner will scrub me with a washcloth."

"Happy to," Jamie said, holding her hand as she got into the tub. "Do you feel like company?"

Ryan grasped the sides of the tub and lowered herself into the water, letting out a sigh as it covered her legs and part of her torso. Her ideal tub was a foot taller than the ones most hotels provided, so she had to soak different parts at different times. "Am I giving off 'go away' vibes or something?"

"No, honey," Jamie said, sitting on the edge of the tub and pulling Ryan's pony tail up to affix it to the top of her head with a clip. "I'm just checking."

"All is well." She bent her knees, and slid down until her chest was covered with water.

"Did you have fun? You guys were gone forever. I was afraid you were going to miss dinner."

"Bren and Maggie were slow to get up, and they stayed up there forever."

"Yipes! I didn't ask if Bren proposed!"

"He did," Ryan said, smiling. "They're going to tell everyone tomorrow night."

"Did Maggie like the necklace?"

"Don't know. Bren and I didn't talk about it. I just raised an eyebrow when they got back to the car, and he gave me a thumb's up."

Jamie rolled her eyes. "For someone who's always talking, you sure do parse out the words carefully sometimes."

"They rode with Ais. I had Donal and Colm."

"Got it. So what did the rest of you do while they were being slow."

She smiled as she sank further down into the water. "Donal climbed the peak twice from different trails, while Aisling and Colm hid somewhere for over an hour." She met Jamie's eyes and said, "And I had…a supernatural experience? Or a vision?" She shook her head. "Not sure what I had, but I had something."

"Um, would you like to give me a few more details? It's not a rule, but I'd think most people would put visions at the top of the list when they're recounting the events of the day."

"I know," she said, with her voice growing quiet. "But this freaked me out." She looked up, adding, "It was incredibly calming when it happened, but now that I've had some time to think about it…"

"What happened?" Jamie asked, ready to shake it out of her.

"I'm not sure what kind of mood I was in, but I was really connected to my body when I was hiking." She met Jamie's eyes. "Usually, I'm all up in my head, but I kept forcing myself to feel my legs and listen to my breathing. Stuff like that."

"Uh-huh. I know what you mean."

"So…I got to the top and I was alone for a while. It was cloudy, but not raining, and the sun kept breaking through, but only for a minute or two. Pretty."

"Sounds it. Were you high up?"

"Yeah. I forget how high we were, but it took two hours to reach the top."

"Two hours for you," Jamie teased. "Three for me."

"It took Maggie about two and a half, and I'm sure you could best her."

"Thanks for the vote of confidence. What next?"

"Let's see." She scooted up enough to rest her head on the back of the tub, with her knees still bent. "I was thinking about how beautiful it was, and feeling pretty Irish," she added, smirking. "Sometimes I feel like I can connect with dozens of generations of my family when I see a landscape that's pretty and undeveloped. The land around there could pass for the thirteenth century if you could ignore a few things."

"Sounds nice."

"It was. Really nice. The sun kept sneaking in and out, and one time I closed my eyes and just felt how great it was to have the heat on my face. After a couple of seconds, I felt like I was being wrapped in a protective embrace. Not by hands or arms or anything like that. Just…a feeling of being loved and protected." She looked at Jamie and added, "But more than that. I don't have words for what else it was, but it was more."

"Go on," she urged, so curious she was beside herself.

"I didn't open my eyes, which was weird. Normally I would have jumped up and tried to figure out what the heck was going on. And then I heard it," she said dramatically. "My mother's voice. Right in my ear. Calling me her child. In Irish," she added, now staring at Jamie with her eyes wide.

"Oh, my God," Jamie whispered. "You had a vision!"

"I know. I just don't know what it means."

"It means… What it means. Your mom reached across the veil that separates us from the other side, honey. She wanted you to know how much you mean to her. Even now." She slid onto the floor, and reached for Ryan, hugging her tightly, even as she got soaked. "I'm so happy for you."

"You are? But…I'm freaked out."

As Jamie pulled away, she peeled off her shirt and put it on the rim of the tub. "You're only freaked out? Or is that one of the things you are."

"One," Ryan admitted. "Some of that deep calm is still with me. And the thought that my mom might have enough agency and power to actually communicate with me is…wow," she whispered. "I've only felt a little like this a few times in my life."

"A few? Tell me about the others."

She waved a hand dismissively. "A few times while I was praying or meditating, I felt some of the…connectedness to something." She looked at Jamie again. "Or everything."

"Right. Right. That's happened to me. Not often. But that sense of being one with the universe kind of thing has knocked me off my feet a couple of times." She grasped Ryan's hands and squeezed them. "Wasn't it magical?"

"It was awesome, but not magical. More…supernatural. If I hadn't recognized my mother's voice, I would have thought a fairy or something was nearby." Her eyes grew wider. "I'm acting like my great-great-great-great grandmother would have, seeing fairies and pookas!"

"Maybe you'll find a pot of gold at the end of the rainbow."

"I already have," she said, smiling warmly. "Its name is Jamie."

"Come on, don't push this aside. This is important, honey."

"I know. I really do know." She looked hesitant when she said, "This is going to make me rethink my atheism. If my mom can talk to me, there's something other than death waiting for us."

Even though the rim of the tub was cold, and she was naked from the waist up, Jamie stretched out to hug Ryan again. "I can't begin to tell you how much I've wanted to hear you say that."

"I'm not sure—"

"No one is, honey. I've only been hoping that you'll be open to the possibility. That's all most of us can summon up on any given day."

"Seriously? You really mean that?"

"Yes!" She sat back on her haunches, saying, "Some days I'll be walking down the street, and something will hit me and I'll think, 'Well, this is all bullshit. The best I can hope for is a long life, because we're all alone in this hell-scape.'"

"You really think that?"

"Yes! But then I'll have a few weeks or a few months or even a few years where everything seems kind of peaceful. I know the world's always a mess, but there's some kind of goodness that I'm very confident of. That's what I want for you. Some periods where everything doesn't seem so…temporary."

"I'm not sure I can get there, but I'm going to try."

"Going back to praying or meditating will help, sweetheart. I promise it will."

"Having that discipline worked for me for years, so I'm going to try to start it up again."

"I'm so happy," Jamie said, feeling tears sting her eyes. "I want you to have a little faith. Just enough to feel like there might be a reason we were born."

Ryan smiled at her, such a touching expression that Jamie was sure she'd start to really cry.

"I know I was born to love you, and that's been enough for me. But I'm going to be open to even more."

Chapter Seven

On Monday morning, Ryan and Jamie waved goodbye to the whole crew. Ryan had arranged for them to take a tour of Inis Mór, a place she and Jamie hadn't yet visited. While she wanted to see it, she wanted to go alone, after everyone else was back in San Francisco. Since they had plenty of time, they didn't have to be on a tourist's schedule.

The group had to travel to Galway to pick up the bus that would take them to the ferry, and after the visit, Colm and Aisling were going to stay in town to shop for tile. That would give them an excuse to be gone for hours, time they needed.

Ryan put her arm around Jamie's shoulders and hugged her. "As much as I love them all, I need a day off."

"Is it a day off when we're meeting with our architect?"

"Sure. We don't have anything else scheduled, and I doubt we'll spend more than an hour with Lucy. What else would you like to do?"

"I don't know." She tilted her head up, checking out the sky. "It's an awfully nice day. Want to walk on the beach?"

"Sure." She waggled her eyebrows. "I could actually use my wetsuit if the surfing school that used to be in Inishcrone is still open and I can get my hands on a board."

Jamie tilted her head as she raised her hand to shield her eyes from the sun. "Does it ever feel like we have different definitions of being together?"

Ryan thought for a minute, going over what she'd proposed. "Oh. You don't think watching me surf is being together, right?"

A smile showed she wasn't annoyed. "Pretty much not. I was thinking of actually being within a few feet of each other."

"My bad. Watching someone do something isn't the same as doing something together." She slapped herself on the side of the head. "Hey," she added. "On our honeymoon, I did something by myself while you watched like every day! Did I bore the hell out of you?"

"No, baby," Jamie said, with her voice taking on the low, sexy tone it got when she was feeling particularly affectionate. "That was two years ago. Back then I would have watched you paint a house and enjoyed the heck out of the experience. Now I've come back down to earth a little. Just a little," she added.

"I hope I understand how to be a good partner one of these days. God knows I need a lot of help."

"You're doing pretty darned well for someone who's just started getting used to being in captivity," Jamie said as she took her hand and led the way to their little rental car.

Jamie sat on a patch of their turf that was high enough to be dry, waiting for Aisling's architect friend, Lucy Daly, to arrive. Ryan was… somewhere. It would have been nice if she could sit down and relax like a regular person, but that simply wasn't in her nature. Jamie would have gone to look for her, since she'd been gone for a half hour, but she wanted to be by the dilapidated gate to wave Lucy down. The entry to their property wasn't obvious.

At ten, a small white car cruised down the lane, and it stopped next to theirs. The driver's window lowered and a woman waved. "Hello," she said, her accent different from any Jamie had heard in the past week. "Siobhán?"

"Jamie," she said, standing to climb over the gate. "Pull up anywhere you'd like."

She did, then got out. Lucy was about Jamie's height, and her pale skin and dark hair made her look very Irish. She was wearing a business suit, with a skirt and heels, not the sort of thing she'd be able to tramp around in. Jamie was just about to suggest they head over to Moira's to chat, when Lucy opened her trunk. "Just give me a moment to get my wellies," she said, with Jamie realizing no experienced Irish architect would arrive at a rural job site without boots. She slipped them on, then clomped over to Jamie and extended her hand. "Lucy Daly. Lovely to meet you, Jamie." She revealed a smile that showed a set of gleaming white teeth. "I should have know you weren't Siobhán, since you look nothing like Aisling."

"Neither does Siobhán," Jamie admitted. "But they're closer than sisters."

From the corner of her eye she saw Ryan loping over to them, eating up the uneven ground like a mountain goat, arms slightly outstretched at her sides to catch herself if she fell.

"Here she is now."

"Oh, my, she's a head taller than Aisling."

"Just about. Her father's side of the family's on the tall side."

"Hello," Ryan said when she reached them, extending her hand to Lucy. She was wearing such a fetching grin it would have pulled the grumpiest person out of a grim mood.

"It's good to meet you, Siobhán. Aisling speaks of you often. And fondly."

"She doesn't do that to my face, so it's nice to hear she's kind to me when I'm not around."

"Oh, you know Aisling. She's rarely serious."

"That I do know," Ryan agreed. "Unlike my cousin, I can be serious when I need to be, and I'm very serious about this piece of land."

"It's a lovely plot," Lucy said. "I assume it's been farmland for generations."

"It has. And even though we're planning on building a big house, we'd like it to look as small as possible. Having it look more like a farm building would be nice, too."

"A farm building?" Jamie said, staring at her. "Is that something we've discussed? Because if it is, I need to work on my memory."

"We didn't discuss that?" Ryan said, unleashing that adorable grin to get herself out of a sticky situation once again. "I could have sworn…"

Jamie looked at Lucy and said, "I'd hate to have the house stick out like a sore thumb, but I wasn't thinking of living in a hay barn, either."

"Let's take a walk," Lucy said. "I'd like to see what we have to work with."

"It's a great space," Ryan said, high-stepping to clear the long grass. "I love the wall that surrounds the pasture."

"Does it go clear around the plot?"

"It's about two hundred feet on three sides. The majority of the land is enclosed in a largely ruined wire fence that we'll probably replace since we plan on having sheep, as well as a horse."

"So you'll need a barn, and a spot for lambing—"

"We've got that," Ryan said. "The only building that's partially intact is a lambing shed, and I'd like to keep it."

"Just needs a roof," Jamie said. They walked for a minute or two, then the lambing shed came into view.

"Oh, but that's a lovely spot," Lucy said. "If you wanted, we could incorporate that into the house…"

"I like the idea," Ryan said, "but you can see the shed from the lane. I think I want the house situated over the rise there. There's a good sized dip in the land, maybe deep enough to hide the house completely."

"Mmm. You can hide the house from view, but you can't hide it from the rain. If you put it in the lowest spot, you'll need to sluice the water away."

"French drains?"

Lucy nodded. "That's a viable option. You can do nearly anything if you have the budget." They walked toward the rise that was just about at the center of the property. Next to it, the land dipped in a depression twenty or thirty feet wide, then rose up again, never quite reaching the same altitude of the high spot.

"I'd love to have the house on the highest point, but there's something very appealing about being screened by the land," Ryan said.

"And the wind," Lucy agreed. "It could be very cosy down there. But, again, you'd have some significant landscaping to do." She peered at Ryan for a moment, clearly assuming she was the brains of the organization. "Do you have a budget in mind?"

"Not really," she said, starting to look uncomfortable. Jamie was tempted to take over and chat about money while Ryan continued to walk around, but she didn't want to treat her like a child.

Lucy laughed a little. "Everyone has a budget of some sort. If you could give me a very rough estimate..."

"I can't. We want to do this right, and build for the long term."

"I understand—"

"I have a large family," Ryan added, "and most of them live in America. So we'd like six bedrooms, and five or six bathrooms for kids and visitors. We'll definitely have a lot of visitors, and we might have a lot of kids," she said, making a face when Jamie caught her attention.

Lucy looked like she wasn't sure she was being serious. "That's a very large house, Siobhán. And with the landscaping you want to do..."

"There's more," Ryan said. "We won't be using much of the house for more than half of the year, but Aisling will share it with us. I hate to heat the whole place if it's just her living here, so I thought we might build a large great room, then have two or three separate buildings, each with a couple of bedrooms and a sitting room."

"You're talking about a compound," Lucy said, clearly even more puzzled.

"I suppose I am. For our bedroom module, we'd like a large bedroom and a bath, then two bedrooms with a shared bath. Maybe the same thing for Aisling. The third building could have two bedrooms of the same size, each with a private bath."

"Three buildings."

"Three *bedroom* buildings. Don't forget the great room, which needs to be large. I want a big kitchen, and I need to be able to seat at least twenty for dinner."

"That sounds like a Viking longhouse," Lucy said, likely now believing Ryan had delusions of grandeur she couldn't possibly afford.

"I know it's a lot. And we might want to hold off on the third bedroom building. But I think we need the others now."

"We also want them to be energy efficient," Jamie said.

"Very efficient," Ryan said. "I was thinking of geo-thermal heat. Do you have any experience with that?"

"I don't," Lucy said. "I'm familiar with the process, of course, but I've not been involved in any projects where it's been utilized." Her eyes were wide open when she said, "I think this project will expose me to *many* things I haven't experienced before."

"That's the O'Flaherty way," Jamie said. "Ryan loves to sail uncharted waters."

After lunch and a very long walk on the beach, they went by Ryan's aunt's house, which had become the gathering place for anyone who didn't have another destination in mind.

The girls were home from school, with Cáit quieter than usual after her history exam, and Brenna her usual chatterbox.

Jamie was sitting on the big sofa, and she turned to peer out the window when she heard a car. "I think Bren and Maggie are here."

Brenna was on her feet in a second, racing to the front door to welcome them.

"She's better than a watchdog," Moira said, "but many times more expensive."

"She doesn't shed," Cáit said, revealing a grin. "If you're trying to think of reasons to keep her, that's a big one."

Moira got up and bent to kiss Cáit's head as she passed. "I love each of you equally, but I'll admit you and Cormac are the easiest to handle."

"I'd hope so," Cáit said quietly.

The door opened, and Brendan and Maggie entered. "Are we the first ones back?" Bren asked.

"You are," Moira said.

"We thought we could eat at Aisling's again tonight. We went to a grocery store she recommended and bought groceries, as well as some treats."

Brenna was in his face immediately. "What kind of treats?"

"Just cheese and crackers and that kind of stuff," he said. "Plus wine."

She dropped to the sofa next to Jamie. "Nothing good."

"What's the occasion?" Moira asked.

"Nothing much. We're both a little tired of pub food, and thought we could save money and have more variety if we shopped."

"Did you buy any vegetables?" Jamie asked. "My craving for something green remains strong."

"We did," Maggie said. "Pubs are not places for people who lean a little to the vegetarian side of the ledger."

"I miss cooking," Jamie said. "Why don't we go prep things so we can have dinner ready when the clan returns."

"I'll go with you," Moira said. "I learned my way around the kitchen the other night."

"Can I go?" Brenna asked. "I can help."

"Do what?" Moira asked, hands on her hips.

"I can…"

"Provide interruption," Cáit said quietly.

"You can come," Moira said. "Maybe you'll learn a few things."

Cáit met Jamie's eyes, then slowly shook her head, with a devilish grin making her even cuter than she normally was.

Having two commercial ovens, as well as a six-burner cooktop, let them roast four chickens in one oven, and two large pork roasts in the other. Cáit had been right, of course, and Brenna was no help at all. But she provided some entertainment as they all worked at their assigned tasks. Moira was really quite good at directing multiple cooks, and Jamie was sure she'd be a big help to Aisling after the grand re-opening.

The rest of the clan wandered in as they returned from Galway, with Martin, Maeve and Conor leading the pack. By seven everyone but Colm and Aisling had returned, and the beer was flowing as the group whipped through all of the snacks Maggie and Bren had purchased.

It always amazed Jamie at how fast just a few large men could destroy a carefully arranged platter. She now knew how caterers felt, when hours of prep was gone in minutes.

They held off on the entrees, waiting for the stragglers, with Kieran saying, "Someone else should have gone with Aisling. Colm's probably spent the whole drive telling her what a great catch he is."

"Colm's not the type to do that," Jamie said, always protective of her second choice of O'Flahertys. "Besides, Aisling's not the type to believe any hype."

"What am I not the type to do?" she asked, having entered the pub through the back door.

"To let some guy talk you into dating him if you weren't in the mood."

She threw her head back and laughed. "I've done exactly that. Many times," she added. "But I've gotten more discerning. Now I find a man I want and pursue him." She shrugged. "The ones who aren't afraid of a decisive woman seem to like it."

"That's how I got Brendan," Maggie said, grasping his hand and holding it to her chest. "I tracked him down and wouldn't give up."

"Like I wanted you to," he said, giving her a lovesick grin. They smiled at each other until it was bordering on uncomfortable, then Bren managed to look away and face the crowd. "Maggie and I were together in our early twenties, and now our early thirties. I wish we hadn't broken up the first time…" He turned and gave her a very sweet smile. "Now I'm determined to never let that happen again. Getting married seems like the best way to keep her close, so…"

Maggie put her arm around him and hugged him tightly. "I'm going to keep this wonderful man right next to me for the rest of my life. He certainly didn't have to talk me into it."

"I did," he insisted, grinning when she pinched him. "I wore her down."

Everyone started to clap, with Martin jumping to his feet to hug both of them, Maeve right behind him. Everyone else got in on the action, with the room buzzing for a long time with lots of questions, most of which they had no answers for.

"We haven't made any plans," Brendan said. "Maggie hasn't even told her family yet."

"No ring?" Colm said when he got to the front of the line. "You got a girl like this and didn't buy her a ring?"

"He bought me a necklace," Maggie said, pulling the piece from where it was hiding under her boat-neck sweater.

Aisling was a few feet away, and she moved over immediately, staring at the necklace like she was under a spell. She looked at Brendan for a moment, then back at the necklace. "For the love of God," she murmured. "You're going to have to travel with an armed guard."

Brendan looked a little sheepish when he said, "When I saw it online I didn't know it was going to be so…impressive."

Jamie clapped Bren on the back and said, "It's the perfect size. You need a necklace to make a statement, and this one truly does."

"It says you emptied your bank account," Aisling maintained. "But you got something truly gorgeous."

Granny made her way past the clutch of bodies and hugged Brendan, then grasped Maggie's hands and smiled at her. Maggie hadn't yet earned a hug, but Jamie was sure she'd get there. It took a while, but you could earn your way into Granny's good graces.

"You'll marry here, then?" she asked, looking at Brendan.

"We haven't even discussed that, Granny. Maggie's got a big family in Chicago, and I've got an awful lot of relatives in San Francisco."

"This is where you'll have the ceremony," she said, unmoved by their concerns. "This is your home."

"We'll definitely consider getting married in Ireland," Maggie said, with Brendan staring at her like this was the first he'd heard of the idea. "We were just talking about the fact that both of our families came from here."

"From Mayo?" she asked, clearly surprised.

"My mother's family is from Kilkenny, and my dad's is from Wexford."

Granny met Brendan's eyes and repeated herself, acting like the previous comments hadn't registered. "This is your home, Brendan. What do you think of June? That's the month people seem to like."

After dinner, Jamie and Ryan sat on a stainless-steel counter in the kitchen, watching the boyos clean. Ryan refused to make cooking and cleaning "women's work," a tenet Jamie had come around to after being in the family for a short time. But even though the boyos did the work, they didn't always do it to an acceptable standard. That wasn't a problem at the O'Flaherty house, since Bren and Conor were well-used to cleaning. But the cousins got away with murder, with their mothers doing everything for them., so they truly needed some supervision.

The kitchen didn't have a regular dishwasher, just a drawer for sterilizing glasses. So they had to fill the sink and wash the dishes and pots and pans by hand.

As they got everything ready to go, Jamie leaned over and said, "Did you have any idea Maggie's necklace was going to be that large?"

"No!" She started to laugh quietly. "That emerald had to be three carats. Given I bought a very nice stone just a year and a half ago, I'm one hundred percent certain that Brendan is only paying for about a quarter of that necklace. Your mom's picking up the rest of the cost—which is nuts!"

"I'd argue, but you've got her dead-to-rights. She's been talking about how to pay Bren back for all of the free legal work he's done for Jen's adoption." She gave Ryan a toothy grin. "I think she's found it."

"I think Maggie knows that stone cost a load, but she's too polite to ask. And Bren doesn't suspect a thing."

"You won't tell him," Jamie warned.

"No way! If he knew, he'd want to take it back. Then Maggie'd be mad at both of us."

"Justifiably," Jamie said, leaning into her playfully. "If you two wanted to make sure you keep to a budget, my mother is the last person you should have called." She tapped on Ryan's temple. "Wise up, bucko."

On Tuesday morning, the work crew assembled once again, with even Jamie getting in on the act. The day started off like most of the projects Ryan had been involved in, with more talk than action.

It took until ten o'clock to have a list of needed supplies, and Ryan sent her father and Jamie to Ballina to pick everything up, making sure they would bring lunch on their return.

Ryan and Donal had rented a jackhammer on their way over, and now she put on hearing protectors and watched him take the bathroom's concrete slab apart. She really wanted to take over from him, but the machine looked awfully heavy and she didn't want to drop it and look like a weakling.

Even though Donal was a muscular beast, he asked for help well before Jamie returned. He'd gotten the bathroom broken up, and now Conor used the jackhammer to break up a stripe of the concrete slab that went through the kitchen to the sewer line. Donal had done a few tests, and had decided the line had either collapsed in part or was fouled in some other disgusting way. He could have investigated further, but Ryan urged him to start fresh. Sewer pipe only lasted so long, and she wanted her cousin to have many headache-free years when it came to a working bathroom.

The bar itself wasn't in bad shape, and the tables and chairs were serviceable, but many of them needed tightening up. Brendan knew how to do that, so he and Tommy took on the task.

Aisling wanted to have live music, and Conor and Niall agreed to build a small, sturdy stage in the corner of the room, with Kevin getting busy running the right kind of conduit along the baseboard to give musicians power for their amps and instruments.

Everyone was working well together, just like they did on the OFC projects when they all knew their tasks. The group only got in trouble when there was a power-vacuum.

Aisling started to go through all of her glassware, dishes and silverware, finding she needed some supplies beefed up. It was a sad pub when you couldn't order a drink because all of the glasses were being used.

Finally, Da and Jamie returned, bearing a van full of the long list of supplies, as well as two giant bags of sandwiches and cookies. In Ryan's view, the day was already a success. They had the right tools, plenty of food, and no significant fights. Days didn't get much better.

When they were ready for their lunch break, Ryan and Conor wrestled a couple of tables outside the back of the pub, where an unattractive concrete pad had been installed in what could have been the garden. A few more trips secured chairs for everyone, and they sat in the sun while they ate.

Ryan was sitting next to Aisling, and she said, "I hadn't spent any time looking around the kitchen before today, so I hadn't noticed this. How did Donnie get away with not having a commercial dishwasher?"

Aisling's eyes widened slightly, then she shook her head. "I hadn't considered that. My mam doesn't have one, and she'll probably continue to provide more meals on a daily basis than I will…"

"I'm not talking about practicality, Ais. Doesn't the health department have to inspect you?"

"It's not unhealthy to wash dishes in a sink. Don't be daft."

"You didn't answer my question. Do you need an inspection?"

She looked away, not responding for a few seconds. "I've a call in to the Food Safety Authority. It's on my list, Siobhán, which is as long as your leg."

Ryan put an arm around her, waiting until she'd settled into the hug to tickle her waist. After Aisling got in a good elbow to Ryan's ribs, she picked up her chair and scooted far enough away to avoid a repeat.

"I assume the FSAI's going to tell you that you need a dishwasher. So let's get one over here and have it installed before your free handymen take off on Sunday."

"How do you know what a regulatory authority in a country you don't live in will have to say?"

"I assume your laws are like ours, if not more stringent. A commercial dishwasher can run through a load in minutes—much faster than a human. I don't want you washing pots and pans after closing, so let's get it done."

"Fine," she said, sighing. "I won't be able to stop you from treating me like a baby chick, so I'll give in to your mother-hen tendencies."

"I don't mind if you call me names," Ryan said, smiling benignly. "I want you to enjoy your pub, and you'll have a better chance of that if you have everything you need. Which reminds me. Call your cook and ask if there was anything she needed and didn't have. I'm sending you and Jamie to Galway tomorrow to a restaurant supply place. You need more glasses and some silverware that isn't bent and nasty, along with whatever the cook recommends."

Aisling looked at her for a minute, then said, "Can I bring my actual mammy? I'd hate to be left without supervision for such a long time."

"You can. Maybe our aunt would like to go, too. You can make a day of it."

Aisling reached out to stroke Ryan's shoulder with tender care. "You're quite the pain, you know. But I wouldn't know what to do without you."

Ryan was creeping out of her room early on Wednesday morning when she heard the door to her right creak open. "Going somewhere?" she asked, making Colm jump.

"Jaysus," he grumbled.

She laughed and gave him a poke to the shoulder. "Since when do you say Jaysus? You've been in Ireland for ten days."

"Since when are you Siobhán O'Flaherty?" he asked, doing a pretty good impression of the Mayo accent.

She shrugged, slightly embarrassed. She knew the boyos had been making fun of her behind her back, but they'd been remarkably sensitive to her face. "I started speaking with an accent while I was in Ireland when I was tiny. It seems silly to stop just because you guys are here."

"But you're doing it now," he reminded her, looking around the empty corridor. "And I'm the only one here."

"I know," she grumbled. "I decided to stick with it so I didn't get confused. I'm full Irish this summer."

"I like it," he said, giving her a smile filled with affection. "I'm full knackered, as you would say. Donal couldn't get to sleep last night, so I had to stay awake listening to him toss and turn for an hour. This schedule's killing me."

Ryan clapped him on the shoulder. "After you've been back home for two days, you'll miss Aisling so badly you'd trade a week of sleep to see her again."

"You're not wrong," he said, casting his gaze at the floor. "I just wish we'd had more time together on this trip. I don't know what I expected, but I hoped it would be like home—where I can sneak away and not raise any eyebrows."

"If you decide to keep seeing each other, you'll tell everyone what's going on. Then, when you come back, you'll have only eight sets of eyes on you, watching you like a hawk to make sure you're treating her right."

"Thanks for the pep talk," he said, thumping her on the head with his fingers. "You really know how to reassure a guy."

Jamie sat in the backseat of Aisling's car alongside Maeve. Aisling and Moira were in the front, all of them chattering away on the long drive to Galway.

She truly loved being a part of this group, feeling closer to Maeve and Moira than she did the O'Flaherty aunts. It wasn't that they weren't friendly. They were. To a woman. But they weren't around as often as Maeve was, mostly since they were all busy playing nursemaid to adult sons and husbands who were as dependent as toddlers. Martin surely wouldn't have agreed, but being alone for so many years had made him a more fully-realized adult than his brothers, and definitely his nephews.

If she and Ryan ever had the chance to go on a trip with the O'Flaherty aunts, she was sure she'd get to know them better. But that was going to have to wait until they built their home. None of Ryan's aunts and uncles went on vacations, preferring to stick close to their routines. But she was sure the aunts would put pressure on the uncles to visit Ireland once they had a free place to stay. One thing you could count on with the O'Flahertys was that they knew a bargain when they saw one.

Jamie swiveled her head to look at Maeve when she gave her a tap on the leg. "Hmm?"

"I was just counting my blessings," she said. "And one of them is being on this little jaunt with you."

Jamie smiled at her. "Same for me. I love being able to hang out with you when Caitlin isn't diverting all of our attention."

"Oh, yes," she said, her smile looking a little impish. "I'm very glad to have time to finish a sentence. But I'm even more glad to not be in County Kerry today."

"Maeve! You let Martin take poor Maggie off to Tralee and you didn't give her a bit of warning."

"Warning? It's every woman for herself," she said, laughing softly. "If I'd warned Maggie and Brendan off, Martin would have insisted I go with him to visit his uncles. Once was quite enough, thank you very much."

"I got away with just meeting Leo and Mary. Even Ryan had her fill after that. We didn't even make an attempt to visit Edward and Jenny."

"I love my personal O'Flaherty," Maeve said. "That love doesn't extend to people who don't treat my husband with respect."

"I hear you. When we were there, Leo complained for a while, then we sat in silence. He was completely uninterested in Ryan, and that's a non-starter for me, too." She gave her a playful elbow to the side. "But throwing Maggie to the wolves was cruel!"

"She'll do the same some day. She can pass the baton to the poor, naive girls Rory and Conor bring to Ireland."

"You have an evil streak I did not know about."

"And I'm going to use it to avoid ever going to Tralee again," she said, her pale green eyes twinkling.

The bathroom floor of the pub had been broken up to replace the sewer line, so Colm spent much of his morning floating a new concrete floor. In a nice commercial setting, or a home, he'd have created a level surface. But here, where the bathroom would get a workout from people not very sober, he sloped it down to a center drain. That would make the floor easier to clean, and given that Aisling had vowed to keep her pub sparkling, Ryan was sure she could use the help.

Since both of Colm's usual helpers were traveling, Ryan worked with him all morning. When it was just the two of them, he was as quiet as a mouse, concentrating on his work like he was in a zen state. She'd always appreciated that about him, and knew that Ais would, too. She loved people who cared enough about their work to do the best possible job.

They finished before lunch, and when they left the small room they met Kevin, who was packing up his tools. "All finished in the kitchen," he said. "You're up."

Colm turned to Ryan with a resigned look on his face. "We'd better get the kitchen floor finished today, or I'll never have time to tile all the walls."

"How long do you think it'll take?"

"Four or five hours, if we're lucky."

She checked her watch. "It's 10:45. Want to have lunch first? Or would you rather take a break in an hour."

"Mmm." He seemed to think for a minute. "We're going to have to move everything out, so we'd better get going now while Kevin and Donal are still around."

"Why don't you go get lunch, Ryan," Kevin said. "We'll have the place cleared out by the time you're back."

She normally hated to be the one sent out to run simple errands, preferring to carry her weight with the boyos. But wrangling the heavy equipment out of the kitchen wasn't something she was looking forward to. As strong as she was, the boyos were easily twice as strong. And nothing made you look more like a weakling than having to put a stove down after moving it two inches. The humiliation was too great to even chance it.

The Ryan family and part of the O'Flaherty family met for dinner at the hotel that night. Jamie didn't care for the limited menu, and the lighting was more suited to a factory, but the restaurant was large enough for them to sit together, and quiet enough to converse.

There were twenty of them, and they'd set up two tables of ten, allowing for plenty of cross-talk, something the family loved to do. Maeve was to Jamie's right, with Ryan on her left.

When Jamie'd gotten home from Galway, she'd found Ryan in the tub, slumped down in the hot water, sipping from a bottle of dark beer. She hadn't had much to say about her day, other than, "Count your blessings you were gone," but the bath or the alcohol had revived her, and she was now joking around with Aisling and Cáit, who were on her left.

After their soup bowls were cleared from the table, Maggie scooted her chair back from behind Jamie and leaned over to address her and Maeve. "Thanks ever so much for abandoning me to the senior members of the O'Flaherty family," she said, giving Jamie a pinch.

"Hey! I was a vital part of an errand. Dishes and glasses had to be ordered today or…" She thought for a moment, unable to come up with a reason.

"Just as I thought. You knew we were going to Tralee. Don't even try to lie to me."

Jamie snuck a look to her left, seeing that Ryan was fully engaged with her cousins. Lowering her voice, she said, "When we visited Martin's family, Ryan was depressed for a full day afterward. And we only saw Leo and Mary."

"I'd never heard of them before this trip, and I'm depressed. Edward and Jenny might be the two saddest souls on the planet," Maggie whispered. "Edward's certain his wife of sixty years is after his money—of which he clearly has none. He keeps an eye on her every minute, but he happily revealed all of his suspicions to me, a woman he's never met."

"Is Jenny's hearing as bad as Leo claimed?"

"Luckily, I don't think she can hear a word Edward says. She's in her own world, sitting in a chair, nodding politely when someone speaks."

"How do they get on?" Maeve asked. "How do they eat?"

"If they didn't have a daughter-in-law who comes by every day to bring their meals, I'm afraid they'd starve to death."

"It's always the daughter-in-law, isn't it?" Maeve asked. "You never hear of anyone saying their son-in-law takes care of his wife's family."

"I've heard that a few times," Jamie said. "But it's always a guy heroically cutting the lawn or something practical. If not for women, we'd need three times more nursing homes."

"And so it shall ever be," Maeve said. "As much as Marty loves me, I can't imagine what would compel him to keep an eye on my mam and da."

Jamie gave her a poke to the arm. "He wouldn't have to, since Ryan would volunteer for that. Thanks for giving me something new to worry about!"

Ryan emerged from the bathroom on Thursday morning and walked over to the dresser to find a pair of shorts to run in. She was certain the weather report was going to be accurate, and wanted to enjoy every bit of the warm, dry sunshine the Irish skies would bestow when the sun eventually rose.

"Slow down there," Jamie said, her voice a little raspy from sleep.

Ryan walked over to her and leaned down to kiss the top of her head. "Did I wake you, baby?"

"Don't think so. I've got a lot on my mind." She struggled slightly to sit up, pushing her hair behind her ear. "I want to show you the mock-up I had done for Aisling's sign."

"Sign? What sign?"

Jamie rolled her eyes. "She needs a sign for the pub, honey. She doesn't want it to say McNulty's forever, right?"

"Didn't think of that. Did she work on the design with you?"

"Nope. I had a graphic artist come up with something. Why don't you show it to her today, then we can hire a sign painter to do it."

"Where's the mock-up?"

"Over on the desk. I think she did a good job."

Ryan walked over and sorted through postcards and other slips of paper, then found a folder tucked under the desk blotter. She opened it to see her cousin's name spelled out with the type of font they'd used for the Book of Kells.

"Very cool," Ryan said, walking back to the bed. "It might be a little Oirish, as she says whenever something refers to an historical Ireland, but she'd be silly to not love this."

"I had the artist put the O'Donohue family crest on the left, and the Ryan one on the right. I thought it was only right to represent both sides of her family."

"You're so thoughtful," Ryan sighed. "And independent! I love how you just pick up an idea and run with it."

"I'm a self-starter," Jamie agreed, scooting back down to lie on her back. "But now I think I'll reset my internal clock for about eight. That's plenty early to self-start the day."

Chapter Eight

It was Brenna's birthday, and as a treat, Jamie convinced Moira to let her skip school. The kid was happy enough at that development to consider that her only present, so when Jamie showed up at nine to announce, "We're going shopping, kiddo," she was so excited she tripped on the way up the stairs to get dressed.

Moira watched her go, quietly saying, "Thank you for reminding me that I can't treat her like I did the others. The child has always needed more attention, but I've always worried I might spoil her by letting the focus fall too heavily on her."

"I have no idea how to raise kids, but it's pretty clear that Cáit and Brenna have different needs. I guess the trick is figuring out how much to let them call the shots."

"That is the trick. Cáit could blend into the pattern on the wallpaper if we didn't draw her out, while Brenna came into the world needing a stage."

"Maybe she'll become an actress and make you all rich," Jamie said, laughing at the thought.

"I'm not sure she could stand the rejection, but goodness knows she'd like the limelight. I suppose we'll find out."

Brenna raced back down the stairs, bright-eyed and bushy-tailed. "Where are we going?" she asked. "Ballina?"

"Let's go a little further, just to mix things up," Jamie said. "How about Castlebar?"

"I love Castlebar," she said, nearly shaking with excitement. "Mammy, this is the best birthday I've ever had!" With that, she grasped Jamie by the hand and headed for the door, not bothering to ask if her mother wanted to come with them. Jamie rolled her eyes, once again reminding herself that parenthood wasn't for a person who needed inclusion or gratitude.

At eleven, Colm tested the concrete of both the kitchen and the bathroom, declaring them dry enough for tile. He started to stack the boxes of tile on one of the tables in the corner of the bar, and Ryan got on the phone. After a few rings, Jamie answered, "Brenna O'Donohue's birthday bash. How can I help you?"

"Oh, what a good cousin-in-law you are. Are you at my aunt's?"

"Of course not. Brenna and I are in Castlebar. We've almost finished our shopping spree down Hopkins Road, and we're considering going to the Museum of Country Life. Then we'll have lunch, of course."

"Of course. Well, after you return, we need you over here. Colm's ready to tile."

"You *need* me?" Jamie asked suspiciously.

"Mmm. Probably not. But you're Colm's regular helper."

"Aisling can fill my role until I get there. Tell him I'll be in charge of clean-up."

"He'll be very grateful. Buy Brenna a little something from me."

"We share our money, sweetheart. Half of everything I buy comes from you."

"I'll remember that the next time you send me to pick up a bottle of wine. If I'm paying for half, we're cutting back."

"Then let's say you're paying for all of the things you like, and I'm paying for all of the things I like. How's that?"

"Much better. Use my money to buy Brenna an ice cream cone. See you later, sweetums."

Ryan waited until the boyos were ready for lunch, then found Aisling outside, helping Kevin place three curved-neck lamps over the old, hand-lettered sign that said "McNulty's." She was good at keeping an eye on the boyos, but not actively interfering. It hadn't taken her long at all to figure out how to manage them.

"Hey," Ryan said. "I've got to make the lunch run. Will you come with me?"

"I suppose I could. I'm sure Kevin needs me here to watch him work, but he can probably get along without me for a half hour."

"I like to eat more than I like to be watched. Feel free to take off, Ais."

"Off I go," she said, turning Ryan around by the shoulders. "We'll return soon with enough food for ten."

"We've got seven here today, so that should work," Kevin called out.

Ryan led the way to her car, and when Aisling was buckled up, she reached into the back seat and handed over the folder. "Jamie had a new sign mocked up for you. Take a look and see if you like it."

Aisling's brows rose, but she dutifully opened the folder and let out a gasp. "It's fairy-tale Irish," she said, letting out a laugh. "But I like it. Actually, I love it. I recognize the O'Donohue crest. Is the other for the Ryans?"

"So the artist says," Ryan said, shrugging. "We're a very, very long way from the people who regularly used a crest, but I suppose there's a chance we're related to them."

"Tourists like this sort of thing," Aisling said, nodding her head decisively. "I want to give a very clear message that the place is clean, updated, and welcomes strangers. I've been in towns where the barman looks you over like he'd rather punch you than pour you a pint. There will be none of that nonsense at Aisling's."

"I love how you refer to yourself in the third person," Ryan said, giving her a slap to the leg.

"There's Aisling the person and Aisling the entity. The entity is going to be warm and friendly." She chuckled a little. "The person will be too, but intermittently." She put her hand on Ryan's shoulder and gave it an affectionate squeeze. "Your Jamie is possibly the sweetest woman on the planet you know."

"I do know," Ryan agreed. "I'm luckier than I deserve to be."

"I sometimes envy you for being able to love women. If I could be just a little more gay…"

"How gay are you?" Ryan gave her a quick glance, having never heard her make any reference to being attracted to a woman.

"Not enough to register," she sighed. "But you can't argue that women aren't easier to love. I'm only attracted to men, but they're a whole different species. It must be nice to love someone who understands you."

"Trouble with Colm?" Ryan asked, slightly uneasy to go down this road.

"Not really. I just wish he understood me better." She shrugged while laughing. "He probably thinks the same."

"He seems happy to me."

"Well, he ought to be! Look at the prize he's getting," she said, pulling down the visor to look at her messy hair and dirt-smudged face in the tiny mirror. "He's a lucky lad, that one is."

Ryan patted her arm after shifting into a lower gear. "So I can tell Jamie to order this up? She's got the name of a sign painter."

"You can. I'd like the name to be colorful. See what the artist thinks about doing the letters mostly in green with gold and red accents."

"You're going all out," Ryan said. "I thought you'd think it was too Oirish."

"Oh, it is. Truly. But I'm happy to give tourists what they want, and a colorful sign is part of it. Aisling's the entity has to be a success so that Aisling the person can afford to pay her taxes."

"There isn't a doubt in my mind you'll be able to do that," Ryan said, sparing a smile for her cousin. "Both of you will be a grand success."

Jamie's usual role as tiling assistant was to consult with Colm about pattern. There were probably unlimited possibilities, but Colm usually stuck to three or four standard ones.

Aisling wanted simple, inexpensive, white tile, and Colm had picked up both four inch square and three by six inch rectangular subway tile.

When Jamie arrived, Colm had already finished two of the walls in the bathroom, and was halfway finished with the third. Aisling wasn't in the room, and when he looked up he spoke quietly. "Is Aisling on a strict budget?"

"Not at all," Jamie said. "Whatever she wants is fine with us. But I'll admit she picks the least expensive thing whenever possible."

"Ahh… She's just cheap," he said, laughing. "She wanted me to do a straight pattern right up the wall. I had to argue with her for ten minutes to convince her it would look like hell because the walls aren't completely plumb."

"Eww." Jamie made a face. "The corner row would stick out like a sore thumb." She took a look at the wall. "I bet it would vary by an inch or more."

"Just what I said. Running bond hides a lot more variation." He took another look at the door. "I'll never admit this in public, but you're my preferred assistant."

"Aww…" She gave him a hug, only to be hit with the door when Aisling pushed it open. "Hands off!" she said, pulling Jamie's hand from Colm's shoulder. "This little O'Flaherty is all mine."

"I'm sticking with the one I've already claimed," Jamie said. "But this one's pretty tempting."

"Knock it off, you two," Colm said, with a very attractive flush starting to cover his tanned cheeks. "We've got to hustle to finish this afternoon."

"Where's Ryan?" Jamie asked.

"In the garden, cutting tiles," Aisling said. "I go out and give her the measurements so that Colm can keep going. She's covered in dust, in case you were thinking of taking her someplace nice."

"She wouldn't go someplace nice even if I had plans," Jamie said. "I'll wait until we're home to torture her with fancy restaurants."

"Just as well," Aisling said, smirking. "We have none."

Jamie kept her promise to clean up, allowing Colm and Aisling to head back to the hotel early. When she emerged from the pub's bathroom, Ryan was alone in the main bar area. The boom box was blaring, so Jamie turned the sound down before she approached. Ryan looked up sharply from her sweeping. "I didn't hear you come in."

"I know. That's why I turned the sound down." She walked over to Ryan and gave her a hug. "Missed you."

"I missed you too." She kissed both of Jamie's cheeks, then released her to finish her sweeping. "I'm just about finished. What are we doing for dinner?"

"Well, they're having some kind of 'do' for one of the teachers in the school who's going on maternity leave, and your granny's going to that. The rest of the clan seems to be leaning toward that newer pub in Ballina."

"The one with like four things on the menu?" Ryan asked, raising an eyebrow.

"That's the one. I said we might join them, but not to wait for us."

"Well, we'll have to show up at some point. Aisling and I ordered a cake for Brenna when we were on our lunch run. Ais is picking it up on her way back to the hotel. But let's have some alone time before we're back in the madness. How about a long walk along the beach."

"Works for me. I brought you a clean shirt, which you desperately need, but it's your jeans that show how dirty you are."

"We've got an air compressor. I'll blow the dust off. Check this out," she said, walking over to put her broom against the wall. "I helped Conor install a sturdy railing around the little stage he built."

"How many people do you think will fit up there?"

"Four…if they're average-sized. But I think Ais was smart to keep it small. Music will help attract a crowd, but you need floor space for patrons."

"Spoken like a not-very-silent-investor."

After her Castlebar excursion, then helping with the tiling project, Jamie was a little tired, but she wasn't about to miss an opportunity to go for a walk with her beloved—a very rare event. She'd seen less of Ryan since they'd arrived than she did at home, which she wasn't thrilled about. But once the boyos left on Sunday, she hoped Ryan's attention wouldn't be pulled in so many directions at once.

Lots of people were walking along the hard-packed sand, relishing both low-tide and the warm temperatures. After three days of rain, everyone had been out in the sun today, soaking it up as eagerly as San Franciscans did after a dreary few days.

They walked hand-in-hand, rarely getting a second look from passersby. It wasn't uncommon for women to walk arm-in-arm in Ireland, and, more than that, people seemed to keep their noses out of your business, unless you were making a holy show out of yourself, as Martin would say.

"I've been thinking," Ryan said, looking down at Jamie with a gentle smile. "Dangerous, right?"

"Often, but not always. What's going on in that pretty head?"

"Um…" She looked out at the ocean, not a promising sign. When Ryan was proposing something good, she looked you right in the eye. "What would you say to staying."

"Staying…where," Jamie said, with her heart rate picking up at once.

"Here."

"Staying in Ireland? For how long?"

"Mmm." She turned and shrugged her shoulders, looking more than a little guilty. "Like…kind of permanently."

"Permanently?" Jamie pulled her to a stop. "You want to move here?"

"Been thinking about it," she said, as if she'd been thinking about buying a new pair of shoes. She started to walk, pulling on Jamie's arm to tug her along.

But Jamie wasn't ready to walk again. She pulled back, holding Ryan in place. "You just drop that on me? Seriously? What about graduate school? You're starting at Cal in a little over two months, Ryan."

"I thought I'd take another year off. We'd be here to get the house finished, then I could maybe get a PhD at Galway in bioinformatics. That's one of their strong areas, and I think I'd like that."

Jamie had her by the shoulders, and was barely able to refrain from shaking her. "You want to leave home, drop your plan to get a PhD in math, and take another year off. You. The person I nearly had to handcuff to convince to take this past year off."

She shrugged again, trying to use her most charming smile to her advantage. "I'm unpredictable."

"Ryan, that's more than unpredictable. That's..." Her whole body shivered from the pent-up frustration that coursed through her. "I don't even have a word for what that is."

"Come on," Ryan said, "Let's keep walking. I can see that you need to vent a little, and I prefer to walk while I'm being yelled at."

"I'm not yelling at you!" She took a breath, then spoke again, much more quietly. "I don't mean to yell at you, but you've hit me with a curve ball here, bucko."

"I know," she said, taking Jamie's hand as they started to walk again. Ryan had taken her socks and boots off and left them in the car, and now her feet made a soft slapping sound as she padded along next to Jamie. "I'm happy here," she said softly. "I feel closer to my Aunt Moira and my grandparents when I'm here. It's become more clear to me that my grandparents' time on earth is limited, Jamers, and I don't want to let their final years pass by with me thousands of miles away."

"I understand that, honey, and I can empathize. But you've let nearly three years pass between visits. That's what's probably made you realize how time is taking its toll."

Ryan met her eyes, looking particularly guilty.

"I'm not giving you a hard time about that, sweetheart, but I think we easily could stay in San Francisco and simply visit more often. I'd be willing to come every month or two if that would help."

She made a face, then started to shake her head. "It's not the same. A weekend is fine for catching up, but it's not like living somewhere. You get into the flow of life when you live someplace, Jamers, and I love the flow here." She nodded decisively. "I like it better than San Francisco, and I think it's a better place to raise our children."

"It might be," Jamie said. "So when you've got your degree, and are ready to get pregnant, we'll talk this all through."

"Um...I was thinking I'd get pregnant soon. Like I might start trying in the fall. Then I'd be able to start my PhD program after I've given birth." Her smile grew to an impressive degree. "We'd be in our new home, we'd have our baby, and you could dote on them while I went to school."

"Are you mad? Seriously! Have you completely lost your connection to reality? You're going to leave me with a newborn while you're gone for twelve hours a day? Who's going to nurse the baby? Me?"

"I wouldn't have to be on campus every day, honey. I'd work things out so I only had to go in two or three days a week."

"That's not the point! Well, it is, but it's only one point. You'd still be gone for twelve hours at a time, and I won't even listen to you tell me that's not true. Galway's an hour and forty-five minute drive, Ryan. That's three and a half hours just for the round-trip. You'd have classes, and you'd need to work on their computers, and you'd have to meet with your advisor... The list goes on, honey. I *know* you."

"I promise I won't try out for any of their teams," she said, grinning like she was enjoying this interchange far too much.

"Are you screwing with me? Seriously. Is this one of your practical jokes?"

"No!" Her grin fell from her face. "I'm totally serious. This plan can work. I can get closer to my grandparents, and our baby can live with cleaner air and healthier food and all sorts of good things."

"And I can be thousands of miles from my mom, and Mia," she said, ready to burst into tears. "It's taken me twenty-two years to really get close to my mother, and now you want me to move?"

"Your mom would love to come visit," Ryan soothed. "We can build her a little house on the property, and Giacomo can hop over here in just a couple of hours. She'd dig it."

"She would *not* dig it," Jamie insisted. "She's firmly entrenched in the city, and she's got Jennie to contend with. The kid needs stability."

"I think she'd fit in great here," she said, as usual, secure in her opinions, no matter how whacky they were.

"Oh, so Jennie and my mom would love to be out in the middle of rural Ireland. Are you going to move your brothers, and all of the rest of your cousins, aunts and uncles? Because you'd miss them like crazy if you weren't close."

"I'll work on them," she said, seemingly seriously. "It would be hard to get Maggie to leave her job, but..."

"You're talking about more than twenty people! You expect all of them to move to Ireland because you want them to?

"There's plenty of work here for good tradesmen," she said, not acting like she could even hear the dismay in Jamie's voice. "And my uncles are all getting a little old to be working as hard as they do. They'd love a comfortable retirement in their home country, and if we built them houses, they could have that."

"I swear to god you're the only person in the world who could bankrupt me, all while spending next to nothing on yourself!"

"You've got plenty of money, and you'll get more in just a few years. That's not an issue, and you know it." She pulled Jamie to a stop and gazed into her eyes. "At least give it some thought. I know it'll be hard to get everyone to move, but I'm sure I could convince at least some of them."

"You couldn't convince my mom," Jamie said. "Or Mia. Or Jordan. Think about *that*," she insisted. "Would you be as close to Jordan if you only saw her a few times a year?"

She closed her eyes for a few moments, then said, "No matter what, I'm going to be a long way from people I love desperately. There's no way to have everything."

"I realize that, Ryan. But as much as I love your family, I need to stay close to my mom. She's been through a lot in the last couple of years, and I wouldn't feel right to abandon her now."

"Not abandon," Ryan insisted. "She'd come visit all of the time. She'd love it here."

Jamie just stared at her for a minute, certain Ryan had learned next to nothing about her mother. She was a cosmopolitan socialite, who loved museums, the symphony, the opera, and fine dining. While Ireland had much of that, it wasn't located in County Mayo. And asking her to leave everything that mattered to her to be close to her first grandchild was absolutely awful. Jamie had no intention of even considering the possibility. But refusing Ryan's clearly heartfelt proposal out-of-hand wasn't fair. She took in a breath and said, "We can continue to talk about this. But you've never asked me for anything that would be more disruptive, sweetheart, and that's saying something."

"I know," she said, dropping her head for a few moments. She lifted her chin and looked out at the sea, which was particularly beautiful tonight, with the setting sun hanging over the calm water like an ornament. "But I love it here, Jamers. I just didn't realize how much I loved it until I experienced it with you."

They made it to the pub in time to watch Brenna blow out her candles and cut into the cake. Jamie smiled at the delight the girl experienced when she was truly the star of the show. And a twelve-year-old girl's birthday was the ideal time to revel in the spotlight.

The guest list was just the people actually related to Brenna. Jamie thought about that for a moment, and realized she put herself in that number. She wasn't related by blood, and she and Ryan weren't even close to getting married, but she easily felt more related to the O'Donohues and the Driscolls than she did to her own emotionally distant family. She had first cousins that she couldn't accurately place in schools or towns, which was really kind of sad. But it was hard to make friends with cousins if you didn't have a close relationship when you were younger.

Looking around the group as she sipped at an overly sweet glass of white wine, her gaze lit on Ryan, who was seated next to Brenna. Ryan was paying close attention to the girl, as usual, and Brenna was making the most of it, talking constantly, with her hands moving expressively.

Jamie was struck, once again, at what a kind, giving person her lover was, always seeking out the person at a party who most needed a willing ear. Ryan looked up, and when their eyes met her gaze slipped away. That was her "I know I'm in trouble" look, one that always made Jamie feel like a bully. While most impartial people would agree that Ryan could test the patience of a saint, she was so damn good-hearted, and tried so hard to be connected that it was impossible to remain miffed for long—no matter what crazy thing she'd done.

Jamie kept her eyes on her, and Ryan tilted her chin to peer back at her. Even though Jamie's stomach was still in knots over the thought of permanently moving to Ireland, she purposefully flushed her unease from her brain and gave Ryan her richest smile.

She returned a dazzler, and for the rest of the night they had eye-sex from ten feet apart. Ryan was world-class at those long, hungry looks, making Jamie feel like she might be lured into the bathroom for a quickie. But she could wait. Actually, waiting was the fun part.

Jamie emerged from the bathroom a few minutes after they returned to the hotel. Ryan had beaten her to the punch when they'd entered the room, and now lay in bed, obviously naked, with the sheet pulled up over her chest against the chilly, damp night.

While Ryan had been brushing her teeth, Jamie had pulled her sexiest undies out of the dresser, and when she stepped into the room Ryan's eyes lit up.

"Respectful lust," Jamie said, chuckling. "That's what I think of when I see that look in your eye."

Ryan laughed too. "That's not inaccurate. I look at you sometimes and have to fight the urge to grab you and toss you onto some kind of soft surface."

"You do?" She was standing by the dresser, and she put her hand on it to steady herself. Sometimes the look in Ryan's eyes made it tough to keep your balance.

"Uh-huh." Now her gaze grew even smokier, giving off a compelling aura that forced Jamie to move closer. "But there's a big part of me that knows it's awful to be that forceful. That's not the kind of relationship I want, or think it's good to have."

"No," Jamie agreed. "If you made a habit of physically yanking me off my feet..." She met Ryan's gaze again, seeing it hadn't grown even one degree cooler. "But there's a big part of me that would love for you to do that." She sighed. "Sex. It's so fucking confusing. Get it?" she asked, laughing again.

"Come here," Ryan said, crooking her finger seductively.

"Come get me."

In a flash, Ryan was right next to her, naked as the day she was born. After a tender wisp of a kiss, Jamie let out a surprised "whoo" when Ryan bent and swept her into her arms. Two long strides had her tossing Jamie onto the bed like a huge sack of potatoes, with the bedsprings screaming for mercy. Then Ryan jumped onto the mattress, hurling herself face-first to land right at Jamie's side. "Couldn't resist," she said, smiling so sweetly that it provided a charming counterpoint to her more lustful instincts.

"I think you want to have sex," Jamie purred, looking into her eyes. "Correct me if I'm wrong..."

Ryan stroked her cheek with her fingertips, suddenly serious. "I want to make love." Her hand moved to glide along Jamie's hair, smoothing the strands so they lay against the pillow. "I know I sprang the idea of moving on you with no warning, and I'm sorry for that. But when I think of sharing our love with a baby—I can only envision it here. I've been fighting it for a couple of months now, but I can't adjust the image to see us in San Francisco."

"Months?" Jamie asked, taking Ryan's hand and kissing the back of it a few times. "That's a long time to be struggling with something, honey. Why didn't you say something sooner?"

"I thought it was only a fantasy. Maybe being here in November brought it up, you know? But it hasn't gone away, Jamers. It's gotten stronger."

"I have fantasies, too, honey, and in mine we're at home, sitting on the deck with our tiny little baby, or over at my mom's house, or in the backyard in Berkeley. In all of my fantasies my mom's there, and your family, and Mia and Jordan. None of that would be possible if we moved here. You'd be closer to the people you miss, but, as much as I've grown to love them, they're not my primary people. Mine are all in San Francisco, Ryan, and that's where they're going to stay."

"I'm losing my boner," Ryan sighed. "Can we make love and argue about this later?"

"Yes and no. We can definitely make love, but I don't want to argue—now or later. We'll work out a compromise. We've had to do that before, and we can do it again."

"Thanks," she said, looking mightily relieved. "I appreciate that you don't let me drive you *too* crazy."

"Just enough." Jamie smiled as she pushed Ryan onto her back and climbed onto her hips. "This is my favorite thing in the world." She bent over and kissed her tenderly, finally sitting up to add, "We're well on the road to making love, I have all sorts of ideas in my head for what I want to do to you, and I still have lots of energy." She reached down and patted her hip. "All of my sensitive parts are touching you, and I can feel your warm skin through my undies." She brought three fingers to her mouth and kissed them. "Magnifique!"

Ryan looked slightly bedazzled when she said, "I love it when you're sitting on me and you start to move your hips a little. I love to watch you turn yourself on." She put her hands onto Jamie's hips and shifted them slightly.

Taking the cue, Jamie put a little effort into it, reaching down to steady herself by holding onto Ryan's shoulders. "Like this?" She had so much sensation flowing already that she was a little surprised. But being seduced for hours at the pub had set her libido on a slow simmer that was ready to reach the boiling point.

"Thank you for packing sexy undies," Ryan purred, staring at Jamie's breasts like she wanted to swallow them whole.

"My pleasure." She put her hands on the outside of her breasts and pushed them together, making the cleavage pop. "I feel sexy in lingerie, and it makes you hot. Everyone wins."

Ryan crooked her finger one more time. "Any way you could bring those babies down here for a minute? I want to lick them like lollipops."

"Odd image, but whatever works." Jamie bent over to let her breasts trail over Ryan's face. Her eyes were closed now, with a beatific smile covering her mouth. "Like that, sweetheart?"

"So much," Ryan purred. "This is *my* favorite part. Where you're in charge, asking for what you need, using me to stoke the fire."

"I'm in charge, huh?" She hovered over Ryan's mouth, with her hardening nipple barely brushing over her parted lips. "As they say, this too shall pass."

Ryan laughed as she flipped Jamie over onto her back. She put her hands on her shoulders, pinning her so thoroughly she couldn't have moved if she'd wanted to—which she didn't. "Yeah, that didn't last long, did it."

"Come down here and kiss me," Jamie demanded. "I might have to top you from below, but I've developed a certain skill in that area."

"You're the master." Ryan lowered herself until their bodies were pressed together from their lips to their hips, ready, willing, and very able to rock her world.

On Friday morning, Ryan skipped her morning run to get a head-start on the remaining tasks for the pub. Colm had to get the entire kitchen finished so he could grout both rooms on Saturday, and given that today was his birthday, she assumed he and Aisling would want to carve out at least a little time alone—which was going to be difficult.

Leaving Jamie to wake up at her leisure, she took the car, knowing Jamie would be able to catch a ride with Aisling. When she got to the pub, she set up her wet saw in the garden, put the boxes of tile on a table, and got the big bucket of mud and all of Colm's tools arranged on another table.

She loved being on the job site before anyone else, relishing the calm before the storm. Early in the morning you could make yourself believe that everything would go smoothly, and that you'd finish early enough to spend some quality time with your girlfriend.

The door opened, and her father poked his head in, smiling when he saw her. "I'm glad my hunch was right." He entered, bearing two paper cups in a carrier, along with a paper bag. "I brought you some tea, since the coffee at the hotel isn't what you like."

"Aww. Thanks, Da. Any food?"

"I'm well acquainted with your appetite, sweetheart. I stopped at the restaurant down the road and had them make you an egg and some bacon on a roll. With cheese," he added before she could ask. "And to wash it down, some oatmeal."

"Best da in all of Ireland," she said, giving him a long hug. "I hate that we've been so busy we haven't had any time alone."

"When I saw you weren't at breakfast, I drove along your usual running route. When I couldn't find you there, I came by here and spotted your car. You can run, but you can't hide from your father."

"I never want to," she said, ripping open the paper bag that held her food. "Have you eaten?"

"Oh, yes. Maeve and I had breakfast with Maggie and Brendan. They're coming by soon."

"I don't think we need the help."

"That's probably why they're coming by." He laughed a little. "Maggie has learned the trick of being a member of a large family. Be elusive."

Colm worked like a man on a mission, getting one wall of the kitchen finished before Aisling and Jamie even arrived. By the time everyone had wandered in, he had more help than he wanted, and he sent nearly everyone off to have some fun, keeping only his able assistants and Donal, just in case a plumbing issue arose.

Ryan went to get lunch at the usual time, but Colm didn't want to take a real break. He ate his meal in stages, taking a bite every time he sent Jamie or Aisling out to relay measurements to Ryan.

By four, he'd placed the last tile, and he stood at the entryway of the kitchen, staring at the floor with a critical eye. "If I'd used a diagonal pattern, the space would have looked fifty percent larger."

Donal had taken off already, so Aisling was able to treat Colm like a boyfriend. She stood next to him and put her hand on his stomach, rubbing it soothingly. "It's brilliant," she said. "You were dead right about the color. The mottled grey won't show dirt, and it makes the white walls look even sharper."

"There's a slight roughness to them," he said. "Helps keep people from slipping." He let out a plaintive sigh. "But the diagonal was the right way to go."

"You told me you'd have to make many more cuts," she reminded him. "This is lovely, Colm. I couldn't be happier."

"Are you sure?" He looked at her like he was on tenterhooks, her opinion obviously critical.

She slipped her arms around him and nuzzled against his chest. He inclined his head and she whispered into his ear. Then a smile covered his face and he nodded enthusiastically. Aisling met Ryan's gaze and said, "We're off, then. Meet you at the restaurant at seven?"

"Are you sure you want a big crowd at your birthday dinner, Colm?"

He cocked his head quizzically. "Can you think of a reason I can give my brothers for having dinner with just Aisling?"

"You could say you've got a date with a local girl, and Aisling could..." She shrugged. "She could say she's not feeling well."

"Wouldn't work. But we'll go back to the hotel as soon as dinner's over."

Aisling looked up at him. "And what will Donal think when he comes home?"

He shook his head mournfully. "Next visit, I'm telling everyone I'm going hiking for two weeks. I just won't add that I'm hiking in Ireland."

"You'll figure it out," Ryan said, feeling a little glum at how disappointed both of her cousins seemed. They'd been able to sleep together every night, which was obviously a good thing. But they'd had very little time to know what kind of chemistry they had outside of bed, which was where they'd spend the majority of their future—if they had one.

Jamie caught a ride back to the hotel with Aisling, leaving Ryan to spend a few minutes cleaning up. When she was finished, she walked over to the church to continue working at re-creating a prayer practice.

Once she'd decided to give it another chance, she'd tried a few ways to get back into the habit. One she was currently experimenting with had her taking Jamie's book of psalms and walking around the church cemetery while she read them aloud.

That wasn't the way she'd done it in the past, but she was trying a lot of different things, seeing what resonated with her.

Today, she had fairly easy access to a meditative state, and she made it through psalm after psalm, letting the ancient words wash over her to reach a place inside her heart that she'd purposefully closed off. She didn't even notice someone was next to her until a hand cupped her cheek, startling her so thoroughly that she almost raised her fist. That would have been a mistake she'd never recover from. Punching your granny wasn't allowed anywhere, but this particular granny would hold it over her head for the rest of her life.

"It does my heart good to see you out here speaking to the Lord," she said, giving Ryan's cheek an affectionate pat.

She was a little embarrassed to be caught, but she'd yet to get away with anything in Ireland. The whole village seemed to know what you were up to before you'd even thought of it. "It's usually quiet here, and I can be by myself without having to watch for traffic."

"Ahh. That helps, does it? There's a fella who built a labyrinth on his property, you know. Not far from here."

"Really? How far is not far?"

"It's between Kilkelly and Kiltimagh. He doesn't mind if people use it, if he's home, that is."

"I think I'll stay here. There's almost never anyone else around."

"You've been here long enough," she said, taking the book from Ryan's hand and putting it into her own purse. "Why don't you make yourself useful and walk me to Moireen's?"

Ryan smiled at the diminutive her Granny used only occasionally, with it quickly dawning on her that Aunt Maeve never got the same treatment. "Don't you have your car?"

"I do," she said, gripping Ryan's elbow and starting to lead her to the street. "But I didn't get my walk in this morning. It was raining stair rods, you know."

"I do," Ryan said, smirking. "I ran right through them."

"No surprise there. I don't see any of those massive lads running with you, though. I suppose they need their energy for closing the pub down every night. You know, if that third one fell over on the way out, he'd be home."

"Do you mean Colm?" Ryan asked, laughing at the expression. "He's only an inch taller than Conor, Granny."

She looked up at Ryan, utterly puzzled. "Why does a man *need* to be that tall?"

"I don't think he made himself that way. The O'Flahertys are just a tall people."

"Your grandfather's taller sitting down than he is standing," she sniffed. "If you can reach the switch to turn off the big light, that's all you need."

"But we come in handy when you don't have a step stool."

"Oh, you're a love, and you know it." She put her arm around Ryan's waist, showing more physical affection on this trip than was her norm. "I wouldn't trade you for any normal-sized cailín in the world."

"Um…thanks," Ryan said, knowing there was a compliment in there if you looked hard enough.

"The rain really lashed down this morning," she said, smiling. "But we were dry as a bone. Not a drop came through our new ceiling."

"I'm so glad to hear that. The boyos will be too, since they've got just enough time to get up there and fix it again, but they sure wouldn't want to."

"They did a fine job. You all did. Now come on and walk me to your aunt's home."

"I have to go back to the hotel and have a shower," she said, checking her watch. "We're having a seven o'clock birthday dinner for Colm, or the third one, as you call him."

"It's only half five. You'll be back here by a quarter past six."

Ryan nodded, knowing resistance was futile. They took the big curve down the hill, and picked up the pace when they got to the center of town. They didn't have any reason to go by the pub itself, but they passed the street it was located on.

"That's Aisling's car," Granny said, observing a small, white car parked in front of the pub. "Did you leave her there to work alone?"

Ais had been gone an hour and a half, and there was no reason for her to be there alone now. If that was her car, she was with Colm, and wanted to be left alone. Ryan was sure of that. "Jamie says every other car in Ireland is a small, white sedan."

"Jamie can say what she wants. I know my little one's run-around. Let's go send her on her way. You're all working too hard."

"She left before I did," Ryan said. "She said she'd meet us at the restaurant, so she must have come by to do something on the way."

"Your dinner's hours from now. If she's here, she's working," she insisted, taking a sharp left.

Ryan grasped her by the arm and tried to guide her back to the main street, but her efforts were rebuffed when her granny shrugged out of her grip to keep going.

"If that's her, which I don't think it is, she'll be along when she's ready. She's probably just measuring something, or picking up some wine or..."

"As if there's any liquor left. Those cousins of yours drink like they've been wandering in the desert like the Israelites."

Ryan ran ahead and turned, walking backwards down the sidewalk. "Let's give her a minute to do whatever she has to do."

Her grandmother stopped on a dime, then narrowed her eyes to gaze at Ryan. "What are you two hiding?"

"Hiding? Why would we be hiding anything?"

Pushing past her, Granny made for the door, with Ryan nearly tripping when she tried to beat her to the punch. "Aisling!" she yelled the minute the door was thrown open.

They entered together, shoulder to shoulder. The boom box Aisling had brought over was on the bar, playing loudly.

"Aisling!" Ryan called out again, at full volume.

"You'll wake the dead with that voice," Granny said, pinching the flesh of her arm in a vise-like grip to hold her still. "Stay right here, Siobhán. I want to see what the girl's up to, even though I know it's no good." She strode to the kitchen and flung the pass-through door open, with Ryan right behind her. It took until that second for the pain from the pinch to reach her brain, and Ryan shrieked from the combination of her flesh being squeezed to the point of gushing blood, coupled with the image of Aisling lying on a counter, Colm's mouth locked against hers, with his left foot on the floor, and his right settling between her legs, allowing him to get some purchase to climb on top of her.

Before Ryan could flinch, Granny grasped the closest large object, a wooden pizza peel, and walloped Colm in the ass.

"Shite!" Aisling yelped, with Granny continuing to hit Colm anywhere she could, the dull thud of wood against fabric-covered flesh echoing through the tiled room.

He was on his feet now, and had turned to face her, crouching down slightly, as if she were a bear he was going to be forced to wrestle to the death—which might have been close to a fact.

"Granny!" Aisling slid off the counter to get between the raised peel and Colm. "Stop it right now!"

Granny slowly lowered the peel, glaring at Aisling with a fire in her eyes that could have seared a steak. "What in the holy name of Jaysus are you up to?"

Aisling's normally pale skin was flushed with color, and her clothes were a bit askew, but she seemed perfectly in control. Ryan envied her ability to face their grandmother and stand up for herself—and Colm. "I can't believe that's a serious question," she said, with Colm gallantly moving to stand beside her, clearly reassured that the five-foot-tall dynamo was not going to actually murder him.

Granny reached for Aisling's arm, but it was pulled away before she could get a grip, once again showing she was quicker than Ryan.

"I've kept both eyes on you for twenty-five years now. I will *not* have you throw away all of that work on an *O'Flaherty*." She made the name sound like the worst curse she could think of, chilling Ryan to the core.

"That's enough!" The words flew from her mouth before she had time to censor herself. "Don't you dare insult my cousin—and me!"

Both Granny and Aisling turned to stare at her, clearly equally surprised at her outburst. Colm took it in stride, his experience with her making it clear to him she wasn't a pushover—in San Francisco, that is.

"This is about me, Siobhán," Aisling said. "I've played along for too long now." She grasped both of Granny's hands firmly, possibly holding them still so she couldn't be slapped in the face. "You know how much I love you," Aisling said, with her words gentle, but the expression on her face stern. "But I won't tolerate your thinking you can dictate who I see." She dropped Granny's hands and put her arm around Colm. He looked like he was ready to run if he had to, but was trying to appear in control. "I've been interested in this lad for years now, and when I was in San Francisco I let him know how I feel."

"I will *not* lose another of my girls to the O'Flahertys!" She lunged for Aisling's arm for no reason at all. Did she think she could physically pull her feelings from her body? But Aisling was once again too quick for her. She turned to the side, putting her arm protectively in front of Colm to push him back a foot.

"I love and respect you, Granny, but you can't beat my feelings out of me. I'm in love with Colm, and you can either accept him or lose me."

Granny glared at her for a few fraught seconds, then turned and stormed out, slamming the door behind her.

Aisling turned and fell into Colm's embrace as he stared at Ryan, completely frazzled. "What in the hell was that about?"

Ryan looked at him for a second, then said, "It hurts me to the core to admit this, but she hates my family. You're obviously guilty by association."

Colm went back to the hotel when Aisling offered that option, and as Aisling watched him drive her car down the street she turned to Ryan and said, "I bet the boy's never been so glad to leave a place in his life."

"Wish I could go with him," Ryan said, still so hurt, so wounded, she was sure she wouldn't be able to disguise her feelings at dinner.

"Come on now," Aisling said. "We'll go back to the hotel so you can have a bath. That will give you time to get yourself in order. Is your car close by?"

"Yeah. Down by the post office. Um… Are you going to alert your mam?"

"No," she said blithely. "If Granny tells on me, I'll deal with it then. If she doesn't, nothing has changed."

Ryan stared at her as Aisling locked the door to the pub, still seeming calm and in control. "That's it? You don't need to plan out your response any better than that?"

She smiled as she put her arm through Ryan's and started to walk. "You need to be quick on your feet, lass. Too much preparation's death. You have to learn to roll with the punches."

Ryan extended her arm, showing the sizable bruise on the underside. "I haven't learned that. I don't think I ever will."

"Ack!" Aisling stopped and touched the angry-looking red welt. "Did she just do that?"

"When we walked into the pub and I tried to stop her."

Bending slightly, Ais kissed the mark. "Thank you, Siobhán. I appreciate that you tried to protect me."

"How about locking the door when you're going to have a ride?" Ryan said, draping an arm around her shoulders as they started to walk again.

"We couldn't figure out a way to be alone at the hotel, so we decided to go for a walk on the beach before dinner. We just stopped here for a moment so I could give Colm my second set of keys. I swear that's the truth. But then…" She shrugged helplessly.

"I understand. When you're trying to keep things on the down-low, you use every opportunity."

"It will be fine," she said, more sure of herself than Ryan would have been—by a long shot. "Knowing her, Granny will keep this between us. But if she doesn't, I'll have to have a conversation with my mam that I've been putting off."

"Maybe it's better to get it out in the open..."

"Not now," Aisling said, shaking her head slightly. "Colm doesn't want his brothers to know yet."

"I don't blame him. Once they know, all of the boyos will too, and they'll harass him on a daily basis."

"I should have fallen for an orphan without siblings," Aisling sighed, holding onto Ryan's arm a little tighter as they continued their short walk.

Chapter Nine

The next morning, Ryan slipped out of the hotel when dawn should have been breaking. But the sun wasn't going to make its presence known any time in the next few hours—or days. The rain was pelting down, but Ryan didn't much care. Her head was full of questions, and talking to Jamie until the wee hours of the morning hadn't helped her clear things up.

It just didn't make sense. How could her grandmother love her, while demeaning the O'Flaherty name on a consistent basis? Ryan *was* an O'Flaherty, and she was proud of the name, even though she had nothing to do with earning it.

Clans had played an important role in Irish history, and they'd given some structure to a wild land. But they'd also allowed the stronger families to ride roughshod over the weaker, the same way every powerful group had behaved since Adam and Eve. Now, many hundreds of years after the power of the clans had been broken, it was nonsense to keep bringing up a family name as if it meant something sinister.

After bending to make sure her laces were secure, Ryan started off across the parking lot, keeping it slow and easy to start. She'd gotten only fifty feet when a car door opened and her grandmother emerged, with her long coat covering her to her knees, Wellies taking care of the rest of her, and the hood of the coat protecting not only her head, but her face. She peered out of the bill of the hood, saying, "We have some things to discuss, Siobhán. Walk with me."

That wasn't much of an apology, and Ryan was tempted to hang a right and take off on her run. But she saw a slight softening in her grandmother's expression, as though she was worried Ryan might refuse.

"All right," she said, waiting for her to lead.

The hotel was on the outskirts of the town, easily close enough to walk to the village shops. But Granny chose the other direction, aiming for the countryside that started not far from the town limits.

They didn't speak for a few minutes, both trying to sync up their strides and get used to the puddles that were sometimes deeper than they looked. Finally, when Ryan was getting anxious because of the silence, Granny said, "I'm sorry for what I said last night, sweetheart."

Ryan stumbled as the sentence registered. She wasn't sure her grandmother had ever issued a true apology—for anything—and it struck her.

"Thank you," Ryan said. "I appreciate that."

"I want you to know that I wouldn't care if your cousin was a complete stranger to you. If he's going to try to take Aisling from home, he's my enemy."

"That's not in the plan. She's not buying the pub and getting her life organized only to leave. But if she did, that would be her choice, Granny."

She looked up sharply. "I couldn't take another loss," she said, with her voice quavering slightly. "Losing Brendan, then Maeve, then Fionnuala, broke my heart in ways I'll never recover from." She gripped Ryan's arm too firmly, adding, "I pray you never know how it feels to lose two children to death, and one to America."

"I wouldn't handle it well," Ryan admitted. "That's actually a huge understatement, but I'm not ready to admit how devastated I'd be."

"I think I know," Granny said, loosening her grip to just hold on like a normal person. "Of everyone, I think you'd understand how losing Aisling would gut me."

"I truly don't think she's of a mind to leave, but it's within the realm of possibility that Colm will move here."

She was expecting another squall, but Granny just nodded. "He seems like a fine man—the best of the bunch, as far as I can tell. But there are almost four million people on this island. There has to be one the girl could fall for."

Ryan wiped the rain from her eyes, annoyed with herself for not having a stouter bill on her rain jacket. "I haven't made a point of this to Ais, but I'd also prefer that she'd met another guy—any other guy."

Her arm was griped hard again. "What's wrong with this one? Is it the drink?"

"No!" Ryan insisted. Of all of the boyos, Colm was the most moderate. That wasn't saying a lot, but she'd never seen him out-of-control, and she was certain he didn't overindulge on a routine basis. "There's nothing wrong with Colm, Granny. He's the cousin I'd choose if I had to pick one for Ais. But he's my *cousin*," she said, still having a sour feeling in her stomach when she thought of them together. Watching Colm climb onto the counter last night gave her yet another image she wanted to erase from her memory bank.

"Ahh. So you're not behind this?"

"Definitely not. And I don't think my brothers will like it, either. And if Colm's mother gets word of him thinking about leaving America..." She met her granny's gaze. "My aunt loves him as much as Moira loves Ais."

Granny waved her hand, like that was a slim possibility. "I'll work on her," she said. "I'll ask around at church to see if anyone has a grandson..."

Ryan put a hand on her shoulder, and met her eyes. "Leave her be, Granny. You're not going to be the first to talk Aisling into doing something she doesn't want to do."

"She's usually so easy," she sighed. "I don't know what's gotten into her." With a sharp look, she added, "Other than an O'Flaherty, that is."

Ryan's eyes nearly bugged out, then she realized her grandmother didn't mean that literally. She had the least dirty mind of anyone on the planet, and double entendres were simply not in her repertoire. She was about to speak when her grandmother said, "Let's turn back now. We might drown."

"Not yet," Ryan said, putting some pressure on her arm to keep her headed in the same direction. "I want to know, once and for all, why you have such distain for my family."

"I don't!" she said, trying to adopt an innocent look. "How can you say such a thing?"

"Because I saw your face yesterday. You weren't upset that Aisling was kissing a man. You were upset that she was kissing an O'Flaherty. You said exactly that."

She looked like she was going to try to slough off the question, but she must have known that Ryan wasn't in the mood for games. "It's not every O'Flaherty," she said, sighing. "It's simply…" She stopped, with the rain hitting the side of her face for a few moments. "It's your father."

"What do you want from him?" Ryan demanded, furious in an instant. "He was an excellent husband to your daughter, and an excellent father to your grandchildren. Now he makes your eldest very happy, and your great-grandchild is over the moon for him."

"Two of my girls," she snapped. "*Two* of them. Lost to one man!"

"They weren't lost, Granny. My mother fell in love with my father, and she probably could have talked him into moving back to Ireland if she'd wanted to. But she chose to stay in San Francisco. She was happy there."

"She was not," she said crisply, continuing to march along the rural road. "She missed Ireland until her dying day. If Maeve hadn't been there…"

"But she was," Ryan said. "Aunt Maeve chose to go to America. That's an indisputable fact."

"Don't you think I know that?" she demanded. "She couldn't be happy here, like Fi and Moira were. She had to have the big city, the *Pacific* Ocean. What was wrong with the Atlantic, I'll never know."

Ryan was tempted to say her aunt hadn't left for an ocean. She'd left primarily because she didn't get on well with her mother. But today wasn't the day for a slap to the face, so she bit her tongue. "Aunt Maeve loves San Francisco, and she loves the life she's made for herself. But now that we're building a house here, I think she'll visit more often."

"Why's that? To see you?" she asked, squinting in Ryan's direction.

"Partly. I'm sure my father will want to come if I'm gone all summer."

"I'll never understand it," she grumbled. "I barely know my grandsons. Tommy waited until his little one was nearly three to bring her. Why is Maeve so cold-hearted to me and her father?"

Ryan knew full well why her aunt kept her distance, but if her grandmother didn't know, it was solely because she didn't want to. "I… um…I can't speak for my aunt. But I do know that she's far from cold-hearted. She's been a second mother to me, and it's only her love that got me through my childhood."

"So you're saying she gave you all of the love she had to give? There's none left for her aged parents?"

"I'm *not* saying that," Ryan said. "Actually, I shouldn't even attempt to speak for her. If you really want to know why she's visited infrequently, why don't you ask her?"

"Ask her?" She raised an eyebrow like she was sure Ryan was joking. "I'm to ask my daughter why she can't be bothered to visit her parents until she finds a reason that suits her? Thank you very much for the suggestion, Siobhán. Now let's get back to the hotel while we still have our shoes. You can buy me breakfast before I dash off to work."

Ryan rolled her eyes, dismayed at her grandmother's steadfast refusal to have a genuine conversation with her oldest child. It was beyond her that you could give birth to a baby you didn't love with your whole heart for all of the days of her life. But it must have been easy for many, since she knew an awful lot of people who were estranged from their families in one way or another. It just made no sense. Why would the people who gave you life not want to hold you close—no matter what?

The whole crew helped out on their final day, but they took it easy, having decided at Colm's birthday dinner that they wouldn't start until ten. With lots of help, and Colm allowing Jamie to grout the bathroom all by herself, they were finished by noon.

The heavy rain had unexpectedly blown away, creating a lovely day, with temperatures in the low seventies, and the threat of more rain minimal. The only task remaining was to put all of the appliances back into the kitchen and hook them up. But they couldn't do that until the grout had time to cure. It was pushing it, but they decided to give it six hours. To while away the time, the whole gang went to the beach with a rugby ball.

With four O'Donohues, four O'Flaherty cousins, three Driscoll cousins, two O'Flaherty brothers, one future sister-in-law, and Jamie, they had enough players to make two teams of eight.

Eamon hadn't played in years, and Cormac, Jamie and Maggie had never played at all. Aisling and Cáit had goofed around with friends, but they were far from proficient. But that didn't stop them from having a blast.

The inexperienced players were spread between the teams, with Jamie sticking close to Ryan. "If I get the ball, I'm giving it to you," she said. "There's no way I'm going to let any of those massive men tackle me."

"That's the fun," Ryan insisted. "Of course, that's when I play on fairly forgiving turf. This sand is nearly as hard as concrete."

"Then you're going to have to use your speed," Jamie said. "The last time I saw you play, you dusted people!"

"Last time I played I hadn't been working like a dog. My legs are toast."

Maggie was on the other team, and she seemed to be using Jamie's tactic, standing about a foot away from Brendan. Ryan was about to suggest she use Conor as a shield, since he was faster, but she didn't want to hurt Bren's feelings.

They didn't have a whistle or a referee, so Kieran just threw the ball into the air and a crowd raced for it, with Ryan holding back a little. She didn't want to have Jamie caught in a scrum and break something, so she'd decided she was going to be laid-back, not a common thing for her.

The ball squirted away from the crowd, flying a few feet in the air to land in front of Brendan. Ryan could see his eyes widen, and he bent to scoop it up, with Maggie turning and running in the opposite direction, clearly trying to avoid seeing any action.

Bren didn't get six feet before Kieran was on him, tackling him as Brendan lobbed the ball to Cormac, who looked like he'd caught a snake. The boy was smart enough to get rid of it in a nanosecond, passing it along to Niall, who actually wanted it.

He scored easily, sailing past Eamon and Annie, who put up a defense they should hope no one caught on film.

From then on, the game was entirely between the seven members of the O'Flaherty clan, with everyone else trying not to get hurt or drenched by skirting too close to the water. Ryan looked up after being knocked on her ass to see Jamie standing next to Maggie, chatting, well away from the action. Some people had no shame.

They weren't keeping score, mainly because they couldn't really tell where the goal-line was. The tide was rising, with an occasional splash from a wave making the line they'd carved into the sand with a stick wash away in moments. But they were having fun, and that was better than notching a win.

They played until her father and aunts arrived with beer and food, then they had a fantastic picnic on the beach. It wasn't even that the food was great. Just sandwiches and crisps. But everyone was there, with Caitlin running around like a duck, heading in every direction, always trying to get to the water before someone could stop her.

They goofed around for hours, with sporadic rugby action when someone got bored. But mostly they lay on the blankets Moira and Maeve had brought, and enjoyed their last day in the sun as a group. Ryan, of course, could have cried at the thought of her brothers and cousins leaving, but she was also glad she was going to have more time for Jamie. If everything went well, they'd have their house in a year or so, and this could become an annual tradition. Having a house full of her American cousins would make her very happy—especially if she no longer lived near them.

It took longer than Ryan would have thought to move everything back into the kitchen. That might have been because they had too many people supervising, or they'd had a few too many beers, but they finally had everything ready for Donal to connect the water lines to the dishwasher and ice maker, and hook up the gas for the stove. Ryan wasn't able to help with anything, but she felt she needed to be there, even though she knew less about the details than just about anyone. Aisling, who should have been keeping an eye on things, had slipped away not ten minutes after they'd arrived. When she didn't return, Ryan looked around to see that Colm was missing, too. She couldn't really blame them, anyone would want to have a little privacy on their last day together, but doing things like that was going to get them caught—again.

It was after six when the job was finished, and Conor walked over to the bar. "Where's Ais? She should pull the first beer to celebrate."

Ryan tried to wave him off. "You can play bartender." She scanned her cousins, all looking like drowned rats, with mud and sand and seawater in their hair and all over their wet clothes. "Do you guys still want to go home and shower before dinner? Or should we just stay here and cut into Aisling's profit margin?"

"Is there any food?" Donal asked.

"No, but Ais could pick some up."

"Stay," Donal said, and eventually everyone but Conor agreed.

"Two weeks," he said, grumbling even as he pulled beers for his brother and cousins. "And Colm's the only one who went home with a girl."

"I did," Kieran said, then Niall raised his hand. Donal looked sheepish for a moment, but he joined in too.

"All of you jerks hooked up?" Conor demanded.

"I would have," Brendan said, laughing when Maggie shot him a dagger-like glare, "but Maggie kept blocking me."

"I would have, too," Cormac said, "but I was well behind all of you on the wish-list."

"What the absolute fuck?" Conor looked like he was about to punch someone, but Ryan found it funny. She wasn't sure why the local women hadn't fallen for his charms, but striking out once in a while was good for him. She wouldn't have thought that if she was playing the game, of course, but from an outsider's perspective, it was good for him.

After Ryan made a few phone calls, they had enough food to keep them going, and since there was still a keg of Murphy's Stout in the storeroom, their beer needs were secure.

Everyone was in attendance, with even her grandparents showing up. Her grandmother acted like everything was fine when she spotted Aisling, so she'd obviously chosen to play it cool. Ryan knew there would be another come-to-Jesus talk, but it wouldn't be tonight.

Brenna had put herself in charge of Caitlin, and as the two of them ran around the pub Annie walked over and pulled up a chair next to Ryan. "I'm doubting my own sanity, but I think we're going to take Caitlin home with us in the morning."

"What?" Ryan stared at her, mouth agape.

"I know, I know. Only an idiot would turn down a vacation after a vacation. But Maeve and Moira spent more time with her these past two weeks than I did. I want Maeve to have time to enjoy Ireland for a couple of weeks, and watching Caitlin isn't the way to do that."

"But I was going to take the lead on babysitting. I was really looking forward to it."

Annie leaned over and kissed her cheek. "I love you like a sister, Ryan, but you're not the type to truly take over unless you have no options."

"What? Are you saying I'd—"

"I'm not giving you a hard time. At all. But I know you. You'll get involved in the planning for your house, or the pub, or something else, and Maeve will wind up watching the baby." She put her hand on Ryan's shoulder and rubbed it gently. "I swear I'm not calling you out. You're Caitlin's favorite sitter, and I appreciate every minute you spend with her. But if you have Maeve and Moira as backups, you'll use them. Then Maeve's still not had a vacation."

Jamie's hands settled on Ryan's shoulders from behind. Then her soft voice said, "She's right, sweetheart. If we were fully in charge, we'd do a fine job. But when there's help to be had…" She let out a soft laugh. "We'd do what Annie does and take advantage of it."

Annie laughed, raising her hand to lean forward and slap Jamie's. "The best advice I've ever gotten was from my mother. When someone is willing to watch your baby—let them."

Well into the evening, after Ryan went to fetch fresh pints, she returned to a table near the back of the room to sit next to Jamie. "Do you think anyone's noticed that only Colm and Aisling are clean?" she said, settling into her chair.

"He really went all out," Jamie agreed. "He shaved, his shirt's pressed, the whole nine yards. Just goes to show how oblivious the rest of your cousins are, since the rest of them look like they've been wrestling alligators in a swamp." She let her gaze hover around Ryan. "That includes you, by the way."

"If you had any pride, you'd be dirty too. But you and Maggie were so far from the ball you wouldn't have known if we were playing rugby or football."

"You were doing what you enjoy, and we were doing what we enjoy," Jamie sniffed. "Chatting."

"The hems of your jeans are slightly dirty," Ryan said, looking her over. "How did you manage to grout a bathroom and not get messy?"

"The grout goes on the tiles, not the tiler."

"I clearly didn't learn that lesson. I got grime from the stove on my T-shirt, and I wasn't even involved in moving it."

"Luckily, I like dirty girls. But I'm going to put you in the shower before I allow you into my bed."

"I wonder if anyone will go back to the hotel? Their flight's at seven thirty, and they have to be there in time to go through security."

"How long is the drive?"

"Two hours," Ryan said, making a face. "I should have put them in a hotel near the airport for tonight."

"Or gotten them a flight that leaves at a decent hour. Seven thirty is harsh!"

"I know. But they decided to leave on Sunday. If both flights are on time, they'll land at two thirty tomorrow afternoon. That'll give them time to go home and crash before they have to go to work on Monday."

"Wow. There are going to be some sloppy jobs done in San Francisco next week."

"I splurged for business class for all of them—both flights," she said, looking proud of herself. "They'll have a drink or two and sleep the whole way."

"Caitlin won't," Jamie reminded her. "I hope Annie's off on Monday. Nurses need to be on their toes."

Ryan chuckled. "Are you saying tradesmen don't? You wouldn't say that if you'd ever used a circular saw."

"Well, I haven't. You're the family circular sawer." She put her hand to Ryan's head and tapped on her temple. "How are you feeling about everyone leaving? I know goodbyes aren't your favorite things."

She shrugged, feeling a little glum. "One way or the other, I have to say goodbye to someone. I want to stay, so I have to put up with some things I hate."

Jamie smiled at her. "I feel like we're just starting our vacation."

Ryan playfully tapped her on the nose. "I'm just starting *my* vacation. You've largely been on one for two weeks."

"What?" she asked, laughing a little. "Are you saying my going to Galway to shop with Ais and putting the grout on the bathroom tile wasn't pulling my weight?"

"You're pretty light, so I guess you pulled your weight. I will admit I'm glad the majority of the work on the pub is over. I feel like I could sleep for a week."

"But you won't," Jamie said, leaning over to kiss her cheek. "You'll be up and at 'em in the morning. Same as always."

"Probably true. But I won't be cutting tile or climbing a ladder."

"You'll just find something else to wear you out." She tucked her arm around Ryan and cuddled up to her. "I've decided I can't change you, so I'm going to enjoy you just as you are."

Before her grandparents left, they went around to everyone who was leaving to bid them goodbye. Ryan was proud of her granny for being just as cordial to Colm as she was to his brothers. Before today, she wouldn't have guessed that her grandmother could put on a polite face when something was bothering her, and it was kind of nice to know she had the capacity.

Tommy and Annie were the next to leave, and Ryan carried a sleeping Caitlin to their car, nuzzling her face into the child's hair just to imprint her smell. "She'll be a different baby the next time I see her," she said, so close to crying she could feel the burn in the back of her throat. She hadn't told anyone but Jamie of her thoughts of staying in Ireland, and now that she considered only seeing Caitlin a few times a year it started to feel like an absolutely crazy idea. But she knew it would be equally hard to leave her grandparents, her aunt and uncle and her cousins. Although she loved having grown up in America, she often wished her parents had never left Ireland. Of course, then she wouldn't have met Jamie. There was truly no way to have everyone she loved in the same place, and that made her sad in ways that she wasn't sure she could ever fully express.

At eleven, Maggie and Brendan got ready to leave. After they'd said goodbyes to everyone, Ryan and Jamie walked them to their car. Jamie touched the chain on Maggie's new necklace and teased, "What are you going to say when the customs people ask if you have anything to declare?"

"I could declare my love for this guy," she said, putting her arm around Brendan's waist, "but other than that, all I bought in Ireland was a load of postcards and some birthday presents for my nieces and nephews." She pulled her necklace from her blouse. "This was a gift, and it didn't even come from Ireland."

"It was an awesome gift," Jamie said, "but I bet the memories of this trip are worth even more."

"Well, I'm not sure how much this cost…" She laughed, leaning into Brendan's body as they walked. "But no matter how much he paid, the thought of marrying him is worth ten times more."

"Don't make any firm plans until we get home," Jamie said. "I love wedding planning."

"Firm plans?" Maggie laughed. "I doubt we'll make any plans at all. I've got a lot going on at work this summer, and I know Bren isn't going to run around looking for wedding venues."

"Ask my mom to share the research she did when Ryan was leading me on about marrying me," Jamie said. "She was very organized about taking notes."

"Knowing your mom, she only checked out nice places. I'll be sure to ask before I do any research on my own."

They reached the car, and spent a minute exchanging kisses and hugs. "Now don't work too hard this summer," Brendan said, holding Ryan for a long minute. "You don't have to build your new house yourself, and Aisling can hire people for the pub."

"I'm on vacation," Ryan said as she pulled away, possibly even believing that. She was a perfect combination of utter practicality, mixed with a fantasy world that only she had access to.

Jamie couldn't keep her head up any longer, but Ryan looked like she still had a little energy left. Conor and the boyos had decided they'd stay up all night, then sleep on the plane. That wasn't an awful plan, but it was one Jamie would have had a hard time mirroring. Since she'd been with Ryan, she'd gone from being a bit of a night owl to a near early-bird. Even though she was young enough to stay up all night without suffering, she now craved a full-night's sleep more than another few hours in a noisy bar—even when she loved all of the customers.

Ryan put her arm around her and said, "You look like you're about to call it a night."

"True. Want me to call the local cab and get a ride back to the hotel? I truly don't mind if you want to stay up with the boyos."

"Tempting," she said, clearly weighing her options. "I hate to be the first to leave."

"The first to leave left five hours ago, honey. We're down to the die-hards now."

"True. But they're my die-hards." She let out a sigh. "I wish I'd had some time alone with Conor. We were in the same place every day, but we never really talked."

"Go talk to him now," Jamie said. "It's two, and they're not leaving until four. You're both very gabby when you've had too much to drink."

"Too much!" She let her head fall back as she laughed. "I'm as sober as a judge."

"Iffy, but don't even think about driving back to the hotel. Speaking of which, how are the boyos going to drive to Shannon?"

"Before I had a sip, I got them to agree that Tommy, Bren, and Maggie would drive. Conor, Niall, Kieran, Colm and Donal are going to squeeze in where they can fit."

"Good girl," Jamie said, kissing both of her cheeks. "I'll go say goodbye to everyone while I wait for my cab." She held Ryan's chin and kissed her mouth gently. "I'll miss you, but not enough to want you to wake me when you get back."

"I know you mean that in the most loving way," Ryan said, with a silly-looking grin showing she'd already been over-served.

After Jamie left, it was just the four O'Flaherty cousins, Aisling, and Conor left in the bar. Ryan wasn't sure what kind of plan Aisling had come up with to have a moment alone with Colm, but she didn't have any ideas to offer. When she'd had too much to drink, the first thing to go was her problem-solving ability, and she had to admit it was officially gone.

Conor was sitting on top of the bar, with his long legs dangling. Ryan had to jump to climb up and join him, but she made it, helped by Conor grabbing her belt loop and pulling hard enough to give her a serious wedgie.

She draped an arm around his shoulders and said, "Can you believe we blew through two weeks this quickly?"

"Fastest vacation I've ever had." He tapped his pint glass against hers, which was nearly empty. She was tempted to have another, but she wasn't going to be able to sleep on a plane the next day, so she held off.

"Did you have fun? I know you didn't have much success with the girls…"

"I could have," he said, seeming perfectly content. "But I didn't want to spend my nights chasing women. It was more fun hanging out."

"Really? You seemed kind of pissed when you learned the boys made a couple of strikes."

"I'm not sure they really did. When it comes to women, you can only believe about half of what they say."

"Half?" She laughed at that. "That's being generous."

"I saw Kieran with a girl who looked like she might buy his bullshit, and I know Colm was with someone. But Niall and Donal might be full of it."

She was drunk enough that she knew she might not be able to play innocent, but she gave it a try. "How do you know Colm was with someone?"

"Donal told me. When he'd get up in the middle of the night to pee, Colm was gone."

"Ahh. I guess I should have gotten everyone their own room."

He let his head tilt until it rested against hers. "If you were any more generous, it would be a crime. Seriously," he said, increasing the force of his voice slightly. "You had to have spent three times what it would have cost to hire the most expensive tradesmen in all of Ireland to do these jobs."

"I wanted them done right. You know it's hard to find people willing to come to Killala."

"Not buying it, little sister. Yes, you wanted it done right, but you also wanted to drag some of our cousins out of San Francisco for the first time in their lives." He gave her a firm pat on the leg. "And you wanted Bren and me to see the family again. You used the jobs as a way to make us not complain about you paying."

"Well, there might be a grain of truth—"

"Admit it. You were up in everyone's business when you didn't have a lot of money to throw around. Now you're going to turn into another Catherine Smith." He playfully bumped her with his shoulder. "Not a bad goal."

"I just want everyone in my life to be happy, and I knew it would make Granny and Granddad happy to get to know Caitlin. Everything else just fell into place."

"Your plan worked. But I think Granny was tired of the kid by the second day."

"Maybe the afternoon of the first," she admitted, laughing at the memory of her grandmother eyeing the spritely child with a certain amount of wariness. "But she liked holding her when she was asleep. I saw her and Granddad do that a couple of times."

"That's when she's at her best. Toddlers are too much for older people. Caitlin's strong enough to knock either of them over."

"I was touched by Annie wanting to take her home so Aunt Maeve could have a real vacation. She's a keeper."

"Yup. We've gotten lucky so far with Annie, and Jamie, and Maggie. Who's gonna screw things up by hooking up with someone who can't get along with the group?"

"Someone will," Ryan guessed. "I just hope it's not soon."

"Well, we don't have to worry that it'll be Colm. At least not yet. By the time he's home, he'll have forgotten all about his Irish fling."

Ryan just nodded, knowing Conor would kick her butt once he found out she'd known about the relationship all along. But she wasn't even tempted to tell him. Having a little time to decide if they were right for each other was important, and once they were thousands of miles from one another, Aisling and Colm could actually have a few conversations where they weren't tempted by the availability of a bed.

A little before four, Maggie pulled up on the deserted street and rolled her window down. "I packed all of your bags," she said, narrowing her eyes at the boyos, who were only slightly wobbly as they lined the sidewalk, waiting for their rides. "I'm warning you now—never let a woman you're interested in see how you live."

"I call dibs on Maggie's car," Conor said. "I'm going to have to listen to Caitlin all the way home on the plane. Adding two hours of her babbling right now is more than I can take." He gave Ryan a hug that yanked her off her feet, then settled her onto the ground and kissed her cheeks. "I love you," he said, adding another hug. "Don't get too used to living in Ireland, because I want you back."

She stared at him, shocked that he'd even think she might be inclined in that direction. "I'll miss you," she said, biting her lip to keep from crying.

He slid into the passenger's side, and said, "The cars aren't going to get any bigger, fellas. Hop in."

Niall took him up on the offer, and Brendan rolled up as he was getting in.

"We've got enough cars so that only one of you has to ride in the back," Brendan called out.

"Fantastic," Kieran said, hugging Ryan and Aisling, then racing for the front seat. Donal ran for the back, pointing at Colm as he laughed. "Have fun with the babby," he said, imitating the local accent.

"I'll get you back when you least expect it," Colm promised. As Brendan and Maggie drove away, Colm grabbed Aisling's hand and pulled her back into the pub. Ryan wisely stayed outside, and when Tommy pulled up Ryan could hear Caitlin chattering away before the window went down.

"Who's left?" Tommy asked.

"She-bon!"

Ryan squatted down and spoke to Caitlin through her window. "Hi, buddy. You're going on the big plane again this morning, aren't you."

"Zoom zoom!"

"That's right. And when I come home, we'll play airplane until my arms give out, okay?"

"Play now, She-bon!"

"I can't, baby. You've got to get going so you can go home."

"Noooooo!"

Ryan shot Annie a guilty look. "I didn't mean to wire her up."

"She was wired ten seconds after she woke. Thank god she likes flying." She turned around in her seat and tried to soothe Caitlin, who had launched into one of her not-infrequent meltdowns. Tommy, ever the pragmatist, reached into his shirt pocket and took out a pair of foam earplugs, which he inserted.

"Is anyone going with us, or did we just stop to upset Caitlin?"

"Colm was here a second ago," Ryan said. "He must have gone in to use the bathroom."

The door to the pub opened and only Colm emerged. "Ahh. Here he is."

"Aisling packed it in?" Tommy asked, with his voice louder now that he couldn't hear.

"Some people can't keep up," Ryan said. She gave Colm a hug and watched him try to get his very long legs into the backseat. The only good thing was that Caitlin was distracted from her tears, and she quieted down when everyone else started to laugh at Colm, who had to pull his right leg into the car with both hands.

"At least the airplane will seem spacious," Ryan said.

"Thanks for the best trip of my life, Ryan," he said, leaning over a little to be able to see her. Caitlin took that opportunity to grasp his ear and tug on it.

"Ear!" she yelped, very proud of her ability to name many body parts.

"Good luck," Ryan said, waving as Tommy wisely started off before Caitlin could realize no one else was going to get into the car.

She watched the taillights grow smaller as the car rolled down the street. Then she was holding Aisling, who'd come out to lean against her. Her voice was rough and a little hoarse when she said, "I wish your uncle Francis had only had girls."

"Uncle Patrick," Ryan said, "but I get your point." She wrapped both arms around her and stroked her back as she started to cry, really letting it out for a minute or two. "Shh," Ryan soothed. "You'll see him again. And next time he'll come alone."

"That will be *months*." She looked up at Ryan, nearly breaking her heart with her red-rimmed eyes and quivering chin. "Could you go without seeing Jamie for months at a time?"

"It almost killed me when she traveled for the golf team," Ryan admitted. "But if you decide to stay together he could move here, Ais. I think he'd do it."

"He said he would. When he pulled me inside, he said he'd start figuring out what he'd have to do to move." She managed a weak smile. "He claims to love me."

"Of course he does. And he'll be able to get citizenship with no trouble, so you won't have to get married right away if you don't want to."

"If I could have pulled him from that car, I'd have married him right here in the street."

Ryan squeezed her tightly. "I've always wanted you to have someone you felt passionately about. Even though I wish you'd chosen a stranger, I'm really happy for you both."

"I think I'm going to have to tell my mam," Aisling said. "She'll know something's wrong."

"Maybe Granny already did."

"No, I'd know if Mam knew. I'll tell my parents when I can talk about him and not cry."

"That might be a while," Ryan said, guiding her back inside so they could call the local cab service to get back to the hotel. It was going to be a long day, with both of them missing the O'Flaherty men—with different levels of affection and connection.

Chapter Ten

Jamie woke up late, with the sun already warming the room. She glanced at the clock, amazed that she hadn't woken when Ryan had come in. As she rolled over, she gasped when she saw the sheet still tucked up under the pillow on Ryan's side.

She wasn't usually the type of person to catastrophize, but her heart started racing. She was sure Ryan wouldn't have driven after drinking all night, but riding home in a cab wasn't completely safe, either. It wouldn't be hard for a cab driver to nod off at four in the morning.

She hopped out of bed, and went into the bathroom, trying to come up with a plan to find Ryan while alarming the fewest number of people. As she opened the door, she gasped again. The tub was filled with six foot three inches of O'Flaherty, wet from the crown of her head down, and so sleepy-looking she might have nodded off any second.

"What in the hell are you doing in the tub?"

"Didn't get home until four thirty, and I was so dirty and sandy that I knew you'd kill me if I didn't shower. Then I thought I might be good-to-go if I soaked for a long time. That was a mistake. I'm even more tired now."

Jamie sat on the edge of the tub and caressed her cheek. "I was coming in here to pee, then gather up a search party."

"Really?" She sat up a little, exposing her shoulders. "I thought you'd see my workboots by the door."

"Seriously? You think I wake up from a sound sleep and search for your workboots?"

"Well, when you put it like that, it sounds silly. Sorry, babe."

"It's all right." She went to grab a towel and held it out for her. "Time to get out now. I've got to pee."

Ryan rolled her eyes, but didn't otherwise complain. She grasped the sides of the tub and pushed herself to her feet. "When you're finished, will you braid my hair? I don't want to bother drying it."

"Sure." Jamie took another towel and helped dry her off. "Give me thirty seconds of privacy."

Ryan left the room, but stood just outside, continuing to talk. Jamie kind of hated that, but she had to be a little flexible, given that Ryan didn't complain about having to leave. "Ready for breakfast?"

"Breakfast? You're not going to sleep at all?"

"Don't think so. I used to stay up all night pretty regularly. I think I can still manage it."

"I've only had five and a half hours, and I feel like I'm carrying a sackful of rocks. But you've always been more resilient than I am."

"Not true," Ryan said. "I just complain less."

Ryan didn't have much appetite for breakfast, but she managed to get some oatmeal and tea down before she pushed the half-eaten bowl away. "Ready?" she asked, standing up.

"For?" Jamie asked, looking up at her.

"For church. Don't you want to go?"

"I *do* want to go. Do *you* want to go?"

"I think so. I'm not ready to make any kind of commitment to the Catholic church, but my granny and my father will be happy if I start to go again, and I can use the time to center myself, if nothing else."

Grinning, Jamie stood and took her hand. "Not to burn the faith of your forebears, but that's what I do during the sermon when I attend a Catholic service. Do they even try to teach priests how to come up with something that people can resonate with?"

"It's a homily," Ryan sniffed, always loving to point out the relatively minor differences in their sects. "And you've got a lot of nerve asking for a good speech when the priest actually turns a piece of bread and a cup of wine into human flesh and blood."

"Uh-huh," Jamie said, her skepticism evident. "You know full well I'd be at the local Church of Ireland if I wasn't trying to make points with your granny. I believe transubstantiation is a symbolic gesture, Ryan, and given that you haven't been to church in ages, you're not one to talk."

"Given how tired I am, I might be one to sleep," she said, thinking that might literally be true.

The youngish priest who'd been assigned to the parish had paid attention during homily class at the seminary. Ryan wasn't even tempted to sleep, and she was pleased when Jamie caught her eye and nodded at the end.

After the service, they stood on the steps of the church, where Ryan was introduced to nearly every person to emerge from the building. Even if she didn't want to continue finding her way back to her faith, she was going to keep going to church. Her presence definitely made her grandmother happy, and her grandfather probably appreciated it as well, although he wasn't the type to make a big deal out of it.

Neither Aisling nor Cormac were in attendance, but the family still took up a full pew, with her father and aunt, Moira and Eamon, and Cáit and Brenna. After they'd all been social to the neighbors, Brenna grasped Ryan's hand and said, "What are we going to do today?"

Ryan looked down at her young cousin's bright, hopeful grin and said, "Whatever you want, kiddo. You're in charge."

"I am?" she asked, her voice rising until it was just a squeak.

"You are. If we can get to where you want to go and get back home in time for bed, I'll do it." She made eye contact with Jamie, whose wry grin indicated she was expecting a request to fly to Italy for a pizza, or something equally outrageous.

Brenna really gave it some thought, with her brow furrowed for a full minute. An idea must have hit, because her face lit up with a smile. "Can I ride a horse? My friend went to a riding center near Galway, and she said it was brilliant."

"A horse?" Ryan said, tilting her head.

Her father was standing close and a teasing grin covered his face when he said, "What are your thoughts about horses, Siobhán? I can't quite recall…"

"Very funny," she said, scowling. "You know I never get on the back of anything dumber than I am. Especially if it can kill me without even trying to."

Jamie tapped Brenna on the shoulder and said, "You won't believe this, but this is one area where I'm more adventurous than Siobhán. I'd love to go riding with you. Cáit?"

She raised her eyebrows while slowly shaking her head. "I've never been. I might side with Siobhán on this one. Besides, I should study. I have my last test on Thursday."

"Thursday? Then you have time to have a little fun," Jamie said. "I took riding lessons from the time I was five until I was in high school, and I never got a scratch. You'll love it."

"We'll go," Ryan said, putting her arm around Cait, "but we might do something else while you two are trying to stay upright."

They didn't reach Galway until one, and by then it was time for lunch. Ryan was in the mood for good fish and chips, and Galway had plenty of good spots. After eating, then goofing around in the tourist-heavy shopping area, they headed for the riding center. When Ryan parked the car, Cáit popped the trunk and pulled out two hurleys and a sliotar. "Care for a little camogie?" she asked. "We can get some exercise without making a poor horse do all the work."

"Done," Ryan said. "No saddle sores for me."

"I'd say you're being silly," Jamie admitted, "but I haven't ridden in about six years. My butt will hurt for sure."

"We're going to do it, aren't we?" Brenna asked, grabbing her hand as she gazed up into her eyes.

"We are," Jamie said. "We'll keep at it until we're too sore to keep going."

"I loooove horses," Brenna said. "Aren't they the best?"

"She's only seen a horse through a fence," Cáit said quietly, so that only Ryan could hear.

"That's pretty true for me," Ryan said. "I saw one in a field when I was very young, and he came over to the fence and clamped down on my arm when I tried to pet him. Scared the hell out of me!"

"The horses won't bite us," Brenna said. She looked to Jamie for confirmation. "Will they?"

"Of course not. I'm sure the horses here are very gentle." She put her hand on Brenna's shoulder and guided her to the office. "We'll have fun while those chickens play their little stick game."

"Camogie!" Ryan yelled after her. "Real athletes don't need other animals to carry them!"

Jamie stuck her hand in the air and wiggled her fingers as they walked away. Ryan bent over to tighten the laces in her shoes, feeling slightly dizzy when she stood back up. "I stayed up all night, so I'm going to be slow today."

"You did?"

"Uh-huh. The boyos were taking off at four, so it hardly made sense to go to bed."

"Sounds like some of my friends. Not me, though. They call me 'Sleepy' since I always find a quiet corner and conk out when we have sleepovers."

"Well-rested people rule the world," Ryan said. "And even if they don't, they're not as grouchy as the ones who stay up half the night."

Apparently, camogie was more tiring than horseback riding. Both Ryan and Cáit were toast after an hour of running around a beautiful field next to the riding rings, but Jamie and Brenna were still at it. Ryan and Cáit went to stand by the ring and watch, with Ryan smiling like a goofball at how cute her fiancée looked sitting tall atop a horse.

"I've never seen Jamie ride. She looks cute, doesn't she?"

"She always looks cute," Cáit said. "It's her nature."

"I can't argue with that." Ryan put her foot on one of the fence rails and leaned on it. "I kind of wish I was interested in riding, since Jamie really loves it. But it's not smart to do something dangerous if you're afraid of it."

"Is it the height? That's what I don't like."

"Nah. I'd go skydiving in a minute. Or bungee-jumping. Or paragliding. Or—"

"I get it," Cáit said, with her mouth quirking up in a grin. "It's not the height."

"It's what I said this morning. Horses can kill you without meaning to. They're smart enough, I suppose, but they don't seem all that interested in pleasing humans. And they spook so easily. I like a nice, docile dog. An animal that's thoroughly domesticated is my kind of thing."

"So if dogs could hold you, you'd ride one."

"I think I would. But that would be one hell of a dog!" She watched for a while, saying, "Brenna looks pretty comfortable."

"Yeah. I thought she'd get out here and change her mind."

"I bet having Jamie close by made her feel safe. She's very patient and calm."

"She's the best," Cáit said. "If I could find a guy like Jamie..."

"That might be a tall order, but I bet you can get close."

"It sounds like it's hard to find a guy you can even stand," she sighed. "Aisling hasn't had a lot of luck, and she's been looking since she was younger than me."

"Things will turn around for Ais. I think being with John showed her she can't settle for a guy she isn't crazy about."

"I'll settle for anyone who'll have me."

"No, you won't." Ryan put her arm around her and gave her a hug. "You've got too much self-respect for that. Once you get to uni, you'll find your people."

"Aisling went to uni. And she had a job after that. Her people have not been found."

"I know. But you can't predict who you'll fall for, or when it will happen." She pointed at Jamie, who looked like the most confident woman in the world, seated upon a tall, tan horse with a blonde mane. "Jamie had a fiancé when I met her. A *guy*," she stressed.

"Yeah. She told me that."

"Right. Well, I'm sure she didn't expect to fall in love with a woman when she signed up for that psychology class, but I'm damn glad she did."

"So…I should study psychology? I was thinking of Irish." She wore the little half-smile that meant she was teasing.

"You can study anything that pleases you. Focusing on the language of our ancestors is awesome, Cáit. I'm really pleased it's caught your interest." She gave her a gentle push. "Not to mention how proud Granny will be of you."

"I love the language," she said, now serious. "I want to teach, I think."

"Like your dad. I love having people in town tell me what a good teacher he is."

"Not just like my dad," she said, her smirk back in place. "I'd like to teach people who've made a commitment to the language. Secondary or College for me."

"Ooo. Sounds like someone's going to grad school." She held out her hand and they slapped palms. "Welcome to the club."

"We'll see. I might change my mind. But that's where I am now."

"I think you're in a good place. And we'll help you get through school, no matter how long you want to stay."

Cáit put her arm around Ryan's waist and gave her a quick hug. "You've always been my favorite cousin, even before you had money."

"Good to know. I'd hate to be turfed out if we go broke."

Cáit laughed quietly. "You're not the sort to go broke. Even though you have money, you still think like a normal person."

Ryan laughed at that. "Jamie would be the first to disagree with that. She's very sure I'm not normal."

Now that the group was smaller, no one was having a birthday, and things were pretty much back to normal, they could have had dinner at Moira's. But with her six, and O'Flaherty four, her normal-sized kitchen couldn't hold them all. When Ryan's grandparents voted to join the group, they were back to either eating at a pub, or at Aisling's. That was an easy choice now that the kitchen was sparkling clean and fully functioning.

Just because the place was hers, however, hadn't clued Aisling in on how to cook, and she seemed entirely uninterested in learning. In all of the times Jamie had been with her, she'd seen her do no more than peel vegetables for a salad.

As usual, Moira and Maeve did the majority of the work. Jamie always tried to help, but the kitchen was really made for a small staff. So she played server while Aisling pulled the few requests for drinks. Aisling stepped out from the bar after everyone was set, saying, "Will you keep an eye on things? I've been summoned."

Jamie started to answer, but Aisling made a bee-line for her grandmother, who was sitting alone at a table near the far corner of the room. Ryan appeared at Jamie's side just a second later. "I wonder if this is going to be a discussion, or a tongue-lashing?"

"Have they spoken since Colm had his arse walloped?"

"Nope. Granny's had a 48-hour cooling off period, so I'm hoping I don't have to pull her off Aisling."

"Mmm. Your uncle is a very laid-back guy, but if his mother-in-law put her hands on Aisling, I think that would change. I can't see Eamon putting up with any nonsense."

"I think you're right. I'm kind of teasing about Granny, but kind of not. Colm looked like he was about to slide into home plate, and Aisling wasn't giving him a 'stop' sign. That's probably the most blatantly sexual thing Granny's ever seen, and I actually feel a little sorry for her. I was uncomfortable, and I don't think of Ais like she does."

"Having kids is hard," Jamie murmured. "Still sure you want to get into all of that?"

Ryan put her arm around her and gave her a quick squeeze. "I'm positive, babe. The promise of kids is worth the certainty that they'll repeatedly shock me to the core."

They'd finished dinner and were breaking up into groups to drive or walk home. After kissing lots of cheeks, Ryan got into the car, joined by Jamie and Aisling. As Ryan put the car into first gear, Aisling started to laugh.

"What's tickled your funny bone?" Ryan asked.

"Granny." She was in the backseat, and she leaned forward and adopted her grandmother's accent, which was just a tiny bit more rural than her own. "Look, I didn't just float up the Moy in a bubble. I know what's going on. If you let a man like that Colm climb on top of you, I can tell you exactly what he'll want next."

"She didn't!" Ryan said, starting to laugh.

"Oh, she did. I don't know what she thinks John and I did while living together, but she seems to worry about my virtue." Her voice rose again as she imitated her grandmother perfectly. "You don't want to have the men think you're like the heel of the bread, do you?"

"Wait!" Jamie said. "Let me guess the punchline of that one." She seemed to think for a minute, then held her hands up. "No idea."

Laughing, Aisling finished it off. "Everyone touches you, but no one truly wants you."

"Oh, god," Jamie sighed. "How did you sit there so politely and not laugh?"

"She's so fecking sincere! Granny only wants the best for me, but we have *massively* different ideas about sex and relationships. I'm sure I'll never convince her that I know what I'm doing, and she'll never convince me to stop. I suppose we're at an impasse."

"As long as she doesn't listen in on your phone conversations, or read your email, you've got some breathing room," Ryan said. "And once your mam knows, she'll be on your side—I think."

"Yeah," Aisling sighed, flopping back against the seat. "That's not a given, is it."

Ryan finished a short run on Monday morning and tried to enter her hotel room quietly. She had a full day planned, and wanted to get over to the pub early. They had to figure out how to order liquor, what supplier to purchase food from… So many things that none of them had any familiarity with.

As the door swung open, she gasped to see Jamie, showered and dressed, standing in front of the mirror that hung over the dresser. She was fussing with her hair, which was finally long enough to pull back into a decent-length pony tail. She didn't pull it back very often, but Ryan liked the look. Less hair near her face showed off her nearly-perfect features.

"Now this is the scene I love to see when I come in from a run," Ryan said, walking over to give her a playful slap on the butt. "Breakfast downstairs? Or do you want to go by my aunt's on the way to the pub?"

Jamie turned to gaze at her, and without a word being spoken, Ryan knew there was trouble afoot.

"What? I couldn't have done anything wrong. I wasn't even here."

Jamie's features softened, and she opened her arms to Ryan, who gratefully slid into the embrace. "Am I really that bad a nag?" Jamie asked softly. "If I am, please tell me."

"You're not a nag. At all. You just point out the stupid stuff I do."

"I'm serious," Jamie said. "I hate to think of your walking into our room, and immediately trying to figure out what kind of trouble you're in. If that's common for you—"

Ryan gently put her fingers over Jamie's lips. "It's not. When you point out thoughtless things I've done, you're almost always justified. I've..." She let herself try to center her thoughts for a moment. "I've been getting justifiably roasted for dumb things my whole life, so I recognize the expression on your face. So what did I do today?"

Jamie turned back to the mirror, making sure her hair was perfect. "It's not a big deal, but I was hoping we could do something touristy today. That's why I got up early. I saw the sun was shining, and I thought it was a good day to exploit it."

"Not a problem. I don't have to punch-in. What did you have in mind?" Ryan hoped a quick walk on the beach would handle it.

"We haven't been to the Aran Isles or St. Kilda..."

"That's in Scotland. You're probably thinking of the Skellig Islands."

"I love islands," Jamie said, meeting Ryan's gaze in the mirror. "If St. Kilda's better, let's head over there."

Ryan laughed at the ridiculous nature of her comment. "Big Skellig is plenty nice."

"Okay, but I'm not married to that. We've got a huge list of possibilities. We haven't been to the Giant's Causeway, or anything in Northern Ireland, for that matter."

"We've done a lot!"

Jamie gazed at her for a moment, her expression one Ryan was very familiar with. It said, "How can we be so close and have such different views?" Her gorgeous green eyes fluttered closed as she turned toward Ryan, then she spoke, obviously trying to hide her exasperation. "We've seen a good portion of Mayo, a little bit of Galway, and a tiny bit of

Kerry. That's it. Nothing of the far south. Nothing of the north. Nothing of the east. I know people who've been here for a single week who've seen twice as much as I have."

"We've seen a lot," Ryan repeated, realizing her certainty was diminishing. "We spent a lot of time in Dingle last trip. Remember how much you liked it?"

Clearly losing her battle to tamp down her exasperation, Jamie's voice started to sound strained. "I *loved* Dingle. I truly did. But that doesn't mean I don't want to see all of the other cities that begin with 'D.' Donegal, Derry, Drogheda… Oh, I don't know… I heard there's a place called Dublin that some people put on their itinerary if they've got days to kill and they've seen everything else."

Ryan backed up and pulled her shirt over her head. "I'm clearly frustrating you, so I'm going to get into the shower. When I come out, I want you to tell me exactly what you want to do." Jamie started to open her mouth, but Ryan spoke over her. "Whatever it is, I'll do it."

Jamie nodded her head, then sat on the chair by their bed, guidebook in hand. That wasn't a promising sign that a walk on the beach would do it, but Ryan was resolved to give her partner a day to do whatever she wanted. It was only fair to let Jamie captain the boat once in a while.

Jamie was just wrapping up her phone call when Ryan emerged from the bathroom, her skin pink from the shower, hair wet. She seemed to think she was covered up when she wrapped a towel only around her waist, even though Jamie's favorite parts were completely bare. She grasped Ryan by the shoulders, and pressed her onto the straight-backed chair by the desk. Taking the wide-toothed comb from her hand, she started to run it through Ryan's hair, getting out the tangles that formed when she roughly ran a towel over it.

"I think I've decided what I want to do," Jamie said. "I'm leaving here on Wednesday, and I'm going to travel across the country."

"Across the *country*?"

"Uh-huh. I might take three days, or even four. Then I want three or four days in Dublin. On the way back, I'll come home a different way so I can see more."

"Am I involved in any of this?"

"All of it, if you want to be. If not, those are my plans."

Ryan reached up to grasp her hand. Then she stood and gazed at Jamie with a concerned expression. "Why are you being so…curt."

"I'm not." Jamie tried to make sure her smile looked genuine. "I was very compliant while watching you work like a dog for the past two weeks. But I've seen everything the Greater Killala Metropolitan area has to offer, and I'm ready to take a peek at some other spots. If you don't want to go, I'll wait for Cáit to finish her last exam, or I'll talk one or both of your aunts into going with me."

"Are you mad at me, or not? I honestly can't tell."

"I'm not angry, Ryan." She put her hands on her bare arms and rubbed them gently. "I'm trying to tell you what my needs are before I get frustrated. Like an adult," she added, with her smile growing brighter. "I'd love for you to be the kind of person who enjoys sightseeing as much as I do, but you're not. So I'm giving you the option—go with me, or wave goodbye."

"Why does it have to be so soon? Couldn't we wait another week or two?"

"Of course we could," Jamie soothed. "But we're…or rather, *I'm* not going to. I'm ready to go." She gazed at Ryan for a moment, truly puzzled by her. "You're talking about wanting to move here permanently, but you don't know the country well at all. I'm happy to have a home here in Mayo for our visits, but if I'm even going to consider living here I've got to know more about the place."

"But I've got so many things I'm going to help Ais with," she whined. "There's a million things to do until she can open."

"Uh-huh. And once you've helped her open, you'll be tending bar, or playing your little whistle, or singing to entertain the crowd." She grasped Ryan by the shoulders and gazed into her troubled eyes. "I know you, sweetheart. Taking a few days to travel around aimlessly is a punishment for you. So kiss me goodbye, and be here to welcome me home in a week or so. How's that?"

"This is important to you?" she asked soberly.

"It is. Besides wanting to look around, we've been around too many people. I love them all, but I need to recharge." She put her arms around Ryan's body and hugged her tenderly. "I feel a little rootless in this hotel. It's hard to center myself. Getting away for a few days will help."

"But you'll just be in another hotel," she said, clearly trying, but failing, to understand.

"True. But now that nearly everyone is gone, being in Ballina makes me feel just far enough away for everything to be inconvenient. I don't want to hang out here, and I don't want to sit at Moira's house for hours a day. It's not working for me."

"Want to move? I heard about a place that's supposed to be nice in Enniscrone."

"We'll see once I get back." She pulled away and opened the dresser to pull out some things for Ryan. "Painter's pants? I don't know how dirty you plan on getting today."

"Jeans and a T-shirt will work." She'd finished combing her hair, and went into the bathroom to blow it dry. Jamie followed her and sat on the edge of the tub, watching her work, admiring how regimented her routine was.

When Ryan had gotten enough of the dampness out to satisfy herself, she pulled her hair back into a pony tail and snapped a band around it. Then she held out her hands and pulled Jamie to her feet. After they shared a few kisses, she gently rubbed noses. "We let our anniversary slip by without even a card."

Jamie smiled at her. "I bought you several, but I didn't give them to you."

"What? Why?"

"Because I knew you'd feel guilty if you hadn't bought me one. But if you gave me one, I was ready for you." She tapped her temple. "I'm prepared."

Ryan closed her eyes for a moment, looking like she might cry. "When we weren't even lovers, I spent hours working on that training book I made for you for Christmas. But now that you're mine, I've started to take you for granted. It's like you're part of the team now, so I don't have to try."

"That's..." She was going to say it wasn't true, but it was true enough. "I know how much you love me. I also know that we're very different. I'm trying to find ways to get my needs met while not making you do things you don't enjoy." She gave her a soft kiss. "But I'll admit that a little anniversary celebration would have been nice."

"We'll have one," she said decisively. "Starting Wednesday. We can drive along the south coast, or head north and go to the Giant's Causeway." She wrapped Jamie in a tender hug, holding on for a long while. "A good relationship is more than just being monogamous and not yelling at you. I've got to step it up."

"Thank you," Jamie said, rubbing her face against Ryan's chest. "I would have enjoyed going with Cáit, but you're my favorite."

On Wednesday morning, Jamie spent a little time nailing down hotel reservations for their trip. She hated to be locked-in to specific stops, but Ryan assured her that they'd be lucky to get anything at all, given it was the beginning of tourist season. It took longer than she'd hoped, but the choice of places available dictated where they'd start. Since she'd found a hotel in Lahinch, in Co. Clare, and another in Kinsale, south of Cork, they'd start off seeing the Cliffs of Moher. While she would have preferred winging it, she'd learned her lesson. If you wanted to stay anywhere unique in Ireland, book early.

Ryan was with Aisling at the pub, leaving Jamie the job of packing for both of them, a task she relished. Ryan was so persnickety about so many things, but she was totally haphazard when it came to packing a suitcase.

After Jamie had everything squared away, she loaded up the car with all of their possessions, checked out, and drove to Killala.

Ryan was outside the pub, supervising the sign painter as he installed the very snazzy-looking sign. Jamie got out of her car and stood next to Ryan. "Now that's a good looking advertisement, isn't it? Someone with great taste ordered that one."

"I got chills when I first saw it," Ryan admitted, smiling at her. "Don't tell her I told you, but Ais got tears in her eyes."

"Aww. I'm glad she likes it."

"Go on in. The girls are inside."

"Aisling and…?"

"Aisling and my aunt are running errands. The younger O'Donohues are here today. Cáit's head is about to explode and she thought a day off before her last exam might be good for her."

"I agree. There's only so much you can cram into a brain. Sometimes it does better with a little room to move."

When Jamie pushed the door open, she saw Cáit and Brenna unboxing pint glasses. Brenna put a glass down and raced over to Jamie, excited and chatty as always. "Siobhán says you're going to Dublin!" Her eyes were bright with interest, and she looked like she might try to stowaway in the car.

"We are. I'm excited."

"I was in Dublin…once, I think," she said, clearly searching her memory. "My aunt lives there, but she usually comes here to visit. I'd like to go again, though. Any time at all…"

"Hey," Jamie said, trying to distract her. "Will you help me with a few things? I checked out of the hotel, so I have two bags full of things I don't need for our trip."

"Sure!" She raced toward the door as Jamie heard Cáit laugh almost silently.

"She gets excited," Jamie said. "Kind of like her older cousin."

"Siobhán's a little more subtle. But I see the similarities."

"I'm glad you're here," Jamie said. "But I thought you might have something more exciting to do to clear your head."

"Maddie's already finished, and she went on holiday with her family yesterday."

"Well, helping out here's better than studying, right?"

"Without a doubt."

Jamie always had to carry the slack when they conversed, and so she kept at it. "So you'll be finished tomorrow, right?"

"Uh-huh."

"Then what?"

She looked up and said, "Aisling will pay me to help with the pub, and since I don't have any way to get to Ballina for a proper job I'll go with that."

Jamie looked at Cáit as she dropped her head to concentrate on her work. "If you want to work in Ballina, go ahead and look for something. We'll figure out a way to get you there."

"I'd happily ride my bike, but Mam doesn't like me going that far alone. There's a bus, of course, but it only makes the trip twice a day."

"Look for something," Jamie insisted. "Unless you'd rather work for your sister."

"I don't mind doing this, but I'm too young to work the bar, and I don't think I'd be of much use in the kitchen." She shrugged. "I think Ais can keep me busy tidying up until she opens, then I'll have to bus tables."

"Not ideal," Jamie said.

"No, not ideal. One of my teachers is tutoring this summer, and she said she'd love to have me help with the beginning students. But she lives a bit north of Ballina…"

"Give her a call," Jamie said.

"Now?"

"Yeah. Right now. See if she needs some help."

Cáit gave her a puzzled look, but she got up and went to the telephone hanging on the wall at the far side of the bar. Jamie went out to help Brenna, whom she was sure was in Ryan's hair at the moment.

After they got the suitcases out, Jamie gave Brenna clear directions on where to put the cases. It was kind of funny watching her try to get them to roll the same way, but she was definitely trying.

Cáit walked over and said, "Mrs. Callaghan said she could keep me busy for three or four hours a day, with more hours on Saturdays. But I'd have to go to her home. She has a couple of small kids, and she has to mind them while tutoring."

"Do you want to do the job?"

"I'd love to," Cáit said, with a hopeful smile covering her face. "It would keep my skills up for college, and I could see some of my friends who found summer jobs in Ballina." Her brow eased into a frown. "But I can't take any of the cars, and I'd hate to ask my mam to drop me over there every day. She's made that trip too many times already, and with Brenna starting secondary this year, she'll be making it for another five years."

"We'll work this out," Jamie said.

Brenna had put the bags in the far corner of the pub, and was now right next to Jamie. "What will you work out?"

"Your sister has a lead on a job. I'm trying to figure out how to get her to Ballina."

"The bus," Brenna said. "Mam won't let her ride her bike." She lowered her voice. "Mam's brother was killed on that road, you know."

"I didn't know," Jamie said. "Well, I knew your uncle was killed while riding his bike, but I didn't know it was on the road to Ballina."

"It was," Brenna said, more sober than usual. "Mam hates the road because of that."

"I don't blame her a bit. It took us a year to drive past the spot where we were carjacked, and what happened to us isn't even close to what happened to your uncle."

"I wish he hadn't been killed," Brenna said, seemingly on the verge of tears. "I'd love cousins who lived here."

Jamie almost smiled at her, but she held back. Twelve-year-old kids had a tough time seeing outside of their own needs, and Brenna was no exception to that. "I have to go check on something with Siobhán. Be right back."

She'd only gone two steps when she heard Cáit say, "Jamie didn't ask you to go along with her, Brenna. Come finish your job."

"But…"

"I'll be right back," Jamie said. "I just need a minute with your cousin."

She exited while trying to ignore Brenna's mild complaint, finding Ryan shaking the sign painter's hand as he was closing up his truck.

Ryan walked over to her and put an arm around her shoulders. "Looks great, right?"

"Extremely." Jamie stretched to place a kiss on her forehead. "What would you rather do? Rent a car for Cáit to drive to Ballina for a summer job, or buy her one?"

"*Buy* her one? I'll admit that she's worked hard, but that's a hell of a graduation present."

"I know, babe. But she has a chance to do some tutoring this summer. Moira won't let her ride her bike to Ballina alone, and the bus only goes twice a day."

"It goes early in the morning and comes back after five. Problem solved." Her smile grew wider. "I'll buy her a bus pass."

Jamie put her arm around Ryan and gave her a squeeze. "She's only going to work a few hours a day. What is she supposed to do if she's finished by one?"

"Um…I think there's a library."

Pushing away from Ryan's body, she gave her a swat. "Forget my question. *I'm* going to buy Cáit a car, so it doesn't matter if you agree. She'll need one to get to university, and there's no reason not to do it now so she can start work this weekend."

"But we're leaving…"

"Our trip can wait. Family can't." She tapped on Ryan's temple. "I thought you knew that."

Ryan was sure her young cousin had a volume button, but she wasn't sure how to adjust it. Brenna was in the backseat with Cáit, excitedly detailing which car they should buy. Ryan had already given her a big, fat, "no" on Mercedes, BMW, and Range Rover, and now they were in the possible category. Cáit hardly said a word, other than a very wan insistence that she didn't need to go to Ballina to work, and that she could come up with some plan to get to university without wheels. But it was clear she was excited, as well. It was just harder for her to show it.

They reached the bigger of the car dealers in Ballina, and as Cáit and Brenna headed straight for the cars on the lot, Ryan held Jamie back for a moment. "You know, Cormac doesn't have a car, either…"

"Cáit and Cormac can share the car to drive to Galway—"

"Don't jinx her! She won't get the results from her leaving cert until August."

"I still haven't got this system straight. How can she know where she's going to school if she doesn't have her exam results?"

"She doesn't. If she's not accepted to NUI-Galway, her second choice is Maynooth. I'm not even sure what her third choice is, but she'll be crushed if she doesn't get her first or second."

Jamie bore a confident smile when she said, "She'll get into her top choice. I can just tell. Then she and Cormac can share the car."

"I guess that can work…"

"Plus, they can use the one we're going to buy."

"We're buying a car?"

"We should. Long term, it'll be cheaper to have one. The rental fees are ridiculous."

"Used," Ryan said, determined to not be moved on this one. "For both Cáit and us."

"No problem. I was thinking used would be best."

"Liar," Ryan said under her breath as they started to walk over to the girls. "I bet you didn't know that used cars even existed before today."

"Did too. My dad has used cars."

"Your dad has classic cars, Jamers, and that's not even in the same ballpark."

By the time Cáit was behind the wheel of her little red car, with Brenna undoubtedly talking her ear off on the way home, it was one thirty in the afternoon. They stopped and loaded up on sandwiches, with Jamie going into the restaurant to order, knowing that Ryan could easily waste a half hour talking to the owner about whether they knew her family. Finally, with Ryan happily munching on a ham and cheese toastie, Jamie was able to relax and think about the trip.

"I'm happy we wasted the best part of the day," she said. "Not that doing something nice for your cousin was a waste, but we sure haven't gotten very far."

"I know what you mean," Ryan said, turning to smile. "I'm glad you shamed me into buying the car. Cáit really will need it, especially if she goes to Maynooth. And with you promising to come back and buy another for us, I think you got a better deal."

Jamie shrugged amiably. "You never know what you're getting with a used car. But it was only two years old, and just coming off lease. I'm sure it's in good shape, which is my main concern."

Ryan's grin widened. "Mine's price."

"No, it's not. Yours is safety and reliability. I know you don't want your cousin stranded out in the middle of nowhere on a cold, rainy night."

"Also true. Now I just hope that by the time we get home, my aunt and uncle will be over however it is they feel about my buying their kid a car without checking with them." She lowered her voice and spoke slowly. "They will not be happy. At first."

"But they'll know that Cáit didn't badger you for one. She's no Brenna, who already told me she'll have her license in exactly five years, and that she will also graciously accept a used car, preferably on her birthday."

"Gotta love her," Ryan said. "All of my cousins have turned out pretty well, but Brenna keeps things exciting."

Jamie didn't have a single complaint about Ryan taking the most scenic route to the cliffs, even though that meant the trip would take longer than it might have. But only a fool would complain about being close to the sea on a warm, dry day in Ireland. The water looked so darned inviting she could have spent the entire day just watching birds fly along the coast, bobbing along on the airstream.

The road went inland for a few miles, and when they jogged towards the water again they hit a spot that gave them a view from a distance. "Gahhh!" Jamie cried, pointing.

Ryan let out a laugh. "Yes, sweetheart. Those are the cliffs. We're going to be there at the perfect time, I'll have you know."

"How far away are we?"

"Mmm. Fifteen minutes? I've been here at least ten times, but I've never seen the sunrise or the sunset. I'm excited about that, so don't think we're leaving until the car park closes."

"I'm getting my camera ready. When I get out of the car, I'm going to snap, snap, snap."

"I'm glad you brought your camera. Even though film is expensive, I see how much you enjoy using it, so I don't even think about the fact that each photo costs around a dollar."

Jamie reached over and placed her hand atop Ryan's, which rested on the gear shift. "I'm not going to let you shame me into taking fewer pictures. This is a very important trip for me. One day I'm going to sit our kids down and show them evidence of the first time their mama brought me here."

"Damn," Ryan sighed. "The thought of that makes me so happy." Their eyes met for a second or two. "I think about our future family all of the time."

"Ooo! A sign! We're close."

"Hold on there, pal. We've got to wait for the buses in front of us to get up the hill. I'd switch to the wide angle lens if I were you. There's a lot to see, but it's spread out." Her eyes narrowed, and Jamie could see her thinking something through. "Want to take a boat ride after we spend some time here? You're guarantied to get wet, and maybe bruised, but it's cool."

"Boat? Me? Always."

"Great. We'll stay up top for a while and take pictures, then we'll go get wet."

After finding what was probably the only spot left in the spacious lot, and striding past the very attractive visitor's center, they continued to climb a relatively gentle incline, with the deep blue sea getting closer and closer. When they reached the edge, Jamie let out another groan of pleasure. "Oh. My. God. This might be the most stunning place I've ever seen."

"And you've seen a lot," Ryan said, grinning like she herself had carved the cliffs.

"I'm…I'm…speechless."

"Best day I've ever seen up here. I've been here when you felt like you were in a big gray ball of cotton candy. You knew the Aran Isles were out there, but you sure couldn't see them."

"They're right there!" Jamie turned to stare at her. "You couldn't see them at all?"

"Like I said, it's never been this clear when I've been here. This is epic." She stuck her arms out and leaned her head back. "My hair isn't whipping around, and the sun is on my face. The gods are smiling on us today. Truly."

Jamie held the camera to her eye and took a photo of Ryan, her smile so filled with pleasure it made Jamie mist up. "You're so pretty," she murmured, snapping away.

"I need some of us together. Hold on." Ryan dashed over to a couple who also had a big camera. Leave it to her to choose a person who'd definitely know how to focus an SLR.

The guy, an American in his thirties, knew what he was doing, since he had them turn so the sun was in their faces. Having been at his spot just a minute before, Jamie knew he would have both the cliffs and at least a portion of the island in the photo.

"Take as many as you like," she said. "I'm happy to waste film to get a good one."

"Give me a different pose," he said, very serious about his task.

Ryan moved to stand behind her, then draped both of her arms around Jamie's neck, clasping her dangling hands together. Jamie was settling her own clasped hands on Ryan's when a soft whisper tickled her ear. "Smile for our kids. I want them to know how happy we were before they wore us down and made us old before our time."

Jamie started to laugh as she heard the shutter click a couple of times. Then Ryan leaned in and placed a kiss on her cheek. A few more snaps and the guy stood up and held the camera out. "Looking good, girls," he said, with a goofy grin on his face.

"Thank you," Jamie said as she looped the strap around her neck. "At least one of those is going in the family album for our kids."

"Kids?" he said, blinking a few times.

"Several," she said, not sure if he looked surprised that they were lovers or that they were old enough to have more than one child. "We're not sure how many, but several is a safe bet."

They had to leave to drive to Doolin to catch the last boat of the day, and Jamie silently praised her prudent choice to leave the camera in the car. She'd have to find some sort of rain/sea protection for it—especially for when they traveled in Ireland.

The boat was crowded, with all of their fellow latecomers extending the lovely day in any way possible. There were only seats for a few, with everyone else holding onto some posts on the otherwise open deck. This was clearly the kind of setup you'd never find in America—the personal injury lawyers had taken all the fun out of risking your neck—but that made it more fun. The boat got close to the face of the cliffs, closer than she would have gone with her own boat, but that made it more fun, too.

The churning water, made more fierce because of the backwash off the cliffs, had her holding on with both hands as Ryan burbled with happiness every time the boat slammed into a gully. "Love this," she kept saying, grinning like a child.

The engines cut back and the boat floated in relative quiet as the captain told them the names of some of the very impressive stacks thrusting up from the water for hundreds of feet. It was truly stunning, and Jamie began to let herself imagine having a boat to do this kind of thing whenever she wanted. Then a significant backwash hit them broadside, and the captain gunned the engine, nearly knocking her off her feet. That was some serious horsepower, and he probably needed every bit of it when the wind caught him unawares. The dream of a boat evaporated as quickly as it had appeared. Letting someone with a ton of experience keep them safe was the better choice. Besides, Ryan would have a fit if Jamie spent what she'd have to to get a boat with multiple powerful engines.

The sun's angle started to reflect off the water, and Jamie desperately wished she could capture the beauty as it began to glow a golden amber. But she had to make do with just her eyes, and her memory. Maybe that wasn't so bad. A camera could never fully capture the joy of Ryan's blissful face as she smiled contentedly, with the glorious sea behind her. Memories were the way to go.

Racing back to the top of the cliffs while the sun was still shining was super cool, in Jamie's opinion. Being able to park closer was awfully nice, too. And having far fewer people around was the icing on the cake.

The path along the cliffs was wide, and paved, but if you were daring you could walk on the long grass and get as close as you wanted. Jamie had her hand in Ryan's back pocket, ready to pull her back if she got too frisky. Her own instincts made her hold tightly to the braided wire that snaked along the path. It was about four feet from the edge, and that made it seem like a waste of money. If it didn't stop people from getting too close, why bother?

The "golden hour" was just about to start, and Jamie couldn't wait to capture Ryan's face in the flattering light.

"The last time I was here was four or five years ago," Ryan said. "I'm not sure why Aisling wasn't with us, but Cormac had just gotten his license and he wanted to roam a bit. We took the little girls along, and I stupidly let them walk up here." She turned and met Jamie's puzzled look. "The wind was blowing so fiercely that I had to hold both Cáit and Brenna's hands in my left, while I hung onto that cable with my right. Cormac, of course, had run on ahead, leaving me to nearly lose both of his sisters."

"Oh!" Jamie said, realization dawning. "This isn't a waste of money." She plunked at the wire like a guitar string.

"Why would you think it was?"

"I assumed it was to keep you from getting too close, but it's on the wrong side of the path for that."

"Nah. People would lose it if their photos were ruined by a protective fence. But trust me, that wire has saved a few lives. The cliffs and a windy day are a bad combination for people who don't weigh much. Add in some fog and…" She faced the water and waved to the depths as she leaned over, laughing when Jamie yanked on her pocket, making her stumble backwards.

"You're the one with the money," she said, her laughter growing. "You gain nothing by killing me."

"I'd have some peace of mind!" Jamie said, grabbing the sleeve of her shirt along with her pocket this time. She was going to *have* to buy a leash.

Jamie had been leery about the hotel in Doolin, but it turned out to be perfectly fine. Utilitarian, but clean and quiet. After they put their things in the room, they took off for dinner, heading to the spot the desk clerk recommended.

It didn't take long to get to the restaurant, a fairly typical pub with a large bar area and an even larger dining room, but they were definitely not the first people to make the trek. Everyone near Doolin was jammed into the place, or so it seemed, but Ryan was able to slide between customers to emerge with a pint for herself and a glass of Murphy's for Jamie.

The crowd was pretty raucous, and was made up of mostly Americans, who always seemed to be the loudest people in any international crowd Jamie had been in. But everyone seemed like they were having fun, which was the point in going out.

Being abroad made people more talkative than they'd be at home, and Jamie smiled as Ryan told her story to at least six people. Everyone seemed charmed by her, which wasn't odd, or maybe they were just curious about why this American woman with Irish-born parents sounded like a local. Jamie wasn't even sure if Ryan realized she was using her Irish accent any more, but now she knew what she'd been referring to when she'd told Jamie it had always taken her a few weeks to ditch the accent after a trip.

A live band started at nine thirty, and they did a great job of playing over the loud crowd. It was actually a little too loud for Jamie, but that gave her an excuse to pull Ryan down and talk into her ear, able to add a discrete kiss while she was at it.

They were both a little flootered when they were finally seated, but it was fun to be slightly drunk and hungry as hell. Ryan ordered the beef stew, and when it arrived she seemed delighted to find two heaping scoops of mashed potatoes swimming in the dark gravy along with chunks of beef and carrots. "This is going to be good," she said, eyes dancing with delight. If there were enough potatoes involved, she was a happy girl.

Returning to their hotel close to midnight, Ryan held the door to their room open, letting Jamie scoot under her arm to enter.

"It's been an hour and a half since we ate, and I'm still full," she said, immediately unfastening her jeans. "If I keep eating like this, I'm going to have to buy new clothes."

Ryan grasped her and held her loosely in her arms. Playfully, she slid her hand into her underwear, poking around her belly experimentally. "If you've gained a pound, I'd be surprised. You drank more beer than normal tonight. That probably makes you feel extra full."

"I'll consider that possibility. Until I decide, I'm going to complain that I'm getting fat."

"Wise choice," Ryan said, kissing her cheek. "Want to get ready for bed first?"

"Sure." She went into the bath and started to put her toiletries on the wide sink. "Can we sleep in tomorrow? I'm not going to want to get up and start driving at the crack of dawn."

"Since I don't know where we're going, I can't render an opinion."

"Oops! Kinsale. Have you been?"

"I have not. I was in Cork for about two hours once, but that's the full extent of my investigation of the area."

"Cool. I like seeing places you haven't been. It's fresh for both of us."

"And what made you choose Kinsale?"

"They've developed a reputation as a foodie town. Their fish is supposed to be extraordinary."

"Works for me." Since the door was open, Ryan walked over and stood in the opening. "Guess what."

"What?" Jamie asked, putting toothpaste on her brush.

"I'm very glad we're taking a vacation from our vacation. I know I don't seem very self-aware, but when I get away from whatever I'm obsessed with, I can step back and see how I've once again let myself get carried away."

Jamie stuck her hand out and patted Ryan's cheek. "So you see that you're not the person opening a pub?"

"Yes, I see that. But when my cousin needs help, I have to step in. I don't think I can stop that instinct, honey."

"I know, babe. That's why I was willing to go on this trip alone. Sometimes you're so involved you can't let go. And I was fully determined not to get aggravated with you. It's not your fault that I need to move around more than you do."

"All true. But I'm still glad you dragged me away. Being alone for a few days is good for us both."

"Agreed. Now I need to be alone for a few minutes. Bye," she said, giving Ryan a slight push as she closed the door.

Chapter Eleven

Jamie had gone to buy snacks while Ryan checked out of their Doolin hotel, but the sack was empty while they were still an hour away from Kinsale. "Late lunch, or early dinner?" Jamie asked as she handed Ryan the last crisp.

"Early dinner. I like eating early on vacation."

Jamie let out a chuckle. "You'd be happy if we ate at five every night. If we ever go to Spain, you're going to be having dinner when everyone else is finishing lunch."

Ryan gave her an impish smile. "Easy solution. Don't go to Spain."

"I'll ignore that comment." She reached into her bag and took out the Irish history book she'd been reading. "Think we'll be able to see any signs the Vikings were here?"

Blinking at her, Ryan said, "Here? Like right here?"

"They were all over the southeast. This was a lively spot," she added. "The Norman invasion started in this area too."

"I know I should know this..."

"It's okay that you don't," Jamie said, laughing at her bewildered expression. "I only know this stuff because I've been reading about it—a habit we don't share."

"I know *how* to read," Ryan insisted, chuckling softly. "I swear I do."

"But you don't like to." Jamie checked the Post-It notes she had sticking out from the pages of her book. "The Vikings started visiting around...eight hundred."

"I know about the Vikings—in general. But I don't know any details."

"Well, when they arrived the first time, they sacked a monastery, stole everything they could sell, then took off. Oh!" A fact moved to the front of her brain, and she added, "The Book of Kells wasn't begun in Kells. It was started at a monastery that disbanded after the Vikings plundered them a couple of times."

"Go figure. I had no idea."

"Yeah. That was their habit for quite a while. Come ashore, steal from the monks, capture some of them as slaves, then leave and sell everything and everyone to the highest bidder. Must have scared the crap out of people." With her hands, she tried to show how big their boats had been. "Thirty or forty guys crammed into boats bigger than the Irish could have imagined. They had keels, too, which let them go farther than anyone on earth had gone before."

"Technology always wins out."

"It kinda does. Anyway, after just grabbing everything they could from coastal areas, they eventually went up the Liffey and landed in Blackpool. Soon, Dublin was a great Viking port. They traded slaves, amber, gold, silver, even silk from Asia."

"Ugh," Ryan growled. "Is there any group of people who don't immediately try to sell other people? What the fuck?"

"It's human nature to exploit whatever you've got. On the plus side, they founded Wexford, Waterford, and Cork. That's why I thought we might see something that showed they were here."

"That'd be cool. Did they thoroughly kick our butts, or did we not mind being plundered. I don't recall hearing about any mass killings."

Jamie shook the book in the air. "According to this guy, they started off small, then gained a little momentum. But it was still just a few raids a year. Then they built settlements. The Irish kings tried to fight back, but even though they had some success, the Vikings kept coming back."

"And this lasted how long?"

"Not as long as you'd think. Around a hundred and fifty years. Then they switched their focus to England and France. After a while, the guys who used to take your stuff and your sons and daughters became merchants. I guess familiarity doesn't always breed contempt."

“That doesn’t sound like us,” Ryan said, grinning. “We’re kind of known for holding a grudge.”

“Maybe so, but within a couple of hundred years, Irish art changed to reflect some Viking themes. It sounds like they civilized you a bit. Your people were pretty wild.”

“Still are,” Ryan said, giving Jamie a sidelong look. “I’ll show you how wild later.”

“I feel like we’ve settled into an every third day schedule.” She touched the upturned corner of Ryan’s mouth. “But those look like bedroom eyes there, O’Flaherty.”

“I think they are. Maybe my vacation vacation schedule’s different than my vacation schedule.”

“You’ve got yourself a date. I’ve never made love in the south of Ireland.”

“Nor have I. I’ve not had so much as a kiss south of Dublin. This is true virgin territory.”

Jamie’s book had recommended a B&B right on the harbor, and she went to check in while Ryan got their things from the car. “We’re set,” she said when she returned. “A lovely woman wanted to help with the bags, but she was about eighty, so I thought we’d better do it ourselves.”

“Don’t go waving my granny off if she ever tries to do something strenuous. She’ll coldcock you.”

“I think I’m making progress with your granny.” Jamie picked up her bag and pulled the strap over her shoulder. “Pretty harbor, isn’t it?”

“Yeah. Really nice. We’ll have to go explore.”

She took a look at the sky, and Jamie did the same, seeing the little bit of sun they’d had now hiding behind a heavy cloud bank.

“I’m praying for sun tomorrow,” Ryan said. “I think there’s a chance.”

“There’s always a chance. Tonight, we’ll go to bed early and pray for sun.”

"I've got some marital duties to take care of first," Ryan said, revealing a goofy-looking seductive gaze. "But if you want to add a good wish for weather while you're screaming your creator's name—go for it."

They reached the landing for the B&B, and an elderly, white-haired, frail-looking woman with bright blue eyes greeted them as she held the door open. "Are you certain you girls can carry all of that," she said, seemingly seriously.

"Yes, ma'am," Ryan said. "We're stronger than we look."

The woman put her hands on her hips and took them in, starting at the top of Ryan's head and working her way down. Her impish smile grew as she proceeded, then her gaze snapped back up to land on Ryan's. "Not possible. You look like you could pull a tree right from the ground if you had a mind to."

"Depends on the tree," she said, flashing that charming grin that worked on young lesbians as well as grannies.

"Let me show you to your room, girls. We have just the one left, but Jamie says you won't mind sharing the bed. It's a large one," she added, then frowned slightly. "Well, it'd be large for me. What do they feed you in America?" she asked as she scampered up the stairs, looking able to take them two at a time, but not wanting to show off. "Ahh, here we are." The door was open, and Jamie moved past her to gaze approvingly at the nicely appointed room. She hated places full of knick-knacks and junk, much preferring a clean, uncluttered look. Besides the dark red rug and red and blue print bedspread, the room was otherwise plain. White walls, dark wood floors and a dark wooden chair. "Perfect," she said, noting the bed was barely queen-sized. They preferred king-sized, but those were not common in Ireland.

"I've stoked the fire to take the chill off," the woman said. "Let me know if you need more turf."

The aroma that scented the room brought a big smile to Ryan's face. "My grandparents burn turf in the fireplace," she said. "When I was young, my grandfather and I helped an old man down the lane dry his turf. My job was stacking it into stooks." She let out a laugh. "I can't believe I remember that. I couldn't have been more than four years old."

The woman gripped her arm, her hand as strong as a vise. "It's the smell. Nothing brings back memories like smell. I can still see my mammy's face when I go into a shop that sells her perfume." She laughed, a light, merry sound. "Not that Mammy wore perfume very often, of course. Not with chasing after the nine of us." She gave Ryan's arm a mild shake. "You're from Ireland?"

"My father's from Tralee, my mother from a small town in Mayo."

"You still have family there?"

"I do. Grandparents, an aunt, and four first cousins on my mother's side, great aunts and uncles and too many cousins to count on my father's. We've been in Mayo for a couple of weeks, and now we're doing a little traveling."

"You'll have a grand time. Let's hope the weather prediction is wrong."

"That's one thing you can almost count on. The weather will rarely match the prediction."

The fire had died during the night, and Ryan's insistence on having the window open was coming back to bite Jamie on the butt. She'd been too enervated after they'd made love to put her shirt back on, and now it was lying on the floor—just far enough that she'd have to get out of bed to reach it. She was snug and warm, with Ryan's body spewing as much heat as that peat fire at its peak. Now a trip to the bathroom was mandatory, but getting across the room and walking on that stone bathroom floor wasn't going to be fun. Turning over to face Ryan, thoughts of leaving bed flew from her head. Staring at Ryan's face while she slept was a pleasure she was rarely able to partake in, and she relished each opportunity. Ryan's eyes were closed, but they weren't moving the way they did when she was dreaming. A ghost of a smile revealed itself, making her even prettier. Leaning close, Jamie kissed her cheek and let her hand settle on Ryan's hip. Immediately, her lashes fluttered, then those crystalline eyes focused. "Are we up?"

"I think I am. I've got to go to the bathroom, but I hate to leave this cocoon." She snuggled against Ryan's heated body. "It's so nice in here."

"Would I be your hero if I got up and shut the window?" her voice, low and rough, vibrated past Jamie's ear.

"No, but you would be if you shut the window, then got my socks." She started to laugh when Ryan did.

"Did you wake me up for that?" She snuck a hand into Jamie's armpit and dug into the muscle that always made her cackle with laughter.

"No!" she cried. "I just kissed your cheek because you looked so pretty. I swear!"

"I'll choose to believe you." Ryan tossed the covers aside and stood, stark naked, then stretched her arms straight up into the air, putting her beautiful breasts on display. She didn't act like she was cold, but her nipples had hardened into pebbles by the time she'd reached the window.

Tucking the comforter around her shoulders, Jamie waited for her socks to be delivered. "Would you like some alone time today, baby?"

"Alone time?" Ryan went to the open suitcase and pulled out Jamie's silk underwear. Then she held up a pair of socks for approval.

"Those are fine."

Ryan handed them and the discarded T-shirt over, looking thoughtful.

"God knows you haven't had much alone time," Jamie said. "I know you need it."

"That'd be great," she said, obviously trying not to look as pleased as she probably was. "But only if that's what you want too."

"I can keep myself busy."

"Super. Want to have breakfast together? 'Cause if you don't…"

"You're ready to take off," Jamie finished for her.

"Well, I hadn't given it much thought, but…"

Jamie had struggled into her clothing and now made a dash to the bath. "Be right back."

By the time she returned, no more than three minutes had passed. Yet Ryan was fully dressed in black leggings, a T-shirt, and her rain jacket. Her hair was back in a ponytail, and her knit hat was perfectly settled onto her head. Garishly colored orange and yellow and green running shoes were just being laced up. "No sense in wasting time," she said, heading into the bathroom. After the toilet flushed, Jamie heard the water running. Knowing Ryan, she was washing her face in ice cold water, a habit that was beyond Jamie's comprehension.

On cue, she emerged, her cheeks pink from the cold. "I'll take some money so I can grab breakfast."

"Will I see you at all today?"

Ryan was already in front of the door. "Uh…sure. When and where do you want me?"

"Go play," Jamie sighed. "I'll make dinner reservations for six. That will give you eleven hours to do whatever it is you're planning on doing."

Ryan took three big steps and stopped in front of Jamie, a big grin plastered to her face. "I'll be missing you. That's the only thing on my agenda."

After giving her a sharp slap on the butt, Jamie turned her and pushed her toward the door. "No one appreciates bold-faced lies, honey. Have fun."

"You too." She was halfway out the door when she said, "Apologize to our host for my skipping breakfast."

"I'll eat your share."

"Good one," she said, laughing as she closed the door and started off. Jamie went to the window, watching her burst onto the street and start running. She couldn't hear her, but was one hundred percent sure she was already singing.

After a very leisurely breakfast enjoyed while chatting with the other guests, half of them American, two Canadians, and the rest from various parts of Ireland, Jamie took a shower, played around on the internet for a while, then went out to check out the town. The day was surprisingly sunny, and she delighted in hearing every single shopkeeper comment on it.

The town was a very cute little place, with narrow streets, brightly colored buildings, and lots of tourists. Tourists were a mixed blessing in every city in the world, but without them, many towns couldn't afford to support more than the basic necessities—towns like Killala.

The main draw in Kinsale, besides the vibrant food scene, was the harbor, which was large and filled with sailboats from all over. She allowed herself the fantasy of buying a good-sized boat and sailing all around Ireland in the summer, but she had a feeling that wouldn't happen. Ryan would never want to be gone for weeks at a time, surveying every port big enough to handle their keel. Unless Jamie could talk Ryan's grandfather into going with them, of course. Then she'd be perfectly happy to take off for points unknown.

Over a light lunch, she started on an Anne Enright novel she'd picked up because of the local bookseller's recommendation, and, before she knew it, she was the only person in the cafe. After leaving a generous tip to make up for hogging the table for hours, she sauntered along the harbor again, snapping photos and enjoying the warmth. It was funny, but even though she'd assumed Ryan would need some alone time, having the day to herself was pretty sweet.

Having a day with nothing to do, and no one to entertain/mind/or communicate with had been just what Ryan had needed to recharge.

She'd seen pretty much everything in town, and had run around the perimeter, spending much of the day along the sea. No matter how many times she saw the ocean, on a clear, sunny day she truly couldn't resist it.

She'd found herself a perch away from everyone, and now sat on a boulder facing the sea, letting the sun warm her completely.

Trying to center herself, she went with the prayer she'd been saying when she had a moment to reflect. It wasn't from Jamie's psalm book, but it felt more authentic, and more reflective of where she was on this journey.

It was still hard to make herself address God, but she was going to make a habit of it, even when it felt weird. She closed her eyes and spoke aloud, trying to start a dialogue with a being she couldn't see.

When I do this, I feel like I'm wasting my time, since just a few weeks ago I was certain you didn't exist. But something keeps calling me back, and I'm not foolish enough to believe I have all of the answers.

I'm seeking…something, and I'm working to stay open-minded. That's all I can do right now. I'm going to sincerely try to find my way back to you—if you're there.

She felt the tears come, as they always did when she got to this point. Ryan had no idea why she cried every time she acknowledged her uncertainty. But it hardly mattered why she did it. This was obviously important to her, and equally important to so many people who loved her. Even if she never got a clear answer, even if she was never sure if the path she was on would lead anywhere, keeping her heart and her mind open to the possibility of God might be enough to let her make some progress.

The worst outcome would be that she'd try to live as a true Christian—loving her neighbor, giving to those less fortunate, and accepting God's grace whenever it appeared, only to have her world end at her death. That wasn't a bad outcome at all, when you thought about it. And the best outcome—being reunited with a loving creator, as well as everyone she loved… That was just too awesome to get her mind around.

She filled her lungs with the sweet, salt-filled air and blew it out slowly. It was impossible to look out at the sea on a beautiful day and feel like all of life was just a cosmic accident. Unfortunately, it was just as hard to turn off the skepticism she'd adopted.

Ryan took another breath and decided to believe. Maybe just for today, but she was going to think back to the easy, uncomplicated relationship she'd had with God just a year and a half earlier. She was going to stop obsessing about things that couldn't be proved, and accept God into her heart.

She spent another few minutes letting that thought warm her, and when she opened her eyes she truly felt lighter and more whole. It might not last—but it might, and she was going to ride it until she was thrown from the horse.

Acting on the advice of their innkeeper, Jamie started to walk toward the Skilly Trail, a path that stayed close to the sea. It was after three, but it wouldn't hurt to be out until close to dinner. God knew Ryan wouldn't rush back.

The trail was superb, and she was so busy snapping pictures of the surprisingly tropical-looking flora that she didn't see the tall, gorgeous woman locked in conversation with an older couple until she was practically even with them. Hanging back, she took some photos of Ryan, loving to watch her when she wasn't aware she was being observed. The sun wasn't directly overhead, but it was still fairly high in the sky, hitting Ryan and her friends with a strong light that made her even prettier. Jamie'd been so intent, she hadn't realized how close she'd gotten until Ryan's hand dropped to her side and gestured with her index finger, beckoning Jamie to come closer.

"Hi," Jamie said as she walked alongside her. She nodded at the couple. "Good afternoon."

"Hello," the woman said, with the man merely adding a quick smile. "Can you believe our luck with the weather? Today was supposed to be nothing but rain, yet here we are."

"It's lovely," Jamie agreed.

"Locals," Ryan said, inclining her head towards the couple. "We were talking about the Lusitania. Did you know it was torpedoed not far from here?"

"Uh-huh. That's why I *read* the tour book," Jamie said. "But I'll admit I was surprised."

"Stop by St. Multose Church on your way back," the man said. "You'll see several graves of the victims."

"I was planning on going to the Old Head of Kinsale," Ryan said.

"Then you'd better shift into another gear," the man said. "That's quite a way from here."

"I saw it this morning," she said. "Now I want to walk all the way out."

"Walk?" The man cocked his head. "You're staying there, yeah?"

"No. We're staying in town."

"Ooo," the woman said, looking strangely…disappointed. "It's private, it is. They've a golf course and a spa. I've heard it's top-notch, but we've not been."

"Private?" Ryan was staring at them like they'd spoken another language. "A head like that? A natural wonder? They sold that to the highest bidder?"

"I'm afraid so. The only way to get close to the head is by boat now."

"Unbelievable," she grumbled. "I thought Ireland was better than that."

"Oh, no," the man said, making a face. "Don't give us too much credit. Money gets what it wants."

"It sure as hell does."

She looked like she was about to cry, and the woman clearly wanted to cheer her up. "Have you been to Charles Fort? We think the view is just as good as from the head." Her voice got quieter when she added, "Of course, we haven't been allowed to walk out to the head since the course opened. It's probably lovely now…"

"We'll try the fort," Ryan said. "We can just continue along this route, right?"

"Right you are," the man said. "Now don't let us slow you down. You've still got some ground to cover."

"She'll have me slowing her down," Jamie said, as Ryan waved goodbye and immediately picked up the pace. "Nice to meet you both."

"Same here," the woman said. "Stay a few days!" she called after them. "There's so much to see."

As they started to walk faster, Jamie said, "Do you know where you're going?"

"I did," she sighed. "The Old Head is super cool, but I was looking at it from a distance. It has to be two miles long." She made a face, looking like she was about to spit. "It infuriates me that they privatized a head like that. It's disgusting."

"We could stay there if you really want—" Jamie shut her mouth when Ryan glared at her.

"Sorry," Ryan said. "I didn't mean to look like I was going to strangle you. But I can't patronize a place that's doing something I think is wrong. There's no valid reason for not allowing people to walk alongside the course at night. If Pebble Beach can allow pedestrians, so can the friggin' head of Kinsale."

"So does that mean you know how to get to this fort?"

"Yeah. Yeah," she said, obviously trying to pull herself out of the snit she'd fallen into.

"I made dinner reservations for eight thirty. We'll be able to walk to the fort and get back to town, right?"

Ryan took a look at her watch. "Yeah. We'll start to head back by seven just to be safe."

Jamie took her hand, partly to slow her down. "I think the woman you were chatting with was right. Even though the city fathers must be idiots to sell off a natural wonder, I could stay here for a while."

Ryan let out a sigh. "Before I heard about the head, I was fantasizing about living here."

"Really? Where have you been that let this pretty place capture you?"

"I didn't do much, actually. Walked around, ran, talked to people. It's just so nice. It's more built up than Killala, with more people to talk to, and more shops to look at. And it's close enough to Dublin to not make it seem like such a slog." She sighed. "But it's Mayo for me. It would be insane to live hours from my family."

"Just a little. But you deserve to live where you want to live. If you want a livelier town…"

"I want that for you," Ryan said, slowing down to give Jamie a long look. "I know you'd be happier if we lived someplace that had more going on."

Jamie squeezed her hand tightly, smiling at her. "Thanks for that. But I can be happy in Mayo. Short term. Just remember that you're going to have to get comfortable with my taking off for quick trips. I wasn't kidding when I said I'd be over at Knock Airport every couple of weeks." She laughed. "I'm sure Brenna would always be up for tagging along."

"Without a doubt."

Jamie gave Ryan a light slap on the belly. "We'll figure it out. Did you fill the beast on your journeys today?"

"Went to a chipper. Grabbed my food and kept walking while I ate."

"Why would anyone sit if they could walk while eating?" Jamie teased. They were walking so quickly she was at her capacity to speak without panting.

"I assume you had a four course meal?"

"Just a salad. But it took me three hours."

Ryan jerked to a halt and stared. "Three hours!"

"I was reading." She pulled out her book to reveal the cover. "Really good. It's about a woman who's visited by an angel."

"Ahh," Ryan said as she started to walk again. "Irish non-fiction."

"It's really good. I think you'd like it."

"Let me know when it comes out on audiobook. I *might* read if I could run at the same time."

"That's my girl," Jamie said, breathing heavily. "Why walk when you can run?"

After two nights in Kinsale, they'd seen nearly all there was to see. They'd wanted to rent kayaks and paddle out to check out the Old Head from the water, but that was not to be. A stiff wind, heavy rain, and a cautious shopkeeper stopped that idea cold. Jamie didn't blame the guy, but Ryan spent a good ten minutes trying to convince him they were both strong enough to get back to shore if the weather worsened. But he had a conscience, and clearly didn't want to be responsible for losing a pair of overconfident tourists.

Now that they were on the road, the weather was clear. A day late, but still welcome. Ryan was driving, and as she guided the car toward Wexford, she said, "You don't want to stop in Waterford, do you?"

"Is it nice?"

"I haven't been, but I've heard it's not particularly pretty. I think it's largely commercial."

"It's not full of glassblowers living in sod houses?"

"Not many of those left," Ryan said, chuckling. "The main Waterford factory closed a while ago, but they have a small one now where their master glassblowers work on special pieces."

"I've seen glassblowers in Italy and Switzerland. If the town isn't charming in some other way, I'm up for skipping it."

"Wexford it is. I'm not sure it'll be charming either, but we've got a place to stay.

Ryan had built up some nervous energy from getting very little exercise the day before, and none at all today. But she wanted to make sure they did some sightseeing that would please Jamie once they got to Wexford.

For most of the three hour drive, Jamie read about all of the sights. They all sounded good enough, but none of them really grabbed Ryan's attention.

"Ooo. How about this?" Jamie said after she'd pulled out a different guidebook and perused it. "They have a replica of a coffin ship. Are you interested in seeing the conditions your relatives lived in when they came to America for those few years during the famine?"

Ryan struggled to keep the scowl off her face. "Not really. I can imagine it well enough without feeling claustrophobic. Anything cheerful in that book?"

"Yes," she said decisively. "The Irish National Heritage Center. As soon as we get to the hotel, I'll get on my computer and check it out."

"I like heritage," Ryan said, not very happy about being stuck inside a museum, but the heavy, dark clouds that were gathering over the sea didn't look like they were going to stay offshore. Being inside might be mandatory.

It was raining pretty hard when they arrived at their hotel, a very neat little place that had a homey vibe. Jamie was on her usual charm offensive, and Caoimhe, their innkeeper, got on the phone and made some calls. When she hung up, she looked a little disappointed.

"I'm afraid the only class the center has space in is an introduction to blacksmithing."

"Book it," Ryan said, realizing she'd spoken pretty loudly.

"And it's tomorrow," Caoimhe added.

"What time?"

"From ten in the morning until four in the afternoon. Your arm will be too tired to hold the steering wheel, I'm afraid."

"I'll risk it. Jamie?"

"Why not." She turned to Caoimhe and said, "When Siobhán really wants to do something, it's best to get out of the way and let her do it."

"Shall I book it for both of you?"

Jamie hesitated just for a moment. "I think so. I can keep an eye on Siobhán to make sure she doesn't overdo it." She paused for just a second, then barked out a laugh. "As if *that* has ever happened."

They went up to their room, a very cute, small space that faced Wexford harbor, which led out to the Irish Sea. "Nice," Jamie sighed. "I love a room where I can see water."

"Me too." Ryan put down their bags and walked over to the window. "Why don't I go get us some lunch?"

"Really?" Jamie moved to stand next to her and wrap her arm around Ryan's waist. "You don't want to go out together?"

"Well, I was thinking of running in the rain for a while, *then* picking up lunch."

"Mmm. Well, I'm not going to run with you, so maybe I'll go find a cafe. The odds are not good at having you return quickly."

"What if I promise to be back in no more than an hour?"

"No more? You *promise*?"

"Scout's honor." She was already opening her suitcase to pull out her running gear, with a happy little smile on her face. Ryan might make it back in an hour, but even if she didn't Jamie wasn't going to give her a hard time. They were on vacation from their vacation, and they each deserved to do what made them the happiest.

An hour and fifteen minutes later, Ryan struggled into the room, carrying two shopping bags that were both beginning to fall apart. A steady rain and paper bags didn't make a good pairing, and these had really gotten soaked.

"Good lord," Jamie said, getting up from her comfy chair to relieve Ryan of her burdens.

"I know I'm late," she said, with some strands of hair plastered to her face. "But the last stop I made was worth it."

"Step into the hall and take off your shoes and jacket. You're getting the carpet wet."

She blinked at Jamie, clearly confused. "There's carpet in the hall…"

"Outside," Jamie said, giving her a slight push.

Ryan shrugged out of her jacket, then kicked off her shoes. After handing them over, she entered the room and started to strip. "That's a righteous rain."

"Those dark clouds over the sea don't promise a nice evening, either."

"They do not." Ryan picked up the bags and carried them over to the bed. Standing there for a second, she took a detour into the bath and grabbed a towel. Once she'd spread it out across the bed she gave a slight tug on the first bag, letting the contents spill out.

"Ooo. You bought good stuff!"

"Really good. There was an excellent farmer's market. Most of this stuff is from individual farms."

"And bakeries," Jamie said, picking up a loaf of fresh bread.

"I bought enough for us to nosh on it all day. We won't have to get drenched looking for dinner."

Jamie stared at her for a moment. "All day? You want to stay in a small hotel room all day?" She checked her watch. "It's only one thirty, babe."

"I'm well aware." She opened the other soggy bag, producing some body butter and a bottle of pink nail polish. "We're going to have a spa day."

"Really? Do you think it will take all day to do my nails?" She tried to sound innocent, but knew she hadn't nailed it.

"It will definitely take me all day to do you—nails included."

Ryan lay propped up by a few pillows, with Jamie using her as a backrest. They'd had a little lunch, and she'd had a little Jamie. Pulling a carton of raspberries close, Ryan popped one in her mouth, and offered another to Jamie, who took it and sucked Ryan's finger into her mouth at the same time. "Delicious," she said, the word a little garbled.

"Why don't we do this more often? I love spending the afternoon with nothing on my mind but you."

Jamie rubbed her head against Ryan's chest. "I'm going to take that as a rhetorical question, baby doll."

Offering up another berry, Ryan said, "I take that to mean you think I'm the problem?"

"You're not a problem. You're…you. And you aren't willing to spend a day doing nothing very often."

"But this isn't nothing," Ryan said softly, with a little emotion in her voice. "Being close like this is relationship glue. It holds us together."

"I know," Jamie said, her own voice growing sober. "Maybe we should move to Ireland. A good cold rain might keep you in the house more often."

"Didn't work today. Although the rain wasn't very cold."

"But it did work. You came back after just an hour. That's something."

Ryan started to run her fingers through Jamie's hair, not speaking for quite a while. Then she let her hands slide down to experimentally touch her face, one feature at a time. "I'm memorizing you for when I'm out running around."

"I'll be here when you get home, baby. You don't have to memorize me." She tilted her head to the side and opened her mouth. "More berries."

"Want a blackberry?"

"I like all berries. Especially ones that taste like they were picked this morning."

"They're pretty awesome." After eating a few more, Ryan slid out from behind Jamie's body and shifted around until they were nose to nose. "So are you." Their lips met for a few long minutes, then Ryan moved away just enough to say, “Your mouth tastes of blackberries. Now I like them even more.”

Jamie gazed at her for a minute or two, with her green eyes searching Ryan’s intently. “You love me a lot, don’t you.”

“With all my heart,” she whispered.

“We’re so lucky. So very, very lucky.”

“I know. I…I hope I never forget that.”

“You won’t, sweetheart. You’re always counting your blessings.”

“I think of it as luck. Or happenstance. I couldn’t believe in a God that rewarded me so richly while so many millions of people suffer. That’s a non-starter.”

“Right. I’m the same. So I’ll change my statement to the fact that you always count your luck.” Her nose wrinkled up in the utterly adorable way it did when she smiled a certain way. “Blessings sounds better.”

“You’re my biggest, best, most wonderful blessing, and I’m damned lucky to have you.”

“Beautifully put.” Jamie put her hand on the back of Ryan’s head and held her still as she kissed her for what seemed like a very long time. “Wanna get lucky?” she asked when she pulled away.

“Double or nothing,” Ryan said, smiling as she tugged Jamie close and kissed her with all of the love she held in her heart.

The next morning, Jamie watched Ryan’s eyes light up as their instructor stoked the fire in his forge and slid a long piece of steel into it. Ryan was the world’s best student when she was interested in something, and hitting stupendously hot things with a hammer was exactly the kind of thing that grabbed her.

They were the only women in the small group, and the only Americans, which was refreshing. Personally, Jamie was only mildly interested in the process. But doing things together made just about anything more fun. The good news was that if she wasn’t in the mood to hammer hot steel, Ryan could be counted on to take over. Her enthusiasm for difficult things knew no bounds.

When it was time to strike a piece of metal so hot it glowed bright yellow, Jamie was tempted to hand the project over to Ryan. But she gathered her courage and gave it a whack. The ringing thud was surprisingly pleasurable, and she hit it again and again, keeping going until it began to lose its vivid color. Then it was back into the fire for another round. She lifted her safety glasses to see Ryan beaming at her, with both thumbs up in the air. It was silly to get so much satisfaction from doing something that impressed Ryan, but she craved her approval as much as she had that of her parents when she was a child. Maybe you never got over that need. One thing she was sure of, though. Ryan would never stop offering praise. If there were a more supportive person on earth, Jamie hadn't met her.

After their class had ended, they walked around the heritage center, checking out the re-creations of homes and clothing and tools from the earliest Celts to the Norman invasion. It was pretty cool to have the things Jamie had been talking about right in front of them.

"I'm not usually much for re-creations of things," Ryan said as they meandered down the paths between exhibits. "But this is pretty cool. Thanks for finding this. If it had been up to me, I'd just be running around Wexford, literally."

"I've had a great day," Jamie said, smiling up at her. "A great two days, actually."

"I loved touching you all afternoon yesterday," Ryan said. "I'll remember that for a long time. But how awesome was it to beat on a piece of steel so hot it was yellow!"

"It was very cool," Jamie admitted. "Now we both have old-style bottle openers." She leaned against Ryan for a moment. "But yours looks better. Your angles are sharper."

She laughed a little. "I'm so proud of it I might start carrying it, even though it will look weird to have a huge bottle opener in my pocket."

"You can pull it off. You've got the butch street cred to make it work."

"I don't think about that much anymore," Ryan said, mulling that over for a moment. "Now that I'm not trying to attract women, I hardly consider what image I'm putting out there. I feel more—myself," she said, nodding. "Just myself. If I look butch, that's fine. If not, that's fine too."

"You're very fine, in every way," Jamie said, as she clasped Ryan's hand while they walked deep into Ireland's past.

Chapter Twelve

Jamie had almost not been able to find a decent place to stay in Dublin, but she'd managed a room for Saturday night. It was far too close to Temple Bar, only merited two stars in the tourist guide, and was more expensive than it should have been. But when you made your plans at the last minute, you didn't always get what you wanted.

They arrived in town at around seven thirty, and Ryan just raised an eyebrow when she pulled up in front of the hotel. Jamie heard her mutter, "Seriously? You chose this?"

"There were very few rooms at the inn," Jamie said. "I found a condo for the next few nights, but this was the best I could do for tonight."

A slow-moving, uniformed guy sauntered out of the hotel and lit a cigarette, acting like he couldn't see their car in the valet spot. Ryan waited patiently for two or three minutes, then she got out and walked over to him. Jamie rolled down her window to hear her say, "If we're not bothering you too much, may we leave our car?"

"Sure. Not a problem." He took another deep drag off his cigarette, then turned his head to blow the smoke away. Ryan was usually very mild-mannered, but the parking attendant should offer up thanks that he'd shifted away from her. Jamie hated to see what Ryan would do if he'd blown the smoke in her face.

They walked into the grim lobby, and approached the front desk. "Jamie Evans," she said to the sober looking guy who was in charge. "We reserved a room."

"Ahh, yes, Miss Evans," he said, cracking the smallest of smiles. "We've prepared a standard suite for you."

"I was hoping for the quietest room you have. We're light sleepers."

"Let me take a look," he said. He'd begun to loosen up, probably revealing his true personality. "We're packed because of the parade."

"Parade?"

"The…" His smile disappeared and he fumbled for a second. "The parade. On O'Connell Street?"

"Is it Pride Week?" Ryan asked.

His smile was back in place in a second. "It is. It is. I was caught short there for a moment. Some guests are interested and some are… not."

"We're interested," Ryan said. "Very interested."

"There are a lot of events going on tonight," he said, with his voice going quiet. "If you go by The George, look for me."

"We will definitely do that. Even though we spent the day blacksmithing, I think we have some energy in reserve," she said, making his eyes go wide. She pulled her massive, hand-wrought bottle-opener from her back pocket. "There isn't a bottle of Guinness I can't open."

Once they'd decided to travel to Dublin, Jamie had gotten on the phone and made dinner reservations for every night. She'd tried to mix it up, with more casual places that she knew Ryan would like, along with some fine dining spots that she craved. After they'd freshened up, they walked out of the hotel to a cool drizzle that had developed in the short time they were inside.

The restaurant was nearby, and by the time they'd crossed the threshold she knew she'd lucked out. It was modern, and sparsely decorated, with lots of youngish people filling the seats. A quiet hum, reflecting good spirits and pleasant conversation, made her smile. Nothing could beat a place with a pleasant hum. Good food followed a good vibe.

A rough-looking guy with a scruffy beard and tattoos along one side of his neck stood by a small desk. "Hello," he said, smiling to reveal a gold tooth right in the front. "Will you be dining with us tonight?"

"We will," Ryan said. "We have a reservation. Evans."

"We're happy to have you. Follow me," he said, leading them to a spot by the window. "We have a few specials, but I'll let you get settled before I tell you about them." After handing over menus, handwritten sheets with a couple of things crossed out, he said, "Let me get you something to drink. What do you think?" He put a hand on the back of Jamie's chair, leaning on it like they were the best of friends.

"We like all sorts of things," she said. "What should we have?"

"Do you like the dark spirits?" he asked, a furry eyebrow lifting.

"We do. Not straight, but in a cocktail."

"I'll have Michael make you up something to take the chill off," he said, nodding before he walked away.

"I like this," Jamie said, noting how pretty Ryan's eyes were as they glimmered in the flattering light of a hurricane candle. "If I can't handle my drink, you might have to have two," she added. "Dark spirits have to be pretty well hidden for me to like them."

"Maybe Michael can tell that by looking at you," Ryan teased. "He keeps sneaking glances at you. Not that I blame him," she added. "You're the best looking girl in the whole place."

"Ha! Every single guy at the bar followed you like they were tomcats and you were catnip. You're going to have half of Dublin in the emergency room by the time we leave."

"Emergency Department," Ryan said, smiling coyly. "And, as usual, you're wrong about this. The guys were looking at you."

"Sometimes that's true in America. Here? You're the catnip, baby. No two ways about it. Irish men have excellent taste."

Their server carried their drinks over on a small tray. "Here we are," he said, "let me know what you think of these. Michael's happy to keep trying if these aren't the tonic for what ails you."

Jamie took a sip, nodded, then looked up and gave the guy a smile. "My compliments to Michael. We might just skip dinner and drink a few of these."

"Ahh, now, don't be too hasty. Some black cod might be nice, or maybe some salmon? I had a bite of both, and I can't for the life of me decide which is better."

"Why not bring us both? We usually eat off each other's plates."

"Brilliant plan. What else do you think you'd like?"

"Surprise us," Jamie said, handing the menus back. "We like everything. Choose whatever you think is best."

He slapped his hand over his heart. "What I wouldn't give to have all of our guests be just like the two of you. We're going to have fun tonight. I promise you that."

"We're already having fun," Jamie said, taking another sip of her drink.

As their server walked away, Ryan clinked her glass against Jamie's and brought it to her lips. "Oh, my. We're not going to be able to resist having another one of these."

"We'll skip the wine and keep these babies coming. Warm whiskey and honey and…"

"Ginger and lemon juice," Ryan added. "But there's a hint of Earl Grey in there. I think I taste bergamot."

"I think you're right," Jamie agreed, taking another sip. "But there isn't any tea, I don't think. Maybe bergamot oil." She held up her glass and revealed a big smile in Michael's direction.

"Stop flirting!"

"Like I'd flirt right in front of you," she said, chuckling. "I'm not a savage. I'm just showing my appreciation. Michael's a craftsman."

The chef was the same, delighting them with all sorts of simple, fresh seafood and perfectly presented vegetables. Jamie was tempted to fight Ryan for the red and golden beets, roasted perfectly and dotted with sultanas and some fresh cheese. But she'd also tried to keep all of the white cheddar mash, a gambit Ryan put a stop to. Quickly, she grabbed the plate and took a heaping spoonful of the potatoes, getting them into her mouth before Jamie could pull the dish back.

"Manners," she whispered loudly.

"You're stealing!"

"I know, but it's so good."

"It really is," Ryan agreed. "We'd come here every other night if this was in Berkeley."

Jamie took a look at the unadorned bowl of boiled new potatoes, a dish they hadn't even touched. "What's with that?" she asked, experimentally poking a potato with her fork.

"The usual." She speared one and popped it into her mouth. "It's fine. Nothing to recommend it, but fine."

"It's odd," Jamie insisted. "And it doesn't fit with the rest of the meal."

Shrugging, Ryan said, "My guess is they didn't offer a bowl of boiled potatoes when they first opened, but enough people asked for them that they started including them. My grandparents would turn the table over if they didn't get a bowl of potatoes with their meal."

"Interesting," she said, taking a tiny bite of one. "There's no reason to eat those when you have these." She dragged her spoon across the bowl of white cheddar mash, filling it to overflowing. The spoon hung in the air for a moment, then she delivered it to Ryan's mouth.

"You do love me," she said, talking around the bite.

"I do. Very much."

Their server came by, put his hands on his hips and frowned. "You ladies didn't eat your spuds."

"We ate the ones with cheese," Jamie said. "Everything was fantastic. Truly excellent."

"I'm glad you enjoyed yourself. So? Another drink? Michael longs to make you something that would go well with our bread pudding."

"Hook us up," Jamie said. "It's our first night in Dublin. We might as well go for it."

"First time ever?"

"For me, yes." She met Ryan's eyes. "My partner was born in Ireland, but grew up in San Francisco."

"Welcome home," he said, giving Ryan a smile so bright and earnest it almost brought tears to Jamie's eyes. "How are you finding it?"

"I haven't been to Dublin in two or three years," Ryan said. "My family's in the west. But I'll come back more often to have a meal like this one."

"We're making progress," he said. "Gone are the days visitors lost weight during their Irish vacations. Will you be visiting family?"

"We've already been in Mayo for a couple of weeks. This is our vacation from our vacation."

"Ach! I'm from Sligo." He extended his hand and slapped Ryan's when she raised her own. "We're neighbors."

"We are. We don't have Sligo on our list of 'must see' places. Should we change that?"

"Not unless you want to visit my parents. They're lovely," he said, "and my mother is a fantastic cook."

"We just might do that. The Ryans aren't known for their culinary skills, but family meals feed my soul."

"As it should be," he said soberly. "Now let me go get those drinks. You need to fortify yourself to kick off your evening."

As he walked away, Jamie reached over and gripped Ryan's hand. "Have I told you how much I love it here?"

"It's great, isn't it? I hope the bread pudding's as good as the rest of the meal."

"Not here," Jamie said, gazing at her intently. "I mean Ireland. There's a friendliness that seems very genuine. At home, people in service jobs sometimes seem like they're forcing themselves to be pleasant."

"Mmm. I'm sure some of the people we encounter are putting on a front, but I get what you mean. People seem a bit more genuine."

"That's it," she agreed. "If there were a few more restaurants like this in Mayo…"

Ryan gave her a smile that had a decidedly wistful edge to it. "You'd still want to go home in August."

They were both slightly tipsy as they walked toward the Liffey to find the gay bar their friend from the hotel recommended. It had largely stopped raining, but there was a lot of moisture in the air. It wasn't cold, though, or maybe the whiskey had warmed them up from the inside.

Ryan wasn't afraid to show a little affection in public, but there were a lot of people on the streets, and many of them looked like they'd already been over-served. Young, drunk men didn't need any temptation when it came to harassing women, and she simply didn't want to have words with anyone. So when Jamie reached for her hand, she held back. "Let's wait until we get to a safe space."

"Really? You think we'll offend people?"

"No, not really. But gay sex has only been decriminalized for what? Seven years? Eight years? People aren't used to seeing much public affection on the streets—straight or gay."

Jamie looked up at her with a wicked smile. "Then we'll just have to show extra affection when we're at the pub."

"That I can do. With pleasure."

"Tell me about your history with Dublin. I'm getting the impression that you haven't been here often."

"What's given you that impression?"

"You haven't been dropping little tidbits of your personal history on me every two seconds. When we're at home, you're always telling me about your adventures in every tiny corner of the city."

"Mmm. I'd guess I've only been here…four or five times."

"Really? That's not very often for your having visited your family nearly every year of your life."

"To drive straight through is only a three hour trip, but it seems much, much farther. The first time I visited, I was with Aisling. Just the two of us." She smiled, thinking of what a production it had been to get permission to go. "We were in high school, and we were going to stay the night with Aisling's dad's sister, but you'd have thought we were going to Katmandu. My granny's still in a snit at Aunt Moira for letting us go."

Jamie laughed at that. "Knowing what you'd been up to at home, that kind of supervision must have felt like being in a straight-jacket."

"Not so much. When I was here, I got with the program pretty quickly. I let Aisling lead the way. If she wanted to fight for something, I backed her, but I wasn't the one straining at the leash."

"Because you didn't have a leash at home," Jamie said, nodding.

"Right. It wasn't a big deal to stay close to home for me. I was usually there for eight weeks. That gave me forty-four others to do as I pleased."

"So what did you and Aisling do when you came?"

"That first time?" Ryan let out a quiet chortle. "Nothing. Walked around until our feet hurt, then went to her aunt's house for dinner. Next morning, up for Mass, then back on the bus."

Jamie's eyes closed as she struggled to keep her laugh down. "That's it?"

"Yep. Aisling had been to Dublin on school and church trips, and to visit her aunt a time or two, but that was her first time without close supervision." Her smile grew as she thought of that weekend. "She was thrilled."

"I assume you grew more adventurous as the years passed?"

"A bit," Ryan admitted. "The first time we ever got truly scuttered was in Dublin. I'm amazed we found our way back to the youth hostel." A quick thought of the future brought her up short. "No daughter of ours will *ever* be allowed to be in the city on her own."

"But our sons can?" Jamie asked, her wry smirk firmly in place.

Ryan waved her fingers dismissively. "Boys create trouble. Girls have trouble foisted upon them."

A frown settled onto Jamie's face. "You had trouble?"

"Nothing bad. But if I hadn't been so totally uninterested in boys, a few of them could have got my knickers off. The last thing I recall of that night is physically holding onto Aisling while a guy tried to drag her out of a pub." She shivered, thinking about the scene. "If I'd lost her, I'd have had to go into the witness protection program. My aunt would have forgiven me—eventually. My granny? Never."

"What if Aisling had lost you?"

Ryan smiled. "Everyone would have been upset, of course, but my granny would have assured them all that whatever happened had been my fault."

Jamie looked down for a moment, and when her gaze lifted she said quietly, "She's tougher on you than I'd like, but I have more empathy for her than I used to. It's clear that she loves you desperately, baby."

"She does. I'm sure of that. But she doesn't understand me very well." She shrugged. "It's dawned on me that she might be disappointed that I'm not more like my mother—either physically or emotionally. Maybe that rankles her."

"If that's true, it's awfully sad," Jamie said, looking like she was close to tears. "She's missing out on so much by longing for something she can't have."

They were just a couple of streets away, and as the crowd of people on the sidewalks grew larger, Ryan grasped Jamie's hand. She didn't honestly think they had anything to worry about in showing they were a couple, but even if there was a slight risk of some taunting she was willing to risk it for the security of keeping Jamie close in a crowd.

"It's on the next street, I think," Ryan said as they moved through the crowd, many of the voices American from the accents she caught. "Yup. Just up ahead."

"Where all of those people are standing?"

"Uh-huh. Big crowd for Pride." When they threaded through the throng, Ryan said, "I hope everyone's smoking out here because they can't smoke inside."

"If you can smoke in Killala, you can smoke in Dublin. Damn. We've only had our smoking ban for two years now, but I've almost forgotten what it's like to be in a smoke-filled room."

Ryan grasped her hand and stepped back out of the crush of people trying to enter. "How much does it mean to you to go inside?"

Jamie looked up and locked on Ryan's gaze for a few moments. "If you're uncomfortable, I'm happy to go right back to the hotel."

She chewed on her lip for a second, uncertain. "I want to be around gay people, but I truly hate being in a noisy, smoky room."

Jamie tilted her chin to look up at the sky. "It's not raining. Let's stay here for a little while and people-watch. We can be gay adjacent." Smiling, she puckered up. "Everyone around us is gay, I think. Time for a kiss?"

"Definitely." She bent over slightly to deliver a soft, sweet kiss to Jamie's lips. "Being gay adjacent is just perfect. Thanks for understanding."

"That's my job," Jamie said, pulling Ryan down for another kiss. "And I truly love my job."

After a delicious breakfast of porridge, fresh cream, and honey, Ryan was ready to get going.

"I'm so glad we came here," Jamie said.

She made eye contact with the server, asking for more coffee. Ryan watched her give her plate a nudge, moving it to the center of the table. She'd eaten most of her baked eggs, nearly all of her bacon, and every bite of a currant scone. It must have been good, since Ryan could see her fighting her instinct to keep nibbling. "Why's that?"

"I like the city, and it gives me a different view of Ireland."

"Mmm. I like it well enough, but I like the wilder parts of Ireland. Dublin's a little too civilized for me."

"I think I like civilization more than you do," Jamie said, wrinkling up her nose.

"So what's on your civilized agenda? Will watching the parade do it for you?"

"Nope. I scheduled a walking tour for three. I think we'll have time to see the whole parade and get a little culture, too."

"What's the culture?"

"I think this is a good day to learn more about James Joyce. Ready?"

"As I'll ever be."

The parade was...cute. Jamie hated to have such a big city view of it, but San Francisco's parade was so many times larger it hardly seemed like the same type of event.

Dublin's parade was similar, conceptually, with lots of floats and affinity groups, and thousands of rainbow flags affixed to people, pets, and vehicles. But it wasn't as aggressively sexual as San Francisco's, which was actually kind of nice. Jamie tried to be as sex positive as possible, but she didn't think she'd ever be comfortable with some of the things she'd seen at Pride. She definitely didn't want to censor it, but she would never display her own sexual interests for the entire world to see.

It seemed to her that the Irish were a little more like her. Not prudish, but also not needing to reveal to the world what flipped their switch.

The parade had started nearly on time, and even though there were some long pauses and a bit of confusion, it moved along much more briskly than Jamie expected.

"This is fun," she said, grasping Ryan's hand as a group of parents and their kids marched by.

"Yeah," she said, grinning widely. "We'll be able to bring our kids to the parade and not have to explain some pretty unexplainable stuff."

Batting her eyes, Jamie said, "Like when you had to school me in pony play?"

Ryan tossed her head back as she let out a hearty laugh. "I still remember the look on your face when I told you how people kept those long tails on."

"Explaining horse-tailed butt plugs isn't something I'm looking forward to. When we bring our kids we'll have to march with the Episcopalians and shield their little eyes from the sex stuff."

"I saw all kinds of crazy stuff when I was a kid growing up in San Francisco."

Jamie looked up at her and waited for her to finish her thought. When nothing more came, she said, "Are you implying that you're well-adjusted?"

"Good point. We'll stick like glue to the group from the Church of Ireland. Our kids can find out about all the wacky stuff on their own."

"Thank god we don't have to worry about that for a few years."

"Fewer if I get pregnant in the next few months…" Ryan flashed that, "You know you can't refuse me" smile, but Jamie wasn't having it.

"You act like you can get pregnant accidentally. Given that's not the case for us, this has to be a unanimous vote, and at this point it's not."

Her smile was still beaming when she said, "If you'll stay I won't complain about the house we build. If you want an indoor pool…" She acted like she was firmly zipping her lips together.

"Oh, right," Jamie said, laughing at the ridiculousness of that promise. "You might convince yourself not to complain, but I'd still have to put up with the anguished looks when I added something you thought was frivolous."

"I never said I was perfect. Just *nearly* perfect." She put her arms around Jamie's shoulders and pulled her close so she was nestled up against Ryan's chest. Ryan bent her head and whispered, "We've made more progress on getting a house in Ireland than we have in San Francisco. Maybe your inner voice really wants to stay."

Jamie grasped her hands and pressed them together. "My inner voice wants to follow through on the reservations we have for our return flight, then send you off to get your PhD at Cal. Once you're Doctor O'Flaherty, we can begin negotiating." She turned her head as far as she could, making sure Ryan could see her eyes. "That's my vote, and I don't think it's going to change."

The festivities were over by two, giving them plenty of time to walk across town to the "James Joyce in Dublin" tour. Ryan had not only skipped reading *Ulysses*, she hadn't read any of Joyce's shorter, more accessible works, and she didn't have any plans to. But Jamie seemed very excited about learning more about him, and Ryan wasn't averse to learning more about Dublin, which she was shockingly ignorant of for someone who'd been to Ireland close to twenty times.

Even though the weather was fine, only the two of them showed up. But their guide, a young PhD student named Liam, didn't seem put off by the poor showing. Over the course of two hours, he led them through the streets of Dublin, stopping at a dozen spots mentioned in *Ulysses*. Jamie elbowed her when she admitted to Liam that she'd never been tempted to read the book, but there was no sense in lying. Jamie's interest was enough to cover both of them, and she peppered Liam with so many questions he must have thought she was a direct descendent of the Joyce family.

Some members of the rowdy gay crowd wound up on the same street where Leopold Bloom had bought some soap. Liam had to raise his voice to be heard over the partiers, while Ryan gave herself a pat on the back for not reading a huge book that made a big deal out of something so dumb. But Jamie's eyes danced with interest. "Can I run in and buy a couple of bars?"

"Of course," Liam said, his Dublin accent softer and rounder than many of the locals. "We're in no hurry a'tal."

Ryan watched the two of them enter the store, certain they could spend the day talking about the book. She was just as certain she'd prefer to go to a local pub and have a pint. Or two. No matter how deep their love was, she and Jamie would never agree that literature was a keystone to a full life. Some of their differences were truly irreconcilable. But she was perfectly fine with that. Actually, having parts of each of them that the other could never understand kept things interesting, and keeping their relationship interesting was one of the keys to happiness.

Early on Monday morning, Jamie stowed their bags with a guy who looked like he might sell them to the highest bidder. She truly didn't want to lose her laptop, but she also didn't want to carry it around on a tour bus, so she accepted the little ticket and hoped for the best. Not long after they stepped outside, a white bus pulled up in front of the hotel, and when the doors opened a friendly female voice called out, "Would ye be looking for the Newgrange tour?"

Jamie poked her head in, noting a man, thin and pale, in the driver's seat, with the front passenger seat occupied by a fleshy, bright-eyed woman with hair dyed as black as coal. She might have naturally had skin the color of alabaster, or the foundation she wore might have accented it, but the contrast between her hair and her skin was shockingly stark.

"We definitely are," Jamie said, then climbed in. "Thanks for picking us up."

"All part of the service. Mary O'Farrell here. You're Jamie or Siobhán?"

"I'm Jamie, and the tall person behind me is Siobhán. It's nice to meet you."

"The same. Have you girls had breakfast? It's a long ride."

"We have," Jamie said. "We're ready to go."

"Sit anywhere," she said, waving her hand. "One more stop, and we'll be off."

There were only four other people on the bus, filling the first two seats behind the driver. Jamie liked a little room, so she walked back a few rows and slid in. "You don't mind if I take the window seat, do you?"

"Nope. I prefer to stick my feet in the aisle."

The bus, a small one, shuddered a little when it started up again, then they crawled through the narrow streets before stopping at another hotel and picking up the last of the guests—who sat right behind the other people in the front.

They all spent a moment introducing themselves, with Jamie surprised to learn all of the other passengers were Irish, mostly from the south, around Cork and Kilkenny.

"You're the only American," Ryan said, sticking out her tongue. "That goofy accent of yours is really going to stand out today."

From that moment until they reached Newgrange, a good hour's drive, Mary barely paused for breath. She started at the dawn of human habitation on the island, only about eight thousand years ago, and proceeded, in great detail, to bring them up to five thousand years ago, finishing her spiel as they turned at a sign indicating the car park was just ahead. "What timing!" Jamie whispered.

"Practice, practice, practice," Ryan said, chuckling. "She's probably been doing this since her hair was naturally black."

"You're not going to do that to yours, are you?" Jamie tugged on some of the dark strands. "I love your natural color but…"

Ryan gave her a look that questioned her sanity. "Can you imagine me going to have my hair touched up every couple of weeks? If I don't like the way it looks when it's grey, I'll wear a hat."

Jamie's head was filled with images of Ryan in various hats, all of which she looked pretty darned cute in, but as they made a final turn the clouds parted to allow a bright golden ray of sunshine to hit the neolithic era mound, making her breath catch in her throat. "More perfect timing!" she squealed, gripping Ryan's arm.

"Epic," she agreed, always less verbal when something truly impressed her.

"I can't believe you've never been here before. It's magical, and we're not even off the bus."

"The list of places I haven't been in Ireland is much longer than the ones I've seen. You keep forgetting I'm a culchie."

"Some culchie," Jamie grumbled. The bus let them off at a visitor's center, where they spent just a minute or two, with Mary cheerily telling the ticket taker that she had only eight guests this morning.

After walking a short distance and crossing the bridge over the Boyne, they got on another bus that drove them up to the site, with Mary continuing to talk.

"I hope you're all already planning your next trip, so if you can manage it, come again during the winter solstice. You'll be here with thousands of others, all hoping for the chance to see a bit of sun streaming into the chamber."

Quietly, Ryan said, "I'm good. I can see the sun any time."

If Ryan had ever liked crowds, her affection for them had evaporated after they'd been carjacked. Jamie loved to be in a sea of people, doing something unique, but she was quite sure she'd have to go to Carnival in Rio, an item on her bucket list, alone. Ryan would probably like seeing the pretty women in elaborate costumes, but that wouldn't trump her aversion to throngs of people.

They exited the bus, finding only about ten other people exploring. *Perfect.* Mary kept talking, which would have been overkill if she hadn't really known her stuff. But she had the whole group listening attentively as they gathered around. "This mound was created at roughly the same time as the great pyramid of Giza," she said, "and about a thousand years before Stonehenge, those Johnny-come-latelies," she added, punctuating her words with a merry laugh.

They followed her into the dark interior chamber, but before they'd gone five feet Ryan patted Jamie on the back and exited. Sighing, Jamie followed her out. "Too claustrophobic in there?"

She shrugged. "I guess." She flicked her hand towards the entrance. "Go on back. I can tell Mary has charmed you."

Jamie paused for just a moment. "Sure?" she asked, already starting to edge back to the entrance.

"Positive. I'll walk around out here and enjoy the sun." She tilted her face up and smiled. "I don't believe in wasting a moment of Irish sun. We might not see it again, you know. We're only going to be here for another six weeks."

"Be back soon." Jamie gripped her hand, then took off, not wanting to miss another minute.

After investigating every nook, the group exited. Ryan was near the big blocks of stone that guarded the entrance, squatting down so her face was close to the intricate decoration. Jamie approached from the side, and ruffled her hair. "It was pretty cool in there, but you didn't miss a lot. No one knows exactly what the site was used for, but it was a burial chamber at one point."

"I love this triskelion," Ryan said, running her fingers over the grooves of the three interlocking swirls.

"Mary says some people think it represents the sun, the moon and the earth."

"Nah," Ryan said, shaking her head.

Jamie backed up a few feet, took her camera out and started taking snaps, catching Ryan in her "professor mode." Brow furrowed, eyes slightly narrowed, she said, "I think these two interlocking ones are the parents, and the one that comes from between them is the child." She'd noticed Jamie was taking her picture, and turned to smile. Getting up, she dusted off her knees and said, "Let me take a few of you."

Jamie handed over the camera and posed, wishing someone would offer to take a couple of them together. But the thin crowd didn't provide many options.

Jamie put her arm around Ryan's back and led her away so they were completely alone. After walking around to the back of the site, where it looked like a simple mound covered in grass, they stopped and looked at it for a while. "I love seeing places like this," she said. "I like to imagine how long it took for them to get the idea, how long they argued about how to design it, and all of the fights they had." She laughed at the thought. "You know someone was pissed that he was doing more than the other guys."

"For sure. But there might have been a big boss, like a king who lopped off people's heads if they complained. I've found that's a way to gain compliance."

"That sounds like you," Jamie agreed, pulling Ryan down for a kiss to her cheek. "Do you like stuff like this?"

"A lot. I think of how little people knew back then. Not knowledge you can gain from experience, but facts. It's hard for me to imagine having to figure everything out, you know? No books, which wouldn't have helped much since no one but the monks knew how to write. If you didn't learn something from your parents, you had to figure it out. Think of how tiring that would be!"

"I went on a great tour of the British Museum once," Jamie said. "I was amazed to learn how static human development had been. Tens of thousands of years using one or two basic tools. Life must have been such a struggle that they didn't have time to create. They just made a new stone ax when the old one wasn't sharp enough to do the job and got on with it."

"I like living now," Ryan said, draping an arm around Jamie's shoulders. "If I'd been here five thousand years ago, I'd be working my butt off hauling these big stones up the river, and wouldn't have you in my hut when I punched out at the end of the day."

Jamie put her hand on Ryan's chest and gazed at her. "How'd you know they brought the stones up the river?"

Her mouth quirked into a sweet smile. "The highway hadn't been built yet. And there weren't many gas stations around, even if they had 4x4s to drag the stones up the hill…"

"Funny girl. I should have assumed you'd figure this out without Mary's help."

"Just makes sense. Rivers were the roads of ancient times."

Jamie took her hand as they continued to walk. "Some of that ancient Celtic knowledge must have seeped into your DNA."

"Most likely," Ryan agreed. "Your understanding of biology is perfection itself."

"Back on the bus," Jamie said. "We're going to jump a few centuries into the present, grab some lunch, then head back to Dublin."

The bus stopped in a small town, its narrow, winding High Street revealing a few small shops and a pub. As the group left the bus, Ryan grasped Jamie by the sleeve and slowed her down. "I made plans for a late lunch," she said. "If you're not starving, you might want to just have a beer." She looked up at the flaking paint that advertised the name of the place, also noting the sour, stale beer scent that wafted out when the first member of their group opened the door. "I guarantee we'll have better food this afternoon."

"Given how this place smells, that won't be a hard promise to keep."

Even though the food looked dismal, their fellow travelers didn't complain about it. But that didn't surprise Ryan. You could almost always count on the Irish to compliment the food and the service of even the worst places, so long as they were treated politely. Everyone would complain when they were alone, but the innate sense of being a good guest truly might have been a part of the Irish genome.

It was almost three when Mary dropped them at the hotel, amidst cheery farewells and many enthusiastic hand shakes. "How much did you tip her?" Ryan asked, laughing a little as they entered the hotel. "Mary truly didn't want to let you go."

"Tip? Was I supposed to tip?" Jamie stopped and stared at Ryan, open-mouthed. "I assumed the fare was all inclusive."

Ryan turned and started for the door, determined to catch the bus at the corner. But a cackling laugh made her stop and slowly turn to give Jamie a scowl. "Very funny," she grumbled.

"When I fail to tip a woman who's spent the better part of her day, and all of her voice, filling my head with facts and figures, you have my permission to take me in for a neurological evaluation. And yes, she was probably surprised at the amount. But she was sweet."

"She was sweet. And smart. My favorite combination."

"We're supposed to meet the owner of our condo at four to get the keys. Should I call him to say we might be late?"

"I think so. I bet we're not finished before five. And we have to dress up a bit."

"Dress up?" Jamie asked. "You made plans at a place we have to dress up?"

"Not dressy-dressy. But you'll feel out of place in your running shoes." She made a face. "The jeans should go too. And the rain jacket."

"Is there an Irish queen I don't know about?"

"Negative. But I know you like to fit in, and that means leather shoes and a proper coat. You brought one, didn't you?"

"In addition to tipping, I will always have a proper coat when I'm on vacation. Now I'm going to have to unpack our stuff here in the lobby, and get dressed in that tiny bathroom. This lunch had better be good."

Properly shod, with nice blouses and slacks, and with only one of them wearing a brightly-colored rain jacket, Ryan led the way down Grafton Street, heading for St. Stephen's Green.

"I'm excited to be going out somewhere nice," Jamie said. She grasped Ryan's arm, but found it unyielding.

"Uhm, it's not a big deal, but we stick out when we walk that way. That's kinda European."

Jamie stared at her, puzzled. "One—we held hands and even kissed yesterday. And two—aren't we in Europe?"

"It's Continental," Ryan clarified. She shrugged, looking a little embarrassed. "I know it shouldn't bother me, but I don't like to have people giving us double-takes—which they have been."

Jamie was fairly sure that was because her partner was strikingly pretty, very tall, and was wearing a jacket bright enough to be seen from a distant star, but she kept her view to herself. "I don't want to make you uncomfortable, baby. We'll act like sisters."

"It bothers me that it bothers me," she said, grumbling softly to herself.

"I'm sorry, sweetheart." She started to reach for Ryan's hand, then stopped herself. "Do you think people recognize us from…?"

"Yes," she said, snapping the word off crisply. "I still get funny looks when I walk around outside Noe. People see me, then their heads jerk up like puppets. For a second, they think they know me. Then they realize I'm famous, but I'm gone by the time they figure it out."

"I'm sorry, Ryan," she said, aching to touch her, but not wanting to further irritate her. "I know how much that bothers you."

"It's draining," she said, her voice quieter now, more resigned. "I should stop bitching about it. It's not like anyone actually hurts me. They're just…"

"They just react, honey. The same way you would if you saw someone you thought you knew."

"Yeah, I guess." She was walking so fast Jamie had to hustle to keep up, but after turning onto another street she slowed, then waited for an ornately dressed man to open the door to a stately hotel.

Trying to lighten the mood, Jamie said, "Ahh… My people," as she purposefully did a full turn, taking in the sumptuous lobby.

That brought a smile to Ryan's tense face, and she held up a finger before peeling off to speak to someone at the front desk. "Right this way," she said. "You're finally getting the kind of lunch you'd eat every day if we had the right amount of servants."

They entered a beautiful, serene, clubby room, richly appointed in velvet covered chairs, small dark tables and generous sofas. Large Chinese rugs covered some of the dark wood floor, creating smaller conversation areas.

A woman in a perfectly tailored dark grey suit approached, beaming a smile. "Welcome. Will you be joining us for tea?"

"We will," Ryan said, "O'Flaherty."

Jamie could feel a smile tug at her lips. Ryan almost always revealed a little Irish flair when she pronounced her last name, but it was stronger today. The "A" was very broad, very cute.

After the woman ticked their names off a list, she picked up menus and escorted them to a spot that was just perfect. A cushy sofa faced an interior courtyard, and an upholstered chair sat at a right angle to the sofa. The furniture was arranged so they'd face only the window, not having to look at anyone else if they chose not to. "This is lovely," Ryan said, giving the woman one of her always charming smiles.

"We have a few options, which you'll note," the woman said. "Other than that, all you need do is enjoy yourselves."

"We can handle that," Ryan said. "We're quite good at it."

As the woman left, Jamie picked up the menu and said, "Full tea with champagne." Closing it, she dropped it to her lap. "That didn't take long, did it?"

"I'll copy you. You always pick the best things."

"You want champagne?"

"Not really. But I know you hate to drink alone."

"I don't hate it a bit. Feel free to stick with tea."

"Then I shall." Ryan put her menu down, then removed her jacket and folded it into a small bundle. "I look like I was out running and dashed in here for a bite."

"You're pretty enough to be able to get away with just about anything. People stare at your face, honey. They don't have time to get all the way down to your jacket."

"Um-hmm." She looked up when another be-suited man approached, ordered for both of them, then spread her arms out across the back of the sofa and crossed her legs.

Jamie watched her, considering her contradictions. She hated to be stared at, yet a part of her went out of her way to act like she owned the place. Her arms were proportional to her height, but considerably longer than most womens', and having them stretched out that way made them look even longer. Not to mention that most straight women didn't sit with an ankle over a knee in a very fancy hotel. All part of the mix of "Ryanness" that Jamie was sure would always confound her. Thankfully, she found almost all of the contradictions adorable.

"It was very thoughtful of you to arrange for this," Jamie said.

Ryan shrugged. "I brought your father here. He shouldn't get to go someplace you haven't been."

"Don't blow off my compliment," she said, reaching over to grip her knee. "I mean it sincerely. You know I love to have tea, and you found a place to make it happen."

Ryan's head tilted a little, and her gaze seemed to drive right into Jamie's soul. "I know you mean it, and I'm very happy I'm able to do things like this every once in a while." She took in a breath and closed her eyes briefly as she let it out. "Since I spent a little time with him recently, I've been thinking about your father more than normal. I keep thinking of the day he said you'd grow to resent me if you couldn't have things like this."

"That's not true!"

"I know," Ryan soothed. "I think I knew it even then, although he scared the crap out of me at the time. It worried me for a while." Surprisingly, she reached over and took Jamie's hand, kissed the back of it while looking deeply into her eyes, then held it tenderly, not letting go even when their server approached with their tea. When he left, Ryan added, "I know you'd love me just as much as you would have if he'd stopped you from having access to your money, but you're used to things like this. It would have been hard for you to give them up completely."

"You're worth a lot more than tea and finger sandwiches, sweetheart." The waiter returned, bearing a three-tiered silver tray, loaded with dainty sandwiches, scones and petit fours. "But I'm glad I can have both."

The tiny little sandwiches weren't very filling, but they kept them coming, silently stocking the empty spots on the tray as quickly as Ryan demolished them.

She'd just finished off the last of the cucumber ones, and held up a hand to stop the server from adding more. "I think I've had my fill of cucumber. Somebody needs to tell these people to add a few slices of ham or bacon to these things."

"This is supposed to be light," Jamie said. "But after we make some progress on those tiny cakes, I won't want dinner."

"Mmm. Then we can stop at a curry place for me." She slid her hand over and gently tapped on Jamie's leg. "You know, I've mentioned your father several times in the last couple of weeks, and you give me a polite nod to show you heard me, then change the subject. Is that the new normal?"

"Mmm. I think so," she said, taking a sip of her champagne while looking at Ryan over the rim of the glass. "You know, you can have a regular drink. I bet they make a cocktail that will go with the sweet part of our meal."

"Seriously? You honestly don't want to talk about him at all?"

"Pretty seriously," she said, breaking eye contact. "I'm also serious about having another glass of champagne. Want to join me?"

That night, Ryan traded places with Jamie as she exited the bath. She was about to slide into bed when she saw a rough-hewn iron triskelion lying on her pillow. She was sure they'd been together every second of their trip, but somehow Jamie had managed to slip into the gift shop and buy the one thing Ryan had seen that appealed to her. Not only that, she'd bought the most rustic of the representations, and, knowing how gift shops worked, she was sure they had some made of twenty-four carat gold. As she gazed at it, she thought of how very thoughtful the gift was. Buying the thing the recipient would most appreciate, rather than what you'd choose for yourself was pure Jamie. "Best girlfriend ever," she called out loudly.

That earned her a quiet laugh. "You've got that title sewn up, sweetums, but I'll gladly take second place."

Chapter Thirteen

Waking to a stream of sunlight pouring into the window from the nearly-closed curtains, Jamie slapped her hand behind herself, landing on Ryan's sturdy thigh. "What a nice surprise," she murmured. "I love waking up and having you next to me." She rolled over and put her hand on Ryan's belly. "Why are you here?"

Smirking, Ryan said, "When two ladies love each other very much, sometimes they sleep together—"

After clapping her hand over Ryan's mouth, Jamie gave it another try. "Why aren't you out running?"

Ryan pried the hand away and kissed it. "I woke up hungry and horny." Her eyebrows moved up and down suggestively. "I didn't want to miss sex if you felt the same, or a big breakfast if you didn't."

Reaching up with a finger, Jamie tapped at Ryan's nose. "Given how hungry I am, I bet you're about to eat the sheets. Let's go have that breakfast, then we can come back here and work it off."

Ryan rolled off the bed in a single, graceful move. "I was crazy to let you talk me into skipping dinner. Remind me that finger sandwiches and scones can't fuel me for over fifteen hours."

Jamie got up and took Ryan's hand, hoping they could manage to fit into the condo's relatively large shower. "Not a problem. Although I can't imagine having you be my afternoon tea partner very often. I think I should continue to have my mom fill that role in my life."

"I enjoyed it," Ryan said as she slipped into the shower to adjust the water. "But I prefer an afternoon snack of a cup of tea and a biscuit or two."

"Yeah. You're all about a biscuit or two."

The day was blessedly warm, with skies so blue you couldn't help but stare at them. They sat together on a bench in St. Stephen's Green, a lovely, formal park right at the end of Grafton Street, to people watch and let their massive breakfast digest. They'd both eaten so much neither of them was in the mood for love any longer, which Ryan had anticipated. She'd purposefully mentioned sex ahead of breakfast, but Jamie hadn't been tempted. Either she truly wasn't interested when she had her period, or she couldn't divest herself of the old messages that most bodily functions were decidedly un-sexual. They were going to have to work to keep from passing on those messages to their kids, a task Ryan was probably going to have to prioritize.

It was a regular Monday morning, but the streets seemed quieter than they should have been, given they were in a thriving metropolis. Maybe people started work later in the city than they did in Mayo.

"If you want to sit and read, I could go put on my running clothes, and go for a jog," Ryan said. "I bet you'd be very happy here for an hour or two."

Jamie took a long look at her, then barely nodded her head. "Why don't you let me read to you for a little while."

Even though she would have never suggested the idea, the fact that it was novel caught Ryan's attention. "I'm in. What do you have?"

"Well…" Jamie reached into her bag and took out what looked like a fresh book. "I'm just getting into this one." She held it up. "Do you know much about Oscar Wilde?"

"Only that he went to prison for being gay."

Jamie waggled her hand. "It was more complicated than that, but that's kind of true. His mistake was loving an unstable guy with a bat-shit crazy father." She fanned the pages of the book in front of Ryan. "I could read the whole thing to you."

"How about a few passages," she said, winking. "I'll take whatever has caught your interest."

She paged through the book carefully, giving the task her usual studious approach. "This part made me think about something you said yesterday," she said when she found what she'd been looking for. "I'm certain you'll agree with this snippet. 'In old days men had the rack. Now they have the press. That is an improvement certainly. But it is still very bad, and wrong, and demoralizing.'" She looked up and met Ryan's eyes for a moment. "He had a tough time with the tabloids of his day."

"When did he live? I can't place him on a timeline."

"A hundred years ago. He was sentenced to prison in 1895. Funny how things don't change much, huh?"

"Not much indeed." She crossed her ankle over a knee and set her elbow on her leg, leaning over slightly. "What do you mean when you say it's more complicated than him going to jail for being gay?"

"Mmm, he was having an affair with a young lord, and the guy's father sent Wilde a note, calling him a sodomite. Wilde sued the father for libel and…" She shook her head. "Bad idea. Especially when you're a well known sodomite."

"Huh." She felt a chill settle onto her body, even though it was a blessedly warm day. "That could have been me."

"What?"

Ryan turned and looked at Jamie for a moment, her gaze roaming around her face. "I could have pushed your father to the point where he did something to hurt me." She shrugged. "It wouldn't have taken much."

"But he obviously likes you now. He wouldn't have called you for advice—or whatever he wanted when you came here to see him."

"Right." Ryan kept her eyes on her for another half of a minute, still amazed that she refused to talk about the visit, or her father in general—at all. That was very much not like Jamie, and Ryan truly couldn't figure out what the silence meant. But those cool green eyes showed not even a hint of interest in diving into the topic, so Ryan let it drop.

"I think your dad does like me. Or at least he doesn't dislike me. But I'm always puzzled by how many people have had their lives ruined because of being gay. It's such a silly thing to hate about someone, isn't it?"

"Very silly." Jamie put her arm around Ryan, then eased it off to rest on the back of the bench. "I think I've made progress with your granny, don't you?"

"Definitely," Ryan said, smiling at the slightly concerned expression on her face. "She's not going to like it when we get married—if we're ever allowed to. But I think that will be partly because we'll never be able to get married in the Catholic church unless something cataclysmic happens, which it won't. Actually, I can't imagine what would be cataclysmic enough for that kind of change to happen."

"Not my circus. Definitely not my monkeys." She put her hand on Ryan's leg, keeping the affectionate pat kind of sisterly. "But if you get to the point where you think there's a god that my grandfather can commune with, we could get married in two shakes of a lamb's tail, as you like to say."

"I rather doubt *that.* Even if we only had a religious service, it would take planning." She didn't add that she wasn't comfortable getting married when Jim wouldn't be invited. If Jamie ever welcomed him back into her life, she'd kick herself for shutting him out.

Nodding, Jamie said, "You're a tough one to pin down, O'Flaherty. But I'm going to keep working on you."

The temperature warmed up to a toasty seventy-five, and everyone who could take to the streets had done so. Given they were in a touristy area, most of the people they saw were visitors, but it was fun walking around at a slow pace, just getting into the flow of city life.

Ryan didn't know the town well at all, but Dublin was small enough to be able to walk around without plans and not get too far off the beaten path. "Is walking around enough excitement for you?" she asked.

Jamie looked up, and a sated smile showed itself. "This is perfect." She slid her arm around Ryan's and hugged her briefly. "I read about all sorts of things we could have done today, but I didn't want to be tied to a schedule. Being with you is all I need."

"Let's walk to the Ha'penny Bridge. We haven't crossed the Liffey yet. Oh! There's a new bridge close by. We can go over on one and come back on the other."

"You're a wild one," Jamie said, giving her another squeeze.

They strolled around for a long time, not talking much. Ryan found herself a little quiet in general, her mind working overtime when she wasn't running or helping on one of the projects. Without making a firm plan, she realized they were close to Christ Church Cathedral. As they got near the nearly ancient building, she noticed small groups, probably on walking tours.

"Do you think the bells ring on the hour?" Jamie asked. "I can't believe people are that desperate for entertainment."

"You never know what a Dub might find interesting. They're quite odd," she said, putting her accent on thick.

There were a few benches near the church, and a couple got up when their baby started to cry. Ryan tugged Jamie along and they grabbed the seats before anyone else made a move. "Nice," Ryan said. "We can move from park to park, just sitting and watching the world go by."

"That's not your normal, but you know I'm happy to do nothing. The church is awfully impressive," Jamie said, tilting her head back to take a good look at it.

"Sure is. It's yours now, you know," Ryan said, trying to temper the sour note that sometimes infused her voice when she thought of the English ransacking the land of her ancestors.

"Mine?" The bench faced away from the church, and Jamie turned all the way around and stared at the building for a minute. "It's Anglican?"

"Church of Ireland. Doesn't that make it Anglican?"

"Uh-huh. They're part of the Anglican Communion." She turned back around. "It was Catholic?"

"Sure was," Ryan said, nodding. "Just for four or five hundred years, though. Your ancestors liked it, so they took it." She couldn't help but shake her head. "Took St. Patrick's too. I don't think the English had to build a single feckin' church after they kicked our butts. Just took 'em."

"I was going to ask about that," Jamie said, looking a little tentative. "I thought there would be all sorts of impressive Catholic churches, but I haven't seen any."

"Aren't any. Well, there's the Pro Cathedral, but it's not all that old. I mean, it's old for America, but it's not old for Ireland."

"To the victor go the spoils. But I don't think you're right about my particular ancestors taking the churches. The Smiths and the Evanses were doing just fine in England. I know my relatives—on both sides—all the way back to the fifteenth century, and not one of them was born or died in Ireland." She bumped up against Ryan with her shoulder. "I checked my mom's genealogy books after we got together."

Letting out a sigh, Ryan said, "It shouldn't bother me. For god's sake, it's been an awfully long time, and we've battled back to be a prosperous country." She made eye contact with Jamie, who was giving her a look filled with understanding. "It still rankles."

"I know. Reading that book about Irish history was sobering. How can you call yourself a civilized people when you have to destroy other cultures to enhance your own."

Ryan took her hand and held it tenderly. "If your ancestors were anything like you, they would have been having a peace march when Cromwell was over here kicking our butts."

"That's a nice thought. Unlikely, but a nice thought. Given that my American relatives didn't mind paying people next to nothing to work in shockingly dangerous coal mines, I have a feeling my family has gone along with whatever lines their purses. But maybe I had some relatives way back when who said, 'No way! Those lovely Irish people are no threat to us.'" She turned and put her lips close to Ryan's ear. "If they'd known how gorgeous the Irish girls were, they would have hustled right over here, but only to marry, not conquer."

Ryan turned before Jamie could move and placed a gentle kiss to her lips. "You've done both."

"Not technically," she said, laughing a little. "But I'm going to wait you out. One day you'll make an honest woman out of me."

"I will that. I assume 'President' Bush will start pushing for same sex marriage any minute now." She stuck out her tongue, making a face. "That was really hard to spit out. I believe in respecting the presidency, but boy, it's hard to believe only six months of that dummy's term is over."

"No politics, please. I'll happily stay here for four years, just to avoid having you grumble the whole time."

"I'll shut up." Ryan made her face comply, showing a sunny smile. "Maybe we'll bring your grandfather over and we can get married right here. I can secretly reclaim the cathedral for the Catholics—at least for one day."

"I'm more Catholic than you are, pal," Jamie said, smiling up at her. "I believe in more of the dogma, and I go to Mass more."

"But I've got the history. And we believe in that a lot more than the silly dogma."

By persistence alone, Jamie managed to snag a dinner reservation at one of Dublin's Michelin-starred restaurants. They had to dine the moment the place opened, but that was what Ryan preferred, making the evening much more palatable for her.

The place was really top-notch, with graceful, efficient service, along with a menu that featured beautifully cooked fish. Their entrees had been placed before them, and Jamie was just about to take her first bite when one of their many servers hustled over to the table to set down a small bowl of boiled potatoes dusted with fresh parsley. Jamie met Ryan's eyes and burst out laughing, drawing a few looks from some of the tables nearby. "I can't believe I did that," she whispered, feeling heat infuse her cheeks. "But that was just too damned funny!"

"I'm not kidding about the potatoes," she said, laughing a little bit as she put one on her plate and took a bite. "Nothing special," she pronounced. "Just the way we like them."

Their condo was over a mile away from the restaurant, but it was only seven when they'd finished dinner, allowing them to walk home in full sunlight. They walked along with the sun hitting them right in the eyes, with Jamie commenting, "I'm not about to say it's too sunny, but I'm tempted."

"Ooo. Don't ever complain about the sun in Ireland. Every ray is precious. Without sun, we couldn't grow potatoes."

"I had fun tonight," Jamie said, reflexively reaching for Ryan's arm, then recalling that she was surprisingly skittish about showing affection in what had to be the most open-minded part of Ireland. "Actually, this trip has been pretty perfect for me. How about you?"

"All good," Ryan said, smiling down at her.

"And you're ready to go back. Right?"

"Um…" She had the grace to look a little guilty when she nodded. "I want to help Aisling, and I'd love to do some sightseeing with my da and aunt. They'll be leaving soon, you know."

"I do know," Jamie said soberly. "But I'm not quite ready to go back."

Looking stricken, Ryan said, "Are you hating being here for so long?"

Ignoring her qualms about touching in public, Jamie gripped Ryan's arm firmly. "I've told you twenty times that I love being here." She met Ryan's troubled gaze and added, "If you were able to relax and goof around a little I'd be perfectly happy. Gleeful, actually. But as soon as we get home you'll be working at the pub full time, and that's not fun for me. So I'd rather keep you out of Mayo for a little longer for purely selfish reasons."

"Mmm." Ryan stuffed her hands in the tiny pockets of her dress slacks, not commenting for a couple of minutes. "I want you to be happy," she finally said. "But I also want to be there for my family." She lifted her gaze and met Jamie's eyes. "Isn't there a compromise we can work out?"

"I'm sure there is, but I'm not sure we'll be able to find it."

"Why's that?"

"Because there are some..." She thought for a moment, trying to make sure she used the right term. "There are some givens we have to take into account."

"Givens?"

"Mmm-hmm. There are some facts that I don't think are going to change." Ryan was already looking a little perturbed, but Jamie wasn't going to let her derail the conversation. They had to face facts. "Your need to pitch in and help every member of your family, no matter how large or small the task, is just that—a need. And that need takes precedence over me." Ryan had a wounded look on her face, and Jamie rushed to finish her thought. "In a perfect world, you'd make everyone happy. But when you can't, you do the work first, then devote whatever time is leftover to leisure, which is where I fit in. Work's always at the pinnacle."

Looking grim, Ryan's gaze shifted to the pavement as they continued to walk. Jamie didn't try to press her point, letting her partner think about it for as long as she needed to. Finally, she nodded decisively. "You're going to have to take over."

"Take over?"

"Uh-huh. You're going to have to tell me I'm not allowed to go to the pub or whatever task I try to add to my list. You could do that like..." She stared into the distance as they waited on a stop light. "Every three days or so. Would that work?"

"Um, sure. That would work great if the goal is to make me the boss of our relationship. We'd probably be happy for a year or two before the resentment got to be overpowering." She looked at Ryan's glum expression. "Is that what you want?"

"Of course not." She was quiet for a few seconds, then said, "I want us both to want the same things. But we don't. If I do what I want, you're unhappy. So I guess I'd rather have you be the boss than have you be unhappy."

"That's not going to cut it. This is a big discussion, honey, and we're not going to figure it out today. So let's start with this week, okay? I need a few more days where I get to do the things I want without first guessing whether you'll be bored to death."

"You've been doing that?" The look on her face was kind of priceless. Clueless, but priceless.

"Yes, sweetheart. Do you think I wanted to take a blacksmithing class?"

"You said you liked it!"

"I did," Jamie soothed. "But mostly because I could see how much fun you were having. Don't you do that for me?"

"High tea," she said immediately. "The whole thing is—" She must have been on the verge of saying something truly insulting, because she didn't even try to finish the sentence. "I had a nice time watching you swoon over those silly lettuce sandwiches but…"

"Watercress, but point taken." She grasped Ryan's hand and held it to her chest. "Go on home in the morning. Leave as early as you want. I'll nose around here until I've had my fill of watercress."

The pleasure in Ryan's eyes must have been impossible to contain, since she didn't have a cruel bone in her body. "Are you sure?"

"I am."

"You won't be bored?"

"I might be. If I am, I'll take the train home."

"Deal," Ryan said, grinning like she'd just won an award she'd coveted for quite a while. Jamie wasn't nearly as happy, but she assumed she'd be able to perk herself up by having a true spa day—with no fresh seaweed, nor Edwardian-era plumbing involved.

Since she was going to be on her own, Jamie stayed up to read. She stretched out on the comfortable sofa and idly paged through her book, looking forward to sleeping in. Her phone rang and she answered it quickly. "Hello?"

"What have you got in your arsenal to cheer a girl up?"

"Why's my bestie down?"

"Jordy," she said, speaking the word through a sigh.

"Care to elaborate?"

"Baby," Mia added. "I'm ready to go, and she'd like to close the discussion—permanently."

"I was afraid of that," Jamie said. "You can't say she didn't warn you, honey. You really weren't listening to her."

"Side?" Mia said, with a hint of sharpness to her voice. "You're on mine, remember?"

"Always. I swear I'll always be in your corner. But I can be on your side while pointing out a fact. Jordan's been telling you she doesn't want kids, and you've been trying to ignore her consistent message."

"Because it's a stupid reason!"

"Are you fighting? Like really fighting?"

"Close enough. Jordy left for Santa Cruz with the volleyball team this morning, and I don't think I'm going to miss her."

"Oh, Mia, don't say that. You love her, sweetie."

"I know I do. But I feel so… I don't even know how I feel. Other than awful. We're tiptoeing around each other, both of us afraid the other one will bring it up again."

"Come here."

"Pardon?"

"Come here. You can take a few days off, right?"

"Um, I guess I could. But…"

"You didn't jump at the chance to come to Dublin. How about Paris?"

"James! You don't have to bribe me!" She waited a few seconds, then said, "Are you serious about Paris?"

"Dead serious. What do you say?"

"Do you think there are flights available?"

"I'll call you back as soon as I find out. Hang tight."

"Hey! I can pay for myself. I'm making a good salary now."

Ignoring the offer, Jamie said, "I'll call you right back."

"James?"

"Hmm?"

"I love you."

"I love you too, Mia. And when I get you to Paris, I'm going to hug you and kiss you until I've made a pest of myself."

"Not possible, but I'd love to see you try."

Ryan woke to the sun hitting the room from a weird direction, then she blinked her eyes a few times and realized they were in the condo Jamie had rented. She checked her watch, and saw that it was just five. Tempted to go for a run, she slipped out of bed, seeing her suitcase by the door. She'd packed everything but a clean set of clothes and her toothbrush the night before, and considered getting her running clothes out. But if she left right that minute…

Taking a look at Jamie, she realized she'd be in trouble for weeks if she took off without saying goodbye. So, she went into the bath and took a shower, brushing her teeth while she washed herself. Jamie thought that was a weird habit, but Ryan found it efficient. She let her armpits soak up the suds while she brushed, letting her finish fifteen seconds faster.

After drying off and getting dressed, she heard a little noise in the bedroom. Poking her head out, she saw Jamie stand up and stretch.

"Need the bath?" Ryan asked.

"Just for a second." Jamie gave her a pat as she walked in and closed the door. "Are you leaving?" she asked. "You've got that look in your eyes."

"I have an 'I'm leaving' look?"

"Not specifically. More like an 'I'm going to get to do something I want' look."

That stung a bit, but Ryan couldn't really argue with her. She just hated that Jamie knew she was forcing herself to act like she was having fun when she would rather have been fixing up an old pub.

Jamie emerged in a minute, then put her arms around Ryan and cuddled her close. "I'll miss you," she said.

"Me too." She held her at arm's length and made sure the sincerity of her words rang out clearly. "I really will, Jamers. There isn't a day that goes by that I wouldn't rather be together."

"I know, honey. You just wish we were together doing what you want to do."

That stung too, and this time she had to mention it. "Um, how is it different for you? You'd have more fun if I loved going out to dinner and shopping and reading."

"True." She looked up and puckered up her lips. "We're both selfish oafs."

"You're a pretty little oaf. And when you get back I expect to be blown away by whatever you buy while you're here. More books, I suspect."

"Mmm." She showed a coy smile. "I'm thinking lingerie, parfum, chocolate… Maybe some beignets."

"Why are you talking about French stuff and using a French accent?"

"Because I'm going to Paris." She walked over to the bed and picked up her suitcase before opening it. "Mia hopped on the last plane out last night. Her flight arrives at de Gaulle at four, and mine should get in around three."

"Paris?" Ryan asked, stunned.

"Uh-huh. Paris had more nonstop flights." She smiled. "More world-class restaurants, too, not to mention the spas."

"I've never been to Paris, you know."

"Uh-huh," Jamie said, not looking up from her packing. "The first time you express a desire to go, we'll hop on a plane." She met Ryan's gaze briefly. "Don't try to guilt-trip me, honey. You're just miffed that I'm going to have fun without you."

It took Ryan a moment to rein in a snotty comment, then she let herself think for another few moments. "Maybe," she said, not willing to give in so easily. "But that makes me sound like a jerk, so I'd rather not have it be true."

Jamie walked over and hugged her again. "I know you want me to be happy. You'd just rather I was happy going back to Mayo today. It's perfectly understandable."

"It is? Really?"

"Sure. All of us have an inner toddler who likes to get what she wants without having to worry about other people."

"All of us? Or just me?" Ryan asked, feeling the bruises start to develop.

"All of us." Jamie pulled her down and gave her a long, sweet kiss. "I'd love to have you go to Paris with me this afternoon. I'd try to do things you liked, but if I couldn't find anything, I'd do what I liked and hope you didn't hate it too much. That's pretty toddler-like."

"When's your flight?"

"Around two. Why?"

She started to pull her shirt over her head, then smiled as a very perplexed look covered Jamie's face. "I'm sparkling clean, and I have nothing on my agenda until I take you to the airport. Hop in the shower and come back out here for a long, sexy goodbye."

"Done," Jamie said, racing for the bath like it was filled with French chocolates.

Chapter Fourteen

By six o'clock, Jamie was exactly where she wanted to be, sitting in the lobby of a chic hotel near the Pont Neuf. The fact that she had a chilled glass of Lillet with a twist, and a French novel at hand made the experience almost perfect. All she needed was her BFF and she'd be set.

She'd always loved the sixth arrondissement, and she'd lucked into a room at the hotel she'd first visited with her mother a few years earlier. The staff was much more deferential, and the furnishings far more elegant than Ryan would have been comfortable with, but Mia had no problem adjusting to the luxe life.

Ryan must have been rubbing off on Jamie at least a little bit, though, since she'd asked for a junior suite rather than one with two bedrooms. Given that Mia always wanted to sleep together, it was madness to throw major money away on a bedroom that wouldn't be used.

Jamie had been watching the door with a portion of her attention, and she smiled brightly when she spotted a curly-haired brunette enter. It took just a second for Mia's gaze to land on her and she rushed over to pull Jamie from the chair she'd been sitting in.

"Love you, love you, love you," she murmured, holding on tight.

"It's a tie for who loves the other more. Come sit down and have a drink. You must be exhausted from flying all night."

A big smile covered her face. "I didn't notice. I had a cocktail and two glasses of wine with dinner over the Midwest, then I conked out and slept until the sun came up. First class is my god," she sighed. "And you're my goddess for booking me in it." She pinched Jamie's cheek firmly.

A half hour later, they went to their room. "I love it up here!" Mia called out from the upper floor. The room wasn't massive, but it was a duplex, with the bedroom and the full bath up a flight of marble stairs.

On the first floor, where Jamie stood, in addition to a half-bath they had an opulent living room with a large sofa, an upholstered chair, and an entertainment center with a TV hidden behind a custom-made cabinet.

The French doors opened onto a perfectly manicured lawn, small, but with little nooks and crannies with arbors and garden furniture tucked away. Right in front of their room a pair of chaise longues were waiting for them if they didn't want to walk to the corner to an historic bistro where Sartre, and de Beauvoir, and Camus had spent many hours knocking back aperitifs.

"I love it down here," Jamie called back. "Want to stick around and have room service? Or would you rather go out?"

"Out." She'd freshened up, getting her hair to behave, and putting on a simple linen dress that looked suspiciously like one Jamie owned. "Do I look okay?"

"You look perfect. Better than perfect." Jamie held her in her arms for a few moments. "People are going to be envious of me for being with such a gorgeous creature."

"You can flatter me until you lose your voice," Mia said, with her own voice quavering a little. "I'm running a little low in the confidence department."

"Come on," Jamie said, taking her hand. "I know dinner and a few cocktails won't fix anything, but they sure as hell can't hurt."

They weren't able to get a table at any of the more elegant Parisian restaurants, even with the help of the very forceful hotel concierge. But he recommended a small place that he claimed was very popular with Parisians, and it turned out to be perfect. The chef was from Morocco, and the menu was laden with dishes from his home country, with some additional French twists.

After they'd demolished a lamb tagine served with some cumin-flecked carrots, they waited for their Grand Marnier soufflé while drinking green tea poured into blue-tinted etched glasses, poured from a great height.

"The first time I came to Paris was with you," Mia said, giving Jamie a fond smile. "Do you remember?"

"I remember your coming with us over summer vacation, but I don't think I knew it was your first time."

"I think it was," she said, looking thoughtful. "But I might have my timeline mixed up. My parents took Peter and me when I was in high school, and I think it was the next year." She smiled, revealing a little of her normal feistiness. "My mom hated it when I did things with you guys before her. I think she was playing catch-up."

"But she let you go with us," Jamie said. "That was nice of her."

"Ehh." She took a sip of her tea and set the glass down on the linen tablecloth that covered a zinc-topped cafe-style table. "She was glad to be rid of me for two weeks. I was a handful when I didn't get my way."

"No!"

"Go ahead and laugh, but we were both spoiled little princesses." She was quiet for a moment, then met Jamie's eyes and said, "Do you think I'm being a spoiled brat over having a baby?"

"No, of course not," Jamie said, covering Mia's hand with her own. "I know how important this is to you. You were certain that being a mom was your thing years ago."

"Forever," Mia said, with her voice barely a whisper.

"Even though Jordan has consistently told you she doesn't want kids, she purposefully hooked up with you after she learned you did. So it's unfair of her to place the blame for the impasse on you."

"Right?" Mia said, clearly begging for reassurance.

"Definitely. When you partner with someone, you have to take them as they are—and you've always made it clear you want to have children."

"I really have," she insisted, as though she had to convince both of them of that fact.

"I've heard you talk about it, Mia. You've been clear. But the fact remains that you're each going to have to give a little on the issue."

Mia tilted her head. "So…I'll have half of a baby?"

Jamie ignored the comment, and said, "Think about delaying. Give her more time to get used to the idea."

"I don't want to! This is the perfect time for me to do it, James. I'm junior enough that they won't miss me at work if I take off six months, and I'll never have more energy than I do now, right? I'm going to need every bit of it if I have to do this alone."

"You sound like Ryan. She's decided she not only wants to have a baby this year, she'd like to stay in Ireland—permanently."

"Don't even joke about that!"

"I wish I were joking," Jamie said, feeling a little tension build in her stomach at the thought of leaving her home. "We haven't really fought about it, but if it comes to that, I'm up for the battle. There's no way I'm staying in Ireland when everyone important to me is in San Francisco."

"I… I don't know what I'd do if I lost you, James. That's not a joke. I'd be…" She bit at her bottom lip, much more emotional than usual. "I'd be a mess."

"I would be too." She grasped Mia's hand and held it firmly. "Don't give it another thought. Ryan thinks she can steamroll me, but she's not going to win this time."

"I always wanted to have a baby when you did," Mia said, looking very blue. "I thought that was our plan."

"It was," Jamie admitted. "But that was when I was going to marry Jack. I assumed I'd jump right in and copy my parents."

"You're not doing very well at that. Luckily."

"Just because I'm not ready now doesn't mean we can't still have a baby at the same time. Wait for me. Please?"

She shook her head a tiny bit. "I'm pretty well set on doing this now. It just feels right."

"*Please* keep an open mind, buddy. You're super young to be a mom, and doing it without a partner would be hard for the baby as well as you. It's *such* a big job. And after being with Caitlin for the past two weeks I can state with authority that having a toddler is tougher than having an infant."

A server approached the table with their dessert, and Mia sat back to give him access to the table. Jamie took the first bite, and made some contented noises while Mia dug in. She looked up with a big grin on her face. "Damn, I love good food."

"That's my girl," Jamie said. "I'll happily spoon soufflés into your mouth to see that smile."

Jamie woke to Mia drooling a little on her back. Actually, she must have been drooling a lot to have it go all the way through her T-shirt. But she'd happily suffer through a spit-soaked back to have Mia next to her again.

When Jamie tried to exit the bed to use the bath, Mia jerked awake, flying into an upright position with her eyes wide. "Where…?"

"Paris," Jamie said, sitting on the edge of the bed and stroking her arm. "With me."

"Oh, fuck," she murmured, collapsing to the bed and draping her arm across her eyes. "Bad dream."

"Want to talk about it?"

"No way."

"Then do you want to get up? It's almost nine."

"Yeah, I think I'm ready." She looked up at Jamie, seeming remarkably vulnerable. "Could we have coffee here? It's going to take me a while to get moving."

"We'll have coffee, then we'll get dressed and go shopping. I'm buying you everything that catches your eye, and I won't hear a word of complaint."

That brought a smile to her face and she gave Jamie a gentle pat. "You can't make all of my worries go away by smothering me with gifts, but I'm not going to stop you from trying."

Mia had a snazzy new bag, along with a matching wallet. They'd just ordered their drinks at a sidewalk cafe, and Jamie noticed that Mia had the strap wrapped around her wrist several times. "Um, I don't think anyone's going to leap over the table to swipe your new purse. You can ease up on the death grip."

"No way." She pulled the purse close and clutched it to her chest. "Except for the diamond earrings my dad gave me for graduation, this is the most expensive thing I own." Her smile grew wider as she reached across the table and gripped Jamie's wrist. "I know it's insane to spend this much on a purse, but I promise I'll treat it like a beloved pet." She squeezed the bag, closing her eyes as she did. "I'll still have this when we're in the retirement home together."

"I've got one of my grandmother's purses from the forties. And my mom has a bag she bought in Paris when she was in college. She uses it all the time." She tapped Mia's bag, a deep rose color that reminded her of some of the flowers in her mom's garden. "It would have been smarter to buy this in black or dark brown so you could carry it more often, but this color reminds me of you." She met Mia's eyes. "It's got depth."

"I have more depth than I want," she said glumly. "Or maybe it's depression."

"You're sad, you're upset, and you're worried," Jamie soothed. "But I don't think you're clinically depressed. Even a great purse can't pull a person out of that."

"I'm holding off on being truly depressed until Jordy leaves me," she sighed. "It looks more and more like she's on the way out."

"Then you have to stop her! Jesus, Mia, if Ryan wanted to adopt an entire orphanage I'd let her do it if the alternative was her leaving." She gripped Mia's hand again. "Doesn't Jordan mean everything to you?"

She sat back when their server came to deliver their drinks, managing to thank him with her very serviceable French. After taking a sip, she nodded her satisfaction, but there was a frown that didn't go away. "You know I love her," she said quietly, staring at the small tabletop. "Jordy's shown me how it feels to love someone, James." Their eyes met again, with Mia looking very pained. "If she had a good reason. Like…" She shook her head. "I can't think of a good enough reason to make me give up a dream I've always had, but if she had one I wouldn't feel this way."

"Isn't it enough that she really doesn't want to be a parent?"

"No," she said, shifting her gaze away again. "Maybe that makes me a bad person. Maybe that makes me an asshole, for that matter. But to ask me to give up my primary goal she needs a kickass reason, and she doesn't have one."

"I think she does, honey. She's worried that your kids will think about her the way she thinks about her own mother. That seems like a damn good reason to me. Hell, I considered not having kids just because my mom and I weren't that close. And believe me, my mom was never like Jordan's mom. That horrible creature broke her in so many ways."

"I'd kill her with my bare hands if that would remove the curse," Mia said, with Jamie tending to believe her. "So we'd take it slow. I'd do most of the work when I was home, and I'd hire someone to watch the baby during the day. That would let Jordy kind of ease into it. If she found she sucked at it, she could act like most of our dads did and just make an appearance at dinner time."

"That's not what you want. You'd actually hate that."

She stared at Jamie for a minute. "I'd like it a fuck of a lot more than having her leave."

Jamie grasped her arm and held on. "Can't you slow down? Take it off the table for now, and revisit the issue in a few years. You've got another ten years of peak fertility, buddy."

"Great. So we'd have a ticking bomb we kept in the closet."

"No, no, I don't think you would. If you wait a while, your relationship would be even more secure. And she'd have a few more years to work on the issue in therapy."

"She says she's working on it now," Mia said, narrowing her eyes, "But I don't believe her."

Jamie stared at her for a moment, stunned. "You think she's lying about that?"

She made a face, waving off the question. "Not lying. At least not technically. But I think she's looking at this whole thing as a test of how lovable she is."

"Oh, shit," Jamie murmured. "There's no way to win that argument."

"Tell me about it. She's the most beautiful, smart, kind, thoughtful, patient woman on the planet, but that ogre of a mother has convinced her she's worthless. And if I prioritize having a baby over her, I'll just be confirming that." She looked at Jamie for a few fraught seconds, then quietly said, "I can't give up on her, James. But I'll lose respect for her if she forces me to give up my dream." Knocking back her drink, she shivered, even though the day was warm and dry. "What am I going to do?"

On Thursday morning, Jamie woke up and rolled over, starting when Mia's big brown eyes were staring right at her. "God," she grumbled. "Ryan does that too. What is it about me that makes women want to watch me sleep?"

"I wasn't watching you," Mia said, surprising Jamie when she didn't have a witty rejoinder. "I was awake and I turned your way when I felt you start to roll over."

Jamie reached down and gently patted her through the covers. "I wasn't upset. I was just joking around."

"Mmm. I seem to have misplaced my sense of humor. It must be bad, since some people at work have asked me if anything's wrong."

"How did you handle that?"

"I'm telling no one. My personal life and my work life will never merge."

"Probably smart." Jamie sat up and scrunched up her big, fluffy pillows to make a thicker backrest. "Are we up for the day?"

"It's after eight, so we should probably go have breakfast."

"That didn't sound enthusiastic enough. Let's go sit on those chairs right outside our room. We can have a light breakfast delivered, then stop at a cafe later in the morning for a little extra."

"Café au lait, bread, and jam," Mia said, finally showing a smile. "I'll put on enough clothes to not get arrested, and meet you downstairs."

"We're in France," Jamie said as she watched her pad over to her suitcase. "There are far fewer Puritans here, so you don't have to wear much."

It was a perfectly beautiful morning in Paris, with clear skies, a few brilliant white clouds, and plenty of sun. The temperature was warm, much warmer than Ireland had been, but not so warm as to be uncomfortable.

The hotel was small, just forty rooms, and no one else was taking advantage of the chairs that rested outside three of the other ground floor rooms. So they were able to lie in the sun and talk in a normal tone of voice without being heard.

Mia ripped off a piece of a crusty baguette and slathered it with jam, after putting an injudicious amount of lightly salted butter on it first. "If I go out of my way, I can get bread this good at home," she said, chewing thoughtfully. "But the butter isn't the same." She cocked her head. "When did you stop having butter shipped in?"

"Take a guess. It was bad enough when I just had Ryan's disapproving eyes. I wasn't up to having Martin notice I was doing it." She let out a laugh. "Ryan thinks we saved money by stopping my regular delivery, but she didn't count on my flying to Paris partially for the butter."

"And the cheese."

"And the cheese. My favorite food."

"Can't say I mind buying a good bottle of wine for the price of an American hamburger, either."

"You can buy a pretty good bottle for the price of a plate of French fries," Jamie said, laughing. "The French know how to enjoy the bounty of the earth."

Mia smiled at her, looking a little misty once again. "The food is a nice perk, but I know you brought me here to cheer me up. Thanks, James. It's helped."

"But only a little." She put the tip of her finger next to the outside of Mia's eye. "You've got some worry lines here that haven't gone away."

"That's the right term," she said, sighing heavily. "I know you don't want to spend our whole trip with me just whining about Jordan, but I can't think of anything else."

"That's where you're wrong. If Ryan and I were having serious trouble…" She shook her head briskly. "There's no way another thought would enter my head."

Mia patted her belly, which was flatter then normal. "I have a sick feeling in my stomach all the damn time. I'll be on BART, going to work, and it'll hit me. I swear I don't go five minutes without feeling like I might have a panic attack."

"Is it time to see someone? On your own, I mean."

"I don't think so. Like you said, I'm not clinically depressed. I'm just anxious and sad and worried." She turned to Jamie and added, "As much as I love being with you and having a willing listener, talking about it doesn't help much. I don't think this is something I can figure out—you know? It's not like there's a right answer."

"No, I guess there's not. But I really wish there was, buddy. I hate to see you so sad."

"I know." She ate a little more bread, and sipped at what had to be cold coffee. "I've decided that if Jordy leaves me, I'm going back to men."

"Jesus!" Jamie sat up and stared at her. "Where in the hell did that come from?"

Her expression turned hard, a very rare occurrence for her. "Let's face facts. When it comes to love, I'm a lot more gay than I am straight."

"So why would—?"

"No one is ever going to mess me up like this again, James. If Jordy breaks up with me, I'm going to keep my distance from women. I can have a perfectly good relationship with a guy, since I'm easily as straight as I am gay when it comes to sex."

"So you're planning on having a loveless life? What sense does that make?"

"Not loveless," she stressed. "I cared for some of the guys I dated. I just wasn't devoted to them like I am with Jordy. If this ends—and I swear to god I'll do anything I can to stop that from happening—my days of devotion are *done*. I've only got one heart, and if Jordy leaves she's going to take half of it with her."

Jamie had called her mom, who'd called Giacomo, who'd called an art dealer he knew in Paris, who'd called in a favor to get them into one of the hottest restaurants in Paris. Located very close to the Rodin Museum, it was an oasis of clean, modern lines, with none of the lavish eighteenth and nineteenth century decorative touches Jamie was used to in Paris. This wasn't your grandmother's Michelin-starred restaurant, a fact that was made clear when Jamie noted that the vast majority of the patrons were on her side of fifty—a rarity when the food was this expensive. Ryan would have hated it. No doubt about it. But from the moment they were gracefully and quietly welcomed, until she was sipping a delightful glass of Champagne, she was a very happy girl.

"You know," Mia said, "I don't think I've ever been to a world-class restaurant without you."

"Really? I thought your parents loved food."

"They do, but my mom won't let my dad pay this kind of money for it. He could afford to, but she's not impressed by the presentation. She thinks it's silly to spend all day making a little nest for a quail's egg." She shrugged. "She'd rather just eat the egg and save fifty bucks."

"Not a bad bit of reasoning." Jamie leaned back when a server arrived with a bite to whet their appetites. It was truly a bite, but it was a beautiful one, with tiny pearls of caviar resting on a quail egg, still in the shell, which had been artfully cracked open to reveal what looked like a tiny soufflé. "How did you know it was going to be a quail egg?"

"Saw a pair of them go to the table across from us. I'm observant," she said, showing a smug smile. She tapped at the shell, smiling when it fell apart without a sound. When she put the world's tiniest soufflé in her mouth, she let out a sensual purr. "My mom might have a point about the money, but this is a mouth orgasm."

"Sublime," Jamie agreed, concentrating to let the layers of flavor reveal themselves on her tongue. "To me, this is art. It doesn't last long, but I love the fact that it's evanescent."

"If I remember my SAT test prep, that means it doesn't last long, and I'm with you. Some of the best things in life last just a second or two." She opened her mouth to add something, then a cloud came over her expression and she blinked a few times as she took another sip of her wine. Knowing how she was feeling, Jamie was sure she was thinking of the first time she kissed Jordan, or some other tender memory. She was tempted to ask what was on her mind, but Mia had revealed enough for one day. Jamie just hoped their lavish meal would give her an hour or two of pleasure to overlay some of her anxiety.

After dinner, they were both so full they couldn't begin to think of anything other than walking off some of the calories they'd so greedily consumed.

They stuck to the main streets, window shopping while they walked slowly, arms entwined. "I didn't even ask when my flight home is," Mia said. "I was in such a rush to get here it didn't dawn on me to care."

"But you do care," Jamie said, giving her arm a squeeze. "I think you should go home and spend the weekend with Jordan. You two need to get unstuck."

"We do," she admitted, "but I don't want to leave you before I have to."

"You've got to prioritize, Mia, and right now, your relationship has to come first."

"You're right," she sighed. "It's just that lately my relationship feels like more work than pleasure."

"Then you've got to turn that around." Jamie put her arm around her shoulders as they continued to walk. "I'm certain you can do it. You've got the skills."

Once back at the hotel, they decided to pull an all-nighter to get the most out of their last few hours together.

They each had a long bath, with the other sitting on the floor, painting the bather's toes with the polish Jamie had brought. Ryan had recently given her a loving pedicure, but she was happy to let Mia start over. Doing something they'd done as high school kids brought back some great memories.

"Hard to believe we did this in my bathroom in Hillsborough just… six years ago," Jamie said. "Before Jack, before Ryan, before Jordan."

"Before you knew I wanted a Jordan," Mia sighed. "Well, that's not true. I wanted one, but I was afraid of wanting one—for a damn good reason."

Jamie grasped her wet toes and gave them a shake. "Please don't think that way. I know it's only been two years, but…"

"One year and nine months," Mia corrected.

"Okay. It's only been twenty-one months, but those have been wonderful months for you. Don't dismiss the joy you've given each other —and still can have if you can work this out."

"I don't dismiss it," Mia said. "Not at all. And if we don't make it, I'm sure I'll look back on the last two years as the best ones of my life."

Jamie took in a breath, trying to get things right in her mind. "Tell me again why you need to get pregnant now? Be specific."

"I want to be a young mom. You know that. If I do it now, I'll only be forty-one when my kid goes to college."

"And if you wait two years, you'll only be forty-three. There's barely any difference!"

Mia was quiet for a couple of minutes, distractedly splashing at the water with her hands. "Do you really think we could put this away and not have it looming over us like a guillotine?"

"I'm certain you can. I wouldn't lie to you, Mia." She put her hands on the slippery foot that rested on the rim of the tub and started to rub it, keeping her touch gentle. "If I were you, I'd spend some time making her believe she's your priority. Let her know she means the world to you."

"She does," Mia said, with her voice cracking.

"She's got to believe that, buddy. Ease off on the goal of having a baby, and work to make her believe how solid you are as a couple." Jamie tickled along her foot, and when Mia started to giggle, she added, "Maybe you could convince her to try a different individual therapist while you're at it. It sounds like she's spinning her wheels with the one she's got now."

"I appoint you my emissary in getting her to switch. I think her current shrink is useless, but I'm never going to tell Jordy that. Up to the task?"

"To keep you two together? Not a problem."

Mia gave her a long look, then said, "Will you hand me my phone?"

Jamie wiped her hands, then gave her the device.

"You can supervise to make sure I'm doing this right."

"Doing what—?"

Mia hit a button, and in a couple of seconds she said, "Hi, sweetheart."

Jamie stared at her, eyes wide.

"I know you're busy, but I wanted to tell you something important." She took in a breath and spit it out in a rush. "I've only been away from you for a little while, but it seems like years. I'm so sorry I've been pressing you about this baby thing." She met Jamie's eyes, with a little of her normal devilish smile showing. "No, it's *my* fault. When I come home, we're going to put the whole question aside and work on having a better relationship. No, no," she said, clearly talking over Jordan. "I know I've made some mistakes, but I'm clear on one thing. You mean the world to me, and I'll do whatever it takes to hold you in my arms for the rest of my life." Her smile faded as her voice broke. "Of course I mean it. You're my life."

They had to get up early to both get to the airport. But their flights were in different terminals, and they had to say their goodbyes in the cab. They were just about to pull up in front of Mia's terminal when she leaned over and put her arm around Jamie's shoulders, letting their heads rest against one another. "I hope I wasn't too much of a bore. I was sick of myself with all of my whining."

"You didn't whine once," Jamie insisted. "You're upset, you're worried, and you're questioning some very big issues. I'm very, very glad you were able to take a few days off work, and I'm very glad we were able to spend the time together."

"Me too." She took in a deep breath and let it out slowly. "I'm going to try to convince Jordy we're two parts of a whole. If she believes that, she'll eventually see that having a baby will only make us stronger."

"Don't get ahead of yourself. Work on one issue at a time. For now, that's to convince Jordan she's your number one. That might take a while." She patted her leg gently. "Seeing a great couples therapist might help."

"Can you get me a referral? I don't want to just pick a name from the phone book."

"I'll do my best." She turned to give Mia the tightest hug she could manage. "I love you so much," she whispered. "We'll be back in a month, and I'll bet you're over the worst of this by then."

"Will you move back in? We'd love it if you would."

"I'll work on Ryan. At the very least, we'll stay in Berkeley during the week." She released her and cupped Mia's cheek. "Jordan and I have to continue our cooking lessons."

"Nothing would make me happier than having you and Ryan sitting in the kitchen when I get home at night." She grasped Jamie's ear and gave it a playful tug. "Even though I'm the only one in the group who'll have a job, I don't mind carrying you bums for another couple of years."

"And once everyone's got their degrees, and we're all settled in our careers, you and I will get down to baby-making."

"Girls," Mia said, kissing Jamie's cheek as she tossed the door open when the cab stopped. "We're having girls. I'm naming mine James," she said, giving her a pointed stare. "But don't let that pressure you."

"Love you," Jamie said one last time as Mia grasped the handle of her bag and scampered across the sidewalk to enter the terminal, her long curls bouncing along behind her.

That afternoon, Jamie walked toward the small parking area near the Ballina train station, with Ryan carrying her bag.

"I don't know what you have in here," Ryan said, "But it's a lot heavier than it was when you left."

"None of your business," Jamie said, sticking out her tongue. "Some of what's in there is a present for you, but I'm not ready to give it to you yet."

"Hope it's lingerie," Ryan said, giving her a wolfish grin.

"Since when do you want me to buy you lingerie?"

"Not for me. For you. I didn't realize how much I liked it until I met you. I guess I hadn't known how hot it was until I saw your sexy self filling it out."

"Nice," Jamie said, giving her a smile. "Giving your girlfriend lots of compliments is a good welcome home gift."

Ryan stuck her key in the door lock, then pressed a button to let all of the doors unlock. Jamie started to grab the handle, but she paused. "The car's different."

"Sure is," Ryan said, smiling. "Brenna and I bought it. She wanted me to buy a sparkling new green Land Rover, but she finally gave her permission for this little white used car."

"You…bought it? You and your cousin bought a car without even mentioning it?"

Ryan immediately got that "I'm in trouble" look, and her body froze.

"Seriously?" Jamie asked. "I'm not angry, Ryan, but buying a car is worth a phone call."

She nodded soberly. "It is." Her gaze shifted to the ground. "I didn't think you'd be into spending a long time looking at every used car in Mayo. God knows Brenna regretted begging to go along."

"Would it have killed you to mention it? Just to keep me in the loop?"

"It wouldn't have even left a bruise," she said, looking like another small push would make her break down in tears.

Jamie grasped her hand and gave it a kiss. "That's all I ask for, honey. Just keep me in the loop." She slid into the car and took a look around. "It's not much different from the rental, but the interior's gray instead of black."

"Nice observation. I'm impressed." Ryan put Jamie's bag into the back seat, then got in and fastened her seatbelt. "My plan was to look around and see what was for sale, but when I mentioned that to the salesman, he told me to go take a peek at my rental agreement. Those people are thieves! Once I saw what we were paying, I couldn't let another day pass. Sorry," she added, looking truly contrite.

"It's because we had to buy the insurance. Our American insurance isn't valid in Ireland."

"So I found out. I bought a policy from the people my aunt uses." She smiled, looking particularly pleased with herself. "I used our new address. We're going to have to put a mailbox up."

"And have someone go check the box when we're gone for nine or ten months."

"Handled," she said, as she started up the car. Ryan hadn't driven ten feet before someone cut in front of her, causing her to jam on the brakes, which made the bag in the backseat topple over. "Hold on," Jamie said. She unfastened her seatbelt and turned around to get the bag settled again. Some pamphlets on the floor caught her eye and she picked them up as she straightened up and got belted in.

The first one had a pregnant woman on the cover, holding onto her protuberant belly the way pregnant women were usually portrayed. At the bottom of the paper, the text read, "Womens' Reproductive Assistance Center, Galway, Ireland."

Her blood ran cold for a second, then she realized the sensation was anger that had built very, very fast. "*Now* you've crossed a boundary. A big one! After I told you in no uncertain terms that I wasn't ready to start a family you went to talk to someone about getting pregnant?"

"No!" she said, looking supremely guilty. "I was in Galway with Aisling and we found ourselves right in front of the place. She'd been telling me she didn't think there were any sperm banks in Ireland, and we…kind of went in just to see how it was done here. It's no big deal."

"That *is* a big deal, Ryan, and if you don't want to wind up where Jordan and Mia are you'll get off this ridiculous idea about jumping into being parents before we're ready!"

"I think we're ready. Actually, I think this is the perfect time, especially if Mia gets pregnant. You've always talked about having kids at the same time. It'd be sweet!"

"It would *not* be sweet. So let me say it another way. *I'm* not ready to have kids yet. I'm only twenty-three, and I've only been out as a lesbian for two years. Let me get comfortable with my identity, our relationship, and my relationship with my mom, Jennie…" She started to cry, holding a hand over her eyes and turning to face the window.

"I'm sorry," Ryan soothed, giving her back a scratch. "Really, baby. I'm sorry I talked to the people at the clinic without telling you."

"It's more than that," she said, her voice hoarse as she whimpered. "You're doing what you do. What you *always* do."

Ryan's face took on the mask of anger that was usually hard to pry off. "Gonna fill me in on my crimes?" she said, her voice cold.

"I have. Many times," Jamie said, now feeling less upset, but angrier. "You decide what you want, then you do it. It might take a while to wear me down, but eventually I give up just to get it over with."

"I don't!"

"You do! But I'm not going to do that this time." She turned to stare at Ryan hotly. "I am *not* moving to Ireland this year. Actually, I'm going to make that even more clear. I'm not moving to Ireland until you're finished with your PhD. And if you get pregnant before you're finished, you're going to have to do it without my consent. Which I *heartily* suggest you not do."

"God damn, Jamers. I'd never get pregnant without your enthusiastic consent."

"Well, you don't have it. And you're not getting it for some time. I know you, Ryan. Once you have a baby you're going to prioritize that child over everything else, and one of those everythings is me." She reached over and gripped Ryan's forearm forcefully. "I want you to myself for a few years. I *need* that."

"All right," she said quietly. "We don't have to talk about it again for a few years. Promise."

"You're not going to bring it up again and again?"

"When have I done that? God, you make me sound like such a—"

"Basketball. Softball. The AIDS Ride after the carjacking—"

"All right," Ryan said, clearly chagrinned. "I know I can be a pain in the ass, but I didn't know I was a constant irritant."

"You're not," Jamie said, wincing when she heard the complete lack of sincerity in her voice.

"Want to try that again?"

Jamie let out a sigh. "It's not that you're a pain in the ass. It's just that you don't have much experience at being in a relationship."

"And that manifests itself how?"

"Simple. You're used to putting your needs first, especially if it's over something that you view as an individual thing. Like sports. You never seemed to understand how your playing basketball affected me and our time together."

"And you think that's what I'm doing now?"

"How would you characterize it? You brought it up, I told you I was not, in any way, willing to leave California now. But you're still thinking about it, probably certain that you'll wear me down."

"God damn it, Jamie, it's kind of awful to keep telling me I try to wear you down. Will you try to tell me how you feel without putting such a negative spin on it?"

She was quiet for a minute, then said, "You're right. I shouldn't characterize what's in your head. So I'll just tell you what's in mine. We need a rock-solid relationship before we have a baby, and I need to be more mature. Ideally, I'd be thirty, or close to it when we have our first baby."

"Thirty? You're serious?"

"Very. That's what I'm thinking now, but I'm open to discussing it as we go." She touched Ryan again, much more tenderly this time. "I'm sorry I got so upset, but I see how a similar disagreement has shaken Mia and Jordan's foundations. I don't want that to happen to us. We've got to keep talking, sweetheart."

"All right," Ryan said, letting out a breath. "I'm sorry for steamrolling you." She was quiet for a minute, finally saying, "You're right. We can both use some extra seasoning. Until I stop trying to push past your limits, I'm not going to be a great partner."

"Thank you," Jamie said. "I hate to fight. But sometimes I just lose it."

"Me too. Having our little ones going through their struggles is tough on us too." She turned and gave Jamie a sad smile. "I miss last year when we all lived together. If we were there now, we might be able to help."

"When we get home, I'd like to live in Berkeley. At least during the week."

"I'd like that too," Ryan said. "I already told Jordan we'd do that."

Jamie just raised an eyebrow, which Ryan saw the next time she turned to look at her. "What?" she asked, clearly not seeing she was making another unilateral decision. *"What?"*

They were in bed that night, at the hotel Ryan had found for them in Ballina. It wasn't a bad place, but Jamie thought she might go shopping for a replacement in the morning. There were a few nice hotels in town, and she bet one of them had newer beds.

She put her hand on Ryan's belly and gave it a scratch, smiling when Ryan stretched out and shivered. "Feels good."

"I love you," Jamie whispered, rolling onto her side to kiss her cheek. "I was thinking about moving here—"

"You brought it up, not me!"

"Yes, sweetheart, I brought it up. I was thinking about why you were hit with the idea now, and I had a guess."

"Hit me."

"I think that your...vision or whatever you want to call your quest to renew your faith is part of it. I think moving here is tied into your longing for a deeper connection with your mom."

"Mmm. Probably true."

"And having a baby, here, in Ireland, would resonate with you because being here, in the place you feel closest to her..."

She seemed to think that over for a minute, then turned and nodded slowly. "Also probably true."

"And since you hate to wait once you've decided on something..."

"Definitely true," Ryan said, looking a little sheepish.

"I think it's a compilation of all of those things, but the longing for a spiritual connection that you used to feel when you were here is probably paramount."

Ryan tucked an arm around her back and pulled Jamie closer. "How'd you get so smart?"

She let out a soft laugh. "By looking before I leap. I don't think you can do that, so it's probably a waste to try."

"Probably not. And you don't always look before you leap. You definitely jumped on me without warning this afternoon."

"Definitely true," Jamie said. "I was rash, and I'm sorry."

"So I'm always rash, but mostly about my decisions. You're sometimes rash, mostly when you're struggling with anger. We've both got to get these rashes under control. They're itchy," she said, starting to tickle Jamie relentlessly.

"Stop! Stop!" She got both of her arms around Ryan, pinning her arms for a second. "Actually, keep tickling me, but focus."

Ryan stopped at once, cocking her head as she waited for instructions that she clearly knew well.

"Slow down," Jamie urged, taking her left hand and sliding it down her belly. "And concentrate on this one little area." She settled the talented hand between her legs and let out a sigh. "You can tickle me right there until your hand cramps."

"Not so fast." Ryan pressed her to the mattress, hovering over her for a moment. "I need some kisses to give me strength."

Jamie puckered up and sank into the mattress when Ryan lay partially atop her and covered her mouth with her delicious lips. "I've got all night, sweetheart. Take your time."

Chapter Fifteen

When Jamie and Ryan walked into Aisling's on Saturday morning, Ais looked up from what she was doing behind the bar, straightened up, then placed her hands on her hips. Her gaze started at Jamie's head and traveled all the way down. "Will you look at the international traveler we have here. What did you do when you woke up this morning and there was no one to serve you a perfect cup of cocoa and a croissant?"

Jamie walked behind the bar and gave her a hug, letting go to kiss both of Ais's cheeks, going for an overly broad French affectation. "It was fantastique. I had my beloved beside me this morning, and that makes up for an awful lot of croissants." She reached into her bag and produced two small boxes. "As for the cocoa, I just need some warm milk and I've got that covered."

Aisling opened the box to remove a tin and gazed at it for a minute. "As soon as we have some of this, I'm going to hide it so Brenna doesn't eat the whole tin."

"And a few chocolates for you," Jamie said, handing over the beautifully wrapped box. "These are from my favorite chocolatier."

"Do you have a favorite chocolatier, Siobhán?" Aisling asked, putting it on thick.

"Butler's gets my vote. But the stuff Jamie likes is pretty darned good."

"I'm taking the mickey," Ais said, giving Jamie another hug. "I'm thrilled that you stopped for even a moment to think of me."

Jamie pulled out the biggest thing in her bag, a loaf of bread large enough to feed a family of four for a week. "There's a boulangerie that I love, and I bought a whole loaf of their bread. It's a mild sourdough that I can't get enough of."

"Will you look at the size of that!" Ais said. "The cousins have gone home, Jamie. There are only about a dozen of us now."

"It can easily last for a week. But it won't. I also brought some lightly salted butter.

"I'm *so* hungry," Ryan said. "Jamie wouldn't let me eat before we drove over."

"Let's have at it," Aisling said. "I was just arranging my beautiful pint glasses on the shelf here." She picked one up and held it aloft. "I could charge an extra pound for every pint because of these. Who would have thought my name could look so lovely."

Jamie took one in her hand and held it up to the dim light that came in through the pub's only window. "That's a nice glass."

"Thanks to you. Now let me get you two fed. Katie, who cooked here under Donnie, is coming over today to talk about a job. You'll help me talk to her, won't you, Jamie?"

"What about me?" Ryan asked as she gathered up the food to carry it to the kitchen.

"Jamie thinks about food, Siobhán. You merely eat it."

Ryan spent the afternoon doing the little manual labor there was to do, while Jamie and Aisling worked on planning the menu.

Jamie clearly had a point of view, but Aisling knew what the locals would want, and when they'd want it.

"I think it's mandatory to have a small menu so Katie can keep on top of things, but you need enough variety to have local people not get bored."

"I agree to some extent, but a lot of people thrive on familiarity," Aisling said. "We need some things we'll have on the menu every night. I was thinking of a good, hearty lamb stew."

Jamie made a face. "No one will want that once summer comes."

Aisling let out a laugh. "Summer comes and goes in Mayo. It's rarely above ten degrees at night, and when there's a wind and a bit of mist, a nice, warm bowl of lamb stew is exactly what people will want."

"No watermelon salad with a salty, fresh cheese and mint?"

"I'd happily eat that," Aisling said, "but you've been stressing how we should use local produce. If you can find a local farmer who's growing watermelon…I guarantee he's praying for a heat wave."

Jamie laughed at her inability to recall Irish weather was simply not what she was used to. "You can take the girl out of California, but you can't take the California out of the girl."

That night, they dined at Kelly's, the only other pub in town that served food. It was bog-standard pub food, with nothing fresh or unique. But that didn't stop people from ordering it up in the convivial place.

Aisling knew the owner's daughter, and she pulled Ryan along when she caught Claire in a quiet moment.

"Well, look who we have here," Claire said, lifting her chin to give Ais a long look. "The competition."

"I'll probably be broke in a year," Aisling said. "But I'm going to give it a go."

Claire came out from behind the bar and gave her a hug. "I honestly wish you all the best, Ais. Two good pubs is better for the town, and McNulty's hasn't been good since Donald took off for the Algarve."

"I hope two pubs can survive. I plan on matching your opening days and hours, by the way."

"Will you really?" She cocked her head and gazed at Ais for a moment. "I thought you might try to get a jump on us. A lot of people go to the first place that opens, and stay until it closes."

"I didn't want to do that to you, Claire. I'm serious when I say I want us both to succeed. That's why I thought it might be a good idea to work out a music schedule. Do you think more people would come out if we both had live music on the same nights? Or should we alternate weekends?"

"I try to have someone in both Friday and Saturday nights," Claire said. "I'd be happy to have you do the same. If we had more variety, people from Ballina might come up."

"Just what I'm hoping for. I'm already at a disadvantage because I'm going to keep the smoking ban."

Claire frowned as she went back behind the bar. "Is that wise?"

"I'm not sure, but I'm going to stress the food, just like Donnie tried to do. I think it's better for the kiddies."

"But she's going to show up on time," Ryan jumped in.

"Ahh. Well, that will be a change, won't it?" Claire said, laughing. "That man will be late to his own funeral. I tried to get him to fix the slow drain we had on our dishwasher. By the time he got to me, the problem had worked itself out."

Brenna threaded through the crowd and slipped between Aisling and Ryan. "I'm going to work at the pub," she said, not bothering to wait for the break in the conversation.

"Are you then?" Claire asked. "Will you be pulling pints?"

Brenna looked up at her sister. "I think so. I can do that, can't I?"

Aisling put her arm around the girl's shoulders and gave her a hug. "You can certainly do that when you're eighteen. Until then, you can work at being my number one table cleaner."

Early on Sunday morning, Ryan sat in a pew at St. Patrick's, with her father on her left, and Jamie on her right. Her grandparents were at the end of the row in front of them, with Brenna and Cáit next to them, their parents to their left.

During the sign of peace, Ryan's father gave her a lingering hug, smiling when he pulled away. "It does my heart good to have you next to me at Mass. Do you think you'll be able to keep this up when you're home again?"

"I think so, Da," she said, seeing how happy that made him. Even if her faith didn't continue to grow, she decided she'd remain a churchgoer. The people she loved loved to have her there. At its worst, it was like going to the opera—something you did because your partner loved it. At its best, it was a good time to collect your thoughts and center yourself. And she would never claim she didn't need time to sit and think about working to be the best person she could be.

The whole gang went to Moira's after church, with everyone under thirty jammed into the living room to sip their tea and eat their toast and jam. Ryan looked up when her Aunt Maeve walked into the room and perched on the arm of the sofa Ryan was sitting on.

"Your father and I think we'd best be making plans to return home," she said. "Annie's mom's been watching Caitlin, and she's about to throw in the towel."

"She's not as tough as you are," Ryan said, smiling up at her. "The baby's never too much for you, is she?"

"I'll admit she tests my limits, but I usually have her only three days a week. I don't know how anyone could watch a toddler every day."

"You did," Ryan said, laughing a little. "I wasn't there, but I'm pretty sure you didn't have a nanny when your boys were young."

"Well," she said, laughing along, "I was a different woman then. "You can do things when you're twenty-five that seem heroic from this perspective."

"You've always been one of my heroes," Ryan said, leaning her head against her aunt. "Sometimes I wish you'd never left Ireland. I think I'd be a different person if I'd grown up here."

"You wouldn't be a person at all, sweetheart. If I hadn't gone, your mother wouldn't have gone. You'd be some average-sized country girl from Killala. For that matter, you might be married to a man, with a couple of kiddies by now."

"Changed my mind," Ryan said, sitting up. "I don't want to change a thing. But you'll come for a long visit in the summer once our house is done, right?"

"We might have to bring Caitlin along, but yes, of course we will. You were younger than she is now the first time you had a summer visit."

"Best times of my life," Ryan said. "I don't recall a lot of details, but spending time with Aisling was always the highlight of my year."

"It still is," Jamie said, leaning over Ryan to address Maeve. "No matter how much she loves me, Aisling will always be first."

"Not…" Ryan shut her mouth, knowing she couldn't win this point, no matter what she said.

"She loves you both," Maeve said. "There's a very large heart in this woman."

Jamie was able to come up with a pair of tickets for Martin and Maeve to leave on Wednesday, and after Ryan moped around for the entirety of Tuesday, they drove them down to Shannon for their flight home.

Maeve hadn't been in their new/used car yet, and she politely commented on all of the features, which were few.

"Jamie's never been in a car this simple," Ryan said, giving Jamie a teasing smile. She seemed better today, but that was common for her. She was gloomier when she was contemplating a separation than when the actual separation took place.

"She's been in my car," Maeve said, "and I don't have a working radio."

"It worked fine before Caitlin crawled around on the floor and managed to rip out the colorful wires that went to the radio," Ryan said. "I think the kid has potential in street crime."

"Don't you go making any comparisons to your little cousin's high spirits," Martin said, reaching up to pat Ryan on the top of the head.

"Have you ever told Jamie about how you learned to vault out of your crib when you were significantly younger than Caitlin?"

Ryan laughed. "I was bored."

"Vault?" Jamie asked. "Is that the right word?"

"Like a gymnast," he said. "She faced the bars, put her little hands on the railing, pulled herself up a few inches, then…" He snapped his fingers. "She was over the bar and onto a pile of stuffed animals that Fi had been too tired to put away."

"How…?"

"Fi was walking by her room when she saw it happen. I can still hear her scream," he added. "I thought a wild animal had gotten into the house."

Jamie stared at the side of Ryan's face for a few seconds, pondering how much money it would cost to have a security monitoring system set up that would keep a constant eye on any of their children that carried even a portion of Ryan's DNA. It would be a lot, but she didn't think she'd ever have a good night's sleep if they left it to chance.

During the second week of August, Cáit finally received her Leaving Cert results, which were excellent. Shortly afterward, she found out she'd gotten her first choice and she'd be starting at NUI-Galway in just three weeks time.

They had a small celebration for her at Moira's, and after they'd all had a piece of her favorite cake Ryan put her arm around her and said, "When's your graduation ceremony? Christmas?"

Cáit looked up at her, clearly puzzled. "It was during my last week of classes." She seemed to ponder the date, finally saying, "I think it was the day before you all arrived."

"No!"

"What's wrong?" Moira asked, approaching Ryan to put a hand on her back. "You look like you've seen a ghost, Siobhan."

"Cáit had her graduation and I didn't even know about it!"

"You were flying across the Atlantic," Moira said. "You didn't miss anything massive."

"It was her graduation!"

"You've not been to any of the graduations we've had so far," Moira said. "They're not the same as the kind you have in America. It was simply Mass for the class and their parents, a few speeches, and we were on our way."

"No caps and gowns?"

"No, no, those are for university graduates. All of the girls wore their uniforms just like any other school day."

"But I didn't buy her a present!"

Cáit looked at her mother and they both started to laugh. "You gave me a car, Siobhan. I think that counts as a gift."

"No, that was because you needed one. A graduation gift is... something else."

Jamie wandered over and gave Ryan a puzzled look. "Everything okay? I keep hearing raised voices."

"Ours aren't raised," Moira said, putting her arm around Cáit. "It's Siobhan who's raising her blood pressure."

"We missed Cáit's graduation," she said. "No one mentioned it," she added, giving her cousin and her aunt a glare.

"Would you feel better if you paid for my Debs ticket?" Cáit asked. "You don't need to, since I've saved up enough to pay for it myself, but..."

"Done," Ryan said. "Do you need a new dress?"

"Of course she does," Jamie said. "I bet she needs a date too."

"I'm going with Maddie," Cáit said. "We finally talked—a little," she said, with Ryan seeing her aunt's head nod discretely. "She admitted she's gay, and I admitted I'm not. I think it will be all right in the end, even though it's a little tense at the moment."

"Good for you," Ryan said, putting her arm around her cousin. "Do you want us to rent you a limo?"

"A limo?" She stared at Ryan for a second. "We're all meeting at the school to take the bus to the hotel where you all stayed. It's not like it is in America, I don't think."

"Nothing is," Aisling said, having walked over to stand by her mother. "They were having proms when I was there in May and I've never seen such carrying on."

"That's what we're best at," Ryan said, laughing a little. "Carrying on."

"Let's go shopping," Jamie said. "You might not have a date, but you can make the guys wish they'd gotten to know you."

Cáit laughed at that. "I doubt that, but I'll take all the help you want to give, Jamie."

"What about me?" Aisling said. "I've been to a Debs myself. I know what's appropriate."

"When do you have time?" Cáit asked.

"I need to make one more trip to Galway to buy some supplies. If Jamie's willing, we'll all go together and buy whatever you need." Aisling shot a look Ryan's way. "You can stay home."

"I'm a girl!"

"After a sort," Aisling said, finding that very funny. "If we had room, you could come. But we don't. Mam, you'll come, yes?"

"I'd love to. We'll make a day of it."

"That's only four people," Ryan said. "There's room for five if we squeeze—"

"I'm coming with you," Brenna called out, having heard their conversation from across the room.

"I'll go to the pub and scrub something," Ryan said, trying to act like she was disappointed.

"Play to your skills," Aisling said, giving Ryan a fond pat on the cheek.

Aisling finally had a license to do business, the health inspectors had given the ok, and all of her supplies were in place. She'd hired another bartender for weekends, and had worked out the menu with Katie. But she didn't want to open until she'd had a week to blast the county with notices about the grand opening, as well as get the local paper over to do an article on it. Jamie thought that was a little presumptuous, but after Aisling talked to someone at the Mayo paper, they happily sent along a reporter, as well as a photographer. Jamie was going to get a color copy of the photo and have it framed for the pub. Aisling had looked like the queen of the castle as she stood proudly in front of her colorful sign.

They'd also made progress with Lucy, and she'd done some very preliminary drawings that Ryan had sent around to everyone who might have an opinion. She and Jordan had conducted a few long conversations about some of the features, while Jamie and Mia had separate conversations exclusively about other things. Even though the house meant a lot to her, she was taking a hands-off approach until they got down to making final decisions. Ryan enjoyed tweaking the plans much more than she did, and Jamie was sure there was a lot of tweaking left to do.

One cool, drizzly morning they'd gone over to the property after taking a long walk. Cormac had decamped for Galway to work on a project for one of his favorite professors, so they'd moved into Moira's for the duration of their trip. It was crowded, but what was the sense of being in Ireland if you weren't surrounded by family?

Through all of their tinkering, they'd stayed true to their original vision of where the house should be placed. It was going to be in the depression right next to the highest point on the land to hide it as well as possible from the street.

Jordan had come up with the brilliant idea of having a tower on the north corner, which would be Ryan's office. Lucy had done some work to find a company that made grain silos, and she'd made plans to have one of the silos fitted with a circular staircase to give them access to the room at the top.

Now they stood on the slight rise above the swale and looked at the view from every direction.

"I think your ivory tower will be another ten feet above this," Jamie said.

"That sounds about right. But it's not going to be ivory. Maybe white, though. We'll see if it's better to paint it or leave it looking like galvanized steel." Ryan took her hand and held it to her chest. "I'm embarrassed to admit how often I think about the house."

"I think about it a lot, too, but I know it's more of a constant for you."

Ryan sighed, tilting her head to gaze up at the spot her tower would fill. "I never thought this was something I could have."

"A house?"

"No," she said, frowning slightly. "I thought I might be able to buy a little fixer-upper in Oakland one day. But I assumed I'd be teaching, and even at a great school you're not going to earn enough to buy a house you design yourself." She smiled down at Jamie. "Besides making me see the whole world in different ways, you've let me realize dreams I didn't even have the nerve to consider."

"Aww, I hope that's true."

"It really is. I know I give you a hard time about your money, but it's been such a godsend." She laughed a little. "I don't mean that literally, of course. I could never believe in a god that rewarded me like this while keeping hundreds of millions of people in poverty. I just mean it's been... kind of awesome."

"Awesome?" Jamie put her arms around her and pulled her in for a hug. "I've never heard you say something like that."

"I struggle with it. That's for sure. But helping Aisling buy the pub, and doing repairs on my grandparents' house, and bringing my cousins over here for a vacation, and getting Cáit a car... That's all been awesome. And you can't have the good things money can buy without some of the bad things."

"All true. It might be more difficult for us to get into heaven than for a camel to pass through the eye of a needle, but we're going to try."

"I don't believe that either," Ryan said, laughing even harder. "But I'm going to do my best to use our money in ways that don't make us bad people."

"You don't have the instinct," Jamie assured her. "You're a giver, and you'll be the same with our money."

Ryan nodded. "Hope so. Right now I'm thinking about how much of our wealth will go to the tradespeople of the West. A lot, I'm thinking."

"Look at it as helping to keep tradespeople employed. They can't work if people don't need their services."

Ryan looked over their land again, then nodded, seeming satisfied. "Think that blanket we stored in the lambing shed's still there?"

"I wrapped it up in a couple of trash bags to keep it dry. Why's that?"

"I think we need to have a little alone time, don't you?"

Jamie took her hand and started to lead her over to the stone structure. "You mean since you refuse to have sex with me in your aunt's home?"

"Pretty much. I've actually been thinking about telling everyone we were going sightseeing and sneaking out to a hotel for some serious sexy-time."

"Oh, you *are* serious. When you're willing to pay for a hotel, you're really sex-starved."

"Once we have our house, we'll be able to chase each other around naked all day long."

"Uh-huh," Jamie said, knowing that had a zero percent chance of happening. The doors would always be unlocked, just as they were in Noe Valley. There would simply be different relatives to poke their heads in. But she didn't need to run around naked on a regular basis. She just needed a little more privacy than they had at Moira's. For now, the lambing shed would have to do.

Ryan was on the verge of pulling the plug on her idea, even though her body was already tingling. She started to lecture herself, then firmly guided her brain back to her original plan.

Jamie was busy placing the blanket on the ground, making sure there were no rocks or sticks that would poke them. Ryan left her to it and stood just outside the enclosure, taking in the fresh, cool air as she tried to center herself.

Her whole goal had been to spend a little time alone with Jamie, completely focused on her. But once they'd gotten to their land, the Jamie-worship had slipped a bit, with Ryan getting carried away by her constant musings about their home. It wasn't even a question that it would be fantastic—Jamie wouldn't settle for anything less. But the house wasn't the fecking point. The point was their relationship. Their love. Their permanent commitment to one another. That was truly what mattered, and when Ryan continually let herself get carried away with plans and dreams and wishes for the future, she necessarily ignored the present. And that was all they had any control over.

Jamie's arms slipped around her waist, and Ryan covered the gentle hands with her own. "Guess what I'm filled with this morning," she said.

That earned her a long hug, and she could feel Jamie's cheek rest upon her shoulder. "I could come up with some funny responses, but you seem pretty serious. So why don't you just tell me, sweetheart?"

"Good answer." Ryan sighed, unable to get enough of the sweet-smelling scent of the grass and the earth into her lungs. "I was trying to think of the right word, and I think I've got it." She turned in Jamie's embrace and put her hands on her pale, smooth cheeks. "Wonder."

"You're filled with wonder?"

"I think that's the word," she said, liking the way it sounded. "I can't think of a better one to describe the mix of excitement and joy I have when I take the time to reflect on where we are, and where we're going."

"It's pretty wonder*ful*," Jamie admitted, gazing up into Ryan's eyes.

"I've always believed you get what you work for, and that's true about us in some ways," she said thoughtfully. "But the bounty of our good fortune is inexplicable, and that's the part that fills me with wonder. I didn't make this happen, but I get to go on the ride."

"You've worked to be a good partner, and to plan for our future—"

Ryan gently pressed her fingers to Jamie's lips, cutting off her words. "Nope. I'm not buying it. We've been outrageously blessed, or lucky, or whatever brought us to this place. It's knowing that it's not a result of our good works or good intentions or good planning that makes it a wonder. It just is... And I think our job right now is to enjoy it, and each other."

Jamie's eyes had taken on a sparkle that gave Ryan chills. "You couldn't stop me from enjoying every bit of you right now, Ryan O'Flaherty. You're the main course of what I'm sure will be a sumptuous banquet—in our humble little lambing shed."

On the walk home, Ryan seemed a little tamped down. That wasn't uncommon for her, especially after they'd been particularly open with each other. She tended to need to recharge a little in her own thoughts after she'd laid herself bare—emotionally and physically. Jamie had been sure that's what was going on when Ryan said, "You know, it's been two full months, and you still haven't been willing to talk about your dad."

"Huh. Talking about my dad was not on the list of things I would have guessed were going on in your head. You continue to surprise me."

"Well, I know *I'm* good at avoiding things I don't want to talk about, but this is odd for you."

Jamie thought about that a minute, then nodded. "It is odd. I don't think I would have been able to put him out of my mind if we'd been at home. But here—I'm in a different world. This is the Irish side of me," she added, chuckling. "I talk to my mom, of course, and Mia, but it's like they both exist in space somehow. I don't think of San Francisco when I think of them."

"But we're going home soon. I mean, it's fine with me if you want to continue to ignore the issue, but that might be harder at home."

"It will be." She pulled Ryan close and whispered into her ear. "I don't want to think about him while we're here. Can you let it drop?"

She made a fist, then shot her fingers out as if what she'd been holding had exploded. "I won't bring it up again."

"Thank you, baby. Once we're back home and you're in school and I'm doing…whatever I'm going to do this year, I'll make some decisions. Until then? My dad is off my radar."

Ryan nodded, seemingly satisfied. "I guess I don't have to understand your reasoning to honor it."

Taking her hand, Jamie held it to her chest as they continued to walk. "Let's stay in the moment. We're here. We're together. We're happy."

"Gotta come up with a better word than happy," she said, her smile making Jamie's knees weak once again. "That's like saying Ireland's greenish."

"We'll work on it," Jamie agreed. "But today, let's just live in it."

Ryan was finding out a lot about her cousin by watching her make decisions about her fledgling business. To Ryan's surprise, she'd learned that Aisling was quite conservative. She had to make sure everything was in proper order before she'd be rushed, and that definitely included making the announcement about her opening. If it were Ryan's pub, she would have made sure she could nab the summer tourist business, even if she wasn't entirely ready. But Ais wasn't like that—at all.

She was sitting at a table in the pub, with Jamie and Ryan making notes while she talked. Ryan had discovered that her cousin needed her hands to express herself when she was being expansive, and if she relied on her own note taking much would be missed.

"I believe the fifteenth of August is the proper date," she declared, looking very sober. "It's a Wednesday, so that will give me two nights to make sure everything is running well before we get a weekend crowd."

"That's not for another week!" Ryan said. "You're giving up a week in August?"

"I'm well aware of the date, Siobhán, and this is the one I've chosen. That will give me time to have Katie come in and cook for family and friends. I want to make sure she's comfortable with the menu. No surprises," she added, her new mantra.

"Damn, Ais, it's not the Mars launch. No matter how well prepared you are you're going to have some screw-ups."

"The more prepared I am, the fewer I'll have," she pronounced, leaving no question about the firmness of her decision.

Over the next few days, Ryan and Jamie got very well acquainted with the people of Killala. Everyone Aisling had gone to primary school with who still lived in the area stopped by, then her secondary school chums filled the place on another night. Every close friend of Moira and Eamon's, some of Cormac, Cáit, and Brenna's friends' families, even Claire Kelly and her father, Big Jim, the owners of the rival pub stopped by.

Ryan was pretty sure it wasn't a great idea to offer free food to the people Ais would need to capture for her clientele, but she had such great trust in Katie's skills as a cook, as well as her own as a publican, that she claimed she didn't mind giving away free food every night. She was canny enough to offer only water with the meals, though, and what she earned from the bar made a dent in paying for the grub.

Each afternoon during the dry run, either Jamie or Ryan plunked Brenna in the car and drove all around Mayo, putting up flyers on every town's and shop's noticeboard, as well as any telephone poles that were already littered with other ads. It was a pretty haphazard way of publicizing the pub, but paying for full-color ads in the regional tourist magazines was a little premature. Both Jamie and Ais thought it better to attract the locals and slowly build their advertising reach.

Ais got a little more nervous each day, and Ryan finally took her aside one afternoon when they were getting ready for their free dinner service to say, "You know, neither Jamie nor I will care if it takes you a while to turn a profit. We want this to be low-stress for you."

"Low stress?" She looked up at Ryan as if she were speaking another language. "My favorite cousin and her partner have lent me an obscene amount of money on a lark. I'm going to pay you back as soon as humanly possible, Siobhán. That's why I have to do this perfectly."

Ryan grasped her by the shoulders and spoke slowly and carefully. "Listen. I didn't want to ever have to admit this, but what we've lent you is less than the interest Jamie makes on her principal in a month. To a normal person what we've lent you is a lot of dough. For us? We won't notice if we never get a dime back."

"But—"

"And we won't care. At all. We both wanted to help you make a run at this. If it doesn't work, we'll try another business. Or a small hotel. Whatever works." She leaned over a little closer and waited until Ais's eyes got wider. "I want Killala to grow, or at least hold on. Now that I have money, I'm going to use it to help the town, and you. So relax," she insisted, giving her a gentle shove. "Go give some food away so you can eventually charge people for a good meal."

"It is good, isn't it?" she asked, clearly needing more assurance than Ryan had ever had to give her.

"Best pub food I've had—in Ireland or the US. So long as we're patient, which we will be, Aisling's will be a tremendous success." She turned her to allow her to go back behind the bar. "As an aside, we're not going to accept any payments for a year, so don't even try."

"But—!"

"No argument. You've got a year to get your feet under you. Then we can look at the books and make up a repayment schedule. A slow one," she added to Aisling's frown.

Chapter Sixteen

On the fifteenth of August, Jamie's main job was keeping Aisling from drinking on the job. The grand opening was set for five, but the woman was so tense by four that Jamie caught her looking longingly at the better whiskey nestled at the back of the bar.

"Hey," Jamie said, going behind the bar to distract her.

"Hmm?"

"You're going to polish off the etching on your new pint glasses." She put her hands over Ais's, stilling her anxious gestures. "It's going to be great," Jamie said. "This is a long race, and you're not going to have a clear idea of how well it will go for quite a few months. So lighten up and try to enjoy tonight."

"Enjoy?" she asked, with the lid of her left eye twitching as she looked at Jamie. "How can I enjoy the night when my whole future's tied up in this place?" She honestly looked like she was about to hyperventilate, and Jamie impulsively wrapped her arms around her and hugged her until she let out a heavy sigh and leaned into her body.

"I know you and Siobhán tell me I've nothing to worry about, but I can't help how I feel. This means so much to me, Jamie."

"I know," she soothed. "But you can only do what you're capable of." She extended her arms and looked at her carefully. "We've watched you work on this place day and night. It's the most attractive pub I've been in, Ais. It's clean, and modernized, the food is great, and the bartender is a charmer."

Aisling gave her a shy smile, shifting her gaze down a few inches.

"It's all true," Jamie insisted. "It will take some time to build a loyal clientele, but you'll get there. You've got the financial backing to be able to weather the slow periods, which is what kills most new places."

"I want to pay you back for your faith in me," she said, looking so earnest it was almost funny. "It means so much to me to be back in my home, but I worry that Killala is simply too small for two good pubs to be able to stay above water."

"We'll figure that out over the next year or two. Not a moment before. So let's go take a walk around town to bleed off some nerves. It's not raining—at the moment."

"All right," she said, shaking her head briskly. "Where's Siobhán? I haven't seen her for hours."

"She's running an errand for me. She'll be back before you ring the opening bell."

"I have no bell," she said, staring at Jamie with her eyes wide open.

"That was a figure of speech, Ais. Come on now. Let's stretch our legs before this place is filled to the gills."

"From your lips to God's ears."

The grand opening of Aisling's was decidedly low-key. An elderly couple who knew Brigid and John opened the door right at five and poked their heads in. "Is this the night?" the woman asked.

"It is, Mrs. Casey," Aisling said, rushing out from behind the bar to guide the couple to a table. "You're my first customers."

"Oh, my," the woman said, looking a little nonplussed by the attention. "I saw your granny at church, and she made me promise to drop by. Are we too early? Aloysius and I like to have our tea early enough to let it settle before we're off to bed."

"Your timing is perfect," Ais said, handing the couple printed menus that were crisp and clean. "Besides our regular menu, we have a delicious summer vegetable soup, and our special entree is poached salmon."

"I do love salmon," the woman said, looking over the menu carefully. "Aloysius likes his meat, don't you Aloysius?"

"I do, Mary Agnes. I do indeed."

The door opened again and Ryan walked in, followed by a very tentative-looking guest. Colm had a big backpack slung over his shoulder, and when he caught Aisling's eye he smiled like a guy who knew his arrival might be a great success—or an utter failure.

"Colm!" Aisling said, dropping the extra menus she held in her hands.

"Surprise," Ryan said. "We would have been here a half hour ago, but some guy had his whole flock of sheep crossing the road outside Ballina."

Aisling was still staring—blankly, and Jamie went up behind her to guide her over to the bar. Colm followed along when Ryan pushed him in the back, and Jamie went back to the table to talk to the customers. She had to pay rapt attention to them to get their order straight, and as she walked toward the kitchen she saw Aisling and Colm standing in the corner of the bar with their heads together, speaking quietly. They both looked like they wanted to be kissing, but this wasn't the place for that. Aloysius and Mary Agnes would have been shocked.

Jamie entered the kitchen and waved the ticket in front of Katie. "We've got our first dinner order."

Moira had been helping to peel potatoes, and she looked up expectantly. "Tourists?"

"No. Friends of your mom's." She took a look at the door, hoping to alert Moira before she walked into the bar and saw their guest. "We do have a tourist in town, though."

"We do?"

"Uh-huh. Colm had a few days off, and he decided to come climb a Munro or two. I convinced him to come for the opening." That was a lie, but not a harmful one. She *had* made his reservations.

"That's lovely! Did he just arrive?"

"He did. Ryan ran over to Shannon to fetch him."

"As soon as we get this order sorted, I'll go say hello." She was grinning brightly when she added, "He knows he has to pay now, doesn't he? If he eats and drinks like his brothers, we'd lose the night's profit."

"Oh, he knows we're open. Colm's the thoughtful one of the group," Jamie added, trying to boost Moira's opinion of the man. He was going to need all of the help he could get if she figured out the real purpose behind his trip.

Word had definitely gotten out about the grand opening. Ryan was thrilled with the turnout, and even more thrilled by how happy Ais seemed. Everyone had bought that Colm had come to climb some hills, which made her doubt her family's intelligence, given he lived within driving distance of taller peaks. But if Colm and Ais could keep things secret for a while longer, it was all the better.

Ryan was serving drinks to the patrons sitting at tables, while Cáit was taking food orders. Jamie was helping Katie keep up with demand, while Ais and Colm worked the bar. Actually, Colm just pulled pints, with Aisling chatting with the customers and pouring shots for the more adventurous drinkers. They would have been in trouble if they had to make complex drinks, but nearly anyone could splash some whiskey into a glass.

They were a little past their capacity, both in terms of how many people were jammed into the pub, as well as how many meals the kitchen could produce. The last time Jamie had poked her head out of the kitchen, she'd clearly been looking for some help, but Ryan had no excess capacity, and there were no other competent helpers.

Around six thirty, Eamon and Brenna walked in, with Brenna running right over to Ryan. "Can I take orders?" she asked, eyes bright with excitement.

"Um…I think we could most use you in helping to clear tables. Remember how we practiced?"

She nodded, with a serious expression taking over her smile. "Don't take the plates away until they've stopped eating. Oh. Don't take one plate away if the other person's still eating. Jamie says that's rude."

"Not to me," Ryan said, "but we're trying to keep up with Jamie's rules."

"Can I wear an apron?"

"Sure. Take mine," Ryan said, removing the half apron she was wearing and tying it around the kid's waist.

"Hey!" Brenna said, almost squealing. "Your cousin's here!"

"Yeah. He wanted to do some more hiking, so we convinced him to come today to help celebrate."

"That's…"

"Colm," Ryan said. "The one who does tile."

"The cutest one," Brenna said. She looked up at Ryan. "He's not *my* cousin, is he?"

"No, Brenna. He's just mine."

"Brilliant," she said, rushing over to the far corner of the pub to scout for diners who looked like they'd had their fill.

Ryan looked around when a hand settled onto her back. "Granny! Granddad!" she said, giving them both hugs. "Great crowd, isn't it?"

"We'll not stay," her grandmother said, having to raise her voice to be heard. "We wanted to have a look about, but now that I see the crowd is good I can stop worrying." She looked around, with her sharp eyes landing on nearly every person in the packed room. "Oh, my, there's Rose McFeeley over in the corner talking to Mary Maloney. There's not a spoon big enough for the trouble that one stirs."

Ryan took a quick look, seeing two frail-looking, elderly women sipping what looked like sodas. "I'll keep an eye on them," she said, sharing a wink with her grandfather.

"I saw that, Siobhán," Granny said, pinching her ear lobe so sharply Ryan gasped. "Have some respect."

"Yes, ma'am," Ryan said, dancing out of the way before her grandmother could get a better hold on her.

By ten, the majority of people who wanted to eat had ordered their dinners. Now the place was packed with drinkers, bellying up to the bar and filling every available spot around the perimeter of the room.

Ryan had all she could handle in keeping the seated patrons satisfied, and even Brenna was running behind, no longer keeping up the blistering pace she'd set when she'd first entered. People were still ordering bar snacks, but Cáit's duties had slowed a bit, and she started to help Brenna catch up.

Ryan looked up when the kitchen door swung open and her aunt exited, flushed and overheated. There was no way she could work in the kitchen six nights a week, but Aisling wasn't willing to hire a prep cook until she was certain they'd have the business to keep one busy. If things kept up at even half of this pace, she'd have no trouble justifying the expense, and Ryan was sure her aunt would happily scale back. Working in a professional kitchen looked like much more fun than it actually was.

The bar was really rocking, and Ryan kept an eye on Aisling to make sure she wasn't falling behind. Jamie was working one end of the bar now, with Ais and Colm having to share the middle of the span. They'd worked out a pretty good system, and had been able to move around one another without any major mishaps. Just as that thought registered, Aisling backed up into Colm, and he laughed as he put his hands on her hips and helped her settle herself. He would have done the same thing to Jamie, or Ryan, for that matter, but he wouldn't have had the hungry look in his eyes that he did when his hands held Aisling possessively for just a second too long.

She looked over her shoulder, and Ryan's eyes nearly popped from her head as she waited for the kiss that Aisling looked like she was going to bestow. She must have realized what she'd been on the verge of doing, and she righted herself and went to get the bottle she'd been heading for. Ryan let out a sigh of relief, then let her gaze scan the crowd. It landed on her aunt, who was staring a hole through Aisling. *Oh, fuck.* The jig was up. Now she was going to be forced to worry about her aunt's reaction until they all had time to have a real conversation. Probably a tense one.

Despite Cáit's protests, Eamon collected her and Brenna and took them home at ten. Since Cáit couldn't serve alcohol, and the food orders were few and far between now, she really wasn't needed—at least this night. But she was going to be leaving for university soon, and Aisling was going to need a full-time server. Only one day in and it was as clear as a bell that Ais was going to be busy. The craic was great in the room, with lots of locals, and a smattering of strangers trying to be heard over the sound system playing Aisling's favorite current pop tunes. Not a trad song to be heard all night long.

Moira hadn't come back into the room, so Ryan spent the remainder of the night thinking of her aunt's reaction. She didn't think she'd mind —so long as Aisling wasn't planning on leaving Ireland—but Ryan wasn't at all sure her granny would be as welcoming once she knew this was a serious thing. Not that any form of disapproval would stop Ais. When she made up her mind, you might as well accept the decision, because it wasn't going to change.

The place was still packed at eleven, but the pace had slowed. Ryan wasn't racing up to the bar as soon as she dropped off a round, and she'd noticed that Jamie was leaning against the back bar whenever she had a chance, taking whatever little bits of rest she could find.

Aisling put the music on hold at a quarter past eleven to call out, "Last orders!" Ryan could feel some of her fatigue come to the fore now that she knew the long shift was just about over. This was only a Wednesday night. What would the weekend be like? She shuddered to think.

Following the law to a T, Aisling poured her last pint at eleven thirty, and Ryan tried to move her seated guests over to the bar. It helped to turn the chairs over and place them—seat first—on the tabletops, but people clearly didn't want to leave. Aisling was smiling and laughing when she resisted the shouted pleas to have a lock in, promising she'd be back the next day at five for all of the people who couldn't wait to wet their beaks again.

Ryan leaned on the end of the bar, feeling completely exhausted. But she got a lot of pleasure out of watching her cousin work her magic on the patrons. She was unflaggingly friendly, and cheerful throughout, but Ryan would have been surprised if anyone tried to push her too far. She was one of those people who'd bend easily—but with a spine of steel.

"Listen up," Aisling called out after she'd cut the music. "We're dead on our feet, and I'm declaring the night officially over. Count your lucky stars you were here for our opening. You'll be able to tell the tale to your grandbabies when they ask about the most important night of your lives. Now get out before I call the Guards!"

That caught everyone's attention, and even the most recalcitrant of the patrons drained their glasses, wished her a good night, and shuffled out.

Aisling leaned over to drop onto the bar, with her arms straight out in front of her, draped over it like she'd been hit on the head. "It's so much easier to drink all night long. What was I thinking?"

The door to the kitchen opened, and Moira walked out, clearly unhappy. "What *were* you thinking?" she asked sharply, glaring at her daughter.

Ais flew into a standing position, staring back at her mother. "What's wrong?"

"You know exactly what's wrong," she said, angrier then Ryan had ever seen her. "As do you," she added, giving Colm the same deadly glance. She turned and went back into the kitchen, dismissing Ryan with a cold, "No one wants to be kept in the dark by her own family." A second later, the only sound in the pub was the door swinging on its hinges.

"Oh, shit," Ryan muttered. She made eye contact with Aisling. "Want me to try to talk to her?"

"She's already gone," Aisling said, letting out a frustrated growl. "Didn't you hear the back door?"

"I was still smarting from that look she gave me," Ryan said. She shook her head briskly. "I've never been the recipient of that one before."

"I have, but not often."

Jamie had been standing like a statue, but she eventually walked down to the end of the bar. "I screwed up. It was my idea to talk Colm into coming over for the opening. Ryan didn't know until this afternoon," she added.

Aisling lifted her arm and put it around Jamie's shoulders, giving her a quick hug. "You were only trying to be helpful. Don't ever apologize for that."

"I shouldn't have tried to surprise you," Colm said. He took Aisling in his arms and held her close, with a small smile coming to his lips now that he'd finally been able to touch her.

"Don't be a plank," she murmured into his shirt. "You just flew a thousand hours to be here for me." She looked up and smiled at him. "I might have to suffer a beating for it, but I'm very happy you came."

"I am too," he said, sighing heavily. He looked down at her like he wasn't quite sure what to do next, but she gave him clear instructions.

"If I'm going to suffer the consequences, the least you could do is kiss me." She tilted her head back, awaiting his kiss. Ryan averted her eyes, regretting that she'd heard the satisfied purr that came out of her cousin when Colm laid one on her.

The front door opened and Moira stood there, with her rain-damp face bearing an expression of perfect frustration. "Now I have to witness this?"

"Oh, Mam," Aisling said, breaking away from Colm to run over to her mother. She grasped her arms and held her for a second. "I'm so sorry I didn't tell you when it first happened, but I didn't want to worry you."

"Worry me? You're not Brenna's age, Aisling. You're free to take up with whoever you want."

"But I knew you'd ask questions, and I didn't want to talk about it until I had some answers."

"What kind of nonsense is that? What questions could I..." She stared at her for a second. "You'd better not be thinking of moving to America!"

"Exactly," Aisling said, moving away from her to go stand beside Colm, who looked like he wanted to dig a hole and climb into it. "I didn't know if we'd get along. And even if we did, I didn't know if I had a future with Colm. Not to mention my doubts about his ability to live in Ireland if it came to that. So why would I tell you I was testing the waters? It would only worry you."

"Well?" Moira said, staring at her as her anger seemed to turn to fear. "Are you leaving us?"

"No," Aisling said firmly. "I never want to leave Ireland. That's why we've intentionally taken things slow." She looked up at Colm, clearly as besotted with him as he was with her. "I've been trying to lure this lad into moving here to be with me, but it's a very big decision for him."

"I'd have to quit my job," he said, his big blue eyes begging for understanding. "It's a very good job." He gazed at Aisling for a moment. "But I'm still tempted to chuck it all and stay, even though it might break my mother's heart."

"And what did you have to do with all of this?" Moira said, walking right up to Ryan. "Is this why you brought your cousins here? So Aisling could test the waters? The good Lord knows you could have saved money by hiring the best builders in Europe."

"Ais had nothing to do with it," Ryan said. "We planned the trip before I learned about her and Colm."

"You didn't tell Siobhán the minute it happened?" Moira demanded.

Ryan stared at her. It hadn't hit her until this minute, but her aunt was mostly angry about being shut out. Now it all made sense. Her feelings were hurt, and she didn't know how to handle that.

"No, Mam. I wouldn't have told her at all, but Jamie caught us kissing one day. She kept the secret for quite a while, but I didn't think that was fair to her."

Moira turned and stared at Jamie. "You didn't tell Siobhán?"

"I didn't," she said, shrugging. "I promised I wouldn't."

"Well, it's time to get this out in the open. You'll have to tell your father," Moira said. "And your grandparents. It's ridiculous to ask people to keep your secret. I certainly won't be a part of it."

"Um…" Aisling looked like she wanted to dash out of the pub and keep running. "Granny caught us in the bar a few days before the cousins left for home."

Moira stared at her, clearly dumbfounded. "My mother caught you… And she didn't say anything to me?"

"I don't think she even told Granddad. She insulted the O'Flaherty family that night, and Siobhán had obviously reached her limit. They had words," she said, making the word sound especially dramatic.

Moira whirled to stare at Ryan. "What in the world happened?"

"Nothing much. I told her I was tired of her slagging off my family, and she admitted she didn't like my father because he took two of her daughters away from Ireland."

"He did no such thing! Your mother was already looking for a way to stay when they met—" She stopped abruptly. "You knew that, didn't you?"

"Not specifically. But my uncles always tease my father that my mother only married him for his citizenship status." She shrugged. "It doesn't bother me why they got together. They were mad for each other."

"They were," Moira said firmly. She took in a breath and faced Aisling again. "So. I have no idea why my mother is being coy, but there's no reason to continue that. I want you to talk to your grandparents about this."

"I'll do it tomorrow. Then we'll be finished hiding."

"Um, not really," Colm said, looking very abashed. "No one in America knows."

"What are *you* hiding?" Moira demanded. "You're not doing anything illegal or immoral, are you?"

"Of course not!"

"Then act like the adults you're supposed to be. Be honest with the people who love you."

Aisling looked like she was going to snap off a smart reply, but she closed her eyes for a moment, then spoke softly. "I'm happy to do that, Mam. And if you want me to, I'll visit Granny first thing and tell her I'm getting serious about Colm. But you'd better be prepared for her to blame *you* for every poor decision I've ever made."

Moira gazed at her for a few seconds. "Did she say anything when she saw Colm tonight?"

"She didn't seem to notice him," Ryan said, jumping in.

Moira hesitated just a moment, then said, "Well, telling your father is a good start. Why don't we leave it at that until you've got your feet settled under you."

"I think that's the wise choice," Aisling agreed, not even trying to hide an obvious smirk.

Chapter Seventeen

Working all night at a busy bar had taken its toll on Jamie, and when she finally woke up, she stared at the clock on her bedside table for a moment, shocked that it indicated it was nine thirty in the morning. Her shock grew when she rolled over to find Ryan lying next to her, sound asleep until that moment.

Blue eyes blinked slowly, then Ryan said, "I'm too old for this."

"So am I, and I'm younger than you." She slid out of bed, annoyed when her legs and lower back felt stiff and unyielding. "How do people work on their feet for their whole lives?"

"I don't think they wake up feeling like a million bucks most mornings," Ryan said. "I assume they get used to it, and just live with a certain amount of pain and stiffness."

Jamie went into the bathroom, and when she emerged a couple of minutes later Ryan was bent over at the waist, stretching her back out.

"Think it's a good idea to go pick up some food and cook brunch for the happy couple? I assume Moira and Eamon would like to get to know something about Colm. I doubt they spoke to him much on the last trip."

"I suppose we could do that. I'm not sure how my aunt and uncle are going to feel about Ais staying with Colm last night, but they didn't give her a hard time when she moved in with John. That's a good sign."

"She's telling your uncle this morning?"

Ryan chuckled softly. "I'm not sure how early in the morning she's planning on doing that, but that's what she said."

"Give her a call. They should be up."

"Says you. They probably didn't go right to sleep like we did. I'm going to call my aunt and see if we can set something up. I'm not going anywhere near her house if my granny's coming 'round."

Jamie made a clucking sound, but Ryan just waved her off and made the phone call.

They all agreed on getting together at one o'clock for lunch. The pouring rain had kept Brenna in the house, and Ryan was sure she'd relish the tension that was sure to be present. The kid loved anything that changed up the routine.

There was a good-sized grocery store in Ballina, and Ryan and Jamie prowled through the aisles, finally coming up with cold cuts, cheese, a couple of cold salads, a soup, and plenty of bread.

By the time they got to the house, the initial stiff greeting had already occurred, and they only had to witness everyone trying to be nice to poor Colm. Ryan had nothing but sympathy for the guy, since she still had a minor case of PTSD from her initial meeting with the Evans clan.

"Who wants lunch?" Ryan asked, brushing by Aisling on her way to the kitchen to set the bags down. "Jamie and I will make sandwiches and heat up some soup. You can all have a seat and get to know one another a little better."

"Thanks," Aisling said, sounding like she might be gritting her teeth.

Brenna was happy to take up the conversational slack, walking right up to Colm to say, "How is it that you're Siobhán's cousin, and not Aisling's?"

"He's not my fecking cousin!" Aisling snapped. "Don't they teach genetics in primary school any longer?"

"Don't snap at your sister," Moira said. She sat down and patted the sofa next to her. "Sit down here, Brenna. I'll explain things to you."

The girl looked like she wanted to continue to question Colm, but she sat down and gave her mother her attention, with Ryan watching not-so-surreptitiously from the kitchen. "You know your Uncle Martin, Siobhán's father, is an O'Flaherty."

"I know that," the kid said, nodding soberly.

"And he's married to my sister, so she's an O'Flaherty by marriage."

"And your other sister was too," Brenna said, still looking up into her mother's eyes.

"That's correct. But my sisters aren't related to the O'Flahertys by blood. Just by marriage. So Colm here is an O'Flaherty because his father and your uncle Martin are brothers. Do you understand that Siobhán has an O'Flaherty side and a Ryan side?"

Brenna chewed at her lip for a moment. "Like I have an O'Donohue side and a Ryan side?"

"Correct. Aisling has the same two sides you do, of course. So you have O'Donohue cousins that Siobhán isn't related to, even though she's related to you."

"Riiiiight," she said. "I think I've got it. So Aisling will be an O'Flaherty by marriage." She looked up at her sister. "You're getting married then, yes?"

"No!" Clearly flustered, Aisling sat down on the other side of Brenna. "I'm dating Colm. We haven't had a lot of time together, and I couldn't possibly ask him to move here until we're sure we'll get along well."

"You didn't come home last night," Brenna said. "Were you getting to know him all night?"

Ryan was *certain* the kid knew she was yanking her sister's chain, but it was clear Aisling wasn't aware. "We were up late cleaning the pub," she sniffed.

"My teacher said you aren't supposed to sleep with people you weren't married to," Brenna added, "but Mam says Siobhán and Jamie can sleep together because no one will marry them and that's not fair." She blinked up at Aisling. "But people would marry you because you're not both girls, right?"

"Right," Aisling sighed. "We're not both girls."

After lunch, which had gone remarkably well, Ryan and Jamie walked out to their car with Aisling and Colm. "Well, that wasn't horrible," Ryan said, giving Colm a hearty slap on the back.

"No, not bad at all. I've never met a girl's parents, so I wasn't sure what to expect."

Aisling stared at him for a few seconds. "You've never met a woman's parents? You're thirty years old!"

"I know. But I've never been serious about anyone, Aisling. You know that."

"Well, you're serious now," she said. "And if my granny thinks you're here to take me away, I might be the first and last woman you can ever say that about."

Once Colm's long weekend visit ended, Aisling put her head down and did little but work. Ryan was sure she was setting a pace that was not only unhealthy, but unsustainable, but it was a waste of time to chide her. So Ryan adopted her schedule, showing up at the pub just nine hours after they'd left the night before. She would have gone even earlier, but Jamie put her foot down immediately, informing Ryan in no uncertain terms that she was going to get eight hours of sleep on her "vacation"—no arguments.

Jamie also worked every night. But she didn't appear until they got busy—about seven o'clock. Each night she strolled in, slid behind the bar, usually giving Aisling a scratch on the back as she took over the right half of the span, leaving Ais to chat with all and serve her half.

Cormac came home for a week before he started his graduate studies, and he helped out as well, leaving Aisling to supervise and be a social butterfly, making everyone who entered feel like she was truly glad to see them.

One morning Jamie lay in bed, watching Ryan get into her work attire of jeans and a knit shirt, and she commented, "We've only got a week left, babe. Are you going to spend every day working a double-shift?"

Ryan sat on the bed, grasping Jamie and settling her onto her lap. Looking down at her, she had the same thought that hit her every time Jamie called her out on her admittedly ridiculous fixations. Why wasn't Jamie *always* number one? What sparked the crazy motivation to do everything anyone else needed before Ryan was one hundred percent sure that Jamie's needs were satisfied?

Those beautiful green eyes blinked slowly, still a little lazy from sleep.

"Why do I do this?" she asked, once again kicking herself for not being able to regulate her behavior before it got out of hand.

"I'm not sure, sweetheart." Jamie lifted a hand and gently stroked Ryan's cheek. "I love that you're so devoted to your cousin. I truly do." Her delicate fingers felt so good as they barely tickled the skin they roamed over. "But your own needs never figure in the puzzle." Her gaze grew more focused. "And you assume I have the same priorities as you do —which is often not the case."

"What should I do?" Ryan asked quietly. "I can't just walk away from helping out when everyone else is there every night."

"I understand that. I do," Jamie emphasized. "But they're not there all day. Moira shows up at five, then your uncle comes by with the girls after he's gotten them some dinner. So they definitely all pitch in, but…" She reached up to tuck some hair behind Ryan's ear, and tickled it while she was there. "You, however, act like you have to be with Aisling every minute—which you don't. And in a week, you're going to be gone, I'm going to be gone, Cormac's going to be gone, and Cáit's going to be gone. If you were smart…" She smiled, showing she was teasing. "And I'm not saying you are… But if you were smart, you'd be helping Ais interview for full time bartenders and servers rather than doing the work of three people."

"You're right," she said, sighing. "I jump in and do what needs to be done at that minute instead of planning for the future."

"Well, that's Ais's job, and I've reminded her to start looking, but she seems to think the crowd will die down. She doesn't want to offer someone a job and not need them after a few weeks."

"Well, that's kind of a good trait…"

"It is. But she could be honest and tell people up front that it might be temporary. Someone who's out of work might take a few weeks pay over none."

"Good point." Ryan picked her up and gently lay her back onto the pillow. "I'll get on her today to make that happen."

"Ryan?"

"Uh-huh?"

"We're leaving next Sunday. I'm not willing to get up at four in the morning to get to the airport on time, so I'm going to stay near Shannon on Saturday night. I'd love for you to join me."

"I will," she said, annoyed with herself for not offering up that small concession on her own. When would she learn?

On their last full day in Ireland, Ryan woke with the dawn—as usual. She started to toss her feet off the edge of the bed, only to quickly pull them back under the sheet. She'd promised herself she'd focus on Jamie today, and she was going to do just that. She didn't allow herself to feel proud of that plan, since she'd nearly forgotten the vow that she'd made just eight hours earlier.

Wide awake, and unwilling to fall back to sleep, she snuggled up against Jamie's warm body and stealthily tucked an arm under her head. That bit of jostling made Jamie turn toward Ryan to toss both an arm and a leg over her. Ryan tilted her head to kiss her cheek, warm from being pressed against her pillow.

Jamie slept so deeply that Ryan was not only able to caress her, she could have basically given her a massage. But she kept her touch light, luxuriating in the intimacy of lying next to someone you loved while she slept.

Unaware of how much time had passed, she started when Jamie's sleepy voice said, "I know I should wake up, but that feels so good I can't keep my eyes open." She moved her head to be able to plant a soft kiss to Ryan's shoulder. "Why are you here?"

"I'm going to stick to you like glue today." She laughed softly. "Will that make up for basically ignoring you for the entire summer?"

With her voice now sounding clearer, Jamie said, "Even though you weren't as attentive as I would have liked, this trip has been what I expected. You had some priorities, sweetheart, and I know you can't just shove your goals aside to focus on me."

"But you're my main goal," Ryan said, hearing the serious tone she hadn't realized she was going to use. "Always, Jamers. I know I let my projects get in the way, but that's only because I'm so sure of our commitment to one another." She moved away a little, having to pick Jamie's head up to get her arm out. "But I realize that's not always fair to you. So I want you to promise to continue to set limits with me. God knows I'll push against them, so feel free to push back."

Jamie gave her such a warm smile that Ryan felt like purring. "You're a silly girl," she said, stroking her cheek while she gazed into her eyes. "I know it would be easier for you if I set limits for you, but I don't think that's good for us as a couple. Over time, you need to learn your own limits. But until you do—I'll continue to take care of myself." She shuffled across the bed until they were nose to nose again. "I wish you were the kind of woman who wanted to do the same things I do, but that's not going to happen. And as much as I try to jump into your projects, I'm never going to have your dedication to fixing roofs and working at pubs." She playfully tried to bite the tip of Ryan's nose, but she was able to stay just out of reach. "I'm always going to be the woman who wants to hire professionals to do the things I'm not able or willing to do, while you'll go to trade school to learn how to give your granny's car a tune-up."

"I could probably do that now—"

"I'm sure that's true, but my point remains. Our relationship will be a success as long as we both try to go out of our comfort zones to accommodate each other."

"Like you working at a bar six nights a week."

"And not going running this morning." Jamie gave her a tender hug. "Which I *know* you wanted to do on your last morning in Ireland."

"How about a walk?" Ryan asked. "We could drive over to Killala and do a long loop around town."

"Let's do that tonight, just before we leave. I'd rather go to your aunt's house for a boisterous breakfast."

"Really? You're not just doing that because you know I want to?"

"Really," Jamie said, giving Ryan a pat to the butt as she started to slide out of bed. "By next year, we'll probably be making breakfast for everyone at our house. I want your aunt to pamper me one last time."

"Aww…" Ryan jumped to her feet. "That makes me feel so good. We're going to love living here."

"For the summer," Jamie said, narrowing her eyes as she stared at Ryan for a few seconds. "That's all I'll commit to."

"That's a start," Ryan said, smirking when Jamie just rolled her eyes and headed for the bath.

Jamie stood next to Ryan as she rapped sharply on Moira's door. It took a minute for her to call for them to come in, and as they did Moira stared at them like they were the last people she expected to see.

"Everyone's gone," she said, looking a little stiff.

"Everyone?" Ryan asked.

"Yes. Almost everyone." She hesitated, then said, "Cáit and Eamon are off for their Saturday morning bike ride, Cormac's taken Brenna to her football practice, and Aisling's still asleep."

"We thought you'd all be in the middle of breakfast," Ryan said. Jamie saw her look toward the kitchen, which was a mess, with bowls and plates and cups and skillets lying on the table.

"We…" Moira followed Ryan's glance, then said, "We had breakfast early. I…" Facing the two of them, Moira said, "I'm amazed at myself for letting this happen, but the cupboards are bare. All I can offer you is some tea."

Ryan looked like she was going to say something, maybe to tease her aunt for being caught short, but she didn't. The vibe in the room was off, and Ryan didn't push things when she wasn't sure of what was going on.

"Come. Sit down," Moira said, acting more like herself when they went into the kitchen. "I'll put the kettle on."

"You don't need to," Jamie said, sure that Moira didn't want company at that minute. "We haven't been to that nice little restaurant in town all summer. We can boost the economy a bit on our last day."

"Please," Moira said, meeting Jamie's eyes. "At least let me make you a cup of tea. I'm ashamed of myself for not being more hospitable."

"You're the essence of hospitality," Jamie said, giving her a quick hug.

"Down you go," Moira said, pressing on Ryan's shoulders to get her to sit. "The kettle will just take a moment. Then we can enjoy a little quiet time."

They sat at the kitchen table and had an uninterrupted, civilized conversation, something they'd had little chance to do, despite spending the summer together. But Jamie was still certain they were interrupting something, and she couldn't get the feeling of unease to leave.

While she tried to keep up her end of the conversation, she kept flashing to the future. If they had as many children as Ryan wanted, their lives would easily be as busy as Moira's, with just as much yearning for the rare empty house.

While Moira seemed perfectly happy being pulled in five different directions at once, Jamie was sure she was often under a lot of stress. Maybe that stress had built to the point where she simply wanted the morning to herself—which she could have had if Jamie could pull Ryan away from the table. But that was going to be tough.

She looked over at her partner, watching her engage with her aunt on a deeply emotional level, revealing everything that Ryan had in her heart. She was such a dear, dear woman. So focused on being both physically and emotionally available for all of the people she held close. That was a goal that was impossible to attain, of course, given there were only so many hours in a day. But Ryan still didn't realize that. All Jamie could hope for was that she would learn. Until then, Jamie would try to be more patient with her. It was churlish to get angry with a woman whose biggest faults were that she was too loving and too giving.

Jamie snuck another look, watching her laugh at a silly thing Moira had said. Even if Ryan never made any progress in limiting herself to realistic goals, Jamie wouldn't love her any less. When you had an almost perfect girlfriend, you had to thank the Lord for your good fortune and keep chasing the little rascal until you caught her.

It was close to ten when they'd helped her aunt clean up after what must have been an epic breakfast, with half of the pots and pans in the house needing a scrub. Ryan took a surreptitious look at her watch, hoping Jamie would suggest they go over to the pub to help Aisling get the place organized for the nightly crowd. But she didn't. After walking into the living room, she said, "What's on your agenda for today, Moira?"

It took her a second to respond, and when she walked into the room, Ryan thought her aunt seemed as ill-at-ease as she had when they'd first gotten there. "Today? The usual, I suppose. When I have no one under foot I usually start to clean..." She didn't get close to saying, "Please leave," but even the hint that she had something she wanted to get to was pretty bold.

Ryan grasped Jamie's hand and started to tug her toward the door, getting a startled look from her partner. "We'll let you get to it," Ryan said. "We were planning on taking a walk later, but it's so sunny and dry we should probably do it now."

Moira smiled while she practically herded them along. "I always tell the kids to never let a dry, sunny day go to waste."

"Why don't you go with us?" Ryan said. "You shouldn't let the fine weather go to waste either."

"Too busy," she said. She leaned in to kiss their cheeks, then began to close the door, forcing them from the vestibule. "Slán leat," she said, firmly shutting the door behind them.

"Does she have a lover hidden upstairs?" Jamie asked quietly as they moved away from the house.

"Horrible thought that I don't want to consider for a second," Ryan said, "but if I didn't know better..."

"Maybe she really wants to get the bathroom cleaned before the kids get back?"

"Maybe..." Ryan stopped at the street and turned to gaze at the house for a moment. "Isn't it funny that Ais was still in bed? We weren't being very quiet, especially when we were banging pots and pans around."

Jamie shrugged. "I thought she was an early riser. Maybe the pace she's been keeping is getting to her."

"Maybe we've overstayed our welcome in Ireland," she said, with a hint of sadness in her voice. "Even though we're loved, we're not part of their everyday schedule." She stuck her hands in her pockets and kept her gaze on the house for a minute. "I think it's probably good that we're leaving. That will let my aunt focus on getting Cormac and Cáit ready to start uni."

"Aww," Jamie said, sliding an arm around Ryan's waist and hugging her. "No one's sick of us, honey. I think your aunt just had a list of things she wanted to do, and a short amount of time to do them. She seemed to be having fun chatting with you for..." She checked her watch. "An hour."

Ryan winced. "I didn't realize we'd kept her that long."

"She didn't mind," Jamie insisted. "Come on now. Let's walk over to Evansville and see what's cracking."

"Evansville?" Ryan asked, with her eyebrows rising.

"O'Flahertyberg doesn't sound very good," Jamie said, showing a charming grin. "Adam Keene said he'd mow for us every few weeks, and we've had a few dry days in a row. I want to see if he's followed through on his promise."

"I can't believe you told our new neighbor you wanted to pay him for his time," Ryan said, still a little puzzled by Jamie's offer. "It'll take years for him to think we're normal."

"He offered to mow our land when he mows his," Jamie insisted, still not getting it. "I wasn't going to have him do that for free, honey."

Ryan rolled her eyes. "You were supposed to refuse the offer!"

Jamie stopped and gazed at her for a moment. "I don't want the grass up to the workmens' knees when they break ground. We needed the job done, and Adam offered."

"He was being neighborly," Ryan explained once again. "You're supposed to thank him and refuse, despite his insistence that he wants to help."

"Then how am I supposed to get my grass cut?"

"You hire someone. A stranger. You can put up a notice at church."

"What if Adam responds?" Jamie asked, giving Ryan one of her sly grins.

"If he knows it's us, and he asks for the job, he's…not Irish. You can pay him as much as you want with no hard feelings."

"If that's all true, it's going to take me forever to figure out who's being honest with me."

"No one is." Ryan laughed at how silly that sounded. "I don't mean people are liars. They're just overly polite. My advice is to post a notice about anything you want to have done, and make it clear what you'll pay."

"We can't negotiate?"

Letting out a sigh, Ryan said, "If we go down that rabbit hole, we'll be at it all day. Negotiating is an advance placement course. Better leave that to me for a couple of decades."

"Hey," Jamie said, grasping Ryan's arm and slowing to a stop. "Someone's on our land."

"What?" Ryan started to walk faster, tempted to leave Jamie and sprint on ahead. "Is that…?"

"I see a man in a flat cap," Jamie said. "And a woman with snow white hair."

"My grandparents! Come on," she said, pulling Jamie along behind her. "They must have come to check the site out."

As they got closer, Ryan saw the whole clan spread out across the land, with Cormac, Cáit, and Brenna kicking around a soccer ball in the fairly short grass, and Eamon and Aisling setting up a folding table near the lambing shed. She was filled with joy when she said, "They're having a party for us! They're not sick of us at all!"

Jamie was panting as she raced to keep up. "They could be having a party because they're so happy we're leaving."

"Ha ha. We're beloved, babe. Come on. Put it in gear!"

"It's in gear. I just don't have all of the gears you do."

"What's this?" Ryan called out when her grandmother turned and caught sight of her. "Is this a farewell party for us?"

She couldn't hide a smile when she said, "We have breakfast out in a field many days, Siobhán." She looked up to gaze at the sun. "When it's gone ten, I might add."

"Why didn't you just tell us to come? We wouldn't have wasted an hour of my aunt's time when she clearly had better things to do."

"I thought you might be the one delaying the production. I should have known we couldn't manage this without a hitch."

Ryan couldn't wait to walk about the perimeter of the property, so she ran for the wall, stuck both hands on it and swung her legs over, landing a little inelegantly, but staying upright. "Ta-da!" she said, bowing.

"How am I supposed to get over there?" Jamie demanded. "I'm not going to impale myself on one of those sharp-edged pieces of stone."

"You'll walk around to the gate like a normal person, Jamie," Granny said. "Don't let Siobhán talk you into her shenanigans."

Jamie stood at the wall and assessed it for a moment. "She couldn't talk me into this if she tried. I'll see you all in a minute or two."

Ryan walked over to her grandmother and hugged her gently. "Thanks for this, Granny. I assumed we'd have to say goodbye at the pub tonight, and I wasn't looking forward to that. Too noisy."

"That's the sound of your cousin's success," she said, smiling up at Ryan. "Don't go wishing for a quiet pub. Lashing rain or a good chill will give her plenty of those."

"Granddad," Ryan said, hugging him as well. "What do you think of our homestead?"

"It's perfect," he said, with his proud smile almost making her cry. "The thought of having you here every summer makes me happier than I can say."

"Come help!" Aisling called out. "I fill hungry gobs every night, but I get paid for that. I expect some help when I do it for the likes of you, Siobhán."

Ryan ran over and helped her uncle and Aisling arrange plates and napkins and cutlery on the table. "We have food for days," Aisling said. "You two had better be hungry."

"We are. At least I am. Jamie's appetite isn't as reliable as mine." She hugged her cousin tightly, speaking quietly when she said, "Thanks for getting up early to not only trick us, but feed us."

Aisling gave her a swat and pulled away. "We can't waste such a beautiful day now, can we?"

"Best we've had all summer," Ryan agreed.

The rest of the cousins walked over from their impromptu game. "It was my idea!" Brenna said, wrapping herself around Ryan until Jamie arrived. Then she let go in a flash to hang off Jamie like a tick. The kid had great taste.

"This seems exactly like the kind of thing you'd think of," Jamie said, stroking Brenna's dark auburn hair. "You're a very thoughtful person."

Cáit rolled her eyes at that, but she gave her little sister a pat on the back. "She's decided it's a goodbye party for you as well as Cormac and me—even though we don't leave for over a week."

"It's efficient this way," Brenna sniffed.

"We appreciate it no matter what," Ryan said. "You're the best family I could have asked for."

"And you'll still have to help clean up, no matter how much you try to flatter your way out of it," Aisling said. "Here comes Mam with the ham."

"That's what was making me so hungry! Your mom told us she didn't have any food in the house, so I assumed you'd had a massive breakfast and the scents had lingered."

Aisling gazed at her for a moment. "For a smart woman, you can be as thick as two short planks."

"Three," Jamie said, quickly running away from Ryan's pinch.

Chapter Eighteen

Jamie had never had a relatively simple brunch served al fresco in a field, but she decided she'd like to do it frequently. There was nothing fancy about the menu or the presentation, but that didn't make it any less charming.

After they'd all eaten, they got up from the blankets they'd spread on the ground and she and Ryan did a slow tour of the place with Ryan's grandparents.

Ryan loved to talk about their plans, and both of her grandparents were respectfully interested, asking enough questions to show they cared, but not enough to reflect any concerns. When they reached the lambing shed, Ryan's grandmother stood in front of it for a minute. "I can still remember having a little time to play with my sister when we weren't keeping an eye on a ewe," she said, sounding a little wistful. "It's been so long since they've kept sheep here that I'm surprised this shelter hasn't fallen." She put her pale, veined hand on the wall and gave it a good push. "Solid," she said, smiling. "Many years of both good and bad on this spot."

Ryan's grandfather said, "I knew your da worked this land, but I didn't realize you were involved with the lambing, Brigid. I thought you'd have been too young."

"My da wasn't always in top form," she said, giving her husband a pointed look. "We all had to help out if we wanted to eat. Every lamb was precious."

"Mmm," he said, looking very sober. "Farming wouldn't have been for me. I wouldn't care to sit in a cold, stone shed, waiting for a sheep to give birth." His eyes twinkled just like Ryan's did. "The fish need no help with that at all."

Jamie expected Brigid to give him a short, stern lecture on how she had no choice in the matter, or something to knock him down a peg, the way she always did with Ryan. But she simply gave him a brief, yet fond smile. "Aren't you the lucky one, then? You've never had a bit of soil under your nails, John Ryan."

He extended his hands, and Jamie had to admit that they were always sparkling clean. "A sailing life for me. Sometimes seasick, never muddy." He took a peek at the sky, just as Brigid had, both of them able to discern far more than Jamie could from the lack of clouds. "Come to think of it, high tide is in an hour. Who's interested in going to the pier?"

"I am," Brigid said, her response startling Jamie. "Let's get moving, girls. If we're lucky, we'll have a fish stew on the menu tonight."

A short time later, Ryan sat on the pier, dangling her legs over, with Jamie right next to her. Her grandfather stood next to Jamie, giving her quiet, patient instruction. Next to him, on a three-legged, canvas-covered stool, Ryan's grandmother tried her luck.

They were spinning, which her grandfather assured her was the proper choice for high tide in the summer at this particular pier, and she had no reason to doubt him. He'd already caught a coalfish, which he generously attributed to Jamie, and he was confident they might take wrasse and pollack. Like most fishermen, he was an inveterate optimist.

When he took Ryan in his boat, they always left well before dawn. But he could find somewhere to fish at nearly any hour. Given he knew the tide the way some men knew the horses at the track, he was never caught unawares.

Ryan couldn't recall ever going fishing with her grandmother, but that was probably because she didn't have to go if Ryan would agree to tag along. Say what you would about her grandmother, she loved her husband fiercely, and would willingly sit in a boat on a cold, drizzly morning to keep him company—when required. Of course, her grandfather spent more time at the church than he would have chosen if left to his own devices.

She took a peek at Jamie, who was trying her best to get the knack of spinning. Ryan smiled at her earnest expression while she tried to follow instructions. Jamie had never expressed an interest in fishing, and Ryan was pretty sure she never would. But she was a trouper, which was one of the many requirements for being a good partner. In Ryan's opinion, Jamie was an all-star in that department, and if she never caught a fish on her own, that was perfectly fine with her. She'd give it a try without complaint, and that was more than enough.

The whole family showed up at the pub that night, as Ryan was sure they would. It was particularly bustling, though, with a trio playing trad music, along with a very spirited crowd. Ryan was sure at least a quarter of the guests were tourists, which was very cheering. The pub could make it if only locals frequented it, but having tourists would give Aisling the boost she needed to be successful. If the pub drew a good crowd during tourist season, it would give her a cushion for the colder months, when even the locals didn't want to walk down the lane for a pint.

The plan was to stay near Shannon so they didn't have a long drive at the crack of dawn. But that meant saying goodbye early—a task Ryan despised. It seemed so much more loving to stay until everyone was dead on their feet. But a promise was a promise, and they'd started saying goodbye the minute they'd arrived at the pub, given that a proper goodbye had to include spending at least fifteen minutes with each person.

They were going to drive their new/used car to a village near Shannon, then one of Cormac's friends from school was going to meet them, drop them off at their hotel, and deliver the car to Cormac at university. That meant they had to get through all eight members of the family right now, one tougher than the next to part with.

Once Eamon, Moira, Cormac, Cáit, and Brenna were ticked off the list, Ryan had to say goodbye to her grandparents. Even though they were both active, in good health, and sound mind, there was always a bone-rattling fear in her heart that each parting might be their last. It was silly to focus on such maudlin thoughts when circumstances didn't merit it, but she had to acknowledge her inner pessimist and try to get through it.

Her grandfather had done his usual—kiss her cheeks while giving her a fond hug, then ruffling her hair like she was a child. He treated Jamie a little more like an adult, but Ryan loved the fact that he was just as warm and loving with her as he was with his blood relatives.

Then it was time to say goodbye to her grandmother. That usually required a long list of things to remember to do or not do or be wary of in America. But this time Ryan was a little dumbfounded to receive only a long hug, then kisses to her forehead and cheeks. "I love you with all of my heart, Siobhán," she said, looking up into Ryan's eyes. "You know that, yes?" she demanded, her eyes burning with their intensity.

"I do," she said, feeling the tears start to build. "Do you know how much I love you?"

"I do," she said, with a smile growing until she showed her teeth. "I'm proud of you, my wee girl. Very proud."

"Thank you, Granny," she said, reaching up to wipe her eyes.

"Enough of that sniffling," she said, taking a handkerchief from her purse and dabbing it beneath Ryan's eyes. "You've finally had a proper visit and we've had a lovely time. There's nothing to be sad about."

"I'll miss you," she said, still sniffling.

Her grandmother grasped her shoulders and gave them a squeeze. "And you know I'd keep you here if I didn't know your father would come and carry you home." Her smile grew a little sly. "He's never shown his temper, and I don't think I'd like to see it."

"It's not very bad," Ryan said, returning the smile. "Unless someone hurts one of us."

"Be off now. I don't want you out on the roads when it's dark."

"Yes, ma'am. I've just got to say goodbye to Ais."

"Lord help us," she sighed. "You'll be here another hour."

"No, no, she's busy tonight."

"Not too busy for you. She'd send this whole bunch back to their homes rather than hurt your feelings."

"Well, I don't know about that, but I know she loves me."

"As well as any sister ever did. Go on now. Go cry over missing your cousin before you've even left the pub."

Ryan shrugged as she backed away, heading for the bar. "It's the O'Flaherty in me," she said, now pretty sure her granny's characterization was accurate. Her branch of the O'Flaherty line was a teary one.

She grasped Jamie's hand and they walked over together. Ryan started to slip behind the bar, but Aisling held up a hand and called her father over. "Take over for a mo, Dad," she said. "I've got to go let Siobhán cry over me."

Moving around Ryan, Aisling grasped the shoulder of her blouse and led her outside. "Now we can have a moment's peace," she said, letting out a tired sigh as she took in some cool, clean air. "They're a lively bunch tonight, aren't they?"

"That's because all of Killala loves you," Ryan said, giving her a playful cuff to the chin. "As do I."

"Me too," Jamie said. "I haven't loved you as long, but I love you fiercely."

"Ahh, and I feel the same for you, Jamie. I'd say you're like another sister, but then that would make you Siobhán's sister too, and that's going too far for even our branch of the family."

Jamie hugged her tightly, and Ryan could hear her say, "We'll send your love to Colm."

"Ach! What I wouldn't give to see my boy again. I'm going to have a proper talk with Granny and Granddad before he comes back." She looked up at Ryan, with the light of the dim street lamp revealing her trepidations. "He'll come back, won't he?"

"Of course he will. I bet you could talk him into coming for Christmas. Or New Year's. If he hasn't told his family they'd freak out if he missed Christmas."

"And I can't go to San Francisco until he's told them. It would look odd." She grasped Ryan's shoulders again and pulled her down so they were facing each other. "Convince him to tell his parents. He needs a push."

"I think it's his brothers and his cousins he's worried about, but I'll do my best. You're talking on the phone, aren't you?"

"Nearly every day," she said, grinning slyly. "He's mad for me, I think."

"I am too," Ryan said, "in a very sisterly way."

"I have all the sisters I need," Aisling said. "You're better than a sister, even though I don't have a word for that." She wrapped her arms around Ryan tightly and held on for a surprisingly long time. "I hate your leaving more than I can say, Siobhán. I love you so much if I could only have one of you, I'd trade you for Colm." She pulled away and started to laugh. "That's a massive lie, but it's a closer call than you'd think."

"Don't tell Jamie," she said, winking at her partner, "but I've been working on her to agree to move here."

"You have?"

"I have. I think this would be a better place to raise our kids."

Aisling reached up and tugged on her ear. "Don't you dare get pregnant before I do. I want our little ones to grow up together, just like we did." She hugged Ryan once more, giving her a robust squeeze. "Having you here with your brood would be more than I could dream of."

"I'll work on her," Ryan promised.

"She's got a lot of work to do," Jamie stage-whispered. "This is one time I'm not going to give in when she begs."

"Work harder, Siobhán," Aisling said, giving her a swat to the arm. "Speaking of work, I can't leave my dad in there alone much longer."

"I love you," Ryan said, kissing her cheeks. "Best summer of my adult life."

"Hey!" Jamie yelped. "It was just two summers ago that you and I fell in love. I've already been demoted?"

Ryan stuck her arm out and Jamie settled under it. "Falling for you was the highlight of my life," Ryan said. "But being with you *and* my family has been awesome."

"Not buying it," Jamie said. "But I've learned that I'll always be a half-step behind Aisling on your favorites list." She gave Ryan a kiss to the cheek. "Ais has seniority."

"Go on now, the two of you," Aisling said, delivering quick kisses to both of them. "Bring Colm with you after Christmas. I know you'll want to check on the progress of your compound."

"I'll book the tickets as soon as we get home," Jamie said. "We'll see you in five months."

"That's five too many, but I expect to be so busy I might not notice the time." She added one more hug, then started for the door. "Even though it's hard work, I love it," she said. "And it's all thanks to you."

"We just lent you seed money," Ryan said. "You're the one who will make Aisling's the most popular pub in Mayo."

"Mayo?" she asked, pulling open the door to let the sound travel out in front of her. "Raise your expectations, Siobhán. I'm going for Connacht, then all of Ireland." With a confident smile, she entered the building and let the door close behind her.

"I miss her already," Ryan sighed.

"Come here, you tender-hearted thing," Jamie said, slipping an arm around Ryan to pull her close. "I want you to step back and look at what you've accomplished this summer."

"I didn't accomplish—"

Jamie playfully slapped a hand over Ryan's mouth, holding on tightly even when she tried to pull away. "Don't you even try to convince me you didn't accomplish an awful lot. Your grandparents have a house that will keep them warm, dry and mold-free for many years, your favorite cousin has a business that will allow her to stay close to home, and we've made a lot of progress on our home. By the time we come back—which I think should be over your winter break, we might be ready to break ground." She pulled her hand away and replaced it with her lips, which Ryan happily met with her own.

"Thanks," she said as they broke apart. "I tend to think of all of the things I didn't get done, rather than the things I did."

"You *tend* to?" Jamie gave her a very dubious look. "For a woman who applauds other people's smallest accomplishments, you're a brutal self-critic."

Ryan shrugged, not willing to concede the point, even though she knew it was valid. "I feel good about Ais," she said, letting herself savor the moment. She took Jamie by the hand and crossed the silent street to take in the view of the pub from a slight distance. "I feel *really* good about the sign," she added, so pleased that Jamie had taken on the task of having such a nice one made. "The sign makes it clear this is a top-notch place."

"It *is* top-notch," Jamie said. "I know you've been in a lot more pubs than I have, but this is the best one I've been to in Ireland. Aisling will make a go of it. I'm certain of that."

"I am, too." She laughed. "I'll send vouchers for a free pint to every household in Mayo if I have to. Once people stop by, they'll want to return."

They stood there quietly, looking into the one window. The glass was so thick it distorted the scene, but colorful shapes moved around inside, making it clear there was a lot going on. The music was loud, but not harsh, and exuberant voices carried through the heavy, moist air.

"We're going to have a *lot* of family time here, baby," Jamie said, smiling serenely. "I know we can't turn a small town into a booming metropolis, but we can make a difference. I'm certain of that."

"I am too," Ryan said, forcing herself to at least try to adopt Jamie's optimism. The fact that there would always be a great distance between her families was never going to be fun. But she and Jamie were on the road to having one foot firmly in each spot, a goal she'd never had the nerve to even imagine fulfilling. She looked over to her partner and smiled. Jamie had the ability to make *all* of her dreams come true.

The End

By Susan X Meagher

Novels

Arbor Vitae
All That Matters
Cherry Grove
Girl Meets Girl
The Lies That Bind
The Legacy
Doublecrossed
Smooth Sailing
How To Wrangle a Woman
Almost Heaven
The Crush
The Reunion
Inside Out
Out of Whack
Homecoming
The Right Time
Summer of Love
Chef's Special
Fame
Vacationland
Wait For Me
The Keeper's Daughter
Friday Night Flights

Short Story Collection

Girl Meets Girl

Serial Novel

I Found My Heart In San Francisco

Awakenings: Book One
Beginnings: Book Two
Coalescence: Book Three
Disclosures: Book Four
Entwined: Book Five
Fidelity: Book Six
Getaway: Book Seven
Honesty: Book Eight
Intentions: Book Nine
Journeys: Book Ten
Karma: Book Eleven
Lifeline: Book Twelve
Monogamy: Book Thirteen
Nurture: Book Fourteen
Osmosis: Book Fifteen
Paradigm: Book Sixteen
Quandary: Book Seventeen
Renewal: Book Eighteen
Synchronicity: Book Nineteen
Trust: Book Twenty
United: Book Twenty-One
Vengeance: Book Twenty-Two
Wonder: Book Twenty-Three

Anthologies

Undercover Tales
Outsiders

You can contact Susan at Susan@briskpress.com

Information about all of Susan's books can be found at
www.susanxmeagher.com or www.briskpress.com

To receive notification of new titles, send an email to
newsletters@briskpress.com

facebook.com/susanxmeagher

twitter.com/susanx